Ans	_____	M.L.	_____
ASH	_____	MLW	_____
Bev	_____	Mt.Pl	_____
C.C.	_____	NLM	_____
C.P.	_____	Ott	_____
Dick	_____	PC	_____
DRZ	_____	PH	_____
ECH	_____	P.P.	_____
ECS	_____	Pion.P.	_____
Gar	_____	Q.A.	_____
GRM	_____	Riv	_____
GSP	_____	RPP	_____
G.V.	_____	Ross	_____
Har	_____	S.C.	_____
JPCP	_____	St.A.	_____
KEN	_____	St.J	_____
K.L.	_____	St.Joa	_____
K.M.	_____	St.M.	_____
L.H.	_____	Sgt	_10/09(Reg)__
LO	_____	T.H.	_____
Lyn	_____	TLLO	_____
L.V.	_____	T.M.	_____
McC	_____	T.T.	_____
McG	_____	Ven	_____
McQ	_____	Vets	_____
MIL	_____	VP	_____
	_____	Wat	_____
	_____	Wed	_____
	_____	WIL	_____
	_____	W.L.	_____

Antony Trew served in the South African Navy and the Royal Navy in the Mediterranean, South Atlantic and the Western Approaches, and was awarded the DSC. He died in 1966.

THE MOONRAKER MUTINY

A tired old freighter, the *Moonraker*, is bound from Fremantle to Mauritius. Haunted by his past, Captain Stone seeks solace in the gin bottle in his cabin. His niece, Susie, flirts with Australian passage worker Hank Casey, and Italian mate Carlo Frascatti grumbles at the motley crew. Then the radio operator receives a warning of a suspected cyclone ahead . . . The panic-stricken crew turn on their captain and abandon ship. Those left behind desperately struggle to keep the battered hulk afloat, whilst nearby, a coaster and an ocean salvage tug are each determined to profit from the *Moonraker*'s disaster . . .

Books by Antony Trew
Published by The House of Ulverscroft:

THE ROAD TO THE RIVER
KLEBER'S CONVOY
DEATH OF A SUPERTANKER
THE WHITE SCHOONER
THE SEA BREAK
TWO HOURS TO DARKNESS

ANTONY TREW

THE MOONRAKER MUTINY

Complete and Unabridged

ULVERSCROFT
Leicester

First published in Great Britain in 2006 by
Robert Hale Limited
London

First Large Print Edition
published 2007
by arrangement with
Robert Hale Limited
London

British Library CIP Data

Trew, Antony, 1906 –
    The Moonraker mutiny.—Large print ed.—
Ulverscroft large print series: adventure & suspense
1. Cargo ships—Fiction 2. Mutiny—Fiction
3. Cyclones—Fiction 4. Sea stories
5. Large type books
I. Title
823.9'14 [F]

ISBN 978–1–84617–979–2

Published by
F. A. Thorpe (Publishing)
Anstey, Leicestershire

Set by Words & Graphics Ltd.
Anstey, Leicestershire
Printed and bound in Great Britain by
T. J. International Ltd., Padstow, Cornwall

This book is printed on acid-free paper

'What is mutiny? There is no doubt that mutiny is a collective offence, that is to say, it cannot be committed by one man. . . . mutiny is an offence which deals with collective insubordination, collective defiance or disregard of authority or refusal to obey authority.'

Lord Chief Justice Goddard,
R. v. Grant (1957)

1

Tugs nudged and hauled the ship clear of the Victoria quay, white plumes hissing from their funnels as they worked industriously like insects worrying at a prey many times their size. When the ship was lined up with the channel, bows to seaward, stern to the Swan River, the Australian pilot muttered into a walkie-talkie and the tugs drew clear. From the wing of the bridge he called, 'Starboard wheel, slow-ahead.' The order was repeated by the helmsman, the telegraph bells rang, and the old, eight thousand ton freighter trembled as her engines began to turn. The sheds on the quays seemed to move aft, a motion scarcely perceptible at first but quickening and so smooth that to those in the *Moonraker* it was as if some unseen force were pulling the harbour past them.

With distance the illusion crumpled and it became evident that the ship was carrying them towards the channel to the sea. Captain Stone crossed to the far side of the bridge, away from the pilot whose presence, like most sea captains, he subconsciously resented. From long habit he focused his binoculars on the Port Authority's office. Hanging from the yardarm of the signal station's mast, two black balls warned incoming vessels of movement in the channel, that they must wait in Gage Roads clear of its mouth. Beyond the signal station the War Memorial stood on its limestone hill, conspicuous and forlorn. Captain Stone shivered. He did not like war memorials. They were evocative of a time which had much affected his life. He shook his head as if to free it from unpleasant memories and looked to seaward.

The long arms of the north and south moles glided by until the *Moonraker* came clear of the entrance, her bows swung to starboard and she headed up through Gage Roads towards the Fairway Buoy.

From the bridge Captain Stone watched two seamen working on a rope ladder at the break of the foredeck. With sheath-knives they cut the spunyarn lashings, unrolled the ladder and paid it out over the side, securing the inboard ends to bulwark stanchions. That done they leant on the bulwarks beside the ladder, looking back at the receding shore with blank expressionless faces.

A breeze came in from the north-west and along the shoals and reefs stretching from Rottnest Island south to Garden Island, patches of broken water showed white and frothing. Sheltered in the lee of Rottnest Island, *Moonraker* moved towards the Fairway Buoy. When it came abeam the engine-room telegraph was put to *stop* and soon afterwards a motor launch came alongside. The pilot went down the rope ladder into the sternsheets and the launch drew clear. He waved to those on the bridge and the launch turned and headed back towards Fremantle Harbour.

Captain Stone ordered *half-ahead* and *port wheel*. When the obelisk beacon on Buckland Hill was astern, he told the helmsman to steady the course.

'Steady as she goes,' repeated the man at the wheel.

At the steering compass the captain checked the course. 'Keep her on nor-west-a-quarter-west,' he said.

'Nor-west-a-quarter-west,' repeated the helmsman watching the heading indicator. With practised hands he turned the wheel slowly, a few spokes at a time. Neglected hands, the captain noticed, nicotine-stained and burnt, scarred and calloused from long years at sea. The man smelt of liquor and his grease and paint-stained dungarees gave off the sweet sour smell of sweat. He had a stubble-covered chin and sunken dissipated eyes. Captain Stone winced. He attached some importance to personal hygiene and smart appearance, aesthetic qualities unusual in this travel-stained old freighter built on Tees-side in 1952, employed tramping the oceans of the world, manned by riff-raff picked up on a dozen waterfronts; a ship registered in Liberia, one of three of its kind operated by Gimbal Ocean Carriers Limited, an undertaking owned and presided over by Mr Hassim Racher from a jaded office near Aldgate Underground Station in the City of London.

With a frown of disapproval, Captain Stone left the wheelhouse. What a man, he reflected, yet not untypical of the crew, and no better than such a ship deserved. With these uncongenial thoughts he went to the chart house.

★   ★   ★

By late afternoon the ship having passed north of Rottnest Island, and Fremantle and the coast of Western Australia being then well astern, course was set for Mauritius some three thousand miles distant. There she was to discharge the two sixty-ton cargo lighters she carried on deck, and take on several hundred tons of sugar before making for the South African coast. At East London and

4

Port Elizabeth she would load five hundred tons of hides and skins. Thence, two-thirds laden, she would sail for Rotterdam and London via the Cape.

Captain Stone had discussed the course for Mauritius briefly with Martinho Lopez the second officer, a softly spoken Mexican who was in theory the navigating officer. But Captain Stone's officers were a mixed bunch with dubious qualifications, their certificates of competence being either Greek, Panamanian, Liberian or Athenian. There was an active black-market in such documents, so he preferred to see to the more important aspects of navigation himself.

Having set course and ordered the man at the wheel to engage auto-steering, Stone went to the wing of the bridge where the chief officer, Carlo Frascatti, was hunched in a corner, smoking a cheroot. He was a narrow-shouldered slouching man with a cadaverous face.

The captain, on the other hand, was tall with greying hair and limpid blue eyes. There was an air of faded distinction about him, heightened by the livid scar which ran up his neck and across one cheek. He looked older than he was and Frascatti, who disliked him, knew why. It was a secret the Italian relished. Not that Frascatti's past was blameless, but he had the advantage since Captain Stone knew nothing of it. Indeed, all he knew was that the Italian was sullen and withdrawn, did not have the tight rein on the deck crew he should, and possessed no more than a Panamanian certificate.

Stopping alongside the chief officer, Stone looked down on the foredeck. It was cluttered with litter accumulated during the five days of loading in Fremantle. He saw much the same thing aft. His eyes travelled meaningfully from his wrist watch to Frascatti, who gazed to seaward as if unaware of the captain's presence.

Adopting the gruff tone he kept for these occasions, Captain Stone said, 'Gang not washing down yet?' He turned his back on the chief officer because he disliked rows and tension and anyway preferred the view of the sea to Frascatti's face. The Italian hunched his shoulders. 'Half the men still drunk,' he said in a throaty voice.

'And the other half?' inquired Stone. 'A hose and two brooms. Three men. That's all that's required.'

'The other men stow wires and ropes and the cargo gear.' Frascatti puffed cheroot smoke to windward and it blew back into the captain's eyes. The Italian knew that Stone, a non-smoker, didn't like that.

6

'Pull the men out, Mr Frascatti. It'll clear their heads. Get the dunnage over the side and the decks hosed down.'

'Okay. I try,' said the Italian grudgingly.

As the captain walked away Frascatti added, 'You know what drink does.' Muttering to himself he went down the bridge ladder.

Captain Stone heard Frascatti's remark and the muttering. Sullen devil, he thought as he went into the chart house, no wonder he has no better than a mate's certificate — and a Panamanian one at that.

★ ★ ★

On *Moonraker*'s fifth night out of Fremantle the moon spread a luminous path astern. Above the ship the southern sky was littered with stars, so bright and numerous they might have been the lights of some great urban sprawl.

A young woman sat on a deck chair in the shadows near the engine-room skylights, screened from the bridge by the fiddley casing and funnel. The moonlight revealed the snub nose and inquiring eyebrows, but not the high complexion, grey eyes and dark hair.

From the engine-room skylights came the

metallic clamour of the engines, a fortissimo of thumping steel, dwarfing the sounds of the auxiliary engines, the generators, circulating and bilge pumps and the whirring fans. It shut out, too, the sound of the sea splashing along the ship's sides. From the skylights came other things: billows of hot air, for instance, impregnated with oil and steam, which added to the heat of an already warm night.

The ship rolled to a long swell, the hull creaking and groaning. Somewhere, a steel door banged at unexpected intervals.

The girl watched the steaming light on the mainmast as it swung slowly across the sky — from port to starboard, and back again. The combination of noise and warm air, the slow roll of the ship, and the movement of the mast across the sky must have made her sleepy for she had no warning of the hands which closed over her eyes and mouth. She tried to scream but couldn't, so she bit.

'Hey. Look out. It's me,' complained an Australian voice.

'Oh,' she said breathlessly. 'Oh, Hank. You scared me. You shouldn't do that. I was half asleep.'

He knelt beside her. She could see his face quite clearly in the moonlight as he leant forward to kiss her. He did this several times and then his hands began exploring and she protested, trying to sound shocked but half laughing.

'No,' she gasped. 'You mustn't. Stop it.'

'What's wrong, Susie? There's no law against it. It's natural you know.'

'Not here,' she said firmly. 'It's too risky even if I wanted to. Which I don't.'

'Where then?'

'Don't ask me,' she said. 'I don't think there's anywhere.'

'Even if you wanted to, which you do,' he said, biting her ear.

'Ow. Don't. That hurts.'

He sat down at her feet, his arms round his knees. 'There's always somewhere,' he said. 'If you really want to.'

'Like where?'

'The lifeboats, the paint locker, the bosun's store, the shaft tunnel, the funnel . . . stacks of them.'

'You're crazy. I've only known you since Sydney.'

'So what? That's twelve days. Long time at our age.'

'It's not. Nothing really.'

'Long enough for me to be crazy about you.'

'I expect you're crazy about lots of girls.'

'Never like this.' His voice was husky.

'Pouf! I don't believe you. It's my body you want.'

'Yeh. Well, okay. It's a beaut. But I mean I couldn't be crazy about a girl without one, could I?'

'You could be more interested in me. What I think. How I feel. What I want to do about life. Things like that.'

'I am interested in you, Susie. Honest. You're always saying what you think and how you feel and what you want to do. But life isn't just talking.'

'So I talk too much about myself do I?'

'No. Of course not.' He got up on his knees and held her in a long extravagant kiss.

'Gosh.' She pulled away from him. 'You're strong. Like a gorilla.'

'Ever been kissed by one?'

She said nothing and he sat down again, and they were silent.

'Why haven't I seen you since Fremantle, Hank?'

'You have. This afternoon. When we made this date.'

'That was about two minutes.'

'It's Garrett,' he said. 'Never gives me time off. A slave driver, that one.'

'No way to talk of the ship's cook,' she said. 'He's an important man.'

'Who says?'

'My uncle. The captain of this ship. *He says*. You know Hank,' she leant forward, breathing into his face, 'you must be careful. Uncle's fed up with you and your rows with Garrett. Says he's not going to have a passage-worker upset the cook. Garrett,' she mimicked the captain, 'is the key to the ship's morale.'

'Key to my foot,' said Hank.

'Don't be like that,' said Susie. 'Uncle means it. And he's right. If Garrett's upset he'll take it out of the crew with his cooking.'

Hank Casey sighed. He was young with longish hair, a lively face and large hands. He played second guitar in a small-time Sydney group in between changing jobs as a motor mechanic which he did pretty often. The longish hair and the guitar were deceptive. He was a burly young man, a strong swimmer who'd been a life-saver on Bondi Beach. That was what he liked to think of as his athletic period. The long hair and the guitar were, he reckoned, his creative period. Hank was all for sampling life. He had his eyes set on the King's Road, Chelsea. He felt sure success awaited him there. But he was a spender and never seemed to get enough money together for the journey. So after a noisy row with the foreman, followed by a briskly assisted walkout — since he'd made the mistake of

backing his views with a monkey wrench
— he'd decided to work his passage. It wasn't
easy to get a ship. There were strong union
laws against passage working, but he found
these could be circumvented if the ship were
registered in Liberia. So he'd settled for the
Moonraker where he'd signed on as a galley
hand, his predecessor having deserted shortly
before sailing. A decision which Hank
endorsed once he'd got to know the cook and
the job, and that hadn't taken long.

Garrett, the cook, was a ponderous man
with a fallen face who sweated profusely,
professed Marxism and detested all passage-
workers whom he called black-legs. He was in
fact not a bad cook.

When Hank Casey signed on in Sydney
he'd not known that the captain's niece was
to be on board. She'd joined as a
supernumerary the day they left Sydney, her
uncle having obtained permission from the
owners to give her passage to London
provided she helped the stewards. He'd put
her in the only spare cabin — one reserved
for pilots — and assigned her to work under
the chief steward, Mr Jenkins. What she did
to help Mr Jenkins was notional, but enough
to satisfy the fiction that she was working her
passage.

On the day they sailed from Sydney she

and Hank had met. Since he was twenty and she eighteen and both were pleasant to look upon and cheerful of disposition, it had been a pleasant surprise. During the long coastwise journey from Sydney to Fremantle, and in the five days spent loading there, the friendship had blossomed.

Now on the boatdeck this moonlight night she was pleading with him. 'Must you quarrel with Garrett. Can't you just take it?' She ruffled his hair.

'Not so sure,' said Hank doggedly. 'Chases the daylights out of me. If I peel potatoes lightly he says I'm skimping the job. If I peel them heavily, I'm wasting good food. If anything burns it's because I've not watched it. If anything breaks it's my fault. And all the time Garrett's slinging off about black-legs taking the bread out of the mouths of honest working men. I get it all day along.' He groaned. 'And half the blooming night.'

She put her cheek against his. 'Poor Hank. But *please* — for my sake — don't fight with him.'

'Fight him?' Hank was incredulous. 'I'd tear him apart if I did. Don't worry. I won't. The last bloke I hit cost me my job.'

'I know. But don't have rows. It makes it more difficult for *us*, don't you see. Uncle's got it in for you already. And he doesn't

13

approve. *The captain's niece and a passage-worker.* I know it's nonsense. But he's old-fashioned.'

'That's great,' said Hank indignantly. 'You're a passage-worker too, aren't you?'

'Yes, I am. But you know it's different. I'm his niece. And he has to think of the officers. They wouldn't approve. Especially Mr Frascatti. He and Uncle don't get on.'

'That makes three of us,' said Hank. 'Okay. I'll do my best.'

'Will you truly, Hank?'

'Honest, Susie.' He knelt beside the deck chair again and put his arms round her. For some minutes they were silent while he kissed and caressed her, his inquisitive hands meeting with rebuffs and muffled protests.

'Can't we go to your cabin?' he pleaded huskily.

Susie stood up in the darkness, smoothing her skirt and blouse and throwing her hair back over her shoulders.

'You must be crazy,' she said. 'They'd see you.'

'Not at two in the morning.'

'What would the fellows sharing your cabin think if you left it then?'

'They sleep like logs. Anyway I'd say I was going to the jazz.'

She pushed him away. 'You know it

wouldn't work. Be terribly risky.'

'It'd be dreamy.'

She laughed and with all the confidence of eighteen said, 'Maybe. But it's not going to happen.' She changed the subject. 'I heard you playing the guitar, Hank.'

'When was that?'

'A couple of nights back. You were playing and some of those fellows were singing. Down by number four hatch.'

'What was the number?'

'Some French song. I don't know the name.'

He laughed. 'You mean *Les Champs Élysées* — like it?'

'It was great.'

'Honest?'

'I mean it, Hank. You're good. I didn't know you spoke French.'

'I don't. It was those black boys from Dakar singing.'

'Are they sailors?'

'No. Firemen.'

'They sing it like they're sad and longing for Paris.'

'Yeh. But it's Dakar they're thinking of. Know what they call it?'

'No.'

'*Paris noir*. Black Paris.'

Above the noise from the engine-room they

15

heard six bells strike on the bridge.

'Gosh. That's eleven o'clock,' she said. 'I promised to take uncle his milk at a quarter to.'

'His *milk*. Hey! The captain drinks milk,' Hank chuckled.

'Yes. Any objections?'

'No. It just seems funny. I mean the captain . . .'

So suddenly that they almost jumped, a voice in the darkness said, 'Is that you there, Susie?'

It was Captain Stone.

2

Captain Stone heard eight bells strike at midnight. They were followed by the sound of tramping feet on the bridge ladders as the watches changed. It was a hot night and he sat in his cabin wearing pyjama trousers, arms folded across his bare chest, head sunk, gazing blankly at the pattern on the carpet.

Though his mood of depression persisted, the knowledge that midnight had struck, that time had passed its diurnal barrier and set off into the unknown of the next twenty-four hours, made him feel more secure. The events of the day belonged now to a time that had passed, to yesterday. There was, too, greater privacy for, other than the watch on deck, the ship was asleep.

He looked towards the door of the sleeping cabin and, though it was shut, his mind's eye saw beyond to the mahogany drawer under the bunk: the top drawer. It was long and deep. I must not think of that, he admonished himself, I must put it out of my mind. There was a dryness in his mouth, a parched feeling in his throat, that nagged and worried. He filled a glass with iced water from the

Thermos and drank slowly, swirling the liquid round his mouth before swallowing. Afterwards he felt better.

The atmosphere in the cabin was oppressive. The windows admitted a breeze made by the ship's forward movement, but it was warm and humid and carried the smell of diesel fuel, of wood-packing, tallow and hides from the ventilators which served the fuel tanks and cargo holds. Captain Stone crossed the cabin and stood under the ventilator trunking. He put a hand to the inlet grille, but it was an old and inefficient system and the incoming air seemed no cooler. Yawning, he scratched his scarred chest absentmindedly, picked up a book, turned its pages, yawned again and put it down.

Back in the easy chair he stuck his legs forward, hung his arms over its sides and let his head droop forward. Once again his eyes focused on the carpet without seeing its patterns.

He couldn't shake off the depression which had been triggered by the row with that cheeky Australian and Susie when he'd found them on the boat-deck.

'What are you doing up here?' he'd asked the young man.

'Talking to Susie.'

'Call me 'sir' when you address me.'

'Sir.'

'Get back to your quarters,' he'd said. 'This deck is for the ship's officers.' As the Australian turned away, Captain Stone added, 'And don't let me catch you with my niece again.'

Casey stopped. 'Why not?' He spoke quietly, the moonlight shining on his expressionless face. 'We weren't doing any harm.'

Susie was alarmed. 'Oh, do go, Hank. *Please* don't argue with Uncle.'

'Leave this to me,' said Captain Stone, 'and be off to your cabin, young woman. I'll deal with you later.'

She looked despairingly at Hank. 'All right,' she said. 'But please don't . . . ' she paused, at a loss for words. ' . . . don't be unpleasant to Hank. I asked him to come and chat. It was my fault.'

'Go to your cabin,' repeated Stone firmly.

When she'd gone the captain turned to the young man. 'I warn you, Casey. Leave that girl alone.'

The Australian shrugged his shoulders. 'I don't see I'm breaking any maritime law talking to a fellow passage-worker.'

'Don't argue with me,' said Captain Stone with acerbity. 'I'm in command of this ship. Leave that girl alone.' For a moment Casey was undecided. 'Okay, Captain,' he said as he walked away. 'We'll see.'

Later Stone sent for his niece and there was another stormy scene. It ended with Susie flinging out of the cabin in tears and slamming the door.

Recalling this, Stone shook his head. Such problems of discipline were foreign to him. His niece had been working as a shorthand typist in Australia for a year and was at her parents' suggestion returning under his care. Not that Susie, or for that matter her parents, had really been concerned about her care. She was quite capable of looking after herself. The attraction was the free passage. But Captain Stone, belonging to an older school, felt personally responsible. He scarcely knew Susie, and having no daughter he knew even less about the behaviour of young women today. But having been a young man himself, and having two sons, he thought he knew what went on when a young man met a girl on the boat-deck in moonlight. The burden of looking after Susie weighed heavily upon him.

At heart he was a man of peace and rows and upheavals upset him. Not that the trouble with Hank and Susie had been the only problem that day. In the forenoon there'd been unpleasantness with Frascatti, the chief officer. Captain Stone, carrying out an inspection of the ship, had not liked what he'd found.

First there'd been the business of the lashings on the heavy lifts on the main deck: two sixty-ton lighters consigned to Mauritius. They'd been loaded in Sydney from the Titan heavy lift barge in Walsh Bay, and the Australian stevedores had made a good job of chocking and securing them. But the movement of the ship in the seaway and the warmer weather as *Moonraker* approached the sub-tropics had slackened the lashings. Not much, but enough for Captain Stone to take notice. 'Why hasn't the slack been taken up?' he'd challenged the chief officer. With a characteristic shrug Frascatti had said, 'Too busy until now, captain. Tomorrow we fix.'

The inspection continued and Stone found untidy storerooms and lockers, lifeboat gripes and other running gear seized up with rust, grease and dirt on decks and paintwork, tarnished brightwork, unscrubbed ladders, crew's quarters dirty with clothing lying about. It was true that the ship had spent four weeks on the Australian coast, but they'd been at sea for nearly a week since Fremantle. In Stone's opinion there was no excuse for what he'd found.

'The *Moonraker*'s dirty. She's not ship-shape, Mr Frascatti,' he'd said, using his gruff voice.

'What you expect, captain?' complained Frascatti spreading his hands. 'With crew like this and ship like this?'

Captain Stone stared at him. 'There is nothing wrong with the ship. I expect it to be clean and ship-shape. No more. No less.'

Frascatti had begun to argue but Captain Stone cut him short. 'That'll do, Mr Frascatti. You've had your orders. Get on with them.' The Italian left the cabin mumbling something in Italian. Some impertinence, I'll warrant, thought Captain Stone.

No wonder, he reflected, stretching himself in the armchair, that he felt depressed. Or was it despair? There was nothing to look forward to. Over the last eighteen months he'd had his first experience of commanding a foreign registered ship and it had not been pleasant. Never before had he put to sea with a bunch of officers and men like *Moonraker*'s. And yet, as far ahead as he could see, it would always be like this. Unless he gave up the sea. But how could he? Where would the money come from? What would his wife and sons say? They had a poor opinion of him as it was. He knew that, though they did their best to hide it.

Miserable and dispirited he looked once more towards the sleeping cabin, seeing with disturbing clarity what lay beyond. Behind the mahogany drawer, once removed, was a plywood panel . . . no, he muttered, it's a coward's way. I mustn't think of it.

The feeling of hopelessness, of being trapped, persisted. He couldn't face going on like this. It was too sordid and humiliating. The arguments with a passage-worker and Frascatti, the dirty ship, the ragamuffin crew. Somehow he must get away from it all. Again he felt the parched dryness, the roughness of lips, tongue and throat, as if he'd been in a desert for a long time. A dehydrated feeling, a sense of imminent collapse.

He stood up, took a towel and rubbed the perspiration from his chest. Pouring another glass of iced water he drank in quick gulps as if his thirst had not been quenched for a long time. He returned the glass to the rack and stood in the centre of the cabin looking round uncertainly, swaying against the roll of the ship.

With sudden decision he opened the door of the sleeping cabin, closed it behind him and turned the key. He pulled out the drawer in which lay shirts and underclothes and placed it on the bunk. Leaning into the space where it had been, he removed the flush fitting panel at the back, thrust his hand deep into the cavity between bulkhead and fitting and withdrew a bottle of Gordon's Gin. Replacing the panel and drawer, he unlocked the door and went back to the day cabin.

The desk clock showed a quarter past one as he removed the lead foil from the top of the bottle and unscrewed the cap.

* * *

Stone helped himself to another gin after which, with some difficulty, he replaced the bottle in the rack beside the armchair. He added a little water, inadvertently pouring some on to his pyjama trousers. For a moment he thought of a touch of angostura but decided it was an unnecessary frill. He drank half the contents of the glass in a gulp, looked at the gin bottle and sighed.

The sigh was not one of despondency, nor of remorse, for the earlier depression had gone. It was regret for the level of gin which had fallen below the label. His mood had in fact changed to one of philosophic resignation. *What had to be, had to be*, but what had to be didn't seem quite so bad now. In the course of two hours, and most of the contents of the bottle, he'd paged mentally through the most difficult chapters of his life and come as always to the conclusion that fate had been unkind to him. As he saw it, what had happened was not so much the result of anything he'd done as of circumstance.

Twice, as a young man, ships in which he was serving had been torpedoed in the Western Ocean. On both occasions he'd had a bad time, first in the water and afterwards on life-rafts. The second time had landed him, broken and burned, in hospital. When he was finally discharged the scars on his body could be seen, those on his mind could not. Because of them he was soon back in hospital. His screaming and waking in the night, his refusal to eat, the festering stomach ulcers, were diagnosed as symptoms of an acute anxiety neurosis.

In time, it was then late 1944, he was discharged from hospital. But his nerve had gone and he could not again face the sea. Ashamed of this discovery, refusing to accept the explanations of those who treated him, he diagnosed his complaint as cowardice and tried to escape from it. In the event he turned, as had so many before him, to alcohol.

The war ended, the fear of being torpedoed, of explosions in the night, of oil-covered water bursting into flame, receded. Harold Stone — the positive elements in his character not yet irreparably damaged — had broken away from alcohol and taken up once more the threads of his life.

He married and installed his wife in a small house in Surbiton where over the years she presented him with two sons. In the post-war build up of Britain's merchant fleet, a time when the shortage of qualified, experienced officers was acute, Stone got command comparatively young.

The Stones moved to a larger house, the sons did well at school and their father's career with the Donnington Steamship Company Limited trading to Africa, India and the Far East seemed assured. Indeed, before long Stone commanded one of their newest and largest freighters, the *Donnington Wave*.

Early in 1968, this ship, outward bound, called at Mombasa to discharge general cargo. Thence she sailed for Madras and Calcutta. Among her cargo was a consignment of arms and ammunition destined for that cold precarious frontier which lies between Nepal and Tibet. An item in the manifest was three hundred tons of land mines.

One evening when the ship was just north of the Equator in longitude 62° east — that is

26

to say about half-way between Mombasa and Madras — there was an explosion in the engine-room which killed two men, injured several others and started a fire. Soon afterwards the engine-room had to be abandoned.

Immediately after the explosion the crew were sent to fire stations, all ventilation was shut down, watertight doors closed, and the emergency generator in the after-castle started up to provide power for pumping water for the fire-mains and lighting.

A radio message reporting the explosion was broadcast on the emergency frequency of 500 kilocycles. It was answered immediately by shore stations and ships in the vicinity, one of them a frigate of the Indian Navy which was within 250 miles.

The Donnington Wave was a motor ship and thus without steam which is a prime weapon for fighting fire in confined spaces. But hoses fed by the fire-mains and other fire-fighting apparatus were brought into action, quantities of carbon dioxide and chemical foam being released in the engine-room. For a time it seemed the fire would be brought under control but the surrounding bulkheads, by now red hot in places, started fires in adjoining spaces and slowly but insidiously the flames spread.

Every man in the ship had, somewhere in the back of his mind, the thought of those three hundred tons of land mines in number two hold. Admittedly the hold was still some distance from the scene of the fire, and there were several watertight bulkheads between it and the engine-room. But the fire was now spreading along the superstructure and if it could not be controlled, it was only a matter of time before it reached the centre-castle. Once established there, the threat to number two hold would be real.

It was a dark overcast night with lightning on the eastern horizon, and a freshening wind which increased the difficulties of the men fighting the fire.

It was fortunate that Captain Stone was regarded by his British officers and Lascar crew as a model of what a ship's captain should be: calm, efficient, a man of few words, with just that degree of aloofness which inspires respect for those in command. These qualities, particularly evident on this night of alarm and distress, somehow communicated themselves to his officers and men. Thus, while they fought the fire and were worried and fearful as men are in such circumstances, there were no signs of panic, not even among the youngest of the Lascars. They had great faith, these men, in their captain.

Yet no man in the *Donnington Wave* that night was more acutely aware of the cargo in number two hold than Captain Stone as he stood on the bridge looking down on to its hatches. For he had a vivid mental picture, as if on a television screen, of what lay beneath.

As time went on other images formed: recalls of 1942 and 1944, of explosions which had rent the night, of wild scrambles for boats which could not be launched, of sheets of flame, suffocating clouds of smoke and the screams of dying men . . . of the fight for survival in oil-covered water which burnt like a bush fire; the acrid fumes choking, the heat scalding, the oxygen in the atmosphere swallowed by the fire so that men's lungs took in only noxious gas, fuel oil and water.

As the fire spread so fear spread in Captain Stone's mind until at last the totality of the old horror returned and his nerve broke. Without consulting the chief officer or chief engineer he gave the order to abandon ship. The chief officer protested, civilly but firmly: admittedly the fire was gaining but it had not yet reached the centre-castle. When and if number two hold was threatened, carbon dioxide could be fed in under pressure through the piping system. The wind might drop, there could be a tropical downpour.

Many things might still happen, urged the chief officer, to enable them to arrest or delay the fire. In the meantime help was on its way. The Indian frigate should be with them within twelve hours and there was a tanker less than 150 miles away.

Captain Stone showed little if any outward sign of the fear within. 'I am not prepared,' he said, 'to risk the lives of my men. For five hours they have fought this fire. Everything possible has been done. Yet it continues to spread . . . ' The fumes of burning paintwork made him choke, and he coughed and rubbed his streaming eyes with a handkerchief already soiled with soot.

'The ship is to be abandoned,' he said, speaking with rather more emotion than the chief officer could recall. 'Get on with it at once, Mr Wilson.'

The chief officer looked at him uncertainly. 'And you, sir. Will you . . . ?'

'I shall be the last man to leave the ship, Mr Wilson,' said the captain who was seized with another fit of coughing.

For the great majority of men the decision was welcome, and since they had every confidence in the captain they believed it to be correct. It was hours now since the explosion and they were beginning to feel the effects of such strenuous and prolonged effort in a smoke-filled atmosphere.

The boats were lowered and manned, a final radio message was broadcast informing the authorities that it had not been possible to contain the fire, that the ship was being abandoned in view of the dangerous nature of the cargo in number two hold.

Captain Stone was the last man to leave. Later, numerous witnesses testified to the calmness and dignity of his demeanour. There were no indications, they said, that the captain feared for his personal safety, though he was concerned about the injured men who had been placed in the boats before lowering. Nothing could be done about the dead bodies in the engine-room.

As the life-boats pulled away the sea mirrored the smoke and flames from the burning ship.

★ ★ ★

Captain Stone commanded one boat, the chief officer the other. The captain told the chief officer that they would lay off to windward, keeping the *Donnington Wave* in sight until daylight. His boat having a motor engine, a line was passed to the chief officer's which was taken in tow. A mile or so from the burning ship the boats hove-to and waited for daylight.

Between two and three in the morning there was a tropical storm. First came the wind in fierce squalls which whipped up the sea, so that Captain Stone ordered the streaming of sea anchors. No sooner had this been done than the rain came. Torrents of it, a blinding deluge which shut down visibility so completely that the *Donnington Wave* was lost to sight. The captain told the men in the boat — they were having an uncomfortable time — that this was a line squall, a not unusual equatorial phenomenon, and that it would soon pass. But it did not. Several violent squalls followed, each blowing from a different quarter, each accompanied by heavy rain.

Later the wind fell away but the rain continued. By daylight that too had ceased and the sea grew calmer. Squalls of wind and rain could still be seen to the westward. It was some time before the light grew strong enough for those in the boats, drenched and wretched, to see the *Donnington Wave*. When they did they found she was some five miles to the west of them, and in place of the billowing smoke expected there was no more than a thin spiral somewhere amidships.

Captain Stone ordered a return to the ship and before long the boats were within a mile.

The nearer they got the more apparent it became that the fire no longer raged. The rainstorms, concluded the captain, and the abatement of the wind had done their work. Nevertheless, mindful of the contents of number two hold and the thin spiral of smoke amidships, he approached with circumspection, making a wide circle round the ship. It was then, with astonishment, that he saw the diminutive shapes of men on the bridge and foc'sle head. But it was not until the boats had rounded the freighter's bows that they saw the small ship alongside. It was a Japanese stern trawler. She was preparing to take the *Donnington Wave* in tow.

★　★　★

The court of inquiry convened by the Board of Trade in London two months later to inquire into the abandonment of the *Donnington Wave* turned out to be a long drawn affair.

The underwriters who were liable for the salvage award — the operation had eventually become a joint one by the Japanese stern trawler and the frigate of the Indian Navy — were substantially interested, as was the Donnington Steamship Company Limited. The award had been a large one because the ship had been abandoned and become derelict. Had the master and some of her crew — or the master alone — remained on board it would have been materially lower.

Lloyd's underwriters and the owners, concerned that the ship had been abandoned, spared no effort to find out why. For this purpose they assembled a formidable array of legal talent. The evidence of the chief officer, and to some extent that of the chief engineer, had not helped Captain Stone. Nevertheless both men had tried, as far as evidence on oath permitted, to protect the captain. It took the court three days to hear the evidence and another two for argument. In concluding his summing up the president said to his assessors, 'You must ask yourselves whether the casualty was due to any wrongful act or default of the master or other person. In particular you must consider whether, having regard to all the circumstances, the decision to abandon the ship at that time was a correct one?' — he paused, looking round the room with stern eyes — 'or whether it was hasty, ill-judged and unseamanlike. That in short is the issue before the court.'

The assessors, themselves master mariners, influenced among other things by the legal luminaries who had dug deep into Captain Stone's past, there to unearth the nervous breakdown of 1944 and the subsequent addiction to alcohol, had decided that the decision to abandon ship had *not* been a correct one, and his Master's Certificate was suspended for two years.

Technically this meant he could not serve in command of a British registered foreign-going ship for the next two years. Its practical effect, however, was to deprive him for all time of such a command, for British owners and insurers shy away from masters whose certificates have been suspended as horses shy from burning fodder. Confronted once again by the spectre of cowardice — for he saw in the court's decision nothing more than reaffirmation of this — Stone, a teetotaller for more than twenty years, sought escape once more in the mists of alcoholism.

A bad time followed. The house in Surbiton was sold, relations with his wife and sons reached breaking point, and he was persuaded to enter an institution for treatment. In time he seemed to respond, was discharged and after months of humiliating endeavour he obtained, with the assistance of Mr Hassim Racher, a Liberian Master's Certificate and command of the Liberian registered *Moonraker*.

There he had been for the last eighteen months but, unlike the post-1944 period, his break from alcoholism this time was by no means complete. For long intervals, many weeks at a time, he would not touch it. Then, under stress of some sort or other, he would resort to the mahogany drawer under the bunk and would not be seen for several days. Dwala would report that Captain Stone was indisposed — the recurrence of a wartime injury, the Ghanaian steward would say, and it was in a sense true. But during that time Dwala would allow no one to see his master.

The polite fiction was not convincing, but its niceties were observed. Particularly by Mr Hassim Racher to whose ears rumours of Captain Stone's weakness came from time to time. For reasons best known to himself Mr Racher was not in the least worried by these which he affected not to have heard.

3

Captain Stone had succumbed to the temptation of the mahogany drawer in the early hours of Saturday the 7th November. Throughout that day he had seen no one but Dwala, the steward. Not even his niece.

'No, Miss Susie,' said the Ghanaian, large and formidable at the door of the captain's cabin. 'You cannot see your uncle. He is sleeping.'

'Sleeping.' She looked at her watch. 'It's after ten o'clock in the morning.'

Dwala regarded her mournfully, 'I think he will sleep all the day long.'

'Is he sick?'

'It is the head. From the war you know.' The African sighed. 'There are bad pains inside. Migraine they call it. He cannot see properly.'

'Poor uncle,' said Susie, who knew he'd been torpedoed twice and burnt severely. 'But can't I help? Do something for him?'

'No, Miss Susie. To-morrow, perhaps the next day, he will be better. Until then he must sleep.' Dwala's eyes were large and sad like a spaniel's.

'No food?' Susie's grey eyes, arched eyebrows and upturned nose registered surprise.

'The captain does not like food at such times. Just a little milk maybe.'

'Aspirins? Something for the headache?'

Dwala nodded. 'He has them. Also pills for the stomach.'

She looked at him uncertainly. 'Tell him I'm very sorry. That I wanted to help. Say I hope he'll be better soon.'

'I will tell him.' Dwala shut the door.

Susie went down to the chief steward's cabin and told him of her uncle's indisposition. Mr Jenkins was an efficient-looking man with a bustling manner. Like many who followed his profession he was inclined to plumpness.

'Yes,' he said. 'Dwala told me the Old Man had a . . . ' He paused, watching Susie with quick inquiring eyes. 'Said he was — ah — er — a bit off colour. Never mind, love. He'll soon be over it. Nearly five weeks now since the last one.'

'It's a shame isn't it?' said Susie. 'That he should still suffer from the war.'

'From the war?' Mr Jenkins' eyebrows lifted in polite surprise.

'Yes. He was torpedoed twice. Had terrible burns. Nearly died, you know.'

'Ah, yes.' Mr Jenkins looked at her with a knowing air. 'Of course. I've seen the scars.'

'On his neck and cheek, you mean?'

'That's nothing,' said Mr Jenkins. 'You should see the rest of him.'

'Bad are they?'

'Shocking. Funny thing. The Old Man's got a hairy chest. But on one side, where the scars are, there's no hair. Won't grow, see.'

'Like napalm in Vietnam, I suppose. The scorched jungle,' said Susie. 'Wars are terrible things. That's why we're going to stop them.'

Mr Jenkins looked up from the stores' ledger he was entering and scratched his head. 'Who's we?'

'Our generation.' She smiled shyly. 'You know. Make love not war.'

Mr Jenkins could see that she was very sincere but he didn't like the sentiment. It conjured up visions of demonstrations in Grosvenor Square, police horses being knocked down and fornication in Hyde Park. So he snorted. 'Oh, that lot.' He put the ball point pen behind his ear and closed the ledger. 'Our lot made love *and* war. Didn't do us no harm, neither. Same as all the others before us. It's natural you see. Fighting and making love. Don't see you can change that.'

Susie didn't want to offend Mr Jenkins who'd been kind to her from the day she had come on board, so she changed the subject. 'Can't I do something to help you?'

'Yes, love.' He pushed across a pile of invoices and duplicate orders. 'Marry that lot for me.'

'Marry them?'

'Yes. Take an order, find the invoice that refers to it, and staple them together. Then put the whole lot in proper date order.'

Susie smiled. 'Oh, yes. I'd like to do that. Shall I take them through to the saloon?'

'That's the idea. You won't be disturbed there. Not even by that passage-worker.' Mr Jenkins winked. 'Got a soft spot for him, haven't you?'

Susie blushed as she scooped up the invoices and orders. 'Oh, he's all right,' she said casually.

'Well, we've all been young once,' said Mr Jenkins. 'Now you run along and don't worry about your uncle. He'll soon be fine.'

'Thank you, Mr Jenkins.'

★ ★ ★

By noon on Sunday Captain Stone had not emerged from his cabin. On the bridge eight bells were struck, the siren was sounded, Lopez, the second officer, took the noon sight and plotted the ship's position on the chart.

40

Doing this alone without the captain gave him especial pleasure. Normally they took the noon sight together and if their readings of the sun's altitude differed, Captain Stone would always prefer his own to Lopez's, however small the difference. Just as he would insist on plotting the noon position on the chart, although that was the second officer's duty.

Martinho Lopez was a tall, olive-skinned man with the long hands and tapering fingers of a woman. He wore sideburns and rather more hair than was usual among second mates in cargo ships. It was of a shining blackness and locks of it hung over his eyes when he leant over the chart room table, so that he had to brush them away with those long fingers.

His main interest in life was music; that is, but for the political activities which had made him a fugitive. Life at sea in the *Moonraker* gave him what he most needed: solitude, privacy, and sanctuary from those who were anxious to find him. Lopez was not his real name, nor was Martinho.

In his cabin were albums of Beethoven, Bach, Mozart, Tchaikovsky, Delius, Prokofiev and others . . . and a stereo hi-fi. With the aid of the carpenter he had sound-proofed the cabin so that even with the volume turned up, he did not disturb others in the officers' quarters.

This was his first voyage in the *Moonraker* and since he was a quiet withdrawn man, no one really knew him. His shipmates regarded him as a strange creature, unusually gentle and reserved for a ship's officer. Little was known of his past except that he was a Mexican, that he had served in Cuban ships and had returned to the sea after some years ashore. He had a Second Mate's Certificate issued in Panama.

Having charted the noon position, Martinho Lopez entered it in the logbook: Latitude 23° 47′ S: Longitude 75° 30′ E: day's run, 332 nautical miles: speed made good 13.9 knots.

Next he measured off the distance to go to Port Louis, Mauritius. It was 1,020 miles. Another three days of steaming. It was Sunday. That meant Mauritius on Wednesday.

★ ★ ★

Later that Sunday, *Moonraker's* radio operator heard a ship reporting the suspected presence of a cyclone.

The corrected barometer reading, radioed the *Southern Sun*, was five millibars below the normal mean, wind force six to seven.

Before the fall in barometric pressure the ship had experienced a heavy easterly swell in which direction her captain suspected lay the centre of a tropical storm.

Port Louis had acknowledged the signal and re-broadcast it as a warning to shipping, adding that it was too early yet to predict the position and possible movement of the storm. The *Southern Sun* — bound for Tamatave, speed 18 knots — gave her position as 18° 33′ S: 68° 40′ E. She undertook to submit further reports as the situation developed.

Kantle, the *Moonraker*'s radio operator, a wizened man with yellow hair and an apologetic face, took the message to the captain's cabin. There he became involved in an argument with Dwala.

'But this is a storm warning,' protested Kantle. 'Get out of my way. I must show it to the captain.'

There was no moving the big Ghanaian standing in the half open doorway. 'Give to me,' he put out his hand. 'I show to captain immediate.'

The radio operator handed over the message, his manner proclaiming how much he disapproved of this procedure, and he went away grumbling. He took his complaint to Frascatti, the chief officer, whom he found in the smoke-filled chart room, a cheroot between his teeth. While Frascatti listened to Kantle he was thinking, not for the first time, that if things went on like this he might yet get command of the *Moonraker*. It would mean obtaining a master's certificate but that could be arranged. It was really only a question of money. When Kantle had said his piece, Frascatti read the message.

'Not my business.' He handed it back and shrugged his shoulders. 'Captain has signal now. That's his business.'

'But he's probably on one of his . . . you know.' Kantle looked embarrassed. He liked the captain.

'Maybe. I don't know. Dwala says the Old Man gotta bad headache. Okay. He can still read radio messages.'

Kantle, for his part, thought he could read the Italian's thoughts which weren't very helpful.

'Don't you think you should — er — discuss it with him?'

Frascatti put up a screen of blue smoke, narrowed his eyes and read the message again. 'Other ship is far — more than 400 miles from here,' he said. 'Plenty time. I see many cyclone warnings before and nothing happen.' He didn't add that, despite his Liberian Mate's Certificate — it had cost him good money in Hong Kong — he was not a qualified mate, that until he'd joined the *Moonraker* his fifteen years at sea had been spent in the foc'sles of Italian ships working as an able seaman. He knew nothing of the complex laws of tropical storms and he'd never experienced one. As far as he was concerned the cyclone — if it were one — was far away and in any case he reckoned that *Moonraker*, a fourteen knot, 8,000 ton ship, should be able to look after herself.

Kantle went next to the second officer's cabin. Martinho Lopez, who'd come off watch at four o'clock, had settled down to a concerto when the knock came on the door. The interruption irritated him but he switched off the hi-fi, opened the door and listened courteously to the radio operator. When Lopez had read the *Southern Sun*'s message he passed it back to Kantle. 'It is the captain's responsibility. This is only warning of a possible cyclone far away. Maybe it does not exist. Let us wait and see. If there is danger, the captain will come to the bridge.'

'If he can.' Kantle looked dubious.

Lopez contemplated him absent-mindedly. His thoughts were with Beethoven. 'I do not wish to make trouble. If it is a cyclone there will be other signals.'

Lopez had been in a cyclone once, in the Caribbean where they are called hurricanes,

45

but it was many years ago and his ship had avoided the storm centre. It did not seem in retrospect to have been a serious matter. He had heard rumours of the captain's attacks but had never seen him drunk. He wondered if Dwala's version was not the correct one. Frascatti made no secret of his dislike for the captain, and it was the Italian, after all, who put out the gossip. Lopez didn't want to offend the captain because he hoped to remain in the *Moonraker*, at least for her next voyage, and he respected Stone who seemed a capable man.

In the circumstances he decided in favour of the Beethoven concerto.

★   ★   ★

The day moved on through afternoon to evening and night. The *Southern Sun* sent further weather reports to Port Louis. As she steamed to the west she was drawing away from the area of disturbance, her barometer was rising slowly and the wind, having veered, had moderated. In her last message, at eight o'clock, she reported that the swell, now diminishing, was from east-south-east.

Apart from these transmissions, Kantle had heard two other ships reporting falling barometers, shifts of wind, and indications of unusual weather. When he'd delivered these to the captain, via Dwala, he discussed them with Frascatti who pointed out that the other ships were even farther from the *Southern Sun* than was the *Moonraker*. Since Frascatti found this reassuring, Kantle assumed it must be and his apprehension faded.

Port Louis re-broadcast a summary of these reports, warning shipping that an area of unusually low pressure, cyclonic in character, existed in approximately 18° south and 70° east; it would probably move in a westerly to south-westerly direction. There was not as yet, concluded the message, sufficient information on which to base more specific predictions.

★　★　★

During those hours between four in the afternoon and eight that evening, *Moonraker* experienced a number of changes in the weather. Endless ranks of cirrus cloud which had all day stretched from horizon to horizon, gave way to dark layers of alto-cumulus: the sky became leaden and the sea took on a grey rather desolate aspect. A pronounced swell came in from the north and in the second dog-watch the prevailing wind, the south-east trades, which had been

47

blowing steadily for days, fell away altogether and the *Moonraker* moved upon a windless sea. The sudden lull, the long swell, the lowering sky, the steel-like greyness of the horizon, filled Kantle with foreboding. But Dwala assured him that the captain had seen the radio messages — as of course had the chief officer — so he concluded that his sense of foreboding was misplaced. Kantle was by nature a worrying man.

The lull was short-lived. The wind came again, veering to the south and before long it was blowing force six. About this time the barometer began to fall, a fact which made little impression on Frascatti then on watch. Knowing as little of the indications of cyclones as he did of the laws of tropical storms, he assumed that this was no more than a local disturbance, which was how he described it when handing over the watch to the third mate at eight o'clock.

None the less, Frascatti was sufficient of a seaman to send for the bo'sun and carpenter and tell them to take a look round the ship to see that all was properly secured.

★ ★ ★

Soon after nine o'clock that night Captain Stone arrived on the bridge. He was correctly dressed but it was evident that he had not shaved for several days.

He'd come up by way of the internal stairway in the officers' accommodation which led to the chart room, wheelhouse and bridge, so that he was not really aware of the weather on his journey upwards. Although the ship's movements in the last hour had indicated a change in the weather, he was shocked when he stepped out into it.

Low scudding clouds cast a blanket of darkness over the night but the force of the wind, the slap and wash of the sea, the cork-screwing of the ship, were things he could feel and hear. And they were more than he'd expected. He went to the windward side of the bridge and saw in the green reflection of the starboard light the heaped seas coming up from astern, lumping as they met the swell, forming sharp watery pinnacles before collapsing.

Tell-tale streaks of foam showed the wind had backed to the east. Watching this angry confusion of water, dimly lit by green light, made him giddy. He rubbed his eyes and went to the steering compass to check the ship's heading. He spoke to the third officer. They agreed the force and direction of the wind . . . east by north, six to seven. The third officer was a silent young Liberian. He'd begun his seafaring in surf-boats on the West African coast and graduated via trawlers to the *Moonraker*. He was quietly proud of his uniform and officer's status. These were things he'd dreamt of as a boy when they'd seemed impossible of fulfilment. His name was Addu Batu, but he was often called *Kroo* because of the surf-boats he spoke of so shyly when pressed. Addu Batu feared Captain Stone. He'd never suffered at the hands of the old man but he *was* captain, and dignified and remote. Addu Batu did not believe the rumours he'd heard of his weakness. Somehow they didn't fit.

Having read through the accumulated radio messages Captain Stone laboriously but accurately plotted the positions, course and speed of the *Southern Sun* and other reporting ships and brought up to date the *Moonraker*'s, last charted by the chief officer at eight o'clock.

There was a persistent buzzing in his head and his vision was blurred, so that plotting took a long time. When he'd finished he mopped perspiration from his face with the chart house towel. Turning to the mercurial barometer swinging in gimbals above the settee he noted the reading and whistled with surprise. The logbook showed it had dropped three millibars in four hours. From the sliding scale he took the correction for latitude and height of eye, and from the *Admiralty Sailing Directions* that for diurnal variation. These gave a true reading of 1008 millibars: five below normal mean. That was a danger signal.

Concentrating his faculties he returned to the chart table. Against *Moonraker*'s position and those of the reporting ships he noted the force and direction of wind sea and swell, and the barometer readings. Once again he turned his attention to *Moonraker*'s charted position. With a Perspex protractor he began to measure . . . what was he trying to measure? His mind switched off as he stared at the chart, unaware of what he saw, trying to remember. A wave of nausea swept him but he fought it off and with an effort of concentration remembered . . . *if the observer faces the wind the storm centre will be nine to eleven points on his left hand side when the storm is about two hundred miles distant.*

That distance was consistent with the fall in the barometer and with the wind they were experiencing, east by north, force six to seven on the Beaufort scale: a moderate gale. It was consistent, too, with the other ships' reports.

He slid the protractor across the chart until the hole in its centre coincided with the pencilled circle of the *Moonraker*'s position.

Nine to eleven points to the left, he kept reminding himself . . . but the staggering movement of the ship, the howl of wind through the chart house ventilators, the slap of flying spray on the windows — these things confused him, and the dull ache in his head made it feel as if it didn't belong. It was difficult to orientate, the chart table and the bookcases seemed to revolve about him — that was it, *revolving storms* . . . cyclones. It all came back. Nine to eleven points to the left . . . left? That was northerly wasn't it? He looked at the compass rose on the chart. Yes. North was left if one faced the wind. With the protractor he measured off nine to eleven points. So the centre of the storm was between . . . between what? His mind went blank again. He sighed. Between what? Through long force of habit an image of the old magnetic compass card formed in his mind. Much better than the 360 degree compass rose on the chart. A seaman knew where he was with the old card.

He studied the image with his eyes shut and the answer came . . . the wind was east-by-north. So the centre of the storm was between north-by-west and nor-west-by-north. Distance? Wind force six to seven, twenty-five to thirty-five knots, backing and increasing in velocity. Better play safe. Say between 150 and 200 miles.

A point difference in the bearing of the centre at 200 miles could displace it by 80 miles. He reached for the dividers, measured a radius of 40 miles on the latitude scale and with shaking hands described a circle. Somewhere within that circle, 150 to 200 miles from the ship, lay the storm centre. By relating his own observations to the information received from Mauritius and the reporting ships, he narrowed the radius to 20 miles and plotted the probable course of the cyclone. It was, he concluded, moving between WSW and SW.

Drops of perspiration were smudging the chart. He stood back, rubbing his face, neck and hands with the towel again. At what speed was the storm moving? He couldn't say with accuracy but probably between ten and fifteen knots. Faster as it moved south into higher latitudes. And it would almost certainly recurve.

Captain Stone knew his laws of revolving tropical storms for he had passed the British Board of Trade examinations three times . . . first for a Second Mate's certificate, then for a Mate's and finally for Master Mariner. What was more he had twice been in ships in such storms: in the China Sea and in the Pacific — *typhoons* they called them in those waters. He'd been in command on the last occasion and kept his ship clear of the storm centre, but even outside it the wind and seas had been something not easily forgotten.

Now, looking at what he'd plotted on the chart and acutely aware of the change of weather, he decided that *Moonraker*'s present course might lead her too close to the cyclone for safety. It was imperative to keep the ship at least fifty miles from the storm centre, preferably more.

With these thoughts in mind he ordered the third officer to alter course to the southward, away from the path of the advancing storm.

That was Captain Stone's first mistake. Not that the alteration of course was by itself irrevocably incorrect, but the reasons his mind furnished for it were. For he had a mental picture of the cyclone recurving before long to the north-east, away from the *Moonraker*. As the situation developed that faulty reasoning would be applied again and again, and the consequences would be disastrous.

Why had he made the mistake? Partly it was the typhoon in the China Sea . . . the constant recollection of that occasion, its nagging intrusion as he considered the problem now confronting him. But mostly it was something else: the steady erosion of his brain cells. Age alone was doing that, but alcohol had accelerated the process. Clinically speaking he was still drunk and though the responsibility of command is said to confer special wisdom, to enable a man to draw on otherwise untapped resources, it cannot perform miracles.

Captain Stone's typhoons, one in the China Sea, the other off the Marshall Islands, had been in the northern hemisphere, whereas the *Moonraker* was in the southern hemisphere. In one hemisphere the habits of tropical storms — cyclones, typhoons, hurricanes, willy-willies, call them what you will — are in important respects the reverse of those in the other. For instance, their habitual path in the northern hemisphere is north and west, usually recurving to north and east. In the southern hemisphere, on the other hand, their habit is to follow a path south and west, recurving later to south and east.

Captain Stone would never in his normal mind — that is to say in those long, predominantly sober intervals between *attacks* — have slipped so easily into this confusion of habits and hemispheres.

That a cyclone should have occurred in the Indian Ocean so early in November was in itself unusual; that it should have coincided with one of Stone's *attacks* was, mathematically speaking, a very high order of chance . . . and that there was on board no officer other than himself who knew anything worth knowing about tropical storms was to prove disastrous.

Back in the chart room he took a radio pad from the shelf above the chart table and groping in his mind for the right words wrote a message for the meteorological authorities in Port Louis. While he was doing this Dwala arrived, black and inscrutable, a Thermos flask and a cup in his hands.

'Your hot milk, captain, sah.'

Without looking up, Captain Stone said, 'Thank you, Dwala.'

The African put the Thermos and cup in the rack and disappeared as quietly as he'd come.

'Christ,' said Captain Stone who was neither blasphemous nor profane. 'That's it. Dwala's like Christ.' He frowned, concentrating once more upon the signal pad.

It took him ten minutes to complete the message. To his clouded mind what he was doing had a spectral quality, as if he were outside himself looking down on a figure crouched over the chart table. He did not, somehow, feel personally involved.

Nevertheless when Port Louis received the

message it would prove to be the most precise report of the estimated position and movement of cyclone *Alpha* — it was the first of the season — so far received from any ship. Indeed, it was the first signal unequivocally to name the disturbance a cyclone. It was unfortunate, though, that the message concluded with: *Am altering course as necessary to avoid storm centre.* Had he informed the authorities that he had altered course to the south-west they would probably, at that stage, have queried his action.

Captain Stone gave the message to Kantle for dispatch, whereafter he sent for Andrew McLintoch and Carlo Frascatti.

4

Andrew McLintoch, chief engineer of the *Moonraker*, was a querulous Scot who should long since have retired. But widowed and childless, his only love was the marine steam engine and his only hope of employment a foreign registered ship. He was seventy-two.

Perpetually grumbling, he spent his life between the cabin amidships and the engine-room. Other activities, like a brief spell on deck to take the air, evening meals in the saloon under the bridge (he often skipped them, preferring the engineers' messroom where he could wear greasy overalls and listen to worthwhile conversation), and rare trips ashore in foreign ports were no more than petty diversions from his real world of *Moonraker*'s machinery and her worn but reliable oil-fired boilers.

They had of course been made in Scotland.

The steam engine was, in Mr McLintoch's opinion, man's fundamental invention. What followed had been built on that great leap forward. The internal combustion engine, he would ask? What was it but a development of the steam reciprocating engine, using petrol or oil mixed with air in place of steam. But the jet engine, his listeners would insist, what of that? Nothing more, he would say, waving his pipe, than the turbine adapted to hydro-carbon fuels. Ah, but the nuclear-powered ships, what were they then? Mr McLintoch would look pained. 'Weel,' he would say in his high pitched tremor, 'I'd ha thought e'en a body that kens nithin' o' marine engineerin', would ken that it's a boiler and a steam turbine they're back to. It's only the fuel to heat the boiler that's nuclear. Nae a thing more.'

Then making a grumbling noise and sucking at his pipe he'd say with quiet reverence, 'Aye. That's the wonder o' it. They had to come back to steam in the end.'

He loved his steam engines, main and auxiliary, and cared for them as if they were his children. But he had no time for the internal combustion engines in the ship: the petrol engine in number one lifeboat and the diesel powered emergency generator in the after-castle. He had assigned responsibility for these to Thoresen, the Danish second engineer, who in turn assigned it to the third engineer, Achmed Khalif, who came from Egypt.

When he was called to the bridge Mr

McLintoch was in his cabin engrossed in an account of a new steam valve. He put down the journal with a gesture of irritation. 'Och, what's he wanting the noo?'

The sides of Mr McLintoch's face had fallen in because of age and an aversion to false teeth. A beaky nose curved down to an upward thrusting jaw, and when he put on his cap and stuck a pipe in his mouth he looked much like Popeye the Sailorman. He would not have liked the analogy because he had a poor opinion of seamen, particularly of ships' captains. They were not, in his view, what they used to be.

He got on well enough with Captain Stone who observed scrupulously the line of demarcation between engine-room and deck. But Mr McLintoch knew of the captain's weakness and, being a lifelong abstainer himself, could not pardon it.

★ ★ ★

When he was called to the bridge Carlo Frascatti was in his cabin feeding a parakeet. It perched on his shoulder making twittering noises as he gave it apple peel. Frascatti mimicked the twittering so well that he and the parakeet seemed able to communicate. The Italian believed they could.

60

The bird, bought in Sydney and very beautiful in blues, greens and tangerines, was a present for his sister Violetta. She lived with his widowed mother in an apartment near the docks in Naples. The mother didn't work. Violetta, a polio cripple, could not be left alone. But for Carlo Frascatti, she would long since have gone to an institution. He was fond of his mother but adored Violetta. Because of them, marriage was something he'd never felt able to contemplate. This had embittered him and had much to do with his surly manner. Between voyages he would spend his time in the little apartment in a back street off the Via Marinella.

Frascatti thought now of Violetta's excitement when she saw the parakeet and learnt that it was hers. It would bring beauty and companionship into her life. They would get on famously. Of that he was sure.

But he was required on the bridge. Muttering and swearing because he resented the call and the weather was bad, he put the parakeet in its cage, got into an oilskin coat, jammed on a cap and with a last look round to see that all was secure, left the cabin. He'd heard that the captain was up and about and the news disappointed him. It meant that Stone was now sober and worrying about the weather.

61

Having had his orders from Captain Stone, the chief officer left the chart house as Mr McLintoch arrived.

The ship was rolling and pitching, an uncomfortable corkscrewing motion, and the wind hissed balefully in the rigging. Now and then she would roll heavily in response to the swell on her starboard beam, then dip and stagger as a sea hit her quarter, throwing up a sheet of spray which the wind dashed across the centre-castle. At times spray went over the bridge and though it was not raining, the *Moonraker* was wet from stem to stern.

In the chart house the mercurial barometer swinging in its gimbals reflected the ship's movements, and the books on the shelf above the chart table flopped from side to side as she rolled. Captain Stone, crouched over the chart table, looked up as the chief engineer came in. 'Ah, Mr McLintoch. You're here.'

The chief engineer took the pipe from his mouth. 'Aye?' he said sternly. 'I am that.'

'There's a cyclone to the north-west of us,' said the captain. 'A hundred and fifty to two hundred miles away. We're experiencing some of the disturbance. It's moving in a south-westerly direction. Should be curving away soon, but I've altered four points to the southward.' He paused, looking at the chart and then back at McLintoch who saw that the captain's eyes were bloodshot.

'The alteration's a precaution,' said Stone. 'We don't want to get too close.' He drew his hand across his forehead as if brushing something away. 'The met. people in Mauritius have sent storm warnings. They can't locate the centre yet . . . nor predict its movements. Too few ships reporting in the disturbed area.' He sighed. 'Not enough data, you see.'

'Aye.' McLintoch fixed him with a coldly critical eye. 'An' ye'll be wantin' me to keep a good head o' steam . . . an' be ready for all eventualities.'

The captain smiled. 'Exactly.' He respected the chief engineer. Too old to be at sea, but a good engineer. One of the old school.

'Then I'll be gettin' along an' seein' to it.' The chief engineer put the empty pipe in his mouth, banged the crown of his cap to make sure it was well seated, and left the chart house.

'Thank you, chief,' Captain Stone called after him, a little taken aback by the old man's sudden departure.

Before McLintoch's arrival in the chart house Captain Stone had given the chief officer his orders. 'Get hold of the bo'sun and carpenter. Make sure everything on deck is ship-shape. Well secured. Rig life-lines. Lashings on the hatch tarpaulins. Ventilators properly trimmed. Plug and screw them down where possible.' While he spoke Stone looked at the chart, not at the chief officer. 'Always best to assume there's going to be trouble, Mr Frascatti. Keep your yard arm clear that way.'

'Okay, captain. Leave it to me. I fix.' Frascatti's speech came in sharp jerks, like the uncertain staccato of a motorbike starting on a cold morning.

As the chief officer was about to leave the chart house Captain Stone said, 'And see to it yourself, Mr Frascatti. When the work has been done, go round and see for yourself. Everything must be ship-shape.'

Frascatti was sick and tired of *ship-shape*. Just as he was of the homilies the captain so often delivered.

★ ★ ★

Moonraker's alteration of course to the south-west had been made at nine-twenty that night. It brought wind and sea on to the port quarter, which was where it should have been had the wind been veering or holding steady. But it was backing. The swell, steep

64

but invisible under the mantle of darkness, came in from abaft the starboard beam causing the ship to roll heavily.

By midnight there was little change in the weather. The wind continued to blow from east-by-north at force six to seven, gusting at times. There was a lumpy confused sea which Captain Stone attributed to the easterly wind and sea jostling the north-westerly swell. The resolution of forces of great magnitude. The motion of the ship was uncomfortable but not unduly so. What water she shipped was mostly spray, though at times the top of a following sea would lop on to the after well-deck.

Having seen to it that a good head of steam would be available Mr McLintoch had gone back to his cabin and the article on the new valve. Frascatti sent for the bosun and carpenter and gave them their instructions. He implied that Captain Stone was unnecessarily alarmed, and hinted at his weakness. Later the bosun and carpenter reported that they'd been round the ship with a couple of hands, everything was secure, life-lines rigged, lashings on the hatches, ventilators trimmed, some screwed down, others plugged.

Frascatti went to the bridge and reported that all was well. Captain Stone, hunched over the chart house table, had replied, 'Very good, Mr Frascatti.'

The captain was tired and his headache worried him. But he'd been busy and the hours had gone quickly. He'd continued to plot *Moonraker's* dead reckoning position and the estimated position of the storm centre. There'd been a further storm warning from Port Louis and messages from other ships, only one of which was still in the disturbed area. Twice he'd written out radio messages for Port Louis, each of them laconic to a degree: *No change in weather experienced since my last signal.*

The chief officer returned to his cabin. Since he would have the watch at four the next morning, he put a cloth over the parakeet's cage and turned in. He'd not gone round the upper deck to see, as the captain put it, that all was *ship-shape*. The bosun and carpenter had said that it *was*: that was good enough for him. It wouldn't have been if he'd known that, their other tasks completed, they'd stood by the rail at the after end of the boat-deck, shining their torches down on the heavy lifts, deciding that with the tops of the waves lopping on to the well-deck when the ship rolled to windward, the prospect of more poking round there in the dark was unattractive.

And the big lighters had looked secure enough.

Neither of these men was unduly conscientious. Had they been, they wouldn't have been serving in the *Moonraker*. Ships tend to get the crews they deserve.

★ ★ ★

At midnight the watches changed. Martinho Lopez came up to the bridge and took over from the third officer, Addu Batu. In the chart house the captain explained the significance of the weather information on the chart. Lopez, who had considerable faith in the captain's wisdom, inclined his head politely from time to time though he was not really listening.

'Weather's been much the same since I came up at nine,' said Stone. 'I think we're running parallel with the storm. Any time now it should recurve away from us. The centre must be somewhere here.' He indicated the position with a pencil. 'To the nor-nor-west. Anything from a hundred and fifty to two hundred miles. No need to worry. I'll be staying up here until daybreak.'

Lopez looked at the tired face of the older man and felt sorry for him. The mild blue eyes were suffused with pink, and over the unshaven face the bristles showed white against flushed skin. For a moment the second officer wondered about the rumours of the captain's weakness. But there was no smell of gin so the Mexican dismissed the idea.

He did not know that Dwala's ministrations had long since purged Captain Stone's stomach of its former contents and replaced them with cornflakes and warm milk. But the alcohol was still in the blood stream, visiting all parts of the captain's body including the brain. This it had deoxygenated and inflamed, causing the severe headache. Lopez did not know that the captain was experiencing the symptoms of a major hangover while marshalling his resources to deal with a problem of considerable magnitude.

'You are not going down, captain?' asked Lopez. 'I can call you if the weather . . . '

'I'll be staying here, Mr Lopez.'

Stone had used his gruff voice so the second officer left the chart house and went out on to the bridge. The wind was from astern and after the third douche of spray, Lopez went amidships where the bridge became the forepart of the wheelhouse. He looked into the night through a clear-glass screen which spun away the water dripping from the wheelhouse roof.

There was nothing to be seen but a wall of darkness, pierced occasionally by the phosphorescent crest of a breaking wave. The wind in the rigging moaned, the notes rising and falling as it gusted. It was blowing at about thirty knots but with the ship steaming downwind it seemed less. Lopez decided that unless it increased he would log it as force 5 at the end of the watch.

Wedging himself against the cork-screwing motion, he gazed into the darkness thinking of Felicia Perez. His mental picture of her was perpetually refreshed by the photographs in his cabin. She had an intelligent forehead hidden by a mantle of black hair; beautiful, limpid almond eyes; high cheek bones, and lips that were always soft and moist. She was as tall as he was until they were in bed. They used to laugh about that. 'I should wear the high heels here. It is not fair that you are longer,' she would say looking down into his eyes, smothering him with her hair. She had firm breasts with upward pouting nipples. They were a challenge to his virility and, when he kissed them, mistily evocative of babyhood.

His thoughts trailed off as he heard above the noise of wind and sea, the chart house door slamming. He turned to see a dark shape cross to the steering compass. Stone's face showed up in the dim light of the binnacle. Then the captain went to the port side of the bridge, disappearing into the darkness. He came back to say, 'Not much change. Wind eased a little maybe. Still from the east. Bit northerly, too, I daresay.'

'Yes, sir.' Lopez was quiet, respectful. His mind still more with Felicia than the weather.

The headache was worrying Stone. Its insistent pressure on the temples, the throbbing. A blood vessel could burst in one's brain, couldn't it? That was how a man got a stroke. Crippled him. All down one side, like that mate in the *Sidonia*. Done in the twinkling of an eye. A fine healthy man struck down. No more than thirty.

The throbbing made it difficult to concentrate. The inside of his mouth, his throat and tongue were parched. Like dry leather he thought. He rubbed the back of a hand across his eyes. One good tot, perhaps two, and the pain and dehydrated feeling would go. He shook the thought away. There were important decisions to be made. In the wheelhouse the luminous dial of the clock showed twenty-two minutes after midnight. Before the alteration at nine-twenty the course for Mauritius had been north-fifteen-west. They'd been steering south-forty-five-west now for three hours. With wind and sea

70

astern he estimated they were making good fifteen knots. He went on ticking off the facts mentally: no current to speak of hereabouts; must already be about thirty miles south of the original course line; wind and weather haven't changed. Moderated if anything. Possibly the cyclone has begun to curve away. No point in overdoing the precautions. Time costs money. Hassim Racher will have something to say if we lose over much. Two and a half days' steaming from Mauritius. That means about eight o'clock on Wednesday morning. Good time to arrive. Get in a full day's discharging and loading. Better come up a couple of points.

He went across to the second officer. 'Bring her up a couple of points, Mr Lopez. West-sou-west, that'll be.'

Lopez said, 'West-sou-west, sir,' and repeated the order to the seaman in the wheelhouse. The man was on standby: messenger, relief lookout, and quartermaster if required. He disengaged the auto-steering and made the adjustment, then locked it back on to the new course. 'Steady on west-sou-west,' he reported. Lopez went over to the course indicator and checked the heading. The ship's motion changed with the alteration of course which had brought the wind more nearly astern and the swell forward of the starboard beam.

Captain Stone realised that since the first alteration of course at nine-twenty *Moonraker* and cyclone *Alpha* must have been travelling on parallel courses. He was right.

What he did not know was that his ship was now on what would prove to be a collision course with the storm centre, at that moment one hundred-and-seventy-five miles to the north-west of *Moonraker*.

5

The coaster *Myfanwy*, displacement 956 tons, registered in Cardiff, was having a wet night of it running before a south-easterly gale. To starboard the light on Cape Point was obscured by rain squalls and low cloud but the coaster's captain, Merfyr Evans, saw from the radar screen that his ship was well clear of the Bellows Rock, two miles off shore on the twenty-fathom bank.

At midnight the light was abeam and he altered course to the north-west. Once round Cape Point, they gained the lee of the land and life became easier for those on board.

Merfyr Evans, a bearded craggy-faced man, had been on the bridge for seven hours without a break. The gale and heavy shipping round the Cape worried him. The mate, Napoleon Calvi, was new to the ship. The second mate, Jan Christopherson, even newer. Both too young and inexperienced for Evans's liking. Calvi, a deep-voiced Corsican with a recently acquired Mate's Home Trade certificate, was twenty-five. Though he'd been at sea since he was fourteen, the greater part of that time had been in fishing boats working out of Ajaccio.

Evans, tough, resourceful, with seventeen years at sea, was sceptical of the Corsican: Too young, too much time in fishing boats, too little in coasters, and too sure of himself by far. Evans had not worried overmuch about concealing his views on this subject. Though the Welshman had some admirable qualities, freedom from prejudice and tact were not among them. In his mind he'd already labelled Calvi 'the fisherman' and it was not a complimentary label. Calvi had been in the *Myfanwy* for only three months, having relieved Old Llewellyn, the coaster's original mate and Evans's trusted friend. After a heart attack, followed by a spell in hospital, Jones had gone back to his native Wales.

Jan Christopherson, a young South African, had been in the ship for less than a month. He'd joined in Durban, a few days after getting his Second Mate's Home Trade certificate. But at least he knew the South African coast and got on well with the mixed crew, mostly Cape coloureds and Zulus recruited on the coast.

One man he didn't get on with was Isak John, the coloured boatswain, who at 28 was a few years his senior. These two men disliked each other intensely, though they'd met only three weeks before. On Isak's side there were deep-seated reasons for this antipathy but since the dislike had been instant and mutual some of it must have been chemical for antipathy, like love, often happens at first sight.

★ ★ ★

Soon after two in the morning when the light at Slangkop was abeam, Merfyr Evans went to the small chart room at the back of the wheelhouse to plot the ship's position. He was writing the new date in the logbook, 3rd November, when he remembered it was his birthday.

He'd been born thirty-two years before at Llandyssul in the Vale of Teivi, within a stone's throw of the river. Years afterwards his mother had told him there was a westerly gale blowing that night, so fierce that even in the Vale it was shaking the house and rattling the slate tiles, and the rain had put the Teivi in a great spate the like of which could not be remembered by the oldest inhabitant.

'You're a child of the storm, Merfyr, and that's why you took to the sea. The gale came right up from Cardigan Bay and blew the waves and the wind of it into the marrow of your bones.' Of course she'd said it in Welsh and it had sounded more like poetry, for Welsh is a poetic language.

Looking at the date in the logbook he recollected these things and thought of his mother. There'd be a letter from her in Capetown. In it she'd wish him a happy birthday and she'd give the news of Llandyssul, of the boys and girls he'd been at school with. Especially would she mention Gwynneth Morgan and, without regard for subtlety, in the next paragraph write, *it's time and more now, Merfyr, that you should be thinking of marriage.*

Dear Mother, he thought, this ship is wife enough for me. In that moment he recalled the numbing shock of the cable he'd opened in Rotterdam three years earlier:

'*Myfanwy died yesterday in road accident. Instantaneous the hospital says. She can have known nothing. Be brave my dearest son.*'

There were no children. They'd not been married long when she died. But they'd known each other all their lives. When he bought the coaster — and that was before they'd married — it had never occurred to him to call the vessel anything but *Myfanwy*, although sailors thought it unlucky to change a ship's name. Because of his wife's death he'd accepted the charter on the South African coast — to get away from where it had happened. He could not bear to walk through the streets of Llandyssul and meet his friends, who were her friends. He could not endure the sympathy, the unspoken thoughts when for kindness' sake nothing was said. So he'd gone.

He would never marry again. He avoided women. To be with them was, he felt, disloyal, an act of betrayal. *Myfanwy* the coaster was wife enough, keeping him busy with work and worry. Though she was running him into debt, he loved her dearly. Freeing himself from these thoughts he leant over the chart table and made the entry in the logbook in slow neat script. Then another look at the chart. In two and a half hours they'd be in Table Bay — an hour and a half before daylight. In the wheelhouse he put the engine-room telegraph to *half-speed*, blew on the engine-room voice-pipe and heard the reassuring lilt of Dai Williams' voice. 'What is it?'

'Revolutions for six and a half knots, Dai.'

'For how long?'

'Into Table Bay. About three and a half hours.'

'Aye, Merfyr.'

Dai Williams was the coaster's chief engineer, the only other Welshman on board now that Old Llewellyn had gone.

Merfyr Evans looked at the steering compass and watched for a moment as the wheel, latched on to auto-steering, turned this way and that as if moved by ghostly unseen hands. Next he checked the radar screen noting the position of the pips of light, the ships within range, and the contour of the coastline, the images glowing and fading each time the scanner swept the screen. Satisfied, he went out to the bridge-walk which ran round the wheel-house. Christopherson was on watch, talking in a low voice to Makona the Zulu lookout, the only seaman in the middle watch.

Evans spent a few minutes adjusting his eyes to the darkness. He could see the lights of seven ships ahead, and three abaft the beam. All seemed distant, cold and anonymous. As he watched, what his eyes saw was signalled to his brain. Working with computer-like speed it told him the direction in which the ships were heading, their approximate course, which could be disregarded and which might be a danger. He said to Christopherson, 'How about some tea?'

'Aye, captain,' the second mate turned to the Zulu. 'Tea, Makona. *Shesha* — hurry-up.'

When the seaman had gone Evans said, 'See those steaming lights dead ahead?'

'Yes, captain.'

'What d'you make of them?'

'Tanker, heading this way.'

'Or maybe ore carrier or container ship,' prompted Evans. 'What speed d'you reckon she's doing?'

Christopherson thought for a moment. 'Sixteen or seventeen knots.'

'Twenty or twenty-one if she's a container ship. And we're doing six. Could be closing at twenty-seven knots?'

'Aye, captain.' There was apprehension in the second mate's voice, as if he knew what was coming.

'How far off d'you reckon she is?'

'Five or six miles, sir.'

'Nearer three. That means we can be in collision in seven to eight minutes.' The captain's voice hardened. 'Jump into that wheelhouse and alter to starboard. Be smart about it.'

When Christopherson came back and reported the alteration of course, Evans said, 'It's better done sooner than later. Never forget that.'

'Aye, sir.'

★ ★ ★

79

As the sun pushed its pink rim above the mountains of Hottentots Holland far to the east, *Myfanwy* entered Table Bay. A pilot came on board and the coaster was soon berthed safely in the Duncan Dock, at the far end near the whalecatchers, the yacht club, the dry-dock and repair yards. Away from the quality, the big liners of Union-Castle, Safmarine and P. & O.

A gangway was run up and harbour officials and a clerk from the agents' office came on board. The clerk handed mail and parcels to the captain, the stevedore foreman came on board with his gang, had a word with the mate and the hatches were opened. Two cranes crawled along their tracks, electric motors whirring. They stopped opposite the fore and main deck holds and lowered their gantries, looking much like the birds of their name.

The harbour officials made for the small saloon under the bridge and got busy with their formalities. When they'd gone Evans sat in his cabin sorting the mail and parcels. Two of them were for him: a long slender tube and a small rectangular package. Both had on them the labels of Capetown's leading ships' chandlers. Evans handed the rest of the mail to Christopherson for distribution. Among the letters for him, Evans saw one from his mother. He was about to open it when a bulky letter from the agents caught his eye. What was in it was likely to be important so he opened it first.

His instinct was right. The letter contained unusual instructions. The two years for which he had chartered *Myfanwy* to a South African coaster company had only six weeks to run. The contract would expire then and he'd take the ship back to Cardiff, a wiser but poorer man for the charter had not worked out successfully. It was his fault, he knew. He'd underquoted because he wanted to get away after his wife's death. He'd cut his margins too fine. The coaster, built in 1955, had suffered weather damage in the heavy seas along the South African coast. There had been machinery trouble and repair and maintenance bills had been higher than he'd estimated. Evans owned the coaster but he'd had to borrow heavily to buy her. Bondholders had a substantial share, and interest charges had risen steeply in recent years.

For these reasons he was glad to be nearing the end of the charter. Once back in British and Continental waters in a trade he knew well he felt *Myfanwy* would once again earn good money. And it was needed. Average earnings of at least £250 a day if he were to

81

cover costs and be left with a reasonable profit.

These thoughts were in his mind as he read the agents' instructions. At times he would re-read a paragraph to make sure he'd grasped its meaning, that he'd understood all its implications. *Myfanwy* was, subject to his agreement, to make a voyage well off the beaten track of the coastal trade in which she was engaged. To Kerguelen Island, in latitude 49° south, longitude 70° east, towards Antarctica. To be made on behalf of the French Government.

She was to call first at Port-aux-Français on the east coast of the island, there to unload stores, equipment and fuel for the French weather station. Thereafter she was to proceed to Port Jeanne d'Arc on the southern side of the Baie du Morbihan to deliver stores, equipment and fuel for a French geological survey party, and to load rock and coal samples. Fuel and weather permitting, she was then to transfer two scientists and their equipment from Port-aux-Français to the French meteorological station on Île Amsterdam, an isolated volcanic islet just under eight hundred miles northeast of Kerguelen. Finally she was to make for Durban to discharge the geological samples for transhipment to France.

Evans knew it was a difficult assignment for his small ship. The voyage was outside the limits of the charter agreement and the agents were offering a bonus. It was too good to be turned down. Not that Evans had considered doing that. This was a challenge. Something out of the ordinary.

The agent's instructions referred him to three charts: the general chart of the Southern Ocean and the large scale charts of Kerguelen and Amsterdam islands: also the *Admiralty Sailing Directions, Volume 9, The Antarctic Pilot*, and *Volume 39, The South Indian Ocean Pilot*. The charts were in the tube which had come with the mail, the sailing directions in the rectangular parcel. Tired as he was he took them to the chart room and worked on them, often referring to the sailing directions, reading the descriptions of the islands and ports he must visit, of the navigational hazards, of the occurrence of ice, and much else that was important.

With parallel rulers and dividers he laid off the compass courses and measured the distances. First to Port-aux-Français, then across the bay to Port Jeanne d'Arc; and finally the return journey to Durban by way of Île Amsterdam. The distances involved were well beyond the normal limits of

Myfanwy's endurance: about 2,500 nautical miles from Capetown to Port Jeanne d'Arc, another 800 on to Amsterdam Island, thence close on 2,400 to Durban, a total of 5,700 miles. The coaster's speed was 10 knots — 240 miles a day — for a consumption of 3 tons of diesel fuel. Her fuel tanks had a capacity of 40 tons . . . that gave her a fairweather range of 2,750 miles. *Problem number one.*

But there would be little fair weather: Kerguelen was far south. Much of the journey would be through the Roaring Forties, the strong westerly winds which increased steadily the farther south a ship ventured. Then there were the currents, particularly the Southern Ocean current — known to sailors as the West Wind Drift. Wind and current, and therefore the sea, would be with the ship on the outward journey and to some extent from Kerguelen to Amsterdam Island. But on the return journey there would be head winds and seas until they reached the latitudes of the south-east trades, about 1,000 miles from Amsterdam Island.

The agents' instructions directed *Myfanwy* to arrive at Port-aux-Français on 25th November — three weeks away, that was. It was the southern summer: the period when ice-bergs and growlers having broken loose from the Antarctic ice-shelf would be on the move. There was small comfort in *The Antarctic Pilot*, so thoughtfully supplied by the agents . . . *both the mean and extreme limits of bergs are farther north in the longitudes of the South Atlantic Ocean. This is also the case in the western part of the Indian Ocean* . . . Farther down the page it went on . . . *the mean limits of icebergs are on the whole farthest north in November and December* . . . He didn't like icebergs, no sailors do. Even radar could fail to detect them. *The Antarctic Pilot* warned explicitly about that.

Then there was the fresh-water problem. Unlike a big ship *Myfanwy* had no evaporator for converting salt water to fresh. She could carry up to twenty tons of fresh water. With her crew of fifteen, consumption was about two-thirds of a ton a day — enough for thirty days. The agents' instructions required the coaster to spend ten days discharging and loading in Kerguelen. There were no port facilities, no tugs or lighters. The coaster would have to lie at anchor and use her own resources backed by whatever help could be given locally. Such assistance, wrote the agents, *might be limited*. Masterly under-statement, decided Evans, who'd the seaman's mistrust of landsmen in nautical matters.

The journey there and back, allowing a day for discharging at Amsterdam Island, should take twenty-five days. To be prudent he allowed twenty-eight. Plus ten days for discharging and loading in Kerguelen — he made it twelve. A total of forty days. Not enough fresh water. *Problem number two.*

When he'd read up Amsterdam Island in the sailing directions he realised why the agents' instructions contained the *fuel and weather* permitting clause. Landing there was only possible in fine weather and since the islet was in the Roaring Forties there wasn't likely to be much fine weather. Problems of fuel and water would preclude waiting any length of time for fine weather. He was glad of the escape clause.

With pencil and paper he worked away at the fuel and fresh-water figures. Then he sent for Dai Williams, the chief engineer, and together they got out some answers. Fresh water would have to be rationed and they might have to top up with it in Kerguelen. But preferably not. Bringing off fresh water in the ship's boats would take time — and delays involved the consumption of more fuel and water, even in harbour.

The fuel problem would have to be met by

carrying extra diesel oil in the ship's double bottom ballast tanks. That fuel would be used first so that the ballast tanks could be flooded to improve stability on the more difficult part of the journey . . . the return to Durban via Amsterdam Island. And it would be cold down in those latitudes, they noted, even in the Antarctic summer. Steam heaters would have to be on a lot of the time. That, too, involved fuel.

Finally they estimated that all being well they'd arrive in Durban with twelve to fifteen tons of fuel remaining. A safe enough margin.

6

To those in the *Moonraker*, caught in cyclone *Alpha*, what had seemed a break in the weather towards midnight proved to be short lived. By one o'clock in the morning the wind had increased and the rolling and pitching of the ship was more pronounced. The barometer reading was still five millibars below normal mean.

The bridge messenger brought oilskins for Captain Stone and Lopez for protection against the heavy rain squalls which swept the ship, slapping and splattering against wheel- and chart house windows, trapped water running from side to side of the bridge as the ship rolled, the scuppers gurgling as it sucked away. The windows rattled with the gusting of the wind which had backed again to blow from dead astern — east-north-east, that was — but it blew harder now and with more noise. The swell remained on the starboard beam.

Four bells struck for two o'clock and Dwala came to the chart house with hot milk and sandwiches. He brought, too, a plastic bag with soap and a steaming hand towel.

'Thank you, Dwala,' said the captain. 'But you must sleep. Turn in, man.'

The dark eyes were grave. 'When *you* sleep, captain, sah, I will sleep.' Then he was gone.

Not long afterwards Kantle arrived in a soaked blue raincoat. His straw coloured hair hung across his face in dank locks so that he looked like a wet dog. 'From Mauritius. Just received.' He handed a radio message to the captain.

Stone smiled sympathetically. 'You could phone these through to the bridge.'

'I prefer to bring them, captain.' Kantle didn't add that he was worried and that it was some sort of comfort to talk to someone and see how the captain — who understood it all — was taking things. Kantle was relieved to find him looking calm though evidently tired.

Stone read the message: *Please report weather and your position course and speed.*

He checked *Moonraker*'s dead reckoning position on the chart before writing the reply: *DR position, latitude 23° 40′ S, longitude 71° 50′ east: course, west-south-west: speed 12 knots: swell on starboard beam, wind astern, force seven: heavy rain squalls, visibility poor.*

Kantle went back to the radio cabin and transmitted the signal, Mauritius acknowledged and told him to stand by. In Port Louis the meteorological authorities, starved for news of cyclone *Alpha,* pondered *Moonraker*'s signal. The course Captain Stone was steering was unusual. They would have expected him to be steaming with the wind on the port bow, hauling round to port as it backed. That would have meant a north-easterly course whereas the ship was on a south-westerly one. On the other hand the *Moonraker* was close to latitude 24° south, and it was common knowledge that these cyclones normally recurved to the south-east between latitudes 15° and 20° south. Her captain would know that. *Moonraker*'s course could only mean he was satisfied that the storm had recurved to the north of his ship, and that he was opening the distance and making longitude in the general direction of Mauritius.

Twenty minutes later Kantle heard *Moonraker*'s call-sign again. It was Port Louis: *Presume you are satisfied your ship is well clear of path of cyclone Alpha.*

Kantle took the signal to the chart house.

Captain Stone read it carefully, then consulted the chart. He wrote a reply: *Your 0253. Affirmative. Will continue to watch situation closely.*

He tore the sheet from the message pad. 'Send them that, Mr Kantle.'

Port Louis received the reply and decided

to take no further action for the time being. There was insufficient information on the recurving of the cyclone to justify a general warning to shipping. The authorities were satisfied that Captain Stone knew what he was about. Shipmasters were well schooled in the laws of tropical storms and every ship carried volumes of the *Admiralty Sailing Directions* which gave detailed information about them.

Port Louis was not to know that Captain Stone hadn't felt it necessary to refer to the meteorological notes in the forefront of the *Sailing Directions*. He knew his laws of storms only too well. Hadn't he been in two of them, in the China Sea and the Pacific? Reading the latest signal from Mauritius he'd seen in his mind's eye cyclone *Alpha*, already well to the north of the ship, recurving to the north-east. He'd felt a distinct sense of relief.

★   ★   ★

The watches changed at four o'clock in the morning when Frascatti took over from Martinho Lopez. With the arrival of Frascatti, Captain Stone took the opportunity he'd long sought to go below.

In the bathroom off the sleeping cabin he shed the oilskin coat, did what he had to,

91

washed his hands and face in hot water and brushed his hair and teeth.

At the back of his mind there was one more thing to be done before he left: to ensure that the bottles were securely stowed. He locked the cabin door, removed the drawer and panel and reached down. The bottles were firmly held, their width being only fractionally less than that of the cavity. He counted them by touching their necks. Ten in all in the top row. There were three rows.

His mouth felt exceptionally parched and the severity of the headache had increased perceptibly. Once free of that, he thought, he'd be able to think straight. He trembled with excitement. Just one tot would put him right. Get rid of the tension. Brush away the tiredness. Sharpen his judgment for what lay ahead.

He pulled out a bottle, took a tumbler from the wash basin and half filled it. The gin went down so quickly that he gasped and his eyes watered. It was extraordinary how it worked. He felt better already. He looked at the bottle. If one tot could do that, two would do more. The second tot was more generous.

When he'd put the bottle back and replaced the panel and drawer, he went to the bathroom, squeezed toothpaste into his mouth and worked it round with his tongue.

Putting on the oilskin coat, he unlocked the door and went through the day cabin to the internal stairway. He felt a different man. Vigorous and ready to cope with the problems confronting him.

At the chart house door a sudden roll threw him off balance and he staggered against it. Watch it, he laughed to himself. Watch it, old boy.

★ ★ ★

A few minutes after Stone's return to the bridge the wind backed a point and blew harder. Puzzled at this development he looked at the barometer.

It had dropped another two millibars.

★ ★ ★

As the morning watch progressed the weather continued to deteriorate. Daylight came officially at about six but scurrying clouds low in the sky, and rain and spray which swept the ship more frequently now, held back daylight and it was not until six-thirty that they emerged from the gloom of darkness.

The wind was shrieking in the gusts and with daylight the swell, now more on the starboard bow than the beam, was seen to be steeper than it had appeared during the night. Broad streaks of foam formed in the direction of the wind and the seas broke frequently, tumbling and collapsing as they overran themselves. Wind whipped foam from their crests and the air was filled with spindrift, reducing visibility to less than half a mile. Radar was switched on.

The wind, blowing now from the northeast, was broad on the starboard quarter. Stone estimated its force as eight, gusting at times to nine. That was getting on for fifty knots, a strong gale on the Beaufort scale. Still puzzled at these developments, he concluded that the ship was experiencing a secondary disturbance formed in the wake of the cyclone. Such things happened. Certainly the weather was behaving in a strangely unpredictable fashion.

Bracing himself he faced the wind and recalled the rule: *if the observer face the wind the storm will be nine to eleven points on his right hand side* . . . no, that was in the northern hemisphere . . . they were in the southern . . . *nine to eleven points on his left hand side.*

Wonderful, he thought, how the headache has gone, and my mouth — why, it feels a part of me again. But this shrieking wind . . . the rain and spray, how they cut into the eyes. Can't see properly. Makes a man feel dizzy. Lose his bearings. He clutched at the bridge rail with both hands, legs apart, fighting the wind. *Nine to eleven points on the left hand*, he repeated. The wind was north-east . . . so the storm's centre should be somewhere between west-nor-west and west.

But it couldn't be? That would mean it was drawing ahead, moving to the west, whereas it should have recurved to the north-east. Either it was a secondary disturbance or a cyclone carrying on to the west, towards the Madagascar coast. They did that sometimes, but not often.

Moonraker rolled to starboard shuddering as a sea broke on the after well-deck. Above the noise of the storm he heard things moving in the centre-castle, crockery smashing, pots and pans falling. A fire bucket came rolling down the bridge with Frascatti in pursuit. The chief officer returned it to its rack. 'Getting worse,' he shouted, his dark face gloomy.

Stone nodded. 'Extraordinary. Should be moving away. Must be a secondary disturbance.' The ship lurched to starboard, shuddering once more as a sea broke abreast the mainmast, water swirling round the winch islands.

'Everything secure there, Mr Frascatti?'

The Italian nodded. 'All ship-shape.'

Stone said, 'Slack taken up on those heavy lift lashings?'

'Sure, captain.' In between thinking he smelt gin, doubt assailed the chief officer. He'd forgotten about the lashings. On the captain's last inspection he'd resolved to deal with them before the next one: five days hence. The doubt evaporated. The bosun and carpenter had gone round the upper deck and reported everything secure. They'd been present at the captain's inspection and heard his complaints about the lashings.

Nevertheless Frascatti decided to look for himself when he came off duty at eight o'clock.

* * *

The ship was labouring badly, shipping such heavy seas that at seven-fifteen Stone ordered speed to be reduced. The standby man in the wheelhouse, a shrunken Cape Verde islander, Juan Tomas, put the telegraph to *slow-ahead* and the bells tinkled as the engine-room answered. The weather was too much for the mechanical responses of auto-steering. Only a seaman could provide the anticipation needed. Such a task was not for Tomas. Stone shouted to Frascatti, 'Send for O'Halloran.'

'Okay, captain.' The chief officer sent Tomas off to fetch the Irishman. O'Halloran, the bosun, was a broad-shouldered giant who'd served in the Royal Navy as an able seaman for fifteen years. An undistinguished career there had ended with his court-martial for striking an officer. When *Moonraker* was in harbour O'Halloran spent much time ashore in the bars along the waterfronts, drinking and fighting and sobering up in police cells before returning on board. Once the ship had sailed he was the best seaman on board though unpredictable. Captain Stone knew that no one was better on the wheel.

O'Halloran appeared, slouching on to the bridge, a smile on his battered face.

'Take the wheel, O'Halloran.' Captain Stone called to him above the storm. 'We need a good helmsman. It's blowing a full gale.'

The Irishman unlatched the auto-steering. 'Aye, sorr.' He grasped the spokes of the wheel. 'It's fair to blowing the balls off a Kilkenny bull, sorr.'

Captain Stone concealed a smile. He had a fellow feeling for this wild Irishman with whom he shared a weakness.

'Watch her head. Sing out if she doesn't answer.'

'Aye, sorr.'

O'Halloran leant forward, watching the compass card with single-minded determination. He was happy because he knew his skill had been respected. In the ordinary way that didn't happen often.

★ ★ ★

Woken from deep sleep by the violent motion of the ship Susie dressed quickly, pulling on shirt, slacks and jersey before making for the upper deck. What she found horrified her. Nothing to be seen but dark lowering clouds, huge seas appearing suddenly from nowhere and rushing at the ship like tall grey buildings with white roofs toppling forward. And the screaming wind, like a thousand banshees wailing. There was a nightmarish quality about it all.

One look was enough. She was scared stiff. I must discuss it with someone, she decided. Uncle or Mr Jenkins or Hank Casey. She went to the captain's cabin.

Dwala shook his head. 'Captain on bridge, Miss Susie. Big storm. Too busy. You no trouble him. You safe. Very strong ship. Good engines.'

Down in the dining-saloon the second steward was no more helpful. He was a frightened harassed Hindu, struggling in the pantry with crockery and cutlery. Mr Jenkins? No, she couldn't see him. He was down in the cold store where there was trouble. 'Too much pieces upsetting and plenty stores wasted.'

She made for the galley. Hank was there, on his knees on the galley floor mopping up a glutinous mess. Behind him portly Mr Garrett was struggling with pots and pans in various places at the same time. Like a juggler. He was swearing horribly.

She said, 'Good morning, Mr Garrett,' tried to look calm and not to notice Hank. The cook's fallen-in, perspiring face was comically mournful. '*Good*, you call it. Diabolical I'd say.'

Hank grinned cheerfully. It seemed a long time since he'd seen Susie. 'Hi, Susie,' he said. 'Just fixing your breakfast. Won't be a sec.'

Garrett snorted disapproval. 'You get on with your job, young fellow me lad.'

'Isn't the weather terrible, Mr Garrett,' said Susie looking at Hank and deciding he was groovy. She grabbed at a handrail as the ship lurched. It was as if the sea on one side had suddenly fallen away. Every pot and pan in the galley seemed to jump, clattering and clanging, a metallic din which drowned

Garrett's curses. The pots on the big stove, held by fiddles, slopped their contents over electric hot plates which sizzled and steamed. Boiling liquid fell on to Hank's arm and he yelped, rubbing the spot fiercely.

Mr Garrett, arms flailing in a brave attempt to contain his equipment, cried, 'You better run along. No place for a girl here. Can't swear proper with you around.'

Susie took the hint. ''Bye, Mr Garrett. I'm really sorry for you. Must be *terribly* difficult. Perhaps the sea will go down soon. 'Bye, Hank. Look after yourself.' She blew him a kiss behind the cook's back and staggered off, bound for the saloon.

★ ★ ★

At twenty minutes past eight the wind backed to the north and blew with such fury that it was not possible to stand on the open bridge without holding on.

Facing the wind, Captain Stone found it difficult to breathe and impossible to see. The human eye could not stand that blast. So he and the chief officer kept to the wheelhouse. The motion of the ship was now so violent and she shipped such solid water that Captain Stone reduced from *half* to *slow-speed*. With a gale force wind on the starboard bow and the reduced engine revolutions, he doubted if *Moonraker* would do more than make steerage way.

There was so much foam and spray in the air that visibility was down to that of a fog. It was difficult to decide from which direction the sea was coming. Great waves loomed up suddenly in the mist of flying scud, sea and swell merging into a lumping medley of high peaks whose crests were whipped away by the wind as they formed.

Looking through a clear-glass screen at the sea beside the ship, Captain Stone had the impression that the *Moonraker* was going astern. The more he tried to counter this with reason, the more the impression gained ground. He felt dizzy and seemed unable to relate to his surroundings. It would be merciful, he thought, if he passed out. A sudden heart attack. A stroke. Then he wouldn't know what was happening. Others would have to make the decisions. But he knew there weren't any others. Only he could save the *Moonraker*.

* * *

At times the fore-well deck was lost to sight under a grey tumble of water, then the bow would lift and become visible again, only to disappear as it buried itself in the next looming sea. A swirl of foaming water would smother everything forward of the bridge until the bow rose once more and the foc'sle and winch islands emerged like surfacing submarines. The wind whipped sheets of spray to leeward, its force breaking them into fine particles of foam.

At some time during the hours of darkness the gale had torn away the lifeboat covers and bridge dodgers, leaving fragments of canvas which flapped in the wind with the sound of pistol shots. Otherwise the ship seemed to have suffered little damage.

Above the noise of the storm and the sustained shriek of the wind, the shrill of steam exhausting from the funnel could be heard at times. Down in the engine-room, Mr McLintoch was grumbling about this waste of power. 'For wha' did the captain want it, ga'ng doon to slow-speed?'

★ ★ ★

Cyclone *Alpha* had recurved to the south-east shortly before half-past five that morning. The storm centre was moving at fifteen knots, but by seven it had reached twenty and was still increasing. It had begun to recurve in latitude 22° south and by seven-thirty was fifty miles from *Moonraker*. These facts were not known to Captain Stone but at eight o'clock he realised that something had gone seriously wrong. There was now every indication that what they were experiencing was not a secondary disturbance but the cyclone itself. It had not, he concluded, recurved to the north-east. With an urgent sense of doubt he went to the chart house and consulted the *Admiralty Sailing Directions* and there discovered what had happened. How could he, he asked himself, have made such an appalling mistake? In the *southern* hemisphere the direction of recurvature was *south* and east, not *north* and east. That was it. The cyclone had already recurved to the south-east, towards the *Moonraker*.

In a humiliating moment of truth he realised he'd failed because he was an alcoholic. But self-recrimination would not help the ship so he looked at the barometer. It had dropped another two millibars. The wind since last backing had remained steady, blowing at hurricane force, while seas like watery volcanoes reared up suddenly around the ship. Not only was *Moonraker* within fifty miles of the cyclone's centre, but since the wind was no longer backing, he knew he'd blundered into its path.

His first instinct was to put the wind on the bow and make ready to haul round to port when it did back, but he decided against it. They'd never get round the centre now. It was too close. The only thing left was to run for it. On an oblique course, he decided, with the wind on the starboard quarter; say south-south-east. In that way the ship might edge clear of the cyclone's path. It was a bad decision, but Captain Stone was in a bad condition. What little nerve and resolve alcohol had left was rapidly crumbling. He went to the wheelhouse. 'Port wheel, O'Halloran,' he ordered. 'Bring her round easily.'

The Irishman repeated the order, turning the wheel gently, nursing the ship round, coaxing her through mountainous seas scarcely visible for flying spindrift. When the ship was almost beam on to wind and sea, Stone ordered *full-ahead*. More power would speed up the turn so that she didn't lie too long in the trough of the sea.

The *Moonraker* received a heavy pounding in the time it took to bring her round, particularly on the after-well deck where the two lighters bore the brunt of the seas which broke aboard. Clinging grimly to the bridge rail Frascatti saw this. It was too late, he knew, to do anything about the lashings if they were slack. Men couldn't work on deck in those seas.

As the stern came up to windward Captain Stone ordered *half-speed* and the motion changed to a series of staggering lurches, the stern lifting high as following seas came up under the counter.

O'Halloran shouted, 'She's coming on to south-south-east, sorr.'

'Hold her there,' replied Captain Stone. 'Watch that she doesn't broach to.'

'Aye, sorr.' O'Halloran leant forward, frowning with concentration, breathing heavily under the strain of special responsibility.

Stone knew there was one other thing he must do now. Let Mauritius know. In the chart house he picked up the phone and spoke to Kantle.

★ ★ ★

Within minutes of the alteration of course, Addu Batu took over the watch from Frascatti.

The chief officer was about to leave the bridge when Captain Stone beckoned him over. 'Look round the ship Mr Frascatti,' he shouted. 'See that all's well. Take O'Halloran with you. Tomas here can take the wheel for a spell. Get the carpenter to sound what tanks he can. With all this pounding she may be taking water.'

'Okay, captain,' said Frascatti, his face making it clear he didn't relish the task.

'Remember,' Stone shouted to make himself heard against the rattle of windows and the shrieking of the storm, 'One hand for yourself and one for the ship.' It was an unnecessary warning. Frascatti was not given to taking chances on behalf of the ship. It would always be two hands for himself.

Stone estimated the wind to be blowing at a hundred knots and a good deal more in the gusts.

★ ★ ★

Frascatti stood at the after end of the boat-deck with O'Halloran. Facing the wind they gripped the rail with all their strength, arching their backs, leaning forward. Flying spray and foam smothered them and breathing was difficult. They were looking down on to the heavy lifts, the two cargo lighters from Sydney. What he saw caused Frascatti to shiver with fear.

The lighter on the starboard side had burst its lashings, come off its chocks and slid forward. It had slewed so that the bow and stern were no longer in a fore-and-aft line.

Frascatti crossed himself. '*Mama mia*,' he muttered.

'Holy mother o' Jasus,' shouted the bosun.

Frascatti screamed, 'Did you and the carpenter check the lashings last night?'

'What's that?' yelled the bosun. He'd heard the question. They hadn't checked the lashings, but he knew the carpenter would no more admit that than he would. He knew, too, that the chief officer hadn't checked them.

The chief officer repeated the question and O'Halloran nodded. This gave Frascatti a grain of comfort. At least the captain couldn't blame *him*.

But the comfort was short lived. As they watched, *Moonraker*'s stern lifted to a great sea the top of which seemed well above the mainmast cross-trees. Her bow dipped until the fore-and-aft angle of the deck was close to forty degrees then, as in a bad dream, they saw the sixty-ton lighter slither towards the centre-castle. *Moonraker*'s stern began to drop and a tower of grey water loomed above the poop in pursuit of the ship. The gale caught the top of it, hurling it over and down, burying the stern and after well-deck.

'Look out,' screamed Frascatti, as the huge sea lifted the lighter above the deck so that for a moment it looked as if it would land where they stood. But as *Moonraker's* stern rose again, the sea drained away and the lighter was launched down and forward, its bows striking the plating of the bulkhead beneath them like a giant battering ram.

7

The plates and frames which the bows of the lighter struck had been sound enough in 1952 when the ship was built, but *Moonraker* had changed hands several times since then and for the last seven years she'd received skinflint maintenance. The bulkhead which should have been chipped and painted with anti-corrosives at regular intervals had been neglected: no more than patched up to meet such survey requirements as existed for Liberian registered ships.

To the astonishment of Frascatti and the bosun the fore end of the lighter had disappeared into the bulkhead. Pale with fright, the chief officer staggered off to the bridge to report, leaving O'Halloran to gape at the disaster.

At intervals immense following seas swept in on the starboard quarter, flooded the well-deck and aided by its steep angle rammed the buoyant lighter farther into the bulkhead. Immediately behind that bulkhead lay the engineers' messroom, forward of it a narrow alleyway ran athwartships. Into it led a door from the messroom, faced on the opposite side by the door in the engine-room casing. This gave access to the landing from which, greasy ladder by greasy ladder, the engineers reached the steel inspection gratings which encircled the main engines in descending levels until the floor of the engine-room was reached.

When the bow of the lighter pierced the outer bulkhead the messroom flooded, tons of water spilling into it and out into the alleyway. That the messroom and engine-room doors should be opposite each other may have been good functional design, but the naval architect could not have reckoned with a sixty-ton lighter coming through the bulkhead into the messroom and then, with the pounding of successive seas, moving forward until it had gone through both doors and pushed several feet of lighter into the engine-room itself. There it remained, firmly lodged, with gaps of torn plating round it. Through these the water surged, spilling down into the engine-room every time a sea broke on *Moonraker*'s after well-deck.

Cries of alarm sounded in the engine-room and men came running up the ladders to find the door in the casing blocked by the bow of the lighter. So they ran down the ladders and made for the exit through the boiler-room. Thence it was possible to reach the boat-deck by way of steel ladders leading up through the fiddley.

All this happened in the time it took Frascatti to reach the bridge. There, frightened and garrulous, he made his report. Appalled at what he heard, Captain Stone at once decided to heave to with the sea on the port bow. In this way he hoped to keep the after well-deck clear of the seas which were flooding it.

His nerves were badly shaken by the disaster and by the fury of the storm which seemed intent on destroying the ship, but he showed none of this as he stood next to Tomas at the wheel. 'Steady her now, Tomas,' he'd say. Then, 'Starboard wheel, Tomas. More starboard wheel, man.' He worked the engine-room telegraph himself, putting it to *half-speed* as they began to turn to windward, then on to *full-speed* just before wind and sea came abeam.

Slowly, with infinite labour, as if she were all but broken by the seas under which she seemed often to disappear, faltering at times, she came up to windward. When the wind was a point or so on the bow, Stone rang *slow-ahead* and though she worked heavily in the seaway she rode better than she had running before it. But it was too late.

Andrew McLintoch, wet as a half-drowned

cat, came to the wheelhouse with grim news. 'The engine-room and stokehold are flooding, captain. There's no' a way of makin' good the damage that lighter's done.'

'Any chance of rigging a wooden bulkhead, chief? Stopping the inflow somehow?'

McLintoch shook his head. 'Every time a sea lands aboard, the lighter moves. It's through three bulkheads a'ready. The rolling and pitching move it, ye ken. E'en if men c'd work there, they'd no' have a verra guid chance. All that jagged metal and the sea rushin' in.'

Stone's face was drawn with worry and exhaustion. He looked many years older. 'Pumps keeping up with what's coming in, chief?' he cried.

McLintoch looked at him grimly. 'No' as yet. Maybe noo we've hove to we'll get the better o' it. Should be less water comin' aboard.'

The captain watched the shrunken old man for a moment, his mind searching desperately for a solution. 'We're not far from the centre of the storm,' he said. 'It's sweeping to the south-east. There'll be a lull when the centre reaches us. Always is. Possibly an area of ten miles of water without wind. Maybe we can do something about the lighter then.'

'How long will the lull last?'

'Twenty minutes or so,' shouted the captain. 'There'll be a heavy swell.'

'An' then?'

Stone looked away from the old man. 'Then? Why, we'll come out on the other side. Into the navigable semi-circle. But I'm afraid . . . ' He shrugged his shoulders in a helpless gesture. 'It'll start again. Second half'll likely be as bad as the first. No point in trying to deceive you, chief.'

'May the guid Lord help us, then,' shouted McLintoch, thrusting an empty pipe into his mouth. 'For there's nae anither body can move a sixty-ton lighter that's driven into the centre-castle.'

'How are things in the stokehold?'

'Nae too good. There's a deal of water there.'

'No way of keeping it out?'

McLintoch shook his head. 'There's a bulkhead screen separating engine-room and stokehold. The wee door in it's nae watertight. Just to keep oot the dust. It'll nae stand pressure.'

'Are you keeping it shut?'

'Aye. It's been shut a' right. More than once. But it's the on'y way oot the engine-room the noo. An' the men are panicky. They keep openin' it to lower the water level in the engine-room.'

Captain Stone frowned. 'The furnaces'll black out soon if that goes on.'

'Aye. They will. But that'll likely be happenin' anyway as the water level rises. There's nae way of keepin' it oot the stokehold.'

'But surely you can delay it.' The captain had to shout into the old man's ear. 'Can't the second and third engineers keep order there?'

'It's nae a question o' that. Water's comin' in tae fast.'

Stone shook his head despondently. 'I don't know,' he said brokenly. 'I just don't know.' He pulled himself together. 'I tell you what, chief. Lock that screen door on the stokehold side. That'll stop any interference from the engine-room side.'

'An what aboot the men in the engine-room?' McLintoch's small eyes glittered in his wrinkled face as he cupped a hand over an ear to hear the captain's reply.

'Put a rope-ladder down through the skylight. When it's time, let them come out that way.'

The chief engineer thought about it. 'Aye. Tha's practical, captain. We'll do tha'. But I doobt it'll help verra much.'

'At least we'll have steam,' said the captain wearily.

'For a while, maybe. And a fat lot of guid that'll be withoot engines to poot it intae,' yelled back Mr McLintoch who felt very strongly that the captain should never have let the ship get into the cyclone. Before he left the wheelhouse he informed Stone that he had shut and screwed down the watertight door which led from the engine-room into the shaft tunnel. At least that would not flood.

★　★　★

At twenty minutes to nine the water in the engine-room — rushing from side to side and end to end with the ship's extravagant gyrations — had gained on the pumps to such an extent that the engines had to be shut down.

Not only the main engines but the auxiliaries, including the pumps, could no longer work. With the generators stopped, there was no electric power. There wasn't a light in the ship nor power for the many electric motors vital to her functioning. On the bridge the clear-glass screens stopped spinning, the lights in the chart house and wheelhouse, in the steering compass and heading indicators went out, and the radar stopped working. The large stove in the galley, heated by electricity, began to cool.

When power failed in the radio cabin, Kantle at once threw the switch to connect with the emergency supply — the batteries on the monkey island above the bridge. He had just tested the transmitter with the new source of power, when the telephone bell rang. It was the captain. Kantle was required in the chart house at once.

★   ★   ★

'Get that emergency generator goin' as fast as ye can, laddie,' Mr McLintoch snapped at Nils Thoresen, the Danish second engineer.

The emergency generator, diesel driven, was in the after steering-compartment. It was intended for just such an emergency as this. Once started it would provide power for lighting, for pumping water through the fire-mains and for other essential purposes.

On leaving Mr McLintoch, the second engineer collected the Egyptian third engineer who displayed a curious reluctance to accompany him. On Thoresen's insistence, however, they made for the poop. This journey involved crossing the after well-deck, a hazardous undertaking even with the lifelines which remained on the port side. Those to starboard had been carried away by the errant cargo lighter.

As they finished their journey with a frenzied dash into the poop deckhouse, a huge sea reared up alongside the ship — a mountain of water. It broke thunderously across the bridge superstructure and the centre-castle and for a moment even the funnel disappeared in a tumble of frothing water. The ship lifted again, slowly as if mortally wounded, and shook the sea clear. Those on the bridge, the moment of terror having passed, were able to take stock of the damage. One of the port lifeboats had gone, two stokehold ventilators were bent double as by the hand of a giant, several windows on the bridge and in the wheelhouse had been smashed, and the starboard bridge ladder had buckled in an extraordinary fashion; neatly, symmetrically, as if in response to the whim of its designer. Though the men on the bridge did not know it, the locker containing the batteries for the radio's emergency supply had been swept off the monkey island.

There was something else those on the bridge did not know: the sea which had done the damage had claimed Mr McLintoch. He'd been busy with two seamen on the engine-room skylights, rigging the rope ladder to be used as an escape route by the men down below. Fortunately for them

O'Halloran, released from the wheel for this task, was one of the seamen.

The chief engineer having disappeared — O'Halloran thought he'd gone to fetch something — the bosun got on with the job of getting the ladder down to where the men were huddled together on the steel grating which ran round the tops of the big cylinders.

Kantle was in the chart house when the big sea broke over the ship. The captain had just completed writing a radio message for immediate dispatch. It was of some length and the wild motion of the ship, the indifferent light, and the alterations Stone made as he wrote had all contributed to the time taken. The message informed Port Louis that the ship had been overrun by cyclone *Alpha* and was now somewhere near the storm centre. The *Moonraker* had, the message continued, suffered severe damage resulting in flooding of the engine-room and stokehold which compartments had been evacuated. The ship was now without power and urgently in need of assistance. The estimated position was given, but Stone well knew that as long as the *Moonraker* remained within fifty miles of the centre of the cyclone no ship afloat could help her.

Back in the radio cabin with this message, Kantle switched on the transmitter only to find that it was dead. He had then discovered that the emergency batteries had been swept from the monkey island.

In the meantime, without power of any sort, unable to steer, *Moonraker* lay beam on to wind and sea, taking the full fury of the cyclone. Because of the flooding, the loose mass of water below, she lay sluggishly in the trough of the sea, a mobile breakwater shaking and shuddering as the confusion of seas broke over her.

It was some time before those on board realised that Mr McLintoch was no longer with them.

★ ★ ★

Aft in the steering-engine compartment the second engineer, Nils Thoresen, looked at the emergency generator with unbelieving eyes.

'Christ!' he shouted. 'What have you done, Khalif?'

The Egyptian was abject. 'It is the fuel injection system. There was a blockage. The day before the storm I was working on it.'

Thoresen surveyed the dismantled engine. There were metal boxes with tools, small components, nuts and oily rags lying about. 'How long to reassemble?'

'Impossible,' said Khalif unhappily. 'The

fuel injector is in the workshop.'

Thoresen turned on him, eyes bright with fear. 'In the engine-room?'

'Yes. I had to take it there. To clear the blockage.'

'So it is under water?'

Khalif averted large spaniel-like eyes. 'Yes,' he said quietly. 'There is no chance of getting it.'

'Jesus Christ!' Thoresen kicked the box of tools and ran his hands through his hair. 'You idiot! You goddam imbecile. This generator was our last chance.'

Khalif's eyes filled with tears. 'How could I tell of the storm. I was doing my best.'

Thoresen knew that even the most skilful craftsman could not make a new fuel injection unit without materials, tools and patterns. And the lathes and drills in the workshop were under water which surged from one side of the engine-room to the other as the ship pitched and rolled.

★ ★ ★

In Stone's mind a plan was taking shape. He sent for Frascatti, the bosun and the carpenter and they gathered in the chart house where the noise level was lower.

'Get as many hands as you can to muster

120

awnings, mattresses, pillows and blankets. Stow them in a dry place near the after end of the engine-room casing. The engineers' cabins will do.'

Frascatti, seldom quick in the uptake, frowned. 'For what, captain?'

'When the centre of the storm reaches us, the wind will drop. There'll be a heavy confused swell, but men will be able to get at the lighter in the alleyway between the engine-room casing and the messroom. There shouldn't be much water coming aboard then. Get together now as much timber as you can. I know you can't get to the carpenter's store, but use tables, bunk boards, cabin furniture. Anything you can lay hands on.'

'You want us to plug the broken plating?' asked Houtman, the carpenter. He was a thin, grey-faced Hollander, working his passage back to Rotterdam.

'Yes. Where the lighter's bows pass through the engineers' messroom. The men will have the protection of the two bulkheads. Put wooden battens in first. Angle them so that the greater the pressure from aft the tighter the plug. One end of each batten against the lighter's side, the other against the inner bulkhead of the messroom. Once you've got the battens in position, cover the inside with two or three thicknesses of canvas. Then pack in the mattresses, pillows and blankets. Throw in plenty of cement with them. Pack it all good and tight to make a plug. It'll swell when the water gets to it. After that, on the fore side of the plug, set up more thicknesses of canvas, and batten them well in,' he paused to yawn, rubbing his hands across his eyes. 'Rig timber shores to hold the foreside battens in place. Get the shores wedged good and tight against the engine-room casing.'

Frascatti looked doubtful. 'We are in big cyclone, captain. When sea breaks on well-deck lighter jumps and plenty water comes through.'

Frowning at the Italian, Stone's eyes, sunken in an unshaven face, reflected the contempt he felt for this man. He yawned again, then pulled himself upright. 'Good seamen overcome difficulties, Mr Frascatti. That's what makes them good seamen.' He used his gruff voice, but he felt exhausted, dazed, and the chart room was dancing before his eyes.

'Sure and we'll give it a go, sorr,' said O'Halloran.

'You'll have to be sharp about it.' The captain stared glassily at them. 'You may have only fifteen minutes. Get the gear ready before we reach the storm centre.'

'At what time are we at the centre?' Frascatti looked at his watch.

'Any time now. The glass should start rising soon. I'll let you know.'

'Okay, captain. We see if we can fix.'

They'd no sooner left the chart house than Thoresen arrived to report that the emergency diesel generator was unserviceable. There was no possibility, he said, of getting it going.

★　★　★

At five minutes past ten the barometer began to rise. Soon afterwards the wind dropped and the sky cleared. The sun shone down on the ship for the first time in two days, visibility improved and though there was still a confused swell, the mountainous seas had gone. At times the tops of swells tumbled on board, flooding well-decks fore and aft and shaking the ship, but not with the fury and frequency of the hours that had passed.

The morale of *Moonraker*'s crew rose with the improvement in the weather. Frightened groups who'd spent hours huddled together in odd corners of the centre-castle broke up and men appeared on the boat-deck looking at the sea and sky, exclaiming at the grotesque aspect of the lighter — one third of it now out of sight — at the spray-encrusted funnel, the bent ventilators, buckled rails and stanchions, the missing lifeboats and other scars of the storm.

Relief from the long hours of strain showed in their faces and they shouted to each other and laughed. Few of them realised that the second half would be much the same as the first, that this was only a lull in the ship's struggle to survive. Those who did, put it out of their minds and lived only for the moment of warm sunshine, of freedom from the screech of the storm.

* ★ ★

Down in the flooded alleyway between the messroom and engine-room casing there was frenzied activity.

Houtman, the carpenter, worked on the torn plating with some of the junior engineers, while greasers and firemen passed material from the cabins where it was stored down the alleyway in which water almost two feet deep sloshed noisily. The task of plugging the gaps was immensely difficult. The motion of the ship was still violent and each time the top of a swell landed on the after well-deck, and *Moonraker's* bows dipped, water would surge forward to burst through the plating.

Time and time again Houtman and his helpers would get the battens in place, only to have them dislodged. But he learnt as he went, got them fixed eventually and the canvas lining was put in place. Mattresses, pillows and blankets were forced in with a liberal addition of cement, and the outer battens fixed. Then work on the shores began. The carpenter found that no man helped him more, worked harder or displayed greater initiative than Hank Casey, the passage-worker. And no one was more cheerful. So the men battled away, urged on by the carpenter and infected by the enthusiasm of the young Australian, knowing that time was limited and that failure would mean the end of the ship once she was caught, as she would be, in the other semi-circle of the cyclone.

★ ★ ★

While the struggle to seal off the plating took place, O'Halloran and a party of seamen were busy on the upper deck. The gripes on the remaining lifeboats and the lashings on the sixty-ton lighter on the port side were hauled taut. Miraculously it had not shifted in the storm, probably because for most of the time it had been on the leeward side. Slack on the hatch tarpaulins was taken up, wedges driven home and the lashings re-secured. Life-lines were hauled taut and lockers and canisters on the boat-deck lashed down. All this had to be done with a sharp eye on the big swells which rolled down on the ship, the men holding on to life-lines as the seas came aboard.

★ ★ ★

In Port Louis the authorities were worried. They had not heard from the *Moonraker* since eight o'clock that morning. It was now eleven. At each hour they called the ship but there was no reply. Her last message had announced that cyclone *Alpha* had caught up with her. Her radio silence could, they knew, be due to several things: static interference from the storm, a breakdown in the radio transmitter caused by sea water or violent motion. In a cyclone waves reached unexpected parts of a ship. One might have engulfed the bridge superstructure and flooded the radio cabin.

Any of these things might have happened, but nevertheless Port Louis was worried.

★ ★ ★

When Kantle discovered that the batteries had gone and the transmitter was out of

126

action, he went to the chart house. There he took from a cupboard a large orange box. It was the emergency radio transmitter intended for use in the lifeboats. It was fitted with a crank-handle to work the generator and could be used either for manual transmission by Morse key, or automatic transmission of the *Mayday* distress signal. Its frequency was the standard maritime wavelength of 500 kilocycles. Its normal range was 300 miles. Kantle set up the machine in the radio cabin. Later he went back to the bridge to get the position of the ship and someone to turn the crank-handle while he worked the key.

All hands were busy so Captain Stone, having given the radio operator the estimated position of the ship, suggested that his niece should assist him. Kantle collected a frightened Susie from the storeroom where she was helping Mr Jenkins clean up the mess. Kantle was pleased to have her. She was a lively girl and though the circumstances were grave Kantle, for long a secret admirer, was stimulated by her presence.

But it was no use. Whether it was interference caused by the violence of cyclone *Alpha*, or that there was no ship within three hundred miles — whatever it was, Kantle got no response to his repeated distress signals. Eventually, tired of using the key, he switched to automatic transmission, pushed the lank yellow hair from his eyes and offered Susie a Mars bar.

It did a lot to restore her morale. If Kantle was offering Mars bars, things could not be as bad as they seemed. Kantle on the other hand, thinking that things could scarcely be worse, was wondering if he would live to finish the stock in the bottom drawer of his desk.

★ ★ ★

Captain Stone had been on the bridge for more than twelve hours and he'd been a sick man at the start. Dwala had brought him milk, sandwiches and apples. These had helped, but Stone was nearing the end of his tether. It was difficult to concentrate, to think straight. His mind kept wandering into fantasies of no particular shape or relevance. Once he was in space, circling the moon. There was a sharp report as the oxygen tank in the power capsule behind him exploded, rocking the command module. He blinked, looking fore and aft. A swell had broken aboard, shaking the ship like a wet dog. Later he was in a lifeboat watching a distant burning ship. From it came a sudden cataclysmic blast. Another sea had struck the

Moonraker. Soon afterwards he was struggling in the water. It was dark and he was trying to call out to a man near him. But his throat was choked with fuel oil. An inflatable life-raft came from the darkness, striking him on the shoulder. It was Addu Batu to report that Kantle could get no answer to the *Mayday* calls.

Stone felt an overwhelming depression, a sense of imminent disaster. Before long they'd be in the other semicircle of cyclone *Alpha.* The loss of Andrew McLintoch affected him deeply. He'd been fond of the little Scots engineer, respected him. Now he was dead. Stone's sense of guilt was acute. There was nothing more for him to do in this temporary lull. He'd already taken a sun sight and plotted a position line. If it was clear at noon he'd transfer the position line and get the sun on the meridian. Then he'd know where the ship was. In the meantime it was all waiting; waiting for news of the plugging operation; waiting to hear if Kantle had established radio contact; waiting while O'Halloran and his men did what they could on deck; waiting, above all, for the tell-tale fall of the barometer — the signal that cyclone *Alpha* was about to strike again.

He couldn't stand waiting with these weird fantasies disturbing his mind. He'd have to pull himself together, get rid of the morbid depression, buck up his morale, sharpen his judgment. There was only one way of achieving these things.

The Cape Verde islander, Tomas, was in the wheelhouse. 'I'm going down to my cabin, Tomas,' said Captain Stone. 'I shan't be a moment.'

8

The crew had more time to work on plugging the damaged plating than Captain Stone had predicted, for it was not until after eleven o'clock that morning that the barometer again began to fall.

The wind when it came struck the ship with expected violence but this time from the south-west, a direction almost opposite to that experienced just before she'd entered the calm at the centre of the storm. Before long the wind had reached hurricane force and once again the *Moonraker* was carried to the south-east in a mist of driving rain and spray. Battered by tumultuous seas, she lay beam on to the storm.

The plugging held: at least for that afternoon and most of the night that followed. It was a terrifying time, that long, seemingly endless night. One of absurd motion, of nerve-chilling sounds, of unrelieved darkness. There were oil lamps in the ship, but the door of the lamp-room under the foc'sle had been warped by heavy seas. In an attempt to force it a young Portuguese seaman was lost over the side. He was the second casualty of the storm.

In the early hours of morning the plug on the starboard bow of the lighter began to work loose. Water got through, but in reduced quantities.

Moonraker had reached the outer orbit of the cyclone on the Sunday afternoon. It was not until midnight on the following Tuesday that it had blown over her and whirled on to the south-east. Had the ship been able to steam, she would fairly soon have drawn clear of the second semi-circle, the navigable half of the storm, but as it was it carried her along with it and her agony was prolonged.

By daylight on Tuesday the worst was over. The wind had dropped, a confused swell remained, the glass rose and the sun shone down from a clear sky. Once more the spirits of the crew rose, for men are infinitely adaptable. In ones and twos they appeared on deck, quiet at first, thankful to be alive, examining with incredulous eyes the damage done by the storm. Before long they were shouting to each other, laughing, joking crudely about their experiences.

Unknown to anyone, the lighter on the port side had at some time during the night been carried away. The broken ends of its wire and chain lashings were all that remained. Both lifeboats on the port side had now gone, and ventilators stood bowed and broken. Whole sections of taffrail, of awning spars and stanchions, had been twisted into strange shapes or carried away. Lifejacket lockers and the canisters containing inflatable life-rafts had been torn from their seating and swept overboard. The gangway on the starboard side, normally stowed on edge against the gunwale, was no longer there. Running gear on the derricks, prised loose by the wash of the seas, lay tangled about the decks or trailed over the side. Virtually everything on the upper deck that was movable, and a good deal that was not, had gone. Everywhere brine had dried white in the sun, as if the ship had come through a snow storm, and the smell of sea salt and fuel oil hung about the upper deck. Down below the odours were mostly of wet things: soaked blankets and mattresses, sodden clothing and flooded alleyways with rotting vegetables, swollen bread loaves, human faeces, toilet paper and other debris floating in them. The sanitary tanks had run dry and it had been impossible to get to the boat-deck to top them up with hand-pumps. Water had entered number two hold where a ventilator had broken at the foot of its trunk.

But there were pleasant surprises too. The hatch tarpaulins, torn in places, had, thanks

133

to their lashings, survived.

The surge of water in the stokehold, the scalding clouds of steam made by cold water striking red-hot furnace doors, had long since caused it to be evacuated. With no one to tend them, the oil fires had blacked out.

Moonraker's big rudder was turned by a steam engine in the steering compartment in the poop. That engine was in turn operated by a telemotor system from the bridge. Without steam the only way in which the rudder could be moved was by means of the big hand-steering wheel in the poop. It was situated one deck above the rudder head, and turned the rudder by means of a worm gear and spindle once it was connected up.

There were no lights in the ship, no way of heating food, not even hot water for making tea or coffee, and though she could be steered by hand there was no use for the rudder if she could not steam.

★ ★ ★

Captain Stone lay on the settee in the chart house in what appeared to be a coma. When the barometer rose and cyclone *Alpha* finally left the *Moonraker* he'd been on the bridge, on his feet, for fifteen hours. With the dropping of the wind he'd sent for Frascatti and Thoresen. They were, he said, to carry out a thorough examination of the ship, reporting back as soon as possible.

No sooner had they left the chart house than he slumped across the table, holding on there for a few seconds before sliding unconscious to the floor. He was found by Addu Batu, who sent for help. Dwala and Susie arrived, but Stone could not be wakened. They laid him on the chart house settee where Dwala settled him with pillows and blankets. 'Captain sick before storm begin,' the Ghanaian explained, his own eyes glazed with exhaustion. 'Too long in cyclone. No sleep. Come short time him be all right. Captain save ship.'

Susie nodded doubtfully, her snub nose twitching. She felt terribly sorry for Uncle Harold and it was marvellous how he'd stayed on the bridge all that time and seen them safely through the cyclone. But she wished he hadn't smelt so strongly of gin.

* * *

Over the next two days, in steadily improving weather, a new pattern of life took shape in *Moonraker*. The door of the lamproom was forced and the general purpose oil lamps

135

found there put into use. Oil navigation lamps were trimmed, placed in position and made ready. At night two all round red lights — the not-under-command signal — were lit and hoisted to the triatic stay above the bridge. By day two black balls were hoisted and told the same story: a ship not under command. The international distress signal, the flags N C — *I require assistance* — were flown from the signal yard on the foremast. Each hour by day, and every other hour by night, Kantle sent out distress calls on the emergency transmitter in the orange box. But there was never a reply and doubt began to grow in his mind. Was the transmitter defective, unable to achieve anything like its claimed range of three hundred miles? With unfailing regularity and increasing despair, he heard Mauritius calling *Moonraker* but could do nothing about it.

The engineers improvised a stove from empty oil drums. It was heated by cotton waste and broken wood sprayed with diesel oil drawn from the gravity tank above the emergency generator. On it Garrett the cook produced the first hot meal for three days and earned unstinted praise from the crew.

★ ★ ★

Frascatti and the second engineer, denied the orders and advice of the captain and chief engineer, had decided that the men must be kept busy. Deck and engine-room staff were put on to making good damage. The plugs round the shifted lighter were repaired and strengthened, it was secured with new lashings, timber shores and chocks made from filled cement bags which hardened with exposure to water. Tarpaulins were patched, stretched and re-secured; the foot of the broken ventilator at number two hold was sealed off; where railings had gone safety lines were rigged and slack lifelines hauled taut. The tangle of cargo gear about the decks was sorted and secured. The remaining lifeboats, the two on the starboard side, were drained, their equipment taken out, inspected, dried in the sun and replaced. The hand-steering gear in the poop was coupled to the rudder-head and with two men on the big wheel, the helm put amidships. Gravity tanks for fresh and salt water were topped up with hand-pumps. The carpenter sounded the ballast tanks and to everyone's surprise reported nothing untoward except in the engine-room and stokehold.

The water in the alleyways and cabins round the engine-room was bailed and mopped up. Brine was cleaned from port-holes and deck windows. These were some of the tasks undertaken, but there were many others.

The principal, the insuperable problem remained: the engine and boiler-rooms were flooded and there was no power for moving the ship, for pumping the flooded compart-ments and bilges, for operating ventilating fans, winches, windlasses and all the other power-driven paraphernalia which keeps a ship alive.

Most fearsome in this catalogue of disaster was the fact that the radio transmitter could not be used.

★ ★ ★

Captain Stone, still in a torpor, had been carried to his cabin on the Tuesday afternoon, since when Frascatti had taken charge. He made it clear that the captain's trouble was gin more than exhaustion; that had he, Frascatti, been in command, the ship would not have been caught in the cyclone. He did not add that, had it so occurred, it would have been pure chance since he would not have known how to avoid it. Nor did he acknowledge that if he'd carried out the captain's instructions about the lighter's lashings *Moonraker*'s disaster might never have occurred.

★ ★ ★

On the Thursday morning Dwala reported that Captain Stone was recovering his strength and would soon be up and about. But the big Ghanaian would allow no one, not even Frascatti or Susie, near his master. At night he slept on the floor against the door of the captain's sleeping cabin curled up in a blanket. A human watch dog if ever there was one.

★ ★ ★

After the cyclone Lopez had taken sunsights in the forenoon and at midday. The first sight gave him a position line which he advanced by dead reckoning to noon when the sun was on the meridian. The point of intersection of the advanced position line and the noon latitude gave the ship's position, plus or minus a few miles. The second officer did not attempt star sights in the evenings and at dawn. He was never quite sure of the formula and found star identification difficult.

Neatly, taking his time because there was

139

little else to do, he plotted the position at noon on Thursday; latitude 29° 05′ S: longitude 69° 32′ E. He measured the distance from the previous day's position, one hundred and eight miles and whistled with surprise. *Moonraker*'s drift over the twenty-four hours had averaged four and a half knots, course made good, SSW. The ship was in the area of the trade winds which blew predominantly from the south-east. But they had been variable, north-east in the mornings, south-west in the evenings. At times they'd fallen away and there'd been periods of calm.

From the chart of Indian Ocean currents he saw that they flowed mainly east in that part of the ocean, but there was a warning to mariners that they were variable and unpredictable. They certainly were, he reflected, looking at *Moonraker*'s position. Drift was made up of two components, wind and current; but he would not have expected her to have gone so far south and west. The ship was, he noted, just over nine hundred and fifty nautical miles from Mauritius. More than four hundred miles south of her original track.

* * *

Not having heard from the *Moonraker* for twenty-four hours after the signal announcing her involvement in cyclone *Alpha*, the authorities in Port Louis warned shipping to keep a look out for her since she might have been disabled. Airlines whose aircraft flew the route from South Africa to Australia were similarly alerted and asked to brief their crews. Thereafter Port Louis began preparations for an air search. This, they decided, would be instituted if nothing were heard of the *Moonraker* for another twenty-four hours. Appeals were made at Government level for search aircraft and responses soon came from Britain and South Africa. The Royal Air Force would provide two long range maritime reconnaissance aircraft of the Beira patrol from Majunga on the west coast of Madagascar, while the South African Air Force would provide two from Saldanha Bay.

These reached Mauritius on the Thursday night. Their captains and navigators conferred with the port authorities and an operational plan was prepared, search vectors were allocated, flight schedules and communication networks settled. At daylight on Friday the 13th November, no word having come from *Moonraker*, the aircraft rolled down the runway at La Plaisance Airport and climbed into a warm starlit sky. Steadily, like a slowly opening fan, they drew away from each other as they made for their areas of search.

★ ★ ★

On the morning of Friday, 13th November, Captain Stone appeared on the bridge looking fresh and spruce. To Lopez who was taking his morning sunsight, and Tomas the Cape Verde Islander on duty in the wheelhouse, it was evident that the captain was quite recovered. Not that he at that stage spoke to either of them. The ship was rolling, a slow unrhythmic motion, the water in the flooded compartments rushing each time to the downward side of the roll, its weight holding the ship there until with a sluggish much delayed action she would recover and roll the other way, the water below cascading across. Adjusting himself to this rhythm, Captain Stone paced the bridge stopping at each extremity to look to seaward or about the ship. Then, frowning at his thoughts, he would begin pacing again.

When Lopez had worked out the sight and plotted the position line, the captain came to the chart house. He examined the chart carefully. 'You have done well, Mr Lopez.'

'Thank you, captain.'

'I see we've drifted well to the south and west.'

'Yes, sir. The ship drifts at more than four knots.'

'Remarkable,' said Stone. 'But the currents here are unreliable. Should set easterly, you know. I've known them do the reverse. Particularly after severe storms.'

'Yes, captain. It seems so.'

'What is our distance from Mauritius?'

'About nine hundred and seventy miles.'

Captain Stone turned back to the chart and worked at it with dividers and parallel rulers, measuring and checking. It occurred to Lopez as strange that the captain should have said nothing of the cyclone nor of the damage suffered by the ship. No questions about what had happened since Tuesday when he'd fallen unconscious to the chart house floor. Lopez knew that the chief officer had not briefed Stone on these matters for the Italian had been on the bridge shortly before the captain arrived. 'I trust the captain still sleeps good,' he'd said with heavy sarcasm.

Lopez's thoughts were interrupted by the captain's voice. 'Mr Kantle had any replies to his signals?'

'Not yet, captain.'

'H'm. That's unfortunate. Tell Mr Frascatti

I'd like to see him.'

'Yes, sir.'

Lopez was glad to leave the bridge. He would take the opportunity to visit his cabin to see if the plastic glue on the pick-up arm had set. During the cyclone the player had been damaged by a bookshelf which had jumped its brackets and fallen, smashing the Perspex cover and damaging the pick-up arm. Twelve of his LPs had been broken: mostly Beethoven and Bach concertos, but some of Tchaikovsky and Mozart. Many of his books had been spoilt by sea water, the cabin porthole not having been properly screwed down while he was on watch on the first night of the storm. Two anthologies of poetry, those of Blake and Francis Thompson, had been ruined. When first he discovered these disasters he'd been far more concerned and upset than about the damage to the ship.

★ ★ ★

Frascatti appeared at the door of the chart house, slouching and scowling. 'You send for me?' he growled.

Captain Stone sensed that the chief officer's manner was truculent, bordering on the insolent. 'Yes,' he said. 'What is the condition of the ship?'

144

Frascatti propped himself against the chart house door, hands in trousers pockets, a cheroot in his mouth. 'You cannot see?' The Italian's voice was more rasping and throaty than usual, as if there were a drought in the vocal chords.

'I have been laid up. Kindly answer my question.'

Frascatti laid a screen of blue smoke between himself and the captain. 'Ah, yes. I forget. You been — ah — sick, captain?'

'Exhaustion,' corrected Stone. 'I was not well when the storm began. A severe migraine.'

Frascatti smiled dryly. 'We all exhausted, captain. But we don't sleep for three days.'

'Answer my question, Mr Frascatti.' Stone's voice was gruff. 'What is the state of the ship?'

The Italian blew another cloud of smoke in the captain's direction. 'She floats. But she is finished. *Finito.*' He spread his hands. 'Engine-room and stokehold flooded. All fires out. No power. Nothing. Emergency generator broken. Impossible to fix. Radio no good. Kantle get nothing for reply.'

Captain Stone turned away, concentrating his attention on the chart. There was a long silence.

Frascatti broke it. 'What to do now,

captain?' With narrowed eyes he watched the back of the captain's scarred neck.

'Make everything ship-shape. That's the first priority.'

Frascatti's lower lip curled. 'You think we do nothing while you sleep, captain?'

'What's that?' Stone's back was still towards the chief officer.

'When we cannot see you, captain, *I* take command.' Frascatti paused to let that sink in. 'Now everything like you say — ship-shape. Everything. Walk round. See for yourself.'

'The plugging round that lighter? Fresh lashings to prevent further shifting?'

Frascatti spread his hands, wiggling the cheroot in his mouth. 'This also we do. First day already. I tell you. Everything. But ship is finished. *Kaput.* What to do now, captain?'

Captain Stone remained silent, examining the chart, tapping with a pencil on the table top. He turned to face the chief officer. 'We're drifting across the main shipping lanes between the Cape and Australia. It's likely we'll see a ship any day now.'

Frascatti went to the chart, pointing to the vast expanse of ocean between Africa and Australia. 'Ship here, captain. Nearly in middle. Like — 'ow you say — needle in haystack. More like we not see other ship.'

146

Captain Stone's pale eyes regarded the Italian coldly. 'We are less than a thousand miles from Mauritius. They'll organise an air search. It's only a matter of time before we are found.'

'I think they will not find us, captain. They must fly one thousand miles out. Then one thousand back. Two thousand before they start search.'

'Modern aircraft can fly five or six thousand miles without refuelling,' said Captain Stone. 'They'll have plenty of time.'

Frascatti shrugged his shoulders. 'You think so, captain. I think not. We have two good lifeboats. One with motor. Better we abandon ship and go for Mauritius. Wind and sea will help us.'

'Have you any idea what that sort of journey in open boats means?' Captain Stone's thoughts went back to his time on life-rafts and in open boats in the North Atlantic.

'I know, I know,' said Frascatti irritably. 'Captain Foster in ship *Trevessa* make this journey already. Two boats. More than fifteen hundred miles they go to Mauritius. This way we have chance. Stay here. Pouf! No chance.' To emphasise his point, he spat out of the chart house door.

Captain Stone stared at him as if he were

the devil incarnate. 'Abandon this ship?' he said sternly. 'You must be mad.' *The decision to abandon the ship was hasty, ill-judged and unseamanlike* . . . the dry unemotional voice of the court's president rang in Captain Stone's ears.

Frascatti grimaced in a strange way. 'Why is mad, captain?'

'To abandon a ship which is still afloat and seaworthy but for power? When help can come at any moment from the sea or the air? A sound ship with more than five thousand tons of cargo aboard? That's why it's mad.'

'You abandon other ships other times. Why not this one?' Frascatti smiled thinly.

Captain Stone stared at him. If he'd had a gun in his hand it was quite possible he'd have shot the Italian. Concealing his emotion, he said, 'That was war. Torpedoed ships.'

'*Donnington Wave* not torpedoed, captain.'

So he knew. This quack of a mate, this wharf rat with a Panamanian certificate knew. Captain Stone concentrated once more on the chart. 'This ship will not be abandoned, Mr Frascatti. Now get about your business. I'll be making an inspection later in the forenoon.'

With the cheroot clamped firmly between his teeth, his hands on his hips, Frascatti stood staring at the captain's back. Laughing derisively, he turned away and left the bridge.

For some time afterwards Captain Stone stood hunched over the chart table, his face in his hands. Then he pulled himself together, went out to the bridge and asked Addu Batu, the officer of the watch, to send for Nils Thoresen.

★ ★ ★

Frascatti had been glad to get away from the bridge. He had important plans for the day, but first there was a private matter to be dealt with. During the storm the parakeet's cage had jumped the hook from which it hung. For hours it must have rolled about the cabin, bashing from side to side, and at some time the parakeet's wing had been broken. Skillfully, tenderly, Frascatti had put the wing in splints. But the parakeet was suffering from shock and he had to feed it from his mouth, pushing chewed apple peel into its beak with his tongue. The parakeet was recovering and Frascatti was happy for it would mean much to Violetta.

★ ★ ★

In his cabin later that day Stone confided the seriousness of the situation to Susie and Dwala, the two people closest to him. He told them of his talks with Frascatti and Thoresen that morning, of his decision not to abandon the ship, to wait for the help he believed would come.

'These men,' he warned, 'may make trouble. I want you to keep your eyes and ears open.'

'Is it possible they are right, sah?' Dwala asked with quiet respect. 'Is the chance in the boats not better?'

Captain Stone looked at the steward thoughtfully. 'With a good crew, first-rate officers and seamen, yes. With the riff-raff we have here, no. It requires good seamanship, strong nerves, iron discipline. Our crew don't have those qualities. One or two good men perhaps, but that's not enough. And there isn't a competent navigator among them.'

'But with you there, Uncle? Wouldn't it be all right?'

'I would not be there.' Captain Stone's pale blue eyes, faintly bloodshot, focused in the distance. 'I shall not abandon this ship.'

'If she sinks?'

'I go with her,' he said quietly.

'I know captains do that,' said Susie. 'But is it really necessary, Uncle?'

'It is necessary for me.' His shoulders lifted in a tired gesture.

'I'd never go in the boats without you, uncle. Some of these men are dreadful. You should hear the things they say.'

'What things?'

'Oh.' She bit her lip. 'I shouldn't have worried you. Just things they say. They don't know I'm there usually. But I wouldn't trust them. Not in one of those boats. And me the only girl.' She shuddered.

Dwala nodded wisely. 'She is right, sah. We gone stay with you.'

'You understand,' said Captain Stone. 'That I will not permit them to abandon ship. But I thought I should tell you that if they try . . . ' he paused. 'If they force a decision upon me, you are free to do as you wish.'

'Yes, Uncle. We understand.'

'I believe,' he added with conviction, 'that your chances in the boats would be less than if you stayed aboard.'

When Dwala had gone, Stone got up from his chair and paced the cabin, hands clasped behind his back, head bowed. 'Good heavens,' he exclaimed suddenly, frowning at Susie. 'This is an eight thousand ton ship. We're drifting across the main sea lanes. There'll be an air search. Long range radar in the aircraft. This is nineteen seventy. We're not back in sailing ship days. Of *course* we'll be found.' He stopped pacing and put his hands on Susie's shoulders. 'The chances are good, my dear. Don't lose heart.'

★ ★ ★

Soon after midday, behind locked doors in the second engineer's cabin, Frascatti and Thoresen had a long discussion. During the afternoon they invited selected officers and men — those they regarded as key personnel — to a meeting to be held in the chief engineer's cabin at eight o'clock that night.

All were enjoined to the strictest secrecy.

152

9

Mr McLintoch's cabin had been taken over by the engineers since their messroom, smashed by the lighter, could not be used. It was a large cabin which the chief engineer had always kept neat and tidy. It had, however, suffered from the flooding, being on the alleyway round the engine-room casing, and the violent motion of the ship had thrown things about though the steward had done his best to clean up. Apart from the smell of sodden things, the clinging whiff of the chief engineer's pipe tobacco, mingled with his shaving soap, hung about the cabin. These odours were so redolent of Mr McLintoch that it seemed to the engineers as if he were still with them.

At eight o'clock that night Frascatti and Thoresen gathered in the cabin with the ship's officers and engineers — all but Addu Batu, the third officer, and Achmed Khalif the third engineer, who were on watch. Mr Jenkins and Kantle were present, as was the carpenter, Houtman, and O'Halloran the bosun. The senior greaser and the senior fireman completed the party. In the dim light of the oil lamp the faces of the men listening to Frascatti were like a group in a Rembrandt painting. He was explaining the alternatives, making plain his views that to remain on board would be suicidal. In speaking of the captain's determination not to abandon the ship he explained with some malice the background to that decision — the *Donnington Wave* affair.

'Because of this he will not leave the ship. In any case he is finished, you understand. So he thinks, why go? How can this help me? But for us it is not the same.'

Lopez's gentle face softened with compassion. 'I see his trouble. It is sad for him. If he tells us we must stay we *must*. Otherwise it is mutiny.'

'Mutiny's a naval term,' said Mr Jenkins knowledgeably. 'In the British Merchant Shipping Act it's called misconduct endangering the ship. Same thing of course.'

'We're a Liberian registered ship,' said Thoresen. 'Don't come under the British Act.'

Lopez said, 'There must be some provision in the Liberian Act. But we are playing with words. No matter how it is described, to disobey the direct orders of the master in such a case is mutiny.'

'No.' Frascatti shook his head emphatically.

'It is not mutiny. The captain is a sick man. He drink too much. Already before cyclone he is drunk. In cyclone he drinks again. This is why the ship is in trouble, you understand. For three days he lie drunk in cabin. How can man like this know what is best?'

Thoresen, the second engineer, supported him. 'What Frascatti says is true. We have the right to save our lives. This is not mutiny. If we stay on board we have no hope. We haven't power even to pump bilges. Every day a little more water comes in. We must use the boats while there is still a chance to reach Mauritius or Reunion.'

'They're bloody small islands,' boomed O'Halloran. 'What if we miss the little buggers?'

'Beyond is Madagascar.' Frascatti flicked ash from a cheroot on to the damp carpet. 'Only another four hundred miles. It is too big to miss.'

'What about food and water? There'll be a lot of us in the boats,' said the senior greaser.

Frascatti pointed to Mr Jenkins. 'Ask the chief steward. He tell you.'

'Plenty,' said Mr Jenkins. 'There's enough tinned stuff in my stores to stock the two boats with a month's supply over and above the iron rations already in them. We'll have to ration water, but it often rains hereabouts.'

'Is there room for all of us, and food and water, in the two boats?' asked the chief fireman.

Frascatti nodded. 'These boats are certified to carry twenty-five people in each. We are only thirty-two.'

'Plenty of room,' said Thoresen. 'And the number's only thirty. We've lost two overboard already.'

'Ah. Yes. I forget them.' Frascatti seemed relieved.

Mr Jenkins scratched his head ruminatively. 'I'm not too happy about this, you know.'

'What is the trouble?' Thoresen frowned.

'Well, like leaving the captain. And possibly the girl. She may want to stay if he does.'

'Don't worry.' The senior greaser exposed gappy teeth. 'We take her anyway. Good to have girl on board. Maybe we come to desert island. Then we make family, heh.' He cackled.

'There'll be none of that.' Frascatti was thinking of Violetta. 'The girl will be treated with respect.'

'And the captain?' repeated Mr Jenkins doggedly.

'We must persuade him to come,' said Lopez. 'For his own good. Also he is a fine seaman and navigator.'

156

Frascatti looked at the Mexican with displeasure. 'You think so. When not drunk, eh?'

Lopez thought he could read the chief officer's thoughts. Explanations to the authorities afterwards would be easier if the captain were not there. But he kept these ideas to himself. 'He will not have the opportunity to drink in the boats,' he said.

Before long agreement was reached on all major points. Since speed was essential — each day the ship drifted farther from Mauritius — it was decided to brief the rest of the crew after the meeting broke up. Those who were on watch would be tackled when they came off at midnight. No difficulty was expected in getting the men's agreement. The absence of the captain and the chief engineer in the critical days after the cyclone, fanned by rumours of the hopelessness of their situation, had spread fear throughout the ship. More and more the men looked to Frascatti, Thoresen and O'Halloran for leadership. It was decided that at two o'clock the next morning, Frascatti and Thoresen, accompanied by O'Halloran, would seize the ship's small arms — four rifles and ammunition — kept in a cupboard in a passage in the officers' quarters. Frascatti held one key, the captain the other.

The final operation would begin at eight a.m., the change of watch at that hour ensuring that more than the usual number of men would be round and about the bridge. As eight bells were sounded, Frascatti and Thoresen would go to the captain's cabin, inform him of the crew's decision and urge him and his niece to accompany them. Should they refuse they would be taken to the boats by force. Justification for this would be the fact that, due to alcohol, the captain was in no condition to make a decision involving his life and that of his niece. Frascatti, who'd been in favour of leaving the captain behind if he would not accompany them voluntarily, had been forced to bow to the will of the majority.

The meeting which had, but for this item, demonstrated a remarkable degree of unanimity, then broke up and the men went off in sober mood to brief their companions.

It had been agreed that Dwala and Susie would not be approached. They were too close to Captain Stone.

* * *

Some time after midnight Hank Casey decided that he must risk going to Susie's cabin. An hour earlier he'd heard of the plan to abandon the ship. The cook had broken the news to him perfunctorily and reluctantly, believing there was little need to consult a passage-worker. When Garrett added that everybody was in the know except the captain, Dwala and the girl, Hank Casey began to have his doubts.

'Keep your mouth shut. They mustn't be told until the time comes,' Garrett had warned him. 'We're leaving things to the mate and Thoresen. They've taken responsibility.'

But the more Casey thought about it the more convinced he became that Susie *should* know. It wasn't playing the game to leave her in the dark about a matter of life and death. When Garrett had gone, Casey went to the boat-deck to think things over. What he'd heard worried him. He spent a long time weighing possible courses of action. Then, taking a torch from the galley, he went off to see Susie. It was twenty to one. She'd be asleep. It was a good time for there was no one about, but for Lopez on the bridge with two seamen.

Casey went quietly along the darkened passageways in the officers' quarters until he came to her cabin and knocked on the door. He had to do this several times, softly, before it opened and he heard her startled 'Who is it?'

159

'It's Hank,' he whispered.

'Hank! You mustn't come here,' she hissed.

'It's not what you think. I must see you. It's very important.'

'Oh!' She hesitated for a moment, wishing she could see his face and read his thoughts. 'All right. Come in.'

Slipping into the dark cabin he bolted the door, fixing the torch against the pillows so that its light was shaded. Susie slipped on a dressing-gown and sat on the only chair, while he leant against the shut door. The ship was rolling, a slow cradling motion, accompanied by squeaks and groans as the hull worked. There was a pleasant suggestion of woman in the cabin, of powder and perfume; very different from where Casey slept. In a whispered conversation he told her of the plans for the next day, of the decision to take her and the captain to the boats by force if they would not go voluntarily. But for small exclamations of surprise, she said nothing.

'Susie,' he pleaded. 'When the time comes — at eight o'clock that is — you *must* agree to come. Persuade your uncle that it's best for him, too. We're in a hopeless position. No power, no radio. Drifting steadily away from the nearest land. And all that water slopping about in the engine-room and stokehold. The ship's slowly sinking.'

While he talked, Susie was thinking that it would be better not to let him know that she and Dwala had already discussed with the captain what might happen. That they'd already made their decision. It was only too evident how concerned Hank was about her. If she told him he might — probably would — tell the others. That would precipitate trouble. It was better that he shouldn't know. Her mind was made up. She wasn't going. He couldn't change that.

'So what'll you do, Susie?' In the dim light of the torch he watched her intently. 'It's a helluva decision to make. They're all going. If the Old Man refuses, you can't stay here in a deserted ship alone with him. You wouldn't have a chance.'

It was best, she decided, to give him the impression that she would go. 'Yes. I can see that, Hank. Isn't it fantastic that we're faced with this decision?'

'Yes. But you'll be okay. I'll see that I'm in the same boat as you and the captain. I'll look after you.'

'Gee, that's sweet of you Hank.' She kissed him lightly on the lips.

He put his arms round her and returned the kiss with interest, smothering whatever she was trying to say. Then, in one powerful movement, he lifted her on to the bunk, slipping in beside her.

'No,' she whispered fiercely, pushing him away. 'Not now. You're crazy, Hank. How can you think of such things at a time like this.'

Shamefacedly he got off. 'Sorry,' he said. 'I know I shouldn't be like that. But when I'm near you — and you in that nightgown — ' He smiled ruefully. 'I reckon I couldn't help it.'

'Go *now*.' She pushed him towards the door. 'Before somebody hears us.'

'Don't forget.' He stood by the door, his hand on the bolt, the torch out, the cabin dark. 'Say nothing about this to the Old Man now. Tell him at eight, when they come to the cabin. It'll only mean trouble, otherwise.'

'Yes, Hank,' she whispered urgently. 'I understand. Thanks for warning me.'

★   ★   ★

After Hank had gone, Susie lay on the bunk in the dark, thinking. She was frantically worried and her head ached. What she'd heard was so awful. Their position was hopeless: her uncle's, Dwala's and hers. They'd be forced into the boats. She thought of some of the crew who'd be there and remembered the things she'd heard them say. Horrible, ugly things — about her. Sex was

162

all right. Marvellous, even. But not if you thought and spoke about it like that. They were animals. It was an impossible situation. To have to decide between staying in a drifting derelict, or going off in the boats with them with land more than a thousand miles away. She thought of the indignities and humiliations a lone girl would suffer in an open boat. *And with those men.*

She turned over, buried her face in the pillows and had a good cry. Afterwards she felt better. But she couldn't just lie there waiting for eight o'clock. She must do something. She slipped on slacks, a shirt and slippers and went along the dark passages and stairs to her uncle's cabin. She knocked timidly. Almost at once Dwala answered. When she whispered her name he let her in. He was dressed. She asked the time. 'Half past two in the morning, Miss Susie,' he said.

★　★　★

By the time she left his cabin Stone had made certain important decisions, some of which he communicated to her. 'You've done the right thing, warning me, Susie. Now listen carefully. Come to this cabin at exactly twenty minutes to eight this morning. In case you are seen, bring a tray with milk, biscuits and an apple. Dwala will be here. Once you're inside we'll lock the door.'

'If they try to force it?'

'Leave it to me,' said Captain Stone grimly.

She looked doubtful. 'I'm frightened, Uncle. They sound determined.'

'I'm sorry it's come to this, my dear.' He patted her shoulder. 'But trust in God. Keep a stout heart. We'll not be going in the boats with them, I'll see to that.'

'I hope you're right,' she said. 'I hope you're right.'

Captain Stone kissed her forehead and she went off in the darkness. As she made her way down the stairs she realised with relief that he'd not smelt of alcohol.

★   ★   ★

When his niece had gone the captain locked the outer door and opened the safe beside the desk. Dwala held the torch while Stone took out ammunition and two .38 service revolvers. He gave one to the steward. 'Load it, and put the spare ammunition in your pocket.' Stone loaded the other revolver, putting ammunition into the pockets of the reefer he'd pulled over his pyjamas.

Having explained his intentions he unlocked the door and went down the

164

darkened passageway to the armoury cupboard followed by the Ghanaian. He inserted
the key, opened the cupboard and felt round
inside it. The four rifleracks and the
ammunition shelves were empy. Without a
word he locked the cupboard, returned to the
cabin, shut the door and turned the key.

'They've taken the rifles and ammunition,'
he said heavily. For some minutes he sat
silent in the darkness, appalled at the reality
of what was happening. 'They mean business,
Dwala.' He stood up. 'Let's get busy. Shut
and secure the windows and portholes. Then
draw the curtains.'

★ ★ ★

No sooner had eight bells struck, than there
came a knock on the door of the outer cabin.
Stone gestured Susie and Dwala to silence,
took a revolver from the desk and stood to
one side of the door. 'Who is it?' he called.

'Frascatti here, captain,' came the reply.

'What do you want?'

'To see you, captain.'

'I'm busy. Can't see you now.'

There was a moment's pause. Then came
Thoresen's voice. 'I am here also, captain. We
must see you at once. It is urgent.'

'What is it that's so urgent?'

There was another pause. 'We have decided . . . the crew has decided . . . to abandon ship,' Frascatti shouted. 'We take to the boats.'

'You'll do no such thing,' replied Stone brusquely. 'I command this ship. I am the only man who can make that decision.'

'No use to talk like this, captain,' retorted Frascatti. 'We decide already.'

Thoresen broke in, his tone conciliatory. 'We wish you to come, captain. You will command. There is a better chance for all in the boats. Especially if you are there. Please come, captain.'

'Under no circumstances, Mr Thoresen. This ship will not be abandoned. The chances of survival are better if we remain on board. Furthermore, it is our duty to stand by the ship as long as there is a chance of saving her.'

'There is no chance,' said Frascatti.

'Nonsense.'

'What of your niece and the steward?' asked Thoresen.

'They'll answer for themselves.'

Dwala and the girl crossed to the door. Stone motioned them to one side of it.

'I'm not going in the boats.' Susie hoped they wouldn't detect the tremble in her voice. 'I'm staying with Uncle. It's safer here.'

'If you stay you die.' The Italian's voice rasped like a file.

'I stay with captain,' said Dwala. 'Not go in boats.'

'You're mad. All of you.' Frascatti spoke with sudden irritation. 'The captain tells you lies. If you stay in ship you have no chance. She will not be found. Radio not working. We see no other ship in five days. All the time we drift south. There is no hope.'

Thoresen said, 'It is the wish of the crew.'

There was a moment's silence after which Frascatti added, 'They make me leader.'

'You are the ringleader, Frascatti,' said Captain Stone. 'That places you in a very serious position.'

'Crew has no confidence in you, captain. You are sick man. Too much alcohol. That is why they ask me to take command.'

There was an embarrassing silence in the cabin. Susie and Dwala found it difficult to know where to look.

'Mr Frascatti, Mr Thoresen, I warn you. To disobey my orders is tantamount to mutiny.' Stone's voice was heavy with emotion. 'You and all who support you. Inform the crew at once that you have given up your plans. That they must continue to obey my orders.'

Muted discussion was followed by Frascatti's voice. 'I am in command, Captain

Stone. You are sick man. The ship cannot be saved. We go. If you and the others not come, we break door. Afterwards we take you. To save your lives, you understand.'

A new voice was heard: O'Halloran's. 'For the Holy Mother's sake, captain, listen to raison. It's for your own good. You and the young lady and that black heathen of a steward.'

'You mixed up in this, O'Halloran? Fifteen years in the Royal Navy should have taught you to obey orders.'

'Begorrah, sorr! There's no sense to staying in a sinking ship.'

Frascatti spoke again, rasping and throaty. 'Is no use to argue. For last time . . . you come or we break door?'

'I warn you, Frascatti,' replied Stone. 'We are armed. Any man forcing that door risks his life.' He fired a warning shot at the cabin deckhead.

'There's more where that came from,' he said in a firm voice.

10

After Stone's warning shot, Frascatti put O'Halloran on sentry duty outside the door. The Irishman had a loaded rifle and orders that no one was to leave. Frascatti and Thoresen then joined Mr Jenkins and Kantle in the saloon. A hurried council of war was held: the firearms in the captain's cabin, and Susie and Dwala's refusal to leave him, had complicated the situation.

After urgent discussion, Mr Jenkins again expressing misgivings, the plan to abandon ship was confirmed. The boats were to be provisioned, watered and made ready for the long journey. Thereafter the men would be mustered and directed to them. A final appeal would be made to the captain and his companions. If they still refused to come there would be no option but to leave them behind. On Mr Jenkins's insistence, supported by Kantle, it was agreed there would be no shooting.

O'Halloran was needed for preparing the boats, so a Brazilian fireman with army experience took over as sentry outside the captain's cabin.

It was a fine day: a blue sky laced with bacon-like streaks of cirrus, smooth sea, gentle swell, light easterly breeze and a sun which shone down warmly on the derelict ship. There was intense activity as the boats were made ready. Tinned foods, biscuits, apples, lime-juice (the last, on Mr Jenkins's insistence, to preclude scurvy), and other provisions were brought up from the storerooms, put in polythene bags and stowed in the boats. These were additional to the iron rations already there. Water tanks under the bench-thwarts were emptied and refilled with fresh water, additional supplies of which were loaded in ten gallon drums. Sea anchors and oil bags for heavy weather were checked: boats' masts, rigging and sails gone over, refurled and restowed. Balers, fishing lines, signal flares and other gear were mustered and stowed. An additional coil of rope was taken on board number one boat — Frascatti's — which would lead. The rope would be used as a painter to keep the boats together during the hours of darkness, and for towing.

Navigation was to be the responsibility of Lopez, the second officer. From the chart house he took sextant and chronometer, navigation tables and nautical almanac, sailing directions for the South Indian Ocean, and charts. Frascatti's boat was given a sextant, deck-watch, chart and nautical almanac. Between them, he and Addu Batu would be able to calculate the latitude, the sum total of their nautical astronomy. The boats' compasses were checked by Lopez and the errors noted.

Kantle fetched the orange box containing the emergency transmitter from the radio cabin and put it in Frascatti's boat. The radio operator had little faith in the emergency transmitter, but there was as yet no definite evidence that it was not working. It was better than nothing. Lopez and two other members of the crew took their transistor radios with them, and each boat was given an Aldis lamp with batteries for signalling.

Achmed Khalif, reputed expert in internal combustion engines, was detailed to Frascatti's boat which had the petrol engine. Khalif put sufficient fuel in the boat for five hundred miles. There was no room for more. Thoresen was to accompany Lopez in the second boat. Frascatti felt that the Danish engineer would provide the resolve and leadership which the gentle Lopez seemed to lack.

★ ★ ★

At times during that morning of high activity Captain Stone inched aside the window curtains in his cabin and looked aft along the boat-deck. What he saw put beyond all doubt the determination of the crew to abandon the ship. From the speed with which they were working he realised that the time of departure was near. At one stage, feeling he could not remain idle in the face of such insubordination, he took a revolver and went to the door of the outer cabin. He had begun to unlock it when a voice on the far side warned, 'If you open I shoot.'

The captain, aware that the mutineers — for as such he now regarded them — had the ship's rifles and amunition and were evidently desperate men, abandoned the attempt. Alone he would have risked armed confrontation, for he no longer attached much importance to his life, but he was not prepared to involve his niece and Dwala in senseless bloodshed to prevent the crew leaving the ship. On one thing he was determined. Any attempt to force him and his companions into the boats would be resisted. If that involved a gun battle then there would be one.

★ ★ ★

Towards half past nine Frascatti knocked once more on the door. This time he was accompanied by Mr Jenkins. 'The boats are ready, captain,' Frascatti shouted. 'We go now. Please — I ask you — please come with us. Weather is fine. We can make good sail for Mauritius.'

Before the captain could reply, Mr Jenkins added his voice to the plea. 'Jenkins here, captain. We don't like having to do this but it's been agreed by all that the chances are better if we take to the boats. Please come with us, sir. I am sure you will . . . '

'You should know better, Jenkins,' the captain interrupted, 'than to get mixed up in this. Now Frascatti, listen here. You and your companions are guilty of mutiny under arms and . . .'

'It is you who fired the shot,' interrupted Frascatti.

The captain ignored the interruption. 'The weather may be fine to-day but that means nothing. The voyage in open boats is a highly dangerous undertaking. More than a thousand miles to go. With the sort of men you've got you'll never make it. If they're prepared to mutiny in this ship, they'll mutiny in the boats. You won't be able to control them.'

'Your mind is not right, captain,' shouted

Frascatti. 'You are not in condition to understand. Too much drink. You think of *Donnington Wave* trouble and you are frightened to leave this ship. So you sacrifice life of young girl and steward. This is very bad, captain. What will people say when we tell them. Better you come with us.'

'You and Thoresen are the ringleaders, Frascatti. You have been conspiring together. I warn you, the consequences will be serious. As for my niece and Dwala, they are free to go. I place no obstacle in their way. You may ask them.'

Frascatti and Jenkins did. But the girl and the African expressed their determination to remain in the ship. They were sure it would be sighted by shipping or aircraft.

At that point Frascatti gave up. Before he left the captain's cabin, Mr Jenkins asked for Susie and through the door explained that there was plenty of food in the storerooms; the keys, clearly labelled, were on the keyboard in his cabin. There were, he said, ample supplies of fresh water and powdered milk. Dwala would know where everything was kept. With these explanations Mr Jenkins bade her farewell, wished her God speed and sighed deeply. There could be no mistaking the concern with which he spoke and Susie, a lump in her throat, thanked him, expressing the hope that he and his companions would come to no harm.

* * *

Frascatti and Thoresen mustered the crew on the boat-deck. Each man wore a life-jacket and warm clothing but beyond these personal possessions were not permitted. The crew were detailed to their boats, deck and engine-room staff being divided equally between the two. Rifles and ammunition were put in the boats, these being the responsibility of the officers in charge.

Fenders were rigged to prevent damage and chafing when the boats were lowered; rope ladders were dropped down to water level, davits and falls were manned and the boats turned out. O'Halloran took charge of this operation though Frascatti, nominally in command, did some shouting. With an eye on the roll of the ship, O'Halloran ordered the men on the falls to stand-by. As she came up from a roll to port, he shouted, 'Lower away handsomely,' and the boats dropped quickly down to the water where fall-blocks were slipped and painters made fast fore and aft. No time was wasted. The crew swarmed down rope ladders and lifelines and soon all were aboard.

Achmed Khalif started the engine in Frascatti's boat, a line was passed to the second boat, the clutch was let in and slowly they drew clear of the ship. When they were half a mile away, the engine was stopped — fuel had to be conserved — the line between the boats was slipped, masts were stepped and the rigging set up. Lugsails were hoisted and trimmed to the easterly breeze and the *Moonraker*'s mutineers set course for the long journey to Mauritius.

★ ★ ★

From the windows of his cabin Captain Stone and his companions watched the lifeboats draw away from the ship. Suspecting a trap, he was determined not to open the door of the outer cabin until they were out of sight. His emotions as the boats grew smaller with distance were a mixture of remorse and humiliation. Frascatti's references to his drinking, to the loss of the crew's confidence and to the *Donnington Wave*, had been deeply humiliating. The more so because they were true. His mistake about the cyclone had been criminally stupid. The ship would have avoided the worst of the storm but for that. And when he knew of the mistake he should never have attempted to run before it with

176

those lighters on the after well-deck. He should have put the wind on the bow and hauled round to port as it backed. Frascatti was right. Alcohol had befuddled his thinking. Nevertheless he did believe that they were safer in the ship than they would have been in the boats, grim though the situation was.

Susie watched the boats go with rather different emotions. Whatever happened to her on board *Moonraker* now would never, she felt, be as bad as what might have happened had she gone in the boats. She was sad about Hank going though she didn't blame him. Even if he'd not wanted to go — and from what he'd said the night before it was clear he did — they'd have forced him to. She prayed for his safety, that nothing awful might befall him. But her woman's intuition told her that she would never see him again and tears gathered in her eyes. She soon pulled herself together and thought of the positive side of things. With her uncle and Dwala on board she would at least have the company and protection of men she trusted. Of course she was frightened. That was only natural, she told herself, but she had child-like faith in her uncle's belief that they would be sighted by another ship or by search aircraft.

She was thinking how marvellous it would be to see a ship coming towards them, or to hear the sound of aircraft engines and look up to see a plane circling, when there came a knock on the captain's door.

'Good heavens!' muttered Stone, signalling silence as he picked up a revolver.

The knock came again, louder this time. Revolver in hand, the captain took up a position beside the door. 'Who is it?'

'Hank Casey, sir,' was the reply.

The captain frowned. Was this a trap? 'What are you doing here?'

'I decided not to go in the boats.'

'Why?'

The Australian paused. 'I was worried about Susie, sir. And I reckoned the chances in the ship were no worse than in the boats.'

'You're not up to some trick, are you?' Stone's tone was severe. 'We're armed, I warn you.'

Susie ran across to her uncle. 'Of course he's not up to tricks, Uncle. Please let him in.'

After a moment of indecision, Stone unlocked the door. The Australian came in covered by the captain's revolver.

Susie ran to him, throwing her arms round his neck and kissing him. 'Oh, Hank,' she cried. 'How fabulous. I can't believe it.'

'Susie,' admonished Stone. 'Watch your behaviour.'

Half laughing, half crying, she turned to

her uncle. 'Oh, Uncle. Don't be silly. Can't you see. It's marvellous having him here. He's young and strong. He'll be a terrific help.'

Captain Stone locked the door, staring dubiously at the young man. 'I daresay. We'll have to see. Quite sure there's no one else on board, Casey?'

'Quite sure, sir. I hid in a locker on the poop. Waited there for more than two hours. Then I took a decco. Lifted the lid a bit. Saw the lifeboats in the distance. After a while I went round the ship to see how they'd left things. Then I came up here.'

'Good,' said Captain Stone, reassured at last. 'I'm grateful to you for staying aboard. You've made a wise decision.'

★ ★ ★

It was not until sunset that evening, when the two lifeboats had drawn together to make ready for the night, that the absence of Hank Casey was discovered. Each boat had, during the day, assumed that the passage-worker was in the other boat.

There were few regrets, the general view being that they were well rid of the Australian. It was one mouth less to feed and water, and if he'd chosen to remain behind that was his business.

11

News of the air search for the *Moonraker* received only brief press and radio mention in London on Friday, 13th November, the mass media being saturated with news of the cyclone disaster in the Bay of Bengal.

Hassim Racher happened to be in Zurich that day and, inadvertently, for the ensuing weekend, the inadvertence being blonde and acquiescent. Such Zurich papers as he read made no mention of the ship, nor had he left a telephone number at which his office might contact him. Thus not until he got to the office in Aldgate on the Monday morning did he learn for the first time that *Moonraker* was missing. With the morning mail his secretary brought him a press clipping announcing the air search and a confirmatory cable from the agents in Mauritius, dispatched on the Saturday, reporting that the ship was three days' overdue.

Trembling with agitation Mr Racher pulled the lobe of his ear. 'Air search, cyclone, three days' overdue!' he shook his head in disbelief. 'I am amazed, Miss Kolbe. But what an extraordinary thing. I mean actually what a terrible occurrence, Miss Kolbe.' Placing his elbows on the desk, Mr Racher sank his head into his hands and groaned.

Miss Kolbe, who knew him well, smiled. Mr Racher always did things so thoroughly, even if it were the portrayal of shock and dejection. 'Oh, well,' she said philosophically. 'The old tub's not been exactly profitable lately.'

'What a thing to say, Miss Kolbe.' Mr Racher's voice was censorious. 'Captain Stone, Mr McLintoch, all those brave fellows. It is not a matter to make light of. Also the ship. Such a fine vessel. And that valuable cargo.' He shook his head, groaning again. 'A tragic disaster if she has been lost.'

'Well, of course, I'm sorry for the sailors,' said Miss Kolbe. 'I mean who wouldn't be. But the ship's well insured. Very well, I'd say. And the cargo, no doubt.'

Mr Racher put his hands to his ears. 'Don't tell me such things, Miss Kolbe. How can you be so heartless.'

Miss Kolbe smiled knowingly. 'I was only trying to comfort you, Hassim.'

'*Mister* Racher please,' said Mr Racher stiffly, suddenly sitting bolt upright. 'You know I don't approve of first names in the office, Miss Kolbe.'

'Of course. I'm sorry.' Her voice was

unrepentant as she opened the bottom drawer of the filing cabinet, bending low to extract a file. The cabinet was opposite his desk and Miss Kolbe knew that Mr Racher, an ardent admirer of the mini skirt, enjoyed the view.

Mr Racher, who'd had an idea, broke the hypnotic spell cast by Miss Kolbe's bottom and said, 'Get me Lloyd's on the phone will you, dear.'

Miss Kolbe resumed the vertical. 'I phoned them first thing this morning, Mr Racher. The ship will not be regarded as a total loss for fourteen days, reckoned from the date on which she was first reported overdue and missing.'

'So,' mused Mr Racher, tapping his pen on a scribbling block. 'Missing on the thirteenth. That would make it the twenty-seventh.' As if he had suddenly remembered something he sank into dejection again. 'Terrible. Terrible,' he muttered. 'To think such things can happen in these modern times.'

'Will you still be needing Lloyd's, Mr Racher?'

'What's that?' he asked, his mind elsewhere.

'Lloyd's. D'you still wish to speak to them?'

'No. No thank you, Miss Kolbe.'

'Don't you think you should ring Mrs Stone and er . . . some of the others?'

Mr Racher looked up. 'Yes. Yes, of course. I was just about to ask you. But not too many. After all the ship is not yet lost. We mustn't be too . . . ' he hesitated.

'Pessimistic?' suggested Miss Kolbe.

'Yes. Of course. Pessimistic. We must always be optimistic.'

Miss Kolbe nodded sagely. 'You always are, aren't you. I mean that's the secret of your success.'

Mr Racher, not altogether happy about this ambiguity, switched the subject. 'Ask Mr Swan to bring me the Lloyd's underwriters' file, Miss Kolbe.'

She closed the filing drawer. 'Certainly, Mr Racher.'

Mr Swan was secretary of Mr Racher's companies which included Gimbal Ocean Carriers Limited, the registered owners of *Moonraker*, *Cloudraker* and *Sunraker*. It was Mr Swan who had persuaded Mr Racher that RAKER could not be spelt RACHER.

★ ★ ★

After five days of continuous activity the air search yielded nothing and was called off, the aircraft returning to their bases in Majunga and Saldanha Bay. It was not surprising that the search had failed. An operation of that nature over vast tracks of ocean requires not only that every square mile be scanned, but that the missing ship and the aircraft which finds her shall be in the same place at the same time. If *Moonraker* had remained somewhere near her last known position she would soon have been found but she was — and that was the searcher's problem — moving at an unknown speed in an unknown direction. This complicated an already difficult task.

Having called off the air search the authorities issued a general warning to shipping to keep a lookout for the missing ship or for boats or rafts from it. At the time the signal was sent, *Moonraker* was eight days' overdue at Port Louis where it was generally believed she must have foundered in the cyclone with all hands.

Aware that it was not possible to launch lifeboats in a cyclone, the authorities allowed the possibility that her damage might have been such that she sank several days after the storm, by which time the crew could have taken to the boats or rafts. But the lack of any radio message after her last report was ominous.

At Lloyd's the Lutine Bell was rung and the *Moonraker* was posted 'missing.'

★ ★ ★

On the last stages of the voyage from Cape Town to Kerguelen, Merfyr Evans, master and owner of the coaster *Myfanwy*, was a tired man. For eight days there had been continuously bad weather, the westerly winds and seas of the Roaring Forties living up to their reputation. For him most of the last five days had been spent in the wheelhouse. Certainly most of the nights, for it was then that danger was at its greatest. Once below latitude 40° south they had sighted bergs and growlers, and as they neared Kerguelen slabs of drifting pack ice appeared. Radar had helped but it was by no means infallible. One wet night during the middle watch, the ship then running before a force seven wind and sea, Evans had gone from the wheelhouse to the small bridgewalk. He'd done so to get away from Calvi, the mate, whose sullen silence was getting on his nerves. He'd recently spent too many hours on the bridge alone with the man. Calvi and Christopherson, the second mate, were working watch-and-watch, four hours on and four off, because of the weather and the danger of icebergs. For most of the nights Evans was up there with them. It was a situation which made for tension, particularly between Evans and the Corsican who felt that the captain's presence on the bridge was a vote of no confidence. In a sense it was, though under those conditions Evans would have been there whoever was on watch.

Standing out on the bridge-walk in freezing weather the night before, he'd heard a roar in the distance and realised that an iceberg had 'calved' a growler — let drop into the sea from one of its high cliffs a slab of ice weighing many hundreds of tons. Evans had at once gone to the wheelhouse and altered course away from the danger. He'd then reprimanded Calvi for not spotting the berg on the radar.

'Look for yourself,' said the Corsican, his deep voice contemptuous. 'There is nothing on the screen.' And it was true. Radar had not yet picked up the hazard. That had been three nights before Kerguelen. The next night, dark with rain and low scudding clouds, Evans and Christopherson had heard the sound of breakers to windward. Since the ship was far from land Evans had realised that the sea must be breaking against a big berg. Unable to pick it up on radar he had turned the coaster downwind.

He had no illusions about what would happen if they hit an iceberg or growler. *Myfanwy* would sink and the chances of rescue in that distant part of the Southern Ocean were remote indeed. For normal purposes the coaster was fitted with radio telephone with a range of three hundred miles. While this sufficed for work on the South African coast, the authorities had insisted that she be fitted with a high-frequency radio telephone — HF R/T — with a range of eight hundred miles for the voyage to and from Kerguelen. The agents had arranged for this to be installed on loan, but Evans was aware that he would, for sizeable parts of the journey, be out of touch with the land and a long way from the main shipping lanes. In any event the coaster's equipment permitted the use of voice radio only, thus messages in Morse code could not be transmitted. Nor received for that matter since she carried no radio operator and neither her master nor mates read morse at standard transmitting speeds.

During the afternoon of the eighth day they sighted the jagged peaks of Kerguelen and as they closed the island and steamed along its northern coast they passed great patches of kelp, glistening and ominous in the dark waters of the Southern Ocean. Evans mistrusted kelp for only too often it concealed rocks. For the rest of the day he held his ship well off the land, reducing speed towards nightfall in order to reach Cape Digby, the north-eastern extremity of the island, at first light the next day. When it came, and they had sighted and rounded the cape, he took his small ship down the eastern coast, round Presqu'ile Courbet and Prince de Galles into the Baie du Morbihan.

Slowly the *Myfanwy* threaded her way through Passe Royale into the deeper reaches of the bay while her crew looked at the encircling land: dark mountains, their slopes laced with the threads of distant torrents, a vast complex of sounds and fjords, islets and peninsulas. Spread like a carpet before this morose landscape the sea mirrored the gloom of a sky into whose clouds mountains thrust snow-capped peaks.

Evans led his ship cautiously in towards the small settlement at Port-aux-Français, keeping the white leading beacons in transit until about half a mile from the shore when he let go anchor in fifteen fathoms and the *Myfanwy* swung to face the westerly wind. Calvi got the deck crew busy, rigging derricks, taking off hatch-covers, and starting up the winches.

As Evans watched the motor boat coming out to the ship he leant on the compass binnacle and sighed with exhaustion. The journey from Cape Town had taken eight days and fourteen hours. It seemed to him more like eighteen days. It had been a hard cold voyage with many worries, though fuel had not been one of them. With westerly winds, seas and currents helping the coaster most of the way, fuel consumption had been less than expected. For which blessing he said a small prayer of thankfulness as he made his way down to the fore-deck to greet the occupants of the motor boat.

★ ★ ★

The men of the weather station who were not on duty turned out to greet the coaster. The arrival of the small ship was a considerable event in the life of this remote community for she brought mail, parcels and new faces. As the unloading got under way there was, in spite of language difficulties, cheerful fraternising between the Frenchmen and the *Myfanwy*'s crew, mostly Cape coloureds and Zulus.

No one was happier than Napoleon Calvi who had not for a long time been among his own countrymen, and for whom the island awakened all the pride in the achievement of France which lies in the heart of Frenchmen. Here, tucked away in the Southern Ocean on the fringes of Antarctica, so remote from

France, Kerguelen was a living testimony to French navigators, explorers and scientists. On the voyage, Calvi had pored over the account of the island in the *Admiralty Sailing Directions*. Every page of it, from the discovery of the island in 1772 by Ives Joseph de Kerguelen-Tremarec, commanding the French frigates *Fortune* and *Gros-Ventre*, to the latest entry about the weather station at Port-aux-Français, was to him a romantic story of French endeavour. The names on the charts fired his imagination: *Pointe-Curieuse* . . . what had happened there? *Crique du Sac á Plomb* . . . boat soundings? Had they left the bag for the lead in the creek? Or was the creek shaped like a bag? *Plage demi Lune* . . . what thoughts had inspired the seaman who gave the beach that romantic name? Had he stood there one night under a half moon, those many years ago, thinking of a girl somewhere in France?

★ ★ ★

With the assistance of the weather station's two motor boats the off-loading of stores and equipment went smoothly despite the westerly wind and cold weather. Cook Glacier which ran diagonally across the island formed a buttress which tamed the wind before it reached the anchorage in the Baie du Morbihan. With Gallic misgiving Calvi noted in the *Sailing Directions* that the glacier was named after Captain Cook who had visited Kerguelen in 1776 on his way to Tasmania.

At Evans' request the agents in Cape Town had provided walkie-talkie equipment and this was proving invaluable in keeping *Myfanwy* and the boats in touch during the unloading operation. The superintendent of the weather station had suggested taking on fresh water at Port Jeanne d'Arc where the coaster could lie close inshore the anchorage there being better protected than at Port-aux-Français.

★　★　★

By mid-afternoon of the second day unloading was completed. They were ahead of schedule and Evans gave permission for as many hands as could be spared to land for a run ashore. But there was little to see. It rained, the wind blew strongly from the west, and the men found walking difficult in the soft yielding ground laced with streams and rivulets. And it was cold; 45° Fahrenheit during the day, falling to 34° at night.

At an impromptu party that night the staff of the weatherstation entertained the crew, plying their guests with such local delicacies as seabirds' eggs, rabbits, the brains, tongues and liver of leopard seals, and an indigenous vegetable, the Kerguelen cabbage. This substantial meal was washed down with ample portions of Burgundy.

Afterwards the party broke up into small groups, some serious, others not. There was endless talk and laughter. A young Frenchman with a guitar sang folk songs, the weatherstation men providing a rousing chorus. This triggered off Merfyr Evans and Dai Williams for no Welshman could resist such a challenge, and the old songs of the valleys rang through the smoke-filled hut. They had needed no accompaniment but later, one of the coaster's crewmen, a Cape coloured, found that his hosts had a concertina. He borrowed it, and *Daar Kom Alabama* and other *liedjes* with their flavour of the spirituals of the deep south took over. After that came the martial voices of the Zulus singing and chanting tribal songs, providing their own accompaniment of stamping feet, clapping hands and animated posturing.

It was not until two in the morning that the party broke up and Evans took his men into the cold night and off to the ship. It had been a gay evening, marred only by a brief but inconclusive fight between the second mate, Jan Christopherson, and Isak John the bosun. Both were young and strong and blood was drawn before Evans stopped it. How and why it started no one knew, nor did they make it their business to find out. Evans resolved to talk to them about it the next day. There was no place in a small ship for feuding, and in his view these two had been guilty of that ever since Christopherson had joined.

★ ★ ★

At daybreak on the third day the *Myfanwy* left Port-aux-Français and began the journey across the Baie du Morbihan to Port Jeanne d'Arc on the southern side: twenty miles as the crow would fly, but nearer to thirty-five for the coaster, for the sea passage involved a tortuous course through clusters of small islands, headlands, inlets and along narrow leads and channels.

The temperature that morning was only two degrees above freezing and the westerly wind, rain squalls, low cloud, and occasional falls of sleet and snow added to the difficulties of pilotage. Evans had to make the most of radar and the echo-sounder. Uncomfortably aware of the possibility of uncharted dangers, he kept the engines at reduced speed throughout the journey.

The odour of kelp, the musky aroma of bog and peat hung in the wind which carried, too, the crisp smell of distant snow and glaciers. Occasionally through the curtain of rain and mist, they would see rookeries of leopard-seals, spotted and glistening, on rocky islets. Sometimes they could hear the seals barking and yet not see them. At others a seal would break water near the coaster in a sudden shining swirl, the sound of its exhalations like those of some giant swimmer. The land and water which enclosed *Myfanwy* on every side was rich with sea birds: albatross, gulls, skuas, terns, penguins — among them King penguins — and, most numerous of all, petrels.

The shrilling of the seabirds, the steady beat of the coaster's diesels, the splash of water thrown aside by her bow, the barking of seals and the occasional sound of crewmen's voices made a pattern of sound which belied the impression Kerguelen had given of a deserted island.

Seven hours after leaving Port-aux-Français they came to Port Jeanne d'Arc. It was not sighted until close at hand when the derelict buildings of the old whaling and sealing stations showed up through the mist and rain. The settlement — abandoned in

194

1909 — had been a large one, and the remains of the factory, the workshops, tanks, storehouses and dwellings lay about in dilapidated confusion.

The coaster's engines were put astern and the siren sounded. Before long a motor launch was seen coming out from the shore.

There were three Frenchmen in it, clad in oilskins and fur caps. A blond bearded man with the pink complexion and blue eyes of a Breton came aboard. He introduced himself as Henri Descartes, leader of the geological survey. A bag of mail and parcels was lowered into the launch and it made for the shore. Descartes spoke good English. '*Bienvenu*. Welcome to Port Jeanne d'Arc,' he said shaking hands with Evans. 'It is good to see you.'

They went to the wheelhouse and Evans pointed to the shore. 'Looks like a deserted film set.'

Henri Descartes laughed. 'Not quite deserted. We 'ave our headquarters for the survey in this place. But alas the stars 'ave gone. Now,' he said becoming serious. 'I show you where we anchor. See the old broken jetty' — he used the French *jetée* — 'There is good water fifty metres from those poles sticking up at the end.'

'What depth?'

'About seven metres at low water.'

'H'm. Three and a half fathoms.'

The Frenchman saw Evans' frown. 'How deep is your ship, *m'sieu le capitaine?*'

'About ten foot six. We're pretty light just now.'

'Then you 'ave enough water.'

'Should be. But I'm worrying about the wind. If it goes north-easterly we'll swing on to what's left of that jetty.'

The Frenchman spread his hands. 'More than ninety percent of the time the wind is from the west. Of course it can change. And there are also sudden squalls from the mountain.' He pointed to where Mount Ross must be somewhere in the clouds. 'You 'ave always to keep the engines ready.'

Evans nodded. 'That's what they say in the sailing directions.' He rang down *slow-ahead* and the *Myfanwy* trembled as her diesels started to turn. When she was near the end of the jetty he stopped, went astern and let go the anchor. He'd been warned that the holding ground was not good. There'd have to be a mate on or near the bridge night and day while they lay at Port Jeanne d'Arc. He was taking no chances.

When the coaster had swung to her cable and he'd plotted the anchor bearings, Evans took the Frenchman down to the saloon.

There they planned the discharging of stores and equipment, and the loading of the ore and coal samples waiting on shore. 'What's the tonnage, *M'sieu* Descartes?' he asked.

'About one hundred and fifty. It is all bagged. Of this only twenty-five is coal. Some is in fifty kilo, others in hundred kilo bags.'

The Welshman was surprised. 'That's a lot more than the agents told me.'

'Any difficulties?'

'Not on account of weight. That'll come in handy in a light ship in these parts. It's the loading time that worries me.'

'We can help, *m'sieu le capitaine*. Ten men and two boats I can let you 'ave. Also the motor boat for towing.'

Merfyr Evans' eyebrows lifted. 'Your boats suitable for carrying this stuff?'

'This is what they are for. We 'ave to bring the coal and ore here by water. The land is too soft. All — 'ow you say — *marais*.'

'Marsh, bogland?' suggested Merfyr Evans.

'Exactly.'

'The agents told me you'd help. I never thought it would be that good.' He looked searchingly at the Frenchman. 'What's the ore?'

Descartes smiled, exposing perfect teeth beneath the blond moustache. 'Unfortunately I cannot tell you *m'sieu le capitaine*. It is not

197

permitted. Actually, we geologists are not quite sure ourselves. There are many different minerals.'

'Sorry, I shouldn't have asked.'

'*Pas du tout*. Not at all. You 'ave to carry it a long way. It is natural to ask.'

Uranium or nickel bearing ores, thought Evans. The French government wouldn't spend all that money carting rock to France unless they'd a pretty good idea what it was. Well, it was none of his business, except to get it to Durban. He said, 'Excuse me for a moment,' and left the saloon. He was soon back with a bottle of whisky, three glasses and some water. He put them on the table. 'No soda I'm afraid, but let's celebrate,' he said. 'The chief engineer'll be along shortly.'

'Splendid. But no water, thanks. Scotch is better *au naturel*.' The blue eyes smiled ingenuously.

Dai Williams arrived and was introduced. Over several whiskies they discussed methods of discharging, loading, and other problems. One of these, how to get fifteen tons of fresh water on board, was soon solved. The survey party's water tank, fed from a mountain stream, was on ground almost seventy feet above sea level. By using flexible piping available on ship and shore — and buoying it from the end of the old jetty to the ship — it would be possible to gravity feed fresh water into *Myfanwy*'s tanks.

With the whisky and the good news about loading and watering, Merfyr Evans began to feel he'd exaggerated the difficulties of *Myfanwy*'s mission in the Southern Ocean. That was on 17th November. Later, he was to feel otherwise.

12

A fierce squall two hours before daylight on 19th November broke the mast of Martinho Lopez's lifeboat. The mast, its galvanised wire stays still attached, went overboard. In the confusion which followed the sheets of the lugsail were let fly and the men nearest the mast panicked in the darkness, cutting any ropes they could lay hands on. The lugsail, thus effectively freed from mast and boat, disappeared into the night. It was fortunate that the mast, floating alongside, was held by wire stays, or it too would have been lost.

The squall had been preceded by a light easterly breeze blowing over a moderate sea. Progress during the five days since they'd left the *Moonraker* had been slow. In the main this was due to a leak in Lopez's boat which required frequent bailing, but the vagaries of wind and current had not helped. Either the south-east trades had blown too hard for sailing the leaking boat, or there were calms with light and variable breezes.

For these reasons Frascatti had that night decided to use the engine. The weather was fine so he could tow the second boat. He gave orders that sails should be hoisted to take advantage of what wind there was and then, with the long painter between them, the boats set off in the darkness steering a north-westerly course.

In Frascatti's boat O'Halloran spotted the squall coming — heard it, he said afterwards — and the lugsail was lowered just in time. The engine was stopped, sea anchors were streamed and both boats lay hove to while the succession of squalls lasted. That was for the best part of an hour.

At daylight, hauling on the painter, Lopez's boat made for Frascatti's.

'Where's your mast and sail?' shouted the Italian as they came within hailing distance.

'Mast broken,' Lopez hesitated, worried about what he had to say next. 'There was an accident. We have lost the sail.' The Mexican's eyes set deep in his haggard unshaven face were bright with fear.

'*Madre de Dios*,' yelled Frascatti. 'What accident?'

'The squall broke the mast.'

'But the lugsail,' shouted Frascatti. 'Why was it hoisted?'

'There was no warning.'

'How then did we have warning? We took in sail.' He did not add that this was due entirely to O'Halloran.

Lopez shook his head. 'It is no use to blame us. We did not wish to lose the sail. In the darkness some of the men cut the tack and halyards. This I did not know until too late.'

'Which men?' Frascatti glared from face to face, baring uneven yellow teeth.

'We do not know,' said Thoresen unhappily. 'It was dark. Now all say they did not do it.' He looked with contempt at the men sitting amidships, their weary bodies sagging on the bench thwarts.

'If you find out, shoot the bastards.' Frascatti glowered at the crew.

The men listened in silence. They looked a sorry lot: unshaven, bedraggled, soaked and dispirited, hunched together in acute discomfort. Five days in the boats had taken the shine off what might, in prospect, have seemed an exciting adventure. The south-east trades had blown hard and though the sun had shone most of the time, it was seldom dry in the boats. Already the effects of exposure to wind, sea and sun were showing on their burnt peeling faces and cracked sore-ridden hands.

There had been grumbling about the rationing of food and water, the men feeling that supplies were sufficient for more generous treatment. In both boats bottles of liquor taken from *Moonraker*'s storerooms had been smuggled on board. To these the men had recourse at night, when there was also filching of food. In the face of growing unrest and muttered threats in the darkness Frascatti had, the day before, increased the rations and ordered Lopez to do the same. In both boats discipline was tenuous and maintained only because the officers and engineers had the rifles in the sternsheets.

Soon after leaving the *Moonraker* it had been found that the second lifeboat was leaking in the bows. It was clinker built and had suffered damage either during lowering or in the cyclone. Whatever its cause, a minor leak had grown over the days into a major one, and all attempts to plug it had failed. The only remedy was constant bailing. Because the water was taken in forward, the boat was down by the bows and this materially reduced speed under sail, the prevailing wind being well abaft the beam. It had also made the boat a sluggish tow when the petrol engine was used.

No ships had been sighted though once an airliner flying high had passed overhead bound for Australia. The trade wind had been boisterous that day, the sea covered in white horses, and the flashing Aldis lamps and the smoke flares the boats released could not have been sighted, for the airliner continued on course and was soon lost to view.

In Frascatti's boat Kantle had with unfailing regularity sent distress calls from the orange box but without result. There were signals in Morse to be heard on the receiver, but as time went on he became more and more convinced that the transmitter was defective. His small wizened face, carpeted with yellow bristles, reflected increasing despair. It was against this background that Frascatti and Lopez confronted each other at daylight after the loss of the lugsail.

'So. Now you have no sail.' The sores on Frascatti's cracked lips thickened his speech. 'How you think you reach Mauritius?'

Locks of hair hung down over Lopez's face where side-burns merged with a half-grown beard to give him the appearance of a bedraggled spaniel. His dark eyes reflected the fear and helplessness of the men in the boat. 'We must repair the mast and make a new sail.' He spoke quietly, watching Frascatti's face for approval.

'New sail. What from?'

'The boat-covers.'

'One boat-cover cannot make a sail.'

'I had thought of that,' said Lopez. 'You too have a cover.'

'We use it for collecting rain water. Also for

shelter from the wind and spray. And to protect the food when the sun is hot.'

'We too. With ours. But you will help us?' Lopez's eyes pleaded.

'You think so?' The angry face and the strident tone frightened the men in Lopez's boat. Perhaps they could read Frascatti's thoughts: if the Mexican's boat had not been leaking the Italian's boat would have made good progress. If it were alone, it would make much better progress.

So far, since leaving the *Moonraker*, they'd averaged less than eighty miles a day. Either the trade winds had blown too hard for Lopez's boat to sail, or there were calms. On three occasions Frascatti had taken the boat in tow using the petrol engine, but they'd found they could only average three knots when towing. And the fuel — enough for five hundred miles under fair conditions — had to be conserved. The current was setting them to the south and west whereas they wished to go north-west. With one boat crippled, progress would be impossibly slow. They would never reach Mauritius at that rate.

Frascatti did some hard thinking about the new sail Lopez's boat needed, and about parting with his own cover. Various courses of action occurred to him in those fleeting moments. One of them seemed promising. 'All right,' he said. 'We shall help you. It is our duty. We can give you half a boat-cover. The other half we keep to collect water.' On his orders the boat-cover — bright orange so that it would be seen by aircraft and ships — was cut in two, one half going to Lopez's boat. 'Now get busy,' growled Frascatti. 'We have not time to waste. If the wind comes we tow you. But then your crew must row with the oars. We cannot use too much fuel.'

'Thank you,' said Lopez. 'We will do our best.'

'You, too, Thoresen,' Frascatti admonished. 'See that these things are done. If you wish to live.' The threat was not lost on the Dane.

As the morning wore on the trade wind blew from the south-east with increasing vigour. In Frascatti's boat the lugsail was hoisted and, far astern, Lopez's boat followed, plunging sluggishly at the end of the long painter. In the towed boat there was much activity. Two men in the bows bailed hard to keep pace with the incoming water while others, mostly firemen, put out oars and rowed, raggedly and ineffectively.

The boat-covers were spread, marked and cut to size with sheath knives. Lopez and a sailor stitched the parts together with palm and needle. But in the cramped heaving lifeboat with wind and spray constantly sweeping over them, it was not an easy task. Thoresen and two engineers cut the boathook into splints which they placed round the break in the mast, lashing them to it. Mr Jenkins and a young engineer worked on an oar, converting it into a yard for the head of the new lugsail, and a sailor spliced a halyard for hoisting it.

All these tasks, working under those conditions and without proper tools, took a long time to complete. Nevertheless by late evening they had re-stepped the repaired mast, hauled taut its stays and hoisted the new lugsail. It was not a very good sail, but it was better than nothing.

When Frascatti saw the bright orange sail go up on the mast of the boat astern, he waved his arms in exaggerated congratulation. This gesture was acknowledged by his crew with a thin cheer.

Less than an hour later the copper disc of the sun slipped below the western horizon. Before long night had fallen.

★ ★ ★

A strange silence lay upon the *Moonraker* in the days after the mutineers' departure. It was a more significant silence than that which had followed the loss of power: the cessation of the beat of main engines, of the suck and plunge of bilge pumps, the hum of generators, the pulsating of condenser circulators and the whirr of ventilating fans.

It was the absence of human noises like the trample of feet on decks and ladders, the shouting and laughter of men's voices, the sounds of the tools they used, the hiss of water from deck hoses, and the noise of scrubbers. The pervasive sounds now were the slap and thump of seas breaking against the drifting ship, the clanging of steel freeing-ports, the slamming of doors in deserted quarters, and incessant water noises in the flooded compartments as the ship rolled — the hissing and breaking of water rushing past machinery and furnaces, shooting occasional wisps of spray through the engine-room skylights.

The voices and movements of the people in the ship — the captain, Susie, Dwala and Hank Casey — were rarely heard above these other sounds. Captain Stone, long indoctrinated in the habits of command, spent most of the time alone on the bridge or in his cabin. Casey, but for the occasions when he was under instruction from the captain, was busy about the ship doing the chores which fell to him, almost always working alone.

Dwala, too, worked much on his own, cleaning the captain's cabin, the saloon and the galley, topping up with buckets of sea water sanitary tanks which could no longer be pumped. When he did work with anyone it was usually Susie who was now cook. Sitting in the saloon together they would plan the day's meals, engaging in long discussion.

Aware how frightened and disturbed the girl was, the African tried to relieve her mind by involving her in problems of *haute cuisine*. In the galley he had found a Cordon Bleu cookery book — one of Garrett's extravagances in Bangkok in a moment of professional aberration following a night on the town — and together they would consider its recipes, gravely discussing their merits and practicality.

Because of the power failure most of the food in the cold store had gone bad and been thrown over the side, but there was a sufficient supply of tinned foods, potatoes, onions and some apples and oranges. The lack of fresh food did not daunt Dwala in these culinary sessions with Susie. As she turned the pages of the cookery book he would point to a dish, *Mousse Apricot Chantilly* perhaps, the word *apricot* having caught his eye.

'That looks good, Miss Susie. What is it?'

After reading the recipe she would look at him sadly. 'It sounds fabulous, Dwala, but how can we? Apricots, shredded orange pulp, whipped cream. Cointreau . . . we just don't have those things.'

Smiling triumphantly, ivory white teeth shining, he would say, 'But we *have* them, Miss Susie.'

'Where?' Her eyes would reflect disbelief. It was expected of her, part of the game.

'In the storeroom. *Many* tins of apricots. Also of cream . . . and that is very good cream. We have plenty oranges . . . all these things we have.'

'And Cointreau?'

He would frown. 'What is Cointreau?'

'A liqueur.'

'Ah,' he would nod wisely. 'We have cognac. It will do just the same.'

She would smile at him, her eyes bright with admiration. 'Oh, you *are* clever, Dwala. That'll be smashing. I'll make it for them tonight.'

Dwala would look round conspiratorially. 'I will put some cognac in a cup and bring it to the galley. It is not good to bring the bottle.'

'Where is it?'

'In the liquor store. I hide the keys. It is better.'

Susie knew what he meant. Each day

discussions of this sort would take place and for the moments they spent in this world of fantasy the girl's mind would be free of worry.

There were other tasks which they tackled together: preparing the saloon table for meals, cleaning and trimming oil lamps, clearing things away and washing up. And Dwala helped her in the galley, keeping the fire going, cleaning it, collecting fuel, peeling vegetables and mopping the floor. When the meal was ready they would sit down together . . . four of them if it was daylight; three at night because one was always on watch then. Even in daylight, Hank or Dwala would leave the saloon every fifteen minutes to see if anything was in sight.

One way and another the days were long and tiring and this was good because it made sleep possible in spite of the nervous strain from which they all suffered. At night there had to be a permanent lookout on the bridge. At first the captain, Hank Casey and Dwala shared this task, taking watches of four hours each. Later this was to change and become more arduous.

And so the derelict ship with its hapless survivors drifted to the south at the mercy of wind, wave and current. Mostly she lay beam on to the sea, rolling drunkenly, a strange interrupted motion with unexpected lurches caused by the rush of free water in the machinery spaces.

★ ★ ★

On the afternoon of the day of the mutiny Hank Casey had taken Susie aside. 'Come with me. I want to show you something.'

'What, Hank?' She looked at him doubtfully, knowing that his mind was never quite free of a certain compelling thought.

'Come along. You'll see.' He smiled. 'It's great.'

'What is? Where?'

'In Frascatti's cabin. Something he's left for you.'

He led the way down to the chief officer's cabin. It smelt strongly of cheroots. A pair of trousers hung over the end of the bunk, a clean shirt and some socks lay on it. It was as if the occupant had put these things out before going for a bath.

Hank pointed to the deckhead where a small gilt cage hung from a hook.

'Oh!' She looked at the bright colours of the parakeet. 'It's gorgeous.' A sheet of paper was fastened with Sellotape to the underside of the cage. Casey handed it to her.

Dear Miss Susie. Please look after the parakeet. She is for my sister Violetta, 1478 Via Marinella, Naples. The bird's name is Zizi. She has broken wing but it comes better. She likes much the peel of apples and also oranges. If the ship is to sink please take from her cage that she may try to fly a little. But I hope you will be rescued and pray for you also.

I am sorry for the trouble but it is not possible to take Zizi in the boat.

Thanking you gratefully and with respects,

Carlo Frascatti.

They took the cage to her cabin and as the days went on she became attached to Zizi and would address child-like monologues to the bird which never answered but looked wise, head cocked on one side, yellow eyes blinking. The wing, still in splints, seemed not to worry it.

★ ★ ★

Caught in the south equatorial current and the south-east trades, the *Moonraker* drifted steadily to the south and west — the best part of five hundred miles since the mutiny — but as she reached and passed the thirty-fifth parallel of southern latitude the trade winds

213

fell away and with them the westerly component of her drift. For some days she moved due south; later, as she entered the zone of the Roaring Forties and began to feel the effects of the westerly wind and current, her track swung to the south and east.

Since the mutiny Captain Stone had been meticulous each day in taking sights and plotting the ship's position: he had taken morning and evening star sights, and latitude by meridian altitude at noon. Conscientiously, and with fortuitous foresight as it happened, he initiated Hank Casey into the ship's navigation routine, teaching him to wind the chronometers each morning, to read a chart and plot a position. The time available — and Hank Casey's mathematics — were too limited for star sights, but Captain Stone taught him how to check the moment of astronomical noon when the sun reached its zenith and its lower limb, seen through the eyepiece of the sextant, no longer climbed but hovered on the horizon before beginning its descent. Then, with the altitude read from the sextant's vernier scale applied to the sun's declination from *The Nautical Almanac*, Hank Casey was able to calculate the latitude.

Other things the captain taught him in those first few days were how to top up the fresh-water tank at the back of the chart house with the hand pump; how to refill, trim and hoist the oil lamps; to read the direction from which wind and sea came; to deduce the current experienced from the daily position plotted on the chart; and to sound the tanks in the ship's double bottom.

These soundings gave cause for gloomy thought. Captain Stone estimated that the ship was taking in water at the rate of ten to fifteen tons a day. This was not coming into the engine-room through the gash caused by the lighter's bow. It was nothing more than the normal intake through the hull which all ships suffer in varying degree and which is dealt with each day by the bilge pumps. But the *Moonraker*'s bilge pumps were not working.

On the credit side, the plugs in the torn plating in the engineers' messroom and engine-room casing held, and the chocks and lashings put on the lighter after the cyclone were still firmly in place. Apart from spray, and the occasional top of a sea which lopped over, little water now came on to the after well-deck.

But the daily intake through the hull was accumulative: over a hundred tons of water in ten days, two to three hundred in twenty days . . . it did not require a genius to conclude that *Moonraker*'s days were numbered unless something could be done. In the meantime it was fortunate that the ship had left Fremantle only two-thirds loaded. But for the reserve buoyancy of two and a half thousand tons this gave her, she might long since have sunk.

The need somehow to pump out the water which was slowly but insidiously sinking the ship became an obsession with Hank Casey.

★ ★ ★

It was on the sixth day after the mutiny, 20th November, that life on board the *Moonraker* underwent a change for the worse. It began with the weather: the barometer fell and the wind came strongly from the west, the sea mounted and buffeted the ship with increasing violence, spray driving over the decks at times. As the day wore on heavy banks of cloud hurried up from the west, the sky took on a leaden appearance and rain began to fall. By late afternoon it was wet and cold, the only warmth in the ship being the homemade stove in the galley where now only one of its two drums was kept alight.

It was this change in the weather which precipitated another and more serious change. Captain Stone's optimism, his belief that they would be sighted, deserted him.

Because of the clouded sky, star sights were not possible that evening but he'd plotted the ship's position by dead reckoning — 36° 30′ S: 64° 30′ E — and written it into the logbook. Then, with growing apprehension, he'd taken a long look at their situation.

The ship had drifted almost a thousand miles to the south since the cyclone. They'd crossed the main shipping routes to Australia and sighted nothing but the masts and funnels of a large liner, hull down below the horizon. That had been three days before, on a bright sunny morning with the trade wind blowing briskly. Without radio they'd had no means of attracting attention. After firing a few rockets and releasing smoke flares they'd given up, knowing only too well that under those conditions there was little chance of being sighted. Captain Stone made no attempt to delude himself: the ship was drifting south at about sixty-five nautical miles a day; they'd reached the Roaring Forties; the days — and especially the nights — were becoming colder and the westerly wind and current had swung the ship on to a southeasterly track. Later, he knew, it would be easterly and they'd be lost in the deep reaches of the Southern Ocean. Maybe, if she floated long enough, the *Moonraker* would in her eastward drift pass south of Australia, south of Cape Horn and . . .

No, they wouldn't drift that far. The Roaring Forties, once they were well into them, would finish off the ship before that. For some time he stood hunched over the chart table, his head in his hands, his nerve gone, his mind confused by these daunting thoughts. Then, a broken man, he hurried down to the sleeping cabin and locked the door. He must, he'd decided, escape from the intolerable burden of reality.

13

When at sunset he'd seen the bright orange sail hoisted in the lifeboat astern, Frascatti made his decision. If the two lifeboats were to keep together, if the leaking boat with the patched mast and improvised sail had to be towed, there was no hope. For Frascatti's boat alone, with the petrol-engine and sound mast and sail, there was a chance.

It was better, he reasoned, that fifteen men should survive than that thirty should die. Not that it was certain that Lopez and his men *would* die. They had the orange sail. They might well be sighted. The *Trevessa's* boats had reached land under the same conditions using only sails and oars.

At the back of Frascatti's mind, behind this façade of reason, the real motives were less complex: firstly, he did not want to die; secondly, he had to think of Violetta and his mother. In his mind the fiction persisted that *this* came first. If he died the impact on their lives would be catastrophic. Violetta would have to enter an institution so that his mother could go out to work. For Violetta it would be like prison. She was too helpless, too gentle, to survive in an institutional jungle at the whim and mercy of every overworked nurse and frustrated petty official. These thoughts of Violetta reminded him of the parakeet. Was the English girl looking after it? Or had the *Moonraker* already sunk so that those beautiful feathers were now just flotsam, bobbing on an empty sea? The sadness which this thought induced was followed by indignation at the injustice of mortality, at the lengths to which the survival imperative could drive a man.

★ ★ ★

The storm came after midnight but this time with ample warning. As the night wore on, clouds gathered in the sky blotting out the moon and stars until the boat was surrounded by darkness. Nothing could be seen but the occasional luminescence of a small wave breaking alongside. The south-east trades stopped blowing and a calm fell over the sea.

Up in the bows O'Halloran shouted, 'Be Jasus, and it's the calm before the storm. It'll be blowing the brass balls off a monkey anny tame now.' On the western horizon flashes of lightning preceded thunder which came rolling across the sea, its reverberations like the rumble of distant gunfire. Lopez will have no excuse, thought Frascatti, as he called to the men forward, 'A squall is coming. Stand by to lower the sail.' He put the tiller hard over and the boat came up in the wind, the lugsail flapping. 'Lower away,' he shouted. When the sail was down they streamed the sea anchor and the boat rode to it, bows to wind and sea.

The storm came quickly. First a subdued roar, the sound of wind and rain on the water. Moments later it was upon them, the wind shrieking, the rain driving with sudden violence. Before it came they had set the boat-cover and sail across the thwarts to catch water. Now the men struggled to hold the canvas against the force of the wind. Silent and drenched, heads bent to avoid the flint-like prick of rain in their faces, they held on grimly waiting for the squall to pass.

The sea grew lumpy, confused by the change of wind, and the motion of the boat became more boisterous as it strained at the sea anchor. Frascatti sat in the sternsheets, one hand on the long tiller, the other shielding his eyes against the rain. When he judged the squall to be at its height he took a sheathknife from his belt. In the darkness he groped for the towline where it crossed the transom behind him. The line was slack.

Lopez's boat, too, would be lying to a sea anchor. With a steady sawing motion the Italian cut through the rope until the last strand parted.

There was not long to wait for the line squall was travelling fast, the wind taking the curtain of rain with it. When he judged the time right, Frascatti shouted, 'Haul in the sea anchor.' O'Halloran reported that it was on board, Achmed Khalif started up the engine and the boat got under way. Frascatti brought her round until the luminous dial of the compass showed they were heading NNW. With quiet satisfaction he saw that the lifeboat travelled through the water with new vigour.

Later that night there were more squalls.

* * *

The lightning and thunder alerted Lopez and his men so that well before the squall struck the orange sail was lowered. When the men in the bows reported that the towline had gone slack, Lopez concluded that Frascatti's boat had hove-to, and he gave the order for the sea anchor to be put over the side. While he waited for the squall he saw, in a flash of lightning, the dark shape of Frascatti's boat as it rode a wave far ahead of them. Its sail was down and it too had swung to face wind and sea.

Soon nothing could be seen for the squall was upon them, the wind and rain coming with great violence. Lopez's boat pitched and tossed, yawing against the pull of the sea anchor, the men sitting with bowed heads, waiting stoically for the storm to pass. When it had gone, the wind was once more from the south-east and the boat swung to face it.

'Tell me when the towline is taut,' Lopez called to the man in the bows. 'Then we shall take in the sea anchor.'

There were still no stars in the sky. The boat pitched and wallowed in darkness, the only sounds the occasional muttering or coughing of men, the splash of bailers and the wash of the sea. A school of dolphins passed close by, their passage marked by leaping dives and phosphorescent trails which glowed and faded.

Sitting in the darkness waiting, infinitely tired, Lopez thought of Felicia Perez, wondering where she was, what she was doing and whether he would ever see her again. Mexico was far to the west. It would be early there. Perhaps only seven or eight o'clock in the evening. He was too tired to work it out. Was she still in Queretaro or had she moved? He imagined her sitting at a table on some pavement. It would be a warm night, the sky bright with stars. Mannos would be there perhaps, and Mona Valdez, and other lecturers and students. They would be talking softly and laughing, some smoking marijuana, others sipping tequila or mescal, looking at the nearby tables for *informadores*. There were always *informadores*. Perhaps one at your own table. Someone you trusted.

Felicia knew this; she had been with him that night. She'd screamed when they'd beaten him up, explaining to her with grins that he was resisting arrest though he never moved from his chair. They'd taken her away for interrogation, too, but let her go next morning. For him there had been months of solitary confinement, broken only by interrogation. No beatings up then. More subtle. Standing in a chalk circle, bright lights in your eyes, relays of interrogators firing questions. Six hours, eight hours, until you dropped. Then a bucket of cold water, afterwards back on your feet in the chalk circle, the lights focused on your eyes, and again the interrogation. He'd known from the questions that somewhere within his circle of friends there was an *informador*.

At last the unbelievable moment of freedom. Because they cannot get what they want this way, they try indirectly. Set you free. Watch you. For weeks, months — years if necessary — until by your movements you betray your contacts. That was why he had gone back to the sea. Through intermediaries he and Felicia had exchanged a few typed letters. Nothing in them but simple commonplaces. No coded messages, nothing that could excite suspicion or incriminate. His signed *Miguel*, hers *Juanita*, no surnames or addresses. But they were at least an assurance to each that the other was alive and free.

Had she slept with anyone since he left? Of course she had. How could someone so beautiful, so compassionate, do otherwise. How could that body, so warm, so alive and vital, live on memories and expectations, denying its natural function. It was of her body he was thinking when Tomas, the Cape Verde islander, called out, 'The line is still slack. It is a long time now.'

Lopez came to with a start and shone the torch on his watch. He'd been dreaming. Tomas was right. It was more than twenty-five minutes since the storm had passed. There must be trouble in the other boat. Maybe the sheets or halyards had fouled in the darkness and they were trying to clear them. 'Haul on the line,' he said. 'Until it comes taut.'

Hand over hand they hauled on the towing

painter until the bare end came into their hands. 'The line has parted,' shouted Tomas.

In the darkness the end of the rope was passed down the boat to Lopez. He focused the torch on it. The rope had not parted. It had been cut. All three strands. Clean cuts, only possible with a sharp knife. For a few moments he failed to comprehend the meaning of what he saw. He passed the rope to Thoresen. 'Look,' he said shining the torch on it.

'My God,' shouted the Dane. 'They have cut the rope.' In a moment Thoresen was on his feet, wedging his knees against the thwarts to counter the pitching of the boat. 'Frascatti,' he shouted into the darkness, shaking his fist. 'You bastard. You've deserted us.' His passion was taken up by others in the boat. Oaths and obscenities were shouted and there were whimpers of fear.

No answering cries came from the darkness. Later in Lopez's boat hysteria gave way to reason, three flares were fired at minute intervals and the Aldis lamp was flashed repeatedly. But there was no response. Somewhere ahead, hidden by the darkness, Frascatti's boat was drawing away from them.

'Listen,' Lopez called in an urgent voice. 'Listen to me.' The noise in the boat subsided and he went on. 'I make you a vow. If I live I will find Frascatti.' He stopped, not sure if the emotion he felt would allow him to continue. The men waited, silent and fearful.

'And then I will kill him,' he said.

'No good making threats,' said Mr Jenkins. 'Won't help us.'

Thoresen said, 'That is right. We must be practical.'

14

Captain Stone was busy in his cabin working on a model of the *Moonraker*. Having fashioned the hull in rough outline, he was fitting masts and Samson posts. They were important to what he had in mind. The precise shape and detail of the hull were not.

Since he'd taken to his cabin on 20th November he had not left it, nor for that matter had he shaved. In those four days he had consumed five bottles of gin. But it should not be imagined that this was all he'd done. There had been remarkable bursts of activity in between sleeping, day dreaming and drinking. These had been inspired by the colourless intoxicant, so pleasantly flavoured with junipers. A nectar which wafted him into a wonderful world of fantasy.

After drinking two bottles within the first twenty-four hours of reaching the cabin on 20th November, he'd had the inspiration — to sail the *Moonraker* to Sydney using the westerly winds and currents of the Roaring Forties. The bursts of activity occurred by day and night. Then he would be immensely busy sketching the sail plan and working on the model. Basically the idea was simple: to make sails from tarpaulins and awnings, set them up as a jury rig on the ship's masts and Samson posts, and sail the ship.

He'd decided on a fore and aft rig. Staysails and trysails. The derricks would be used as booms at the foot of the triangular sails, and the topping lifts as hoisting halyards. It was as simple as that. Using two masts and four Samson posts he estimated a sail area of about seven thousand square feet. With twenty knot winds — common in the Roaring Forties — plus the westerly current, he thought *Moonraker* might make four to five knots under such a spread of canvas.

At the moment he was drilling holes in the wooden hull. That done, he'd step the masts and Samson posts, then add the derricks and rigging. From a bunk sheet he would cut out the model sails — everything exactly to scale of course — and, using them, he'd work out the details of hoisting and trimming. He intended to do the job very thoroughly; to take no chances.

He inserted the foot of the foremast in the hole he'd just drilled and tapped it home. He was surprised at the ease with which he did this. Things didn't go quite so well with the mainmast, however. For one thing he couldn't see properly. The hull was blurred and it was difficult to get the foot of the mast into the hole.

'Good,' he muttered as he at last succeeded. 'Now for the hammer.' It too proved elusive. He stood up — rather too quickly as it happened — and suffered an attack of dizziness. The ship chose that moment to lurch to starboard, throwing him across the low table, whence he rolled to the floor. For a few moments he lay there, breathing heavily. Then he hoisted himself on to his hands and knees and found his way back to the settee. 'Confound it,' he said glumly, looking at the broken masts. 'Most unfortunate that she rolled then.'

A combination of weariness and an inordinately dry throat persuaded him to leave the model, the litter of tools and wood shavings which surrounded it, and go to his night cabin. Once there he took a bottle of gin from the hiding place and a tumbler from the wash basin. Unlocking the door, he returned to the day cabin. The roll of the ship exaggerated his stagger, but he reached the leather armchair safely and flopped into it. 'Well done,' he beamed at the bottle. 'Shows what determination can do.'

On the table beside the chair there was a tray with apples, biscuits and red Cheddar, his favourite cheese. There was, too, a glass of milk. Dwala had put the tray there at noon, but Captain Stone had been too busy with the model to worry about food. Being a great believer in milk as an antidote to stomach ulcers, he drank it first, then some gin. After that he had a go at the biscuits and cheese. Exceptionally good, he decided. Feeling better, he poured a second gin and after downing that began peeling an apple. He did this with fuzzy determination, muttering complaints about the movement of the ship, the bluntness of the knife, and the tendency of the apple to slip from his hand.

Only when he'd cut his thumb rather badly did he desist, clucking with annoyance and throwing the bloodied apple into the waste-paper basket. 'Bad time of year for apples,' he decided, returning to the biscuits and cheese. 'And these Aussie apples don't compare with a good English Cox or pippin.'

It had been a useful day, he decided, holding a handkerchief round the cut thumb. In spite of the accident to the masts he'd got through a lot of work. The Samson posts and derricks were now ready. He'd fit them the next day. Remaking the masts wouldn't take long. Cutting out the sails would require care. He might ask Susie to do that. No. On second thoughts, better not. Didn't want her poking round the cabin.

It was important to keep everything to scale, to be precise and methodical. That was the real secret of what he was doing. Not charging in like a bull at a gate, cutting up precious tarpaulins and awnings before he really knew what was wanted and how it was going to work. After the sails he'd see to the rigging. Then the model would be ready for the tests. Shouldn't take more than two or three days now to complete the job.

After that the real thing. That'd need all hands. Stretching and cutting the huge tarpaulins and awnings. Marking them out, cutting them to size. Then the seaming and roping with palm and needle, punching in the brass eyelets to take the iron hanks — there weren't any hanks in the ship, but small shackles would do. They'd be the runners on the wires rigged vertically on the after side of the masts to act as travellers. Wonderful what you could do if you put your mind to it. Sailing an eight thousand ton steamship over three and a half thousand miles through the Roaring Forties into Sydney. Sounded difficult but nothing to it actually for a seaman.

With the fourth tot of gin, Captain Stone's thoughts leaped ahead to the arrival in Port Jackson Harbour, Sydney. He'd have to time it for daylight. What a shock the men in the signal station on Outer South Head would get when they saw an eight thousand ton freighter closing the land under full sail. They'd have had no warning, and communication wouldn't be possible until he was close inshore because *Moonraker* had nothing better than a ship's torch with which to signal. The mutineers had taken the two Aldis lamps.

On second thoughts he realised that the authorities probably *would* have had some warning. *Moonraker* would have been sighted by another ship by then, especially on the last lap into Sydney. It was a focal point for shipping. The other steamer would close them, her captain and crew amazed at what they saw, and signal, 'Do you require assistance?'

He'd reply, 'No, thank you. We've come three and a half thousand miles with this rig and can manage very well.'

'What ship and where from?' would almost certainly be the response.

'*Moonraker*. Disabled in cyclone on voyage from Fremantle to Mauritius.'

He sighed. Sydney would know all right. A frigate would probably be sent out to meet them at sea. He'd refuse assistance. Tell the frigate to lay off: *Thank you for your trouble but help not needed*. He couldn't stop it acting as escort. That was the business of her captain.

Where was he? Ah, yes. The signal station on Outer South Head. Well, he'd hoist on one halyard the International Code flag G — *I want a pilot*, and on the other, Z — *I require a tug*. Apart from that he'd do a Nelson on them. Pretend he couldn't read their signals which would certainly tell him to lay off and await the arrival of pilot and tugs.

He'd stand on until he'd passed between the Heads and entered the Sound. Then the sails would come down smartly. The pilot cutter from Watson Bay would be waiting for them off Inner South Head. *And* the tugs. The Chief Harbour Master would have seen to that. Stone imagined the conversation with the pilot on *Moonraker*'s bridge, after they'd exchanged the customary courtesies.

'You mean to say, captain, that you've sailed her three thousand miles through the Roaring Forties with that rig?'

'Three *and a half* thousand miles.'

'Three thousand five hundred miles?'

'Yes. And with hand steering. We've no power. Not even the emergency generator.'

'How many crew?'

'Myself, an African steward, my young niece, and a passage-worker. Motor mechanic. Not a bad lad.'

'It's unbelievable, captain. *Absolutely* unbelievable. You mean to tell me you made, rigged and handled all that sail with only four hands?'

'Yes. Seamanship is not yet a lost art.'

'It's — it's a fantastic achievement, sir.'

'If you've got to do these things, you somehow do them.'

'You know of course that your ship was reported missing, believed foundered, weeks ago.'

'I daresay,' Stone would say with a quiet smile.

The pilots would pass these details to the tugs by walkie-talkie and in no time the news would be all over Sydney.

Nature broke into this chain of thought. Captain Stone got up reluctantly and staggered through to the bathroom. Due to difficulties with his vision, the roll of the ship and his flies, he peed uncertainly but at length into the white porcelain bowl. Pulling the chain he returned to his cabin deep in thought. There was a good tot left in the bottle. With a contented sigh he emptied it into the tumbler, ate a lump of red Cheddar and leant back in the armchair.

Where was I, he asked himself? Ah, yes. The news would be all over the place in a trice. As the tugs towed *Moonraker* down towards the inner harbour, past Bradley Head and Shark Island, by Rose Bay, Double Bay and Rushcutter Bay, making for the anchorage in Woolloomooloo Bay, near the graving dock — why, then the ships in harbour, hundreds of them, would be sounding their sirens, bunting fluttering aloft, motor launches and yachts out in their hundreds, the whole harbour alive and vociferous in its welcome to the crippled ship as she limped in from her epic voyage.

He supposed the City would lay on some sort of official reception. The Lord Mayor, representatives of the Governor-General, the State Governor and the Prime Minister, the Naval Commander-in-Chief, the Chief Harbour Master, and a lot of other local dignitaries. A band and guard of honour too, he imagined.

The Lord Mayor would make the speech of welcome, congratulating him and his companions on a great maritime feat, perhaps one of the greatest. At the end of it the Lord Mayor would break the news that the Board of Trade in London had quashed the findings of the court of inquiry into the *Donnington Wave* affair. There would be a climactic moment when the representative of the Governor-General announced to the vast crowd on the waterfront that Her Majesty the

Queen had graciously assented to the conferment of a knighthood — Captain Sir Harold Stone of the *Moonraker*, worthy successor to Captain Sir Cecil Foster of the *Trevessa*.

Quite carried away by this vision, yet appalled at the prospect of having to reply to such weighty speeches, Stone decided that the occasion called for the opening of another bottle.

★ ★ ★

Hank Casey looked up at the steel grating where Dwala held the rope. 'Stand by,' he shouted. 'As she rolls I'll jump.'

There was a scum of froth on the dark water in which floated greasy cloths, cotton waste and soggy pieces of emery paper. It was, at that moment, ten feet deep. When the ship came on to an even keel it would level off at about six. Then she'd roll to port and the water on the starboard side, where he was, would be waist high. That was when he'd jump.

He'd been down in the engine-room many times in the last few days, taking soundings, timing the rolls with the second-hand of his watch, making a plan of the layout where the workshop was, measuring the distances by eye, estimating the time it would take to wade them and explaining the drill to Dwala.

The sky had cleared shortly before midday and shafts of sunlight pierced the engine-room skylight, diffusing the dimness below. Slowly the *Moonraker* came upright and water flooded through the main engines, past the motionless piston arms and crankshafts, hissing and spouting. For seconds she remained on an even keel before lurching to port, the water cascading across.

Casey jammed the rubber torch into the waistband of his shorts, called out and jumped down. Wading through waist-high water, he faltered at times when his feet failed to grip the oily steel of the submerged deck. In eleven seconds he'd almost reached the workshop door. 'More line,' he shouted to Dwala. Up on the gratings the African paid out the lifeline. If Casey couldn't get back, if something went wrong, it would be vital.

Casey felt the ship recovering and wedged himself against the rail round the crankshaft well, grasping it with both hands. The water surged over him with a dull roar. With eyes shut, he held his breath, tightening his grip on the rail. *One-un, two-oo, three-ee, four-or, fi-ive:* the seconds ticked away while he fought the pull of water and buoyancy. Eleven seconds went before he could breathe again. That was all right. He'd reckoned on nine to fifteen — an average of twelve.

He covered the last few feet to the workshop door as the water level fell from his shoulders to his waist. The door was shut. He struggled with the oily handle but before he could open it, was submerged again. The ship stayed down on the roll for fourteen seconds. Hunched under water, holding on grimly, knowing the depth now was at least twelve feet, he wondered if she'd ever roll back. She did, and he wrenched the door open, latched it against the bulkhead and wedged himself in the doorway as the water came flooding back.

Next time his head was clear he called to Dwala, 'Going in now.' He switched on the torch and waded into the workshop. The size and appearance of the object he sought was deeply etched in his mind. If he saw or felt it he'd know all right. Using the gasket on the intake port of the diesel generator as a base pattern, and the illustration in the manual for detail, he'd made a full scale drawing of the missing unit.

But the search was proving more difficult than he'd expected. Keeping down when the compartment flooded was not easy — he'd hold on to a lathe or drill, or wedge himself under the work-bench — and the oil fuel was worrying him. The torch-light couldn't penetrate its surface, and his feet kept encountering obstacles which slid about as the ship rolled. It was like walking on a shifting heap of slippery rubble. He had to search in short bursts: action-filled seconds when the water on the starboard side was waist-high as the ship rolled to port. Then he'd duck down under water to grope for the missing part. It was exhausting work, particularly the intervals of submersion when he couldn't breathe. It was frightening, too — the pressure of water, the noise magnified by the confined space, and the darkness when he shut his eyes to keep out the oil.

Several times he struggled back from the workshop to the grating where Dwala waited. There he rested while the African rubbed him over with cotton waste soaked in kerosene, removing the worst of the oil fuel, cleaning his face and eyes with fresh water.

'The stuff gets in everywhere,' Casey complained.

'You think you'll find it, Hank?'

'Sure. If it's there I'll find it.' He breathed heavily like a tired boxer in his corner waiting for the bell. 'But Jesus, there's some junk in that workshop.' Soon he was continuing the search. Each thing his hands encountered under water was brought up, examined and thrown out of the workshop. He wasn't going to check the same thing twice.

Some time later Dwala heard a triumphant shout, followed by Casey's yell, 'Got it.' The African looked down and saw the water surge over him. The ship rolled the other way, and Casey waded towards the ladder. He slipped and fell, the next rush of water washing him off his feet. Dwala hauled on the lifeline, pulling him to the ladder. The Australian struggled to the lower grating where he collapsed. Dwala secured the line and hurried down. Casey lay spread-eagled, shaken with fits of coughing, the injector unit in one hand, torch in the other. The ship lurched to starboard and water spilled over the grating forcing him against the rail. Dwala got his arms under the young man's armpits. 'Come on, fella. You gotta get out of here,' he shouted.

Casey was racked by fits of coughing and retching. He looked up at Dwala, shaking his head, clutching the fuel injector to his chest. The Ghanaian dragged him up the steel ladder to the higher gratings and laid him on his side. 'You done good job, fella. Take rest. Bye and bye you breathe okay.'

Casey's face was contorted with pain. His chest felt as if it was on fire. When the spasm

241

of coughing passed he managed to smile, held up the lump of metal and croaked, 'We've got it.' He attempted to sit up but Dwala pushed him back. 'No. You rest some more, man.'

15

As the *Moonraker* drifted south the weather grew steadily colder and temperatures in the ship's living spaces, usually heated by steam radiators, crept closer to those outside. The only real warmth was in the galley where the improvised stove burned day and night. It was there that Casey, Susie and Dwala took their meals.

They wore warm clothing now and piled extra blankets on their bunks. Though he did not tell them, Casey knew it would get colder.

★ ★ ★

Unable to see the captain and aware of his condition, Casey had taken on himself the responsibility of winding the chronometers each morning and of calculating as best he could the ship's position. The sun had been visible only twice in the last six days, so that both latitude and longitude were often by dead reckoning. He also wrote up the log book. From the latitude and the increasingly strong westerly winds, reinforced by what he'd read in the *Admiralty Sailing Directions*, he realised the ship was in the Roaring Forties. On 26th November he'd got a sight of the sun at noon and made the latitude 41° 10′ S: the longitude by dead reckoning, 71° 30′ E. He knew there was a lot of guesswork about that longitude.

He knew, too, that their chances of rescue were now remote. The *Moonraker* had already drifted south of the established shipping lanes between the Cape and Australia. No air routes traversed that part of the Southern Ocean. But he kept his fears to himself, went about his work whistling and singing and occasionally, if he were not too tired, he'd play the guitar, choosing numbers Susie knew and getting her to sing with him. Like Dwala he was doing what he could to bolster her morale. As to the Ghanaian — he was all right, decided Casey: calm, well adjusted, accepting his lot as Africans do with dignity and composure.

But Dwala, though he told no one, had a problem which bore on him more heavily than Susie's morale: it was Captain Stone. Protecting the old man's privacy, trying to hide his disgrace; patiently keeping up the pretence, long since worn thin, that it was the old war injuries. In a sense, of course, that was true but to Susie and Hank the African's efforts seemed like those of a mother

244

protecting a wayward child from the scorn of prying neighbours.

Susie's shame when she'd learnt the real nature of her uncle's attacks had given way to despair, and latterly to pity. Once, when Dwala was in the galley and had forgotten to lock Stone's door, she'd got into his cabin and found him on the floor working on the model. She'd listened to his stumbling speech as he explained how he would sail the ship into Sydney. Bursting into tears, she'd run off to Hank for comfort. He'd told her to leave the old man alone. There was nothing they could do to help him. Dwala, he said, had searched every nook and cranny of the day and night cabins but couldn't discover where the gin was hidden. He'd never found a bottle. Not even empties, presumably because Stone threw them out of the porthole at night. Indeed, but for the smell of gin and his behaviour, there was no evidence that the old man did drink.

★ ★ ★

Since the mutiny Susie and the Australian were often together. Not for long, though, because of daily chores and the watches kept on the bridge each night, a task she now shared with Hank and Dwala. When she and

Casey were alone together they would plan for the future. Absurd, romantic plans of a dream-like texture. Sometimes they realised the futility of these and would look at each other hopelessly and fall silent, resigning themselves to the realities of life in their floating limbo. Then when reality once more became intolerable, they'd fall back on their dreamworld.

After the mutineers had gone, Casey and Dwala had left the deserted crew accommodation and moved up into the officers' quarters under the bridge. Casey took over Lopez's cabin and Dwala installed himself in Mr Jenkins's which was handy to the saloon, storeroom and galley. It was after ten o'clock on the third night — Dwala was on watch and Stone had gone to his quarters — that Casey said to Susie, 'Come along to my cabin. Show you something great.'

'Better be,' she said severely. 'None of your tricks.'

He laughed mischievously. 'Why d'you always go on like that, Susie?'

'Because you always *act* like that.'

'You're prejudiced. Don't recognise my good points.' He grinned guiltily. 'But honest. This is the goods.'

With a show of reluctance she didn't really feel, she followed Hank down to the second officer's cabin.

Hank shut the door. 'Why d'you do that?' she eyed him suspiciously.

'Want it to bang each time the ship rolls?'

'There's a latch.'

'Yeh. I forgot that.'

'Sit down, señora,' he pointed to the settee.

'Señorita,' she said. 'Anyway what's so wonderful?'

He looked mysterious. 'Hang on a jiffy.' From the bottom drawer of the desk he produced a chocolate box.

'Chocolates,' she sighed happily. 'Smashing.'

He shook his head. 'Used to be. Not now.'

He took a batch of photos from the box, some in black and white, others in colour, and passed them to her: a black and white of Fidel Castro, one of Ché Guevara. Then the coloured photos. The first was a young woman — dark, almond-eyed, high-cheekboned — in black slacks, red shirt, spurred riding boots and a black sombrero. She was standing beside a white stallion, holding its bridle. It was signed *Felicia*. Then Felicia in a night club, Martinho Lopez beside her, both incredibly handsome. Felicia in a bikini, close-up, the sea Kodak blue, the sand white, snow-capped mountains high in the background. Felicia on skis, black and red skiing suit, the snow white and gold in the sun. She was smiling at the photographer.

'My, she's beautiful.' Susie's eyes narrowed. 'Who is she? One of your girl friends?' Hank shrugged his shoulders. 'Not mine. His. Her name's Felicia.'

'Brilliant,' said Susie. 'Are they all of her?' She looked at those still in his hand.

'Yeh. You haven't seen anything yet. Take a decco at this.' He passed it to her, chuckling. It was Felicia lying on a couch, naked, her body as beautiful as her face. Across the foot of the photo she'd written, *Para mio carissimo Martinho. Felicia.*

Susie looked up from the photograph, her face expressionless.

'They get better,' said Hank ingenuously. 'Try this number.'

With sudden rage she threw the photos at him. 'Take them. I don't want them.'

He stooped to gather them and she got up. 'You're kinky, Hank. You're looking at something private. Something which has nothing to do with you. Those two are in love. And you . . . ' she hesitated. 'You're just leching.'

He was putting the photos back in the chocolate box when she made for the door. He grabbed her.

'Leave me,' she blazed. 'Let go. I loathe you.'

Hank was strong and his arms were round her. 'What's wrong, Susie,' he pleaded. 'What's so terrible about looking at pictures of a dishy bird?'

'Let me go — you . . . ' She got a hand free and scratched his face. A thin line of blood appeared as if drawn by an invisible pen.

'Jesus!' He drew his fingers across his cheek, looking at the blood with unbelieving eyes. 'What's got into you?' He held her with one hand.

'You showed me those photos because you thought they'd get me going, didn't you? Well you're wrong, mister randy Australian. All you've done is *revolt* me.'

He let her go. 'I suppose you'll be telling me you're a virgin next.'

'Whether I am or not is none of your business,' she stormed. 'But one thing for sure. You'll never have the opportunity of finding out.' His eyes were angry and she thought he might hit her.

'Oh, for Chrissake, Susie, be natural. Of course I want to sleep with you. I'm a man and you're a woman. What's so wrong with that?'

'Plenty,' she said, hoping she wasn't showing the affection she felt for him. 'Listen, Hank. There's a time and a place for making love, and it's not now or here. We're in terrible danger. Anyway, I've made a pact.'

'Who with?'

'With God. After the crew left.'

'What sort of pact?' He was puzzled.

'That I wouldn't — we wouldn't.' She hesitated. 'Do something He wouldn't like us to do — if . . . '

'If what?'

'If He'd save us. All of us in the *Moonraker*.' The grey eyes above the turned-up nose challenged him.

'How d'you know He wouldn't like us to?'

'Because I do. My conscience tells me.'

'Mine doesn't. We wouldn't be made the way we are if we weren't meant to.'

'*You* didn't make the pact. Anyway, I'm keeping it.'

With a muffled groan he flopped on to the settee, ruffling his hair into a tousled mop. 'Jesus, what a voyage. That bastard Garrett, a cyclone, a mutiny, stuck in this abandoned tub with a drunken skipper, and now,' he laughed hysterically, rolling sideways on the settee as the ship lurched, ' . . . and now a Pommy virgin who's a religious maniac.' He sat up suddenly, staring at her. 'And to think all I wanted was a nice quiet ride to the King's Road, Chelsea.'

'Thank you very much.' She flung out of the cabin and slammed the door.

From that moment onward Casey never did or said anything which could have offended Susie's God. They would kiss and caress at times, but the more desperate their situation became the more genuinely they seemed in love. Unknown to her, he'd later made the same pact. He wasn't at all sure if there was a God, but maybe there could be and if there was — well, it might make a difference.

★　★　★

If sailing the *Moonraker* to Sydney was Stone's obsession, getting the diesel generator to work was Casey's. It had taken a day and a long night's rest — Dwala had kept his bridge watch for him, doing a double stretch — to get over the physical exhaustion of recovering the missing part. Since then he'd spent two days and most of two nights working on the diesel generator. First he'd read the manual of instruction, then cleared the blockage in the fuel injector, completing the task which Achmed Khalif had begun. For tools he'd had to rely on the few left in the steering flat by the third engineer, and some he'd found in the radio cabin. By noon of the second day he'd reassembled the injector unit and bolted it back into place. As a motor mechanic he'd

251

had experience on diesel engines: in trucks and tractors mostly. But in spite of that he couldn't get this one going. In the course of five hours — working by oil lamp and torch light, for there was no natural light in the steering flat — he checked through the fuel system, clearing the fuel lines and ensuring that the injector unit was functioning properly. But the engine wouldn't start.

Next he tackled the electrical system. After many hours he found the trouble. At the back of the control panel there was a concealed safety switch, a recessed button, presumably to prevent the curious from starting the engine. There was nothing about it in the manual. Hank's anger at this discovery was soon dissipated by the most beautiful sound he'd ever heard: the explosive staccato of the engine as it came alive. There was no audience as he danced and capered round it, waving his arms and shouting, 'The old bastard's working. Oh, boy. What d'you know. It's bloody working.'

When the engine had warmed up, he let in the clutch and engaged the generator drive. The needle on the voltmeter climbed until it reached the green sector marked 110/115 volts. He adjusted the throttle to keep it there and let the engine run while he tested the controls and switches on the panel. When he'd finished he checked the fuel level in the overhead tank. It was low. Dwala had been drawing fuel for the galley stove. Casey worked the handle of the priming pump until the tank was full.

With a last affectionate look at the engine, he went off to break the news. Susie would be on the bridge but she could come down to the galley for a few minutes. He didn't think he'd ever been so excited.

★　★　★

Her eyes shone. 'Oh, Hank. You're fabulous. How did you do it?'

He tried to look modest but failed. 'Starting it wasn't too bad. It was finding the fuel injector unit down in the workshop. That crooked me.'

She gave him an affectionate hug.

Dwala beamed. 'You been done good job, man.'

They were sitting in the galley. It was lit by an oil lamp which swung from the deckhead as the ship rolled, shuddering when big seas caught her out of rhythm and broke against the side. There was a line of washing — jerseys, sea boot stockings and other garments — strung across the galley drying, a smell of damp wool, of cooking, of diesel fuel and human bodies. Through the ventilator over the stove came the sound of the wind in the rigging and the splash and break of the sea. Above the small table where they sat, the parakeet was asleep in its cage.

Dwala took a pot from the improvised stove, and they held out enamel mugs. As he poured, the pleasant aroma of coffee hung in the air.

'What does it mean, Hank?' Susie leant forward, eyes bright. 'Can we have lights and heaters now?'

'Not to-night anyway. I've got to figure things out. The control panel has two switches: *Fire-Mains* and *Emergency Lighting*. The fire-mains side's okay. Switch that on and the pump starts. But nothing happens when I turn the lighting switch. Must be another one somewhere. Perhaps in the engine-room.'

Susie sat with her chin on her elbow, thoughtful and serious in the dim light. 'What are fire-mains, Hank?'

Dwala said, 'For fighting fires. The pumps pick up sea water and pipe it round the ship for the fire hoses.'

'Another thing.' Hank fought down a yawn. 'We must get power to the radio. Send out messages for help. Haven't a clue how it works. Any ideas, Dwala?'

'No sah. Not my business. I am steward. Maybe captain understand. He's clever man.'

'Sure,' said Hank avoiding the girl's eyes and failing to stifle the yawn. 'Gosh, I'm tired.' He rubbed his eyes.

'Go and turn in, Hank.'

'That's the big plan. To-morrow I'll get cracking. Rig temporary leads from the generator. There's plenty of insulated wire in the store. Fix it somehow. Great thing is the generator's working.'

'It'll be smashing,' said Susie. 'Real lights and heaters, *and* the radio working.'

Hank looked at his watch, 'I'm short on kip right now. 'Bye. See you later.'

When he'd gone they agreed not to call him that night. They'd share his watch — the morning — between them.

'Now I must get back to the bridge.' Susie was business-like. 'I've been away for ten minutes. But I just had to hear what Hank had to say. He's terrific isn't he, Dwala?'

'Sure. He's a good boy.'

'Thanks for the coffee. 'Bye now.'

16

The chart room clock showed an hour and seventeen minutes past midnight. Merfyr Evans looked at the barometer. It wasn't encouraging. For two days low cloud and rain squalls had precluded star or sun sights. The previous noon he'd made *Myfanwy*'s position by dead reckoning 43° 20′ S: 74° 30′ E. Course for Amsterdam Island, N 25 E; estimated time of arrival, daybreak, 30th November. With wind and sea abaft the port beam the coaster, rolling boisterously, was making good nine knots.

Steam heaters warmed living spaces, wheelhouse and chart room, but it was cold outside. Since leaving Port Jeanne d'Arc he'd spent most of the time watching the radar screen in the wheelhouse or scanning the sea from the bridgewalk. Icebergs and growlers continued to haunt him. Kerguelen was five hundred miles astern, but for the next fifteen hours, until they were north of latitude 40° S, they were still within the area of drifting ice. The last lap was no time to relax.

Now, in the chart room, he worked on another problem: diesel fuel. They'd left Cape

Town with forty tons in the fuel tanks, and seventy in number one double-bottom tank. It had two compartments; each held thirty-five tons. On leaving Kerguelen there were sixty-eight tons remaining: forty in the fuel tanks and twenty-eight tons in number one double-bottom tank, port side. Assuming a stay of two days, there should be fifty-five tons remaining on leaving Amsterdam Island: forty in the fuel tanks and fifteen in the d.b. tank. That should leave at least twelve/fifteen tons of fuel in hand on arrival in Durban — an adequate safety margin. But until they'd used that fifteen tons — five days' consumption — the tank couldn't be flooded for ballasting. If really bad weather came along they might have to flood with the oil still in it. That would reduce the safety margin to five tons. Pretty chancy for a long voyage, much of it into head winds and seas. Putting away the notebook he decided to postpone crossing that particular bridge. But he was grateful for the one hundred and fifty tons of ore samples in number two hold. They helped the coaster's stability.

He checked the radar screen again. Nothing but dancing particles of light: wave cluster. Turning up the collar of his duffle coat, he stepped out on to the bridgewalk. Rain and wind cut into his face, cold and pricking. He wedged himself between the bridge rail and the wheelhouse, accustoming his eyes to the darkness. While he searched the black void ahead he thought of the time in Kerguelen. They'd completed their assignment there in eleven days — one ahead of schedule. Things had gone more or less according to plan. More ore to load than expected, but the fresh water problem had been easier.

The geologists from the survey party and their equipment had been embarked. The two Frenchmen were in the spare accommodation — a double berth cabin off the saloon. Little had been seen of them in the two days since leaving Kerguelen, and they'd not shown much interest in food. A small coaster in a big sea took some getting used to.

Two incidents in Port Jeanne d'Arc had upset Evans. There'd been another fight between Jan Christopherson the second mate, and Isak John the bosun. On shore, near the boat jetty, the afternoon before leaving. No one knew how it had started. Christopherson had knocked Isak John down and was standing over him when Evans appeared, accompanied by Henri Descartes, the chief geologist.

Evans had shouted, 'Stop that, Christopherson. Get back to the boat.'

The second mate had looked up, seen Evans and ignored him. As Isak John got to his feet, Christopherson went for him again. Evans had thrust himself between the two men. Christopherson, white with anger, and a bigger man than the captain, pushed him out of the way. Evans stood back for a moment, gathering himself. Then with his right hand he grabbed the young man's shoulder and spun him round. With his left he hit him full on the chin. It was a solid workmanlike blow with one hundred and seventy-five pounds of thickset Welshman behind it. The second mate went down. Evans examined his fist with a critical eye and decided it was all right. He said to Henri Descartes, 'My apologies. I don't like fighting.'

'So I notice.' The Frenchman smiled. Christopherson, still dazed, dragged himself to his feet. Evans beckoned to the men at the jetty. 'Help him to the boat.' He glared at Isak John. 'I'll deal with you later.' And he had, the next morning. Told them what he thought of them and warned that they'd be logged next time. But he couldn't get to the root of the trouble. Neither man would talk. Evans suspected it had to do with race and colour. It worried him. They were good men.

The other incident concerned the mate. Calvi had come back on board late the night before sailing, a good deal the worse for wear, having wined and dined with members of the survey party. By itself that wouldn't have mattered, but he'd made such a song and dance of his return on board — literally — that it did matter. Having performed a French folk dance under arc lights on number one hatch to the accompaniment of wild Gallic cries, he'd marched up and down the foredeck beating an empty oil drum and singing the *Marseillaise*. Finally he stood on the foc'sle proclaiming the glories of France in a deep voice and in what promised to be a long speech. Some of the crew had applauded but others, not pleased at being disturbed, had hurled insults. That was bad for discipline, so Evans had intervened and once again one hundred and seventy-five pounds of Welsh flesh and blood had gone into action.

Next morning a sober Napoleon Calvi reported to the captain's cabin half an hour before sailing. He had a black eye.

'Well,' said Evans coldly. 'What have you to say for yourself?'

'Nussing,' said Calvi. 'Nussing at all.'

'Not my business if you get drunk. But if you raise hell when you get back on board it is. Understand?'

'I am of France, captain. I was with

Frenchmen. We were *en fête*.'

'Don't let it happen again,' said Evans. 'A mate *earns* respect.'

Napoleon's good eye glared. 'I wish to go now. Make ship ready for sea.'

The captain nodded. 'You can go.' As the Corsican reached the door Evans said, 'The *Marseillaise* is a fine song. Better sung in a higher key.'

Calvi turned, his eyes sullen. 'It is not a song. It is the anthem of France.'

Outside the wheelhouse in the cold darkness Evans smiled at the recollection. But the incident had upset him. Not good to have crewmen shouting insults at a drunken mate. Evans didn't really know what to make of Calvi. He'd done well with the discharging and loading in Kerguelen, overcome the many difficulties which had arisen. But he wasn't sure of the man. A strange mixture: hard-working, tight-fisted, reserved. Saved almost all his pay. Spent his time in port skin-diving, collecting mussels, spearing fish. An unsailorly recreation in Evans' opinion due, he supposed, to the man's fishing origins.

Evans' thoughts were interrupted by Jan Christopherson's voice. 'Radar contact, captain. Bearing o-two-o, six miles. Fine on the port bow.'

Evans searched along the bearing with binoculars but saw nothing save darkness. He went to the radar screen and watched the scanner sweep. Each time it passed 020 degrees a pip of light showed brightly, fine on the port bow, distance five and a half miles. He had no doubt it was a berg and judging by the pip a large one. 'Steer twenty degrees to starboard,' he ordered. 'Keep a sharp watch on the bearing. Let me know if it doesn't change.'

Christopherson repeated the order and Evans went to the forepart of the bridge.

★ ★ ★

Christopherson had reported the radar contact at 0127 — twenty-seven minutes past one o'clock. With the coaster's alteration of course the radar bearing changed from five to twenty-five degrees on the bow. By 0142 it had opened to forty degrees, distant two and three-quarter miles. Fearful of surrounding 'growlers', Evans altered the coaster's course a further five degrees to starboard. Nothing could be seen with night glasses, but that was not surprising. Icebergs were difficult to pick up even on a clear night.

When the bearing of the pip was abeam to port, two miles away, he breathed a sigh of relief. Soon afterwards there was a clearing in the clouds, the rain stopped and in a brief moment of moonlight he saw, where the berg should have been, what looked like a ghost ship lying beam on to the sea. The lookout shouted, 'Ship on the port beam.'

The moon went behind the clouds and the ship was lost to sight. Two dim red lights in a vertical row had taken her place. At times, as the coaster sank into the trough of a sea, they would disappear, only to reappear as she rode the next sea.

Evans made for the wheelhouse. 'Slow ahead. Port wheel,' he ordered. Christopherson unlatched the automatic steering and took the wheel. Evans swung the azimuth ring for a bearing. 'That radar contact's ship. Not a berg,' he said. 'She's lying beam on to the sea. Not-under-command lights hoisted.' The whistle of the voice-pipe shrilled. It was Dai Williams in the engine-room wanting to know what was happening. Evans told him.

As the coaster closed the drifting ship a light began to flash from her bridge. There was no mistaking the crudely transmitted signal. *S O S — S O S — S O S*. Evans aimed an Aldis lamp at the stranger and made: '*What ship? What is your trouble?* The only reply was a further series of *S O S*s. It seemed the signaller couldn't read morse. Several times, slowly, Evans signalled *Will stand by you until daylight*. There was no intelligible response.

The coaster closed to within half a mile, pitching steeply as she headed into the twenty-knot wind and sea. Then Evans hove her to in the lee of the unknown ship, engines turning just enough to keep her bows on to the weather. It was too dark, even with night glasses, to make out detail. At times a phosphorescent veil drifted across the black hulk of the stranger as a sea broke against her side and the spray was caught by the wind. He saw that she was a freighter. Deep in the water. Between seven and eight thousand tons, he judged.

Napoleon Calvi and the bosun, wakened by the change in engine speed and alteration of course, arrived in the wheelhouse. Evans explained what had happened. 'I'm not doing anything until daylight,' he said. 'Then we'll see how things are. She's riding all right. Doesn't look in any immediate danger. Maybe an engine defect or steering trouble. Don't understand why they can't read signals.'

'Maybe they cannot speak English?' suggested Calvi.

'Why don't they use the International

Code then? That way they'd tell us a lot more than SOS can.'

For some time the SOS's continued to flicker in the darkness. Calvi took the Aldis lamp and made, OK — OK — OK, a number of times, slowly, and the unseen signaller stopped sending.

Evans realised that with daylight he'd have to decide whether to attempt salvage or simply take off the crew. The terms of his charter permitted him to deviate for the purpose of rendering assistance to another vessel, so he had no worries on that account. On one point he'd already made up his mind: he would not — not yet at any rate — let Kerguelen or Amsterdam Island know what he'd found. If he did the news would be broadcast and ships — especially ocean salvage tugs — would make for the scene hell bent on salvage money.

He felt instinctively that this disabled ship might be the answer to the exigent demands of *Myfanwy's* bondholders. As a seaman his first concern was for those on board, but he'd decided with quiet determination that if any ship was to make money out of what he'd found it would be his.

The decision made, he called Kerguelen. Port-aux-Français answered and to the French operator, whose voice he recognised, he said: *Trouble with radio transmitter. Shutting down to effect repairs. Weather bad, otherwise all well.*

Unknown to those in the wheelhouse he had, as he spoke, several times released the on-off switch in the handset. The interruptions were slight. Not enough to mutilate the message but they made his point. Next he called Amsterdam Island and gave the operator the same message, adding: *Weather bad. Fuel position may compel me omit call at Amsterdam Island in terms of my charter.*

The operator on Amsterdam Island heard the breaks in transmission but they did not interfere with the substance of the message. He replied: '*Roger, Myfanwy. We understand but 'ope you shall come all the same.*'

Evans replaced the handset and switched off the transmitter.

'The transmitter is defective?' Calvi's tone conveyed surprise.

Evans pointed through the wheelhouse windows to the not-under-command lights blinking in the darkness. 'There's a salvage job out there. If we broadcast the news there'll be others after it.'

The men in the wheelhouse nodded approvingly. The captain was shrewd. They could do with the salvage money.

The rain came again, swathes of it, slapping

against the wheelhouse windows where the wind flattened it into quivering streaks.

★ ★ ★

Susie had been on *Moonraker*'s bridge as the curtain of rain lifted and the moon shone through a rift in the clouds. Her heart had all but stopped when she saw a small ship on the starboard side, a mile or two away. It was drawing ahead. With a shriek of excitement she ran to the ship's bell and rang it furiously. It was the signal they'd agreed upon should anything be sighted. When she got back to the wing of the bridge the moon had gone and though she couldn't see the ship its lights were still there. Through binoculars she saw the white masthead steaming lights and between them, closer to the water, a red light. As she watched, the space between the steaming lights grew smaller. So did the ship.

'Oh, my God,' she gasped. 'They're not going to leave us?' With a sick feeling she kept the binoculars trained on the lights. When she'd all but given way to despair, the red light was joined by a green one, the two set apart like eyes of ruby and emerald. The ship had turned and was coming towards the *Moonraker*. A moment later Casey arrived on the bridge, Dwala close behind him.

'What's up?' Casey shouted.

'Look,' said Susie in a choked voice. 'Oh, look.' The darkness hid her tears.

'Jesus!' he yelled. 'It's a ship.'

'Coming this way,' said Dwala as if this were the most ordinary occurrence. 'They gone seen us, man.'

'Oh, thank you God,' sobbed Susie.

Hank put an arm round her while he watched the approaching ship. 'Everything's okay now, Susie. Don't cry.'

'I'll be all right. I'm excited.' She rubbed her eyes with her knuckles. 'It's the vow, Hank. Remember?'

But he'd gone. Run for the wheelhouse. In a moment he was back, aiming the torch at the approaching lights, cold fingers pressing the signal button, sending the message he'd so often practised: *S O S — S O S — S O S.*

The small ship signalled a reply but he couldn't read it, so he kept on sending *SOS*'s. An idea occurred to him. 'You and Dwala go down and tell the captain, Susie. If he's still — well, you know — get cracking and for chrissake sober him up somehow. He *must* come up here.'

★   ★   ★

268

There were four hours left to daylight. Throughout them Dwala and Susie worked on Captain Stone. First several doses of an emetic — mustard and warm castor oil — which Dwala said always worked. It certainly did. The captain retched and groaned, not once but many times. Then steaming towels and bicarb, Dwala racing between the galley and the night cabin. And later, when it was getting towards daylight, warm milk, biscuits and slices of apple.

By then Captain Stone's groans had given way to protests. 'For Heaven's sake leave me alone. Please. I beg you.' But eventually, near to dawn, their message seemed to be getting through: *a ship has arrived and is standing by. A very small ship — you understand, sah? — do you hear me, Uncle? — but nevertheless a ship.*

When daylight came — with what seemed to them the most wonderful morning of their lives — they got him up the stairway and into the wheelhouse. Then, after a rest and more coaxing, out on to the bridge. There he peered with incurious apathy at the coaster hove to in their lee, her hull glistening wetly in the early morning light, bows lifting high to meet the oncoming seas, red boot-topping showing clear down to the fore-foot, then disappearing into the troughs until only her masts and upperworks were visible.

Captain Stone continued to peer and apathy gave way to concern. What on earth was a coaster doing deep in the Southern Ocean? And what did it want? Instinctively he sensed the threat to his plan to sail the *Moonraker* to Sydney. The master of the coaster would be after the salvage money. Blurred as his faculties were, Captain Stone realised that he was in no position to refuse help. He hadn't yet got the sails on the model, let alone cut, sewn, rigged and hoisted on the *Moonraker* herself. Once again Fate had dealt him an unkind blow. Robbed him of the opportunity of performing a great maritime feat. There was only one grain of comfort in this new development. At the court of inquiry — for assuredly there would be one — they would not be able to say he had abandoned his ship.

In the meantime there was this coaster to be dealt with.

17

Dawn came with a lowering sky and tumbling seas. To windward the freighter bulked dark against leaping spray. In her lee the coaster climbed to meet the oncoming seas, riding the crests, falling into the troughs beyond.

With full daylight they read the name on the freighter's bow: *Moonraker*. It meant nothing to Evans. The signals about *Moonraker* and cyclone *Alpha* had been sent in Morse code. *Myfanwy* didn't read messages in Morse code. Flying from the signal yard on the foremast were two tattered pieces of bunting. Evans examined them through binoculars and realised they were the badly faded flags NC — *I require assistance* — the International Code distress signal.

He manœuvred the coaster round the freighter's stern and read the port of registration — *Monrovia*. Liberian flag. That wasn't encouraging. Next he took *Myfanwy* to windward, keeping well clear of the bigger ship but able now through glasses to see something of her external damage against the light quarter of the sky. The lifeboats had gone; ventilators, rails and companion ladders were twisted and smashed; windows on the bridge superstructure were broken; a tangle of bent rail hung down from the monkey island.

On the after well-deck, to starboard, there was some deck cargo. Not until they were back in the freighter's lee did he realise that it was a lighter. In some extraordinary way its bows had penetrated the centre-castle. His main concern was the state of affairs on board. What was the trouble? Had she any power? What crew? Were other ships already coming to her aid? It was not easy to get that information from a ship that couldn't read signals.

Waiting for daylight he'd read up salvage in *Brown's Nautical Almanac* and *Lloyd's Calendar* and one central fact was fixed in his mind. If salvage were to be undertaken, the freighter's captain must accept *Lloyd's Open Form* — the internationally approved contract. Unless Evans got that acceptance there'd be no salvage. Again he took the coaster upwind through long seas and stationed her on the *Moonraker's* weather-side. Attempts to communicate by loudhailer failed. Under those conditions they were hopeless. It'll have to be rocket or drift line, he was thinking when a signal winked uncertainly from the *Moonraker's* bridge.

Through glasses he saw four people there. Otherwise the upper deck was deserted. That was strange. The signaller was using a torch. Evans called to Christopherson, 'Tell him to go ahead.' The second mate aimed the Aldis lamp and made: *Pass your message.* Slowly, unevenly, the blinking light on the freighter's bridge replied: *Disabled in cyclone two days from Mauritius.*

'Mauritius,' echoed Evans. 'Why, that's fifteen hundred miles to the north. They must have been drifting a long time. Ask him what crew he's got?'

Christopherson, recently qualified, was quick on the Morse key. The distant torch interrupted: *Too fast. Signal slowly.*

'Slow it up, lad,' snapped Evans. 'It's not a competition.'

During the exchange of messages which followed a sketchy but disastrous picture emerged: engine-room and stokehold flooded, no power, four people on board — the captain, two men and a woman — no radio, no help on the way.

'Otherwise fine,' was Merfyr Evans' laconic comment. It would be far more of a task than he'd imagined while waiting for daylight. He'd not underestimated it even then: the laden freighter, deep in the water, would be the most difficult of tows for the coaster with her low power and light draught. Especially in those high southern latitudes, and with the long distances involved.

If only Old Llewellyn Jones were still in *Myfanwy*, he thought. Towing would need good seamanship and steady nerves. Old Llewellyn had those qualities. Evans wasn't so sure about Calvi. Standing by during those long hours of darkness he'd not reckoned on a flooded engine-room and stokehold, no power, no radio, virtually no crew. It was the last which worried him most. Frustrated by the slow signalling, the paucity of information — the difficulty of summing up the situation in *Moonraker* — and knowing that he would have to put someone aboard her sooner or later, he signalled: *Will attempt tow you. Salvage basis Lloyd's Open Form. Do you accept?*

Delay followed. He saw the shapes on the freighter's bridge gather. Discussing it, he said to himself. Not that they have much option. Who and what was the captain, he wondered? Greek, Lebanese, Pakistani ... young, old, middle-aged? He felt sorry for him.

The torch was flashing again. *Thank you*, it said.

You don't get away with that, decided Evans. He tapped back: *Do you accept*

Lloyd's Open Form?

Further delay. Then: *Yes. We accept.*

Evans made: *Will attempt transfer a mate to you immediately.*

The freighter replied: *Thank you but consider impracticable in this weather.*

The signalling was taking too much time; and time, limited by fuel, was critical to the operation. Evans said to Calvi, 'He doesn't want our man, then. But I'll not put a line across until I know more about things over there.'

Calvi agreed. 'Always they are like this, captain. They want help but they like to make they can manage. Then not so much of the salvage money. Same in fishing boats.'

Evans watched the distant bridge through glasses. 'We haven't the fuel to waste time arguing. We must get a man across.'

'How?' Calvi's face was expressionless.

'We can't put a boat down in this,' Evans admitted. 'We'll put a line across by rocket. Or drift one downwind to them. When they've got it they can haul across a heavier rope. Afterwards a life-raft.'

A sea broke against the *Moonraker*'s weather side and spray swept the ship. Calvi shook his head. 'No good to drift a line, captain. They can't work on the weather side. Rocket from leeward maybe okay.'

Evans looked at him coldly. Was this Frenchman from fishing boats trying to teach him seamanship. 'Starboard wheel. Half ahead,' he said, turning to Calvi. 'Tell Isak John to make a two-and-a-half inch manila ready for running. At least a hundred and twenty fathoms.'

Calvi went off. Evans spoke to Christopherson. 'Fetch the line-throwing gear from the wheelhouse. Look sharp.' He turned *Myfanwy* downwind, passing ahead of the freighter. When she was some distance downwind of the bigger ship, he brought her round, bows on to wind and sea. With the engines turning at slow-speed, the coaster edged up towards the *Moonraker*. Evans's mind was occupied now with another problem: who should he send across? Calvi or Christopherson? The young second mate seemed more dependable: strong, taciturn. Not temperamental like the Frenchman.

Christopherson came back with the box containing the Schermully apparatus.

Evans said, 'Know how to make it ready?'

'Yes, captain.'

'Then get busy, lad.'

The second mate opened the box, took out the Schermully pistol, connected the half-inch line to the wire tail of a rocket, inserted a cartridge in the pistol, placed the rocket in

276

the barrel and checked that the line was clear for running. 'All set, sir,' he called to Evans.

Calvi came back to report that one hundred and twenty fathoms of two-and-a-half-inch manila were flaked out ready for running.

'Bring the end up here. Outboard of everything,' said Evans. 'Make it fast to the bowline on the lower end of the rocket-line.' While this was being done a signal was made to the freighter to stand by for a rocket-line. When Evans judged the coaster to be within two hundred yards, he said, 'Right. Put it across.'

The second mate aimed the pistol and fired. The rocket soared away in a high arc taking the line with it. It fell short of the *Moonraker*. Evans swore. 'Should carry a good three hundred yards, even in a twenty-knot wind. Get another ready.'

The coaster's bow was falling off the wind and he had to take her round again and come up into it. Once more he took her to within two hundred yards of the freighter. He didn't like to go closer in those big seas. The second rocket missed the ship altogether, the line crossing ahead of her. The third fell short. There was only one rocket left. When Evans had brought the coaster round into wind again, he took the Schermully pistol himself, aimed with an elevation of about thirty degrees and pressed the trigger. The rocket crossed the *Moonraker* forward of the bridge as a sea broke across her fore well-deck. She rolled to windward and the line washed back with the sea spilling, over the bulwarks.

Evans's face was puckered with anger and frustration but he kept a rein on himself. 'We'll have to drift a line down to her then,' he said, handing the pistol to Christopherson. 'I'll take her up to windward again. Tell the bosun . . .'

'Don't go to windward, captain,' interrupted Calvi. 'Take her as close as you can in the lee. Then . . .'

Evans' eyes shone with sudden anger. 'Then what?'

'I swim with the line.'

'You crazy? You can't swim in this. It's not a bloody bathing pool.' Evans had all the seaman's mistrust of the sea as a means of supporting the human body.

Calvi shrugged his shoulders. 'I can,' he said. 'If you get close enough.'

Evans' anger evaporated. The Frenchman was serious. He looked at him with detached curiosity. The man had guts anyway. 'It's not long you'd last in that cold water.'

'I can do it,' said Calvi stubbornly. 'If you can go close.'

Evans was aware of the implied challenge. 'If you don't make it we'll not have a line across and I'll lose a mate.'

'If necessary haul me back on the line. But it will not be necessary.'

Evans frowned at the turbulent sea, the wind creaming the crests, snatching them away in spray. 'I don't like it,' he said.

Calvi's good eye smouldered. The other was still black. So the Welshman didn't think much of him? As for that, Calvi didn't think much of Evans's chances of getting a line across by drifting it downwind. The few hands in the freighter would never pick it up on the windward side in that weather. Calvi needed the salvage money. With it he could marry Marie Louise. His chin thrust forward. 'If I am in that ship, captain, *perhaps* we can salvage her. If not?' He spread his hands and shrugged his shoulders.

The Corsican's arrogance was so sincere, so naïve, it took the wind from Evans' sails. For a moment, unable to answer, he stared at Calvi. Then with quick decision he said, 'Good. You can bloody swim.' He, too, had doubts about the freighter's ability to pick up a line on the windward side. But he wasn't telling Calvi.

While the coaster turned in a wide circle, opening the distance before coming up in the

279

big ship's lee, Evans typed a brief note to her captain. Beneath his own signature he added an acceptance for signature by the other man. Not worth taking chances with a Liberian registered ship, he decided. *A man's word is his bond* didn't apply in certain circles. Briefly he discussed with Calvi what to do when he'd boarded the *Moonraker*. Not that Evans was at all sure the Corsican would board her, but he felt it unkind to say so. 'Make sure he signs that acceptance.' He handed Calvi the typed note. 'Until he does, we do nothing.'

'Except I swim.' There was the shadow of a smile on Calvi's face.

'Yes, you swim.' Evans watched him with quizzical eyes. Was he bluffing? The Corsican went off to make plans with Isak John, the bosun: then he went to his cabin and changed for the swim.

As the coaster made up through rolling seas towards the *Moonraker*, Evans signalled: *Put ladder over starboard side fore well-deck and stand by for swimmer.* From the wheelhouse he saw Isak John and a Zulu seaman working on ropes under the foc'sle. Soon a thickset figure in a skin-diving suit went forward, balancing against *Myfanwy's* corkscrewing. It was Calvi. He had a small canister tied to his belt and was carrying flippers. Merfyr Evans had not realised that his mate would be using *that* sort of gear. He'd forgotten the man's unsailorly hobby. Well, we shall see, he reflected. As he watched Calvi put on the flippers and rubber cap and fix the lifeline round his waist, he felt a sense of guilt. He'd never given the Frenchman much encouragement and here was the youngster risking his life to get a line across in half a gale. And with that black eye to boot! It was a strange world, reflected Evans. You didn't know the stuff a man was made of until you saw him in a tight spot.

Calvi gave the thumbs up sign to the bridge. Slowly the coaster made for the *Moonraker*. Evans determined to get her in closer this time. He owed it to Calvi.

When the coaster was less than a cable's length from the *Moonraker*, engines were stopped and the wheel put to port. The wind caught the bow and it began to pay off. Evans looked down to where Calvi was standing and raised his arm. The Corsican dived from the starboard bulwarks, neat and clean, surfacing to tread water for a moment, to adjust his goggles and check the lifeline. Then he made for the freighter, a steady purposeful crawl, the water churning behind him, Isak John paying out the lifeline.

Juggling with wheel and engines, Merfyr

Evans held the coaster a hundred yards or so down wind from the *Moonraker*. The distance looked a lot less when the freighter rose on big seas and towered over the coaster down in the valleys below. Busy handling her, Evans had little time to watch the man in the water. But Calvi's powerful crawl never faltered as he made his way towards the big ship, climbing the slopes of the seas, disappearing into the troughs, the lifeline trailing behind him. As he drew near the freighter the seas flattened in her lee, the wind cutting rippling swathes across the heaving water.

★ ★ ★

The coaster came up in the lee of *Moonraker*, and Casey and Dwala put the rope ladder over the side. Clad in yellow oilskins they stood by it, backs to the spray which swept the deck, keeping a wary eye to windward, grabbing at the lifelines when seas broke aboard. The coaster stopped within a few hundred feet of the *Moonraker* and the little ship's bow paid off to port. A dark shape hovered on her bulwarks, dived, surfaced and was soon moving towards the freighter. 'Jesus, that guy can swim,' said Casey. Coming from an Australian who'd grown up on surf beaches, it was more of a compliment than Dwala appreciated.

'Where I belong they come like this, good swimmers.' Dwala, too, was no stranger to surf beaches.

'Sure, Dwala. But in warm water, heh?'

The African grinned. 'Oh yes. Plenty warm there in Accra. Of the strong sun, you know.'

Casey watched the sea surge up the side, floating the foot of the ladder up with it as *Moonraker* rolled to starboard. 'We must look out for the roll,' he said.

When Calvi was thirty yards away Captain Stone shouted from the bridge. 'Throw that heaving line.' Casey whirled the line above his head and let go. The knobbed end sailed downwind, striking the sea ahead of the swimmer. With a few powerful strokes Calvi reached it, treading water while he made it fast round his waist. Then he came on, the crawl slower. Hank Casey took in the slack of the line as the distance closed. Twenty feet from the ship's side Calvi stopped and trod water again. The ship rolled towards him and he spurted for the ladder as its foot rose with the sea. He grasped it well up its length. Casey and Dwala hove on the line and before the next roll to starboard he was aboard.

The Australian shook him by the hand. 'Boy. That was great.'

Calvi pulled up his goggles, unhitched the line from his waist. 'Help with this,' he said. 'Quick. We mustn't lose it.'

A sea struck the ship's side, the spray sweeping over them and they held on to the lifelines. As the water washed away they climbed the companion ladder to the centre-castle, helping Calvi to pass the end of the line outside stanchions and railings. At the fairleads under the bridge, it was passed in and made fast to the bitts. Calvi signalled with his arms to the coaster. An answering wave came from Isak John.

'Haul on this line to bring over a manilla,' the Corsican said. 'Quick.' The three men hauled away. Over on the coaster a metal can was lowered into the sea. 'It is made fast to the manila,' explained Calvi. They hauled hand-over-hand, the load becoming heavier as the weight of rope in the water increased. Calvi saw the can approach the ship's side.

'Easy now,' he said. 'Next time we roll, haul quick.'

The roll came. 'Haul away,' he yelled. The eye of the manila came through the fairleads. 'Give me enough slack to lift the can over the rail,' he shouted. A moment later he had it on deck. They hauled in more of the manila and he made the rope fast to the bitts. 'Watch that line,' he said. 'It is important for the ship. *And you.*'

There was a gleam in his eye as he looked back at the coaster. It wasn't pride of achievement or conceit. Something more simple. He'd shown the Welsh captain how to get a line across in bad weather. It wasn't in the seamanship manuals but it worked. The fear of that last moment when the *Moonraker* rolled down on him, the water surging up her side as he'd made a dash for the ladder, was already forgotten.

★　★　★

Calvi introduced himself to the stooping English captain with the unshaven face, pale bloodshot eyes and halting speech. At once, and with some emotion, this man told him of the mutiny. 'Lot of foreign scum,' he finished gloomily. 'Don't understand loyalty and discipline.'

Calvi said, 'We wondered why you had no crew.'

'Come to the chart house.' The stooping figure led the way. Once there Calvi, his skin-diving suit still dripping, removed the waterproof seal and lid from the canister and handed Stone the typed offer of salvage. The captain put on his spectacles and read the letter, breathing heavily. He turned to Calvi.

'Yes. I accept. I've already done so by signal.'

'Sign please, captain.' Calvi was polite but firm.

'Now?'

'Immediately, please.'

'Are you swimming back with this, Mister . . . ?'

'Calvi. Napoleon Calvi.' The Corsican frowned. He didn't like his name forgotten so easily. It was a famous name. Even to an Englishman. 'No. I do not swim back. I stay here for the salvage. Sign, please, captain. Then we can begin.'

Captain Stone shook his head in doubt, sighed deeply and wrote his name with a shaking hand. He gave the note to Calvi.

The Corsican looked at the signature. 'Thank you, captain. Now I inspect the ship, please. You come also?'

The captain frowned, put his head out the door and called a name. A girl with grey eyes and an upturned nose came into the chart house. Her jersey and denim slacks were soiled and her hair untidy. She had a dark sun tan. Not so pretty decided Calvi, but *sympathique*.

'He wants to inspect the ship.' Captain Stone's voice was gloomy. 'Get Hank Casey to take him round. I can't leave the bridge.'

Pity you didn't always feel like that, she

thought, looking at the skindiver and wondering how he'd got the bruised eye. 'Come with me.' She smiled, but he looked serious. He didn't know she was trembling with excitement, that he was to her a heroic figure. Hadn't he just done the bravest thing she'd ever seen. He followed her on to the bridge and down the ladder. They found Casey and Dwala watching the manila rope, wondering what was to come next.

'Hank,' she said. 'The captain wants you to take this . . . ' she hesitated, not knowing the skindiver's name. 'Take *him* round the ship. He must inspect it.'

She smiled at Calvi. 'My name's Susie. What's yours?'

'Napoleon,' he said.

It would be, thought Casey, wondering how Napoleon had got the black eye. 'Sure,' he said. 'I'll show him round.'

Susie looked at Calvi with shining eyes. 'I don't know how you did it.' She blushed. 'It was sensational.'

Calvi smiled for the first time. 'It was nussing,' he said shrugging his shoulders. 'Please, some dry clothes. I stay in the ship now, you understand.'

'Stay in the ship?' Hank Casey didn't sound madly enthusiastic.

'Yes. For the salvage.'

Susie said, 'Oh, that's marvellous. Fix him up with dry clothes, Hank.'

Casey nodded. 'Yeh, sure.'

'Quickly please,' said Calvi. 'There is much to do.' He took the two-gallon-can from Dwala and tucked it under his arm. 'And now?'

'Follow me, Napoleon.' The Australian winked at Susie.

She was not amused.

18

At nine o'clock, fitted out in warm clothing, mostly Lopez's, Calvi began his tour of inspection.

First it was the lighter. He sized up the damage, checked the cement plugs, the chocks and lashings. 'Later we make tight the lashings,' he said. 'Now the engine-room.' They went down to it through the skylight using the hanging rope ladder. Calvi examined the flooding, jotting down his estimates in a notebook. 'The shaft tunnel. Also flooded?'

'Haven't a clue,' said Casey.

Calvi found the horizontal iron wheel on the upper grating which turned the spindle and worm for closing the watertight door to the tunnel. 'It is shut,' he said. 'We must see what water it has. Through the escape hatch, you know.'

Casey did not know.

'What are you?' Calvi looked at him curiously. 'Seaman? Steward?'

'Passage-worker. Motor mechanic by trade.'

'Ah,' said the Corsican. 'I think so.'

The Australian didn't much like the way he said that.

'What is wrong with the emergency generator?'

'It's okay,' said Casey laconically.

'But you signal this morning that you have no power.'

'That was the captain. I fixed the generator yesterday.' Casey told him of the recovery of the missing part, of the two days and nights working on the engine.

'You did well,' said Calvi. 'But why is it not working?'

'Haven't found the circuit switches for the lighting yet.'

'They will be here.' Calvi's eyes searched the engine-room bulkheads. 'Possibly that one.' He pointed to a rectangular box high up on the after side.

'Planned to hunt round to-day.' Casey was feeling inadequate.

Calvi opened the cover. There were switches and fuses, marked *Mains Supply* and *Emergency Lighting*. He shut the switch on the emergency side. 'Now the steering compartment, please.' When they got there Casey started up the diesel, let in the clutch and engaged the generator, setting the throttle for the correct voltmeter reading.

'*Bon*,' said Calvi. 'Now we make the emergency lighting.'

Casey shut the switch and the lights in

the steering compartment came on. They switched off their torches.

'*Magnifique*.' Calvi patted his back. 'I wish the engineers who desert you can see. They were rats, *n'est ce pas?*' Calvi examined the fire-mains pump, paying particular attention to the inlet side. He read the maker's tag on the generator. Going over to a circular hatch, he slipped the double sided locking device and opened it. 'The escape hatch from the shaft tunnel,' he explained, aiming his torch down it. 'Only a little water. *Bon*. We shall flood it.'

'What's the big idea?'

'It will make lower the level in the engine-room and stokehold. That is good. It means also we can pump. That is better.'

'Pump with what?'

'This.' Calvi pointed to the fire-mains pump.

'Dwala says that's for pumping water from the sea. Circulates it through the fire-mains to hose points on deck.'

Calvi nodded. 'Yes. And he is right. But a pump is a pump. I think we make this one do other things. But I explain. First we flood the shaft tunnel by opening the watertight door to the engine-room. Then we take off this.' He tapped the inlet pipe with his foot. 'It comes from the sea. Next we put a hosepipe in its place. The hose we put through the escape hatch into the shaft tunnel. Then it sucks water from the tunnel into the fire-mains. In this way we take the water from the stokehold and engine-room.'

'Where does it go then?'

'To the hose points on deck, then into the scuppers and over the side. *Voilà*.' Calvi thought, there is little time but he must understand these things if he is to help.

Casey was thinking, he's making out what a great guy he is and what a twit I am. He said, 'How much d'you reckon that pump can handle?'

'The output of the generator is fifteen kilowatts.' Calvi frowned with concentration, leaning against the bulkhead, supporting himself against the roll of the ship with one hand, stroking his dark chin with the other. 'I think at least ten thousand litres in one hour.'

'Greek to me,' Casey was unimpressed. 'What's that in tons?'

Calvi did some mental arithmetic. 'About ten tons.'

'Two hundred and forty a day.' The Australian brightened up. 'That's great.'

'It is better to rest the diesel.' Calvi looked at the engine thoughtfully. 'We can pump sixteen hours in twenty-four. Always at night for this makes also some lights. Then a rest.

Then more pumping in the day.'

'Yeh, that's not bad. If there's fifteen hundred tons down there, that would empty it in about ten, twelve days.'

'So. We begin to-day. But first we try the hand-steering.' Calvi walked over to the big wheel, stepped on to the wooden grating, examined the overhead compass, the telephone to the bridge, and the helm. 'The rudder is admidships. *Bon.*' With difficulty he turned the wheel through thirty degrees. '*Merde!*' he said. 'Come. We try together.'

Between them they put the wheel hard over both ways. 'It is heavy work.' Calvi shook his head. 'These old ships. The arrangement is bad. There must be two men all the time. And this means four. Working two hours on, two off.'

Casey laughed dryly. 'Hey. That's bloody great. We've only got Dwala, myself and the girl.'

Calvi's good eye was fixed on the Australian. 'How is the captain?'

Casey didn't want to let Susie down, but what was the use of bluffing. The Frenchman would find out soon enough. 'Okay. When he's not stoned.'

'He drinks?'

Casey nodded. 'His nerves are shot to hell. Last war they say. We haven't seen him since the twentieth. At least not until this morning.'

Calvi ran his hand across his chin. 'This makes for difficulties. *Alors.* We shall manage somehow. Now we go to the foc'sle. I must see the anchors and cables. Also the wires and ropes. Afterwards I speak with my captain.'

Casey said, 'How old is he?'

'Quite old. At least thirty-two.'

'Goodo.' Casey chuckled. 'Is he French, too?'

'A Welshman. It is a British ship. From Cardiff.'

'Cardiff! Bit off course aren't you?'

Calvi shrugged. 'It is a long story. Sometime I tell you. Come! *Mon ami.* To the foc'sle.'

★ ★ ★

On *Moonraker*'s boat-deck, screened from the bridge by the funnel, Calvi opened the two-gallon can with a tin-opener provided by Dwala. Dai Williams had soldered a neat rectangular panel on one side; Casey was busy on the other. When he'd got it open he removed a layer of cotton waste and lifted out a polythene bag. In it was one of the two walkie-talkies used in Kerguelen. And spare batteries.

He extended the pole aerial and switched

on. 'Calling *Myfanwy* — calling *Myfanwy*. Do you read me?'

A strong Welsh accent came on the air. 'I read you, Calvi. Go ahead.'

Briefly, succinctly, Calvi made his report, prefixing it with the news that Captain Stone, British, had signed the acceptance for salvage. He covered everything: *Moonraker*'s damage; the flooding, the plan for pumping, the mutiny; the anchor cables, wires and ropes available; brief details of those on board, including a frank reference to the captain's condition.

'So what do you need, then?' asked Evans.

'We must have three seamen and one engineman.'

'You won't bloody get them,' was the abrupt reply. Calvi realised his captain hadn't liked the *must*.

'How can we manage a tow if you take half my seamen?' demanded Evans.

'We also must manage the tow.' Calvi wasn't giving in. 'And the hand-steering. *And* the pumping. With myself there are only three men. The girl cooks and cleans. Hand-steering takes four men. Two in each watch. I must be on the bridge. This is five. We must run the diesel-engine and generator. Refuel the diesel tank with the hand pump. For these I want the engineman. Casey, the passage-worker, is a motor mechanic. He can help when the engineman sleeps. But he must also assist with the steering. And he must sleep.'

'Roger,' replied Evans. 'I need to think on this. Call you back later.'

He soon did. With another problem. 'Now then, Calvi. Who'll be on the bridge when you sleep? The captain?'

'It is not possible. I have told you of the captain.'

'And so, when you sleep?'

This was the one problem Calvi had not faced. He paused to consider it. 'Send the French geologist, captain. Le Clerc.'

'Le Clerc's not a seaman. I can't use passengers.'

'Ask him, captain. He is a Frenchman. He will volunteer.'

'But he's no seaman, I tell you.'

'He's a scientist. Intelligent. He will learn quickly. And Bartot, the other, can help you.'

'Very obliging of you,' said Evans.

There was further discussion and in the end, grudgingly, the Welshman gave in. It was agreed to transfer the men by inflatable life-raft as soon as possible. They would use *Moonraker's* lee. The raft to be hauled across on the two-and-a-half-inch manilla, and back on a line supplied by the coaster.

Next they got on to details of the towing

rig. Evans outlined what he had in mind. At *Moonraker's* end the tow would begin with twenty fathoms of her starboard anchor cable. To its outboard end would be attached one hundred fathoms of six-inch wire rope, the heaviest the freighter carried. On board *Myfanwy* the coaster's cable would be led aft along the starboard side. To distribute the weight of the tow, it would be taken clean around the deckhouse on the poop, thence to the stern capstan and outboard through the after fairleads. When *Moonraker's* towing wire was secured to *Myfanwy's* cable, twenty fathoms of that cable would be paid out. In all the length of tow would be eight hundred and forty feet. The weight of the cables at either end, acting on that length of tow, would ensure spring and minimise the chances of parting because of a taut wire.

Since *Moonraker* had no power, the coaster would haul out the bigger ship's cable once the wire hawser had been passed. Next they discussed and agreed the method of making fast *Moonraker's* cable on her foc'sle. To Casey, listening, the whole thing was incomprehensible. Finally, they agreed that the messenger for passing the tow would be the two-and-a-half-inch manila linking the two ships. To this would be bent on a four inch manila to take the weight of the wire.

This item became the only subject of disagreement.

'We must keep the messenger between the ships *after* the tow is passed,' said Calvi.

'What would that be for now?' There was a chilly note in Evans's voice.

'*La corde paresseuse*. It is essential.'

'The what?'

'In English I do not know. Perhaps — *the lazy line*.'

'And what the bloody hell's that?'

'If the tow should break we do not have to pass it again. It is already there.'

'What is?'

'The lazy line. The messenger.'

'Now, look here, Calvi. Once the towline is secured I'm not having a lot of rope hanging in the water between the two vessels. In no time it will be around our screw.'

'We keep half the length out. The rest we use only if the tow parts. Then it runs free. There is another thing, captain. If the tow parts,' he lowered his voice, 'the Captain Stone here cannot say, 'Now you no longer have a line on me. You have lost the salvage. Now I let another ship tow me?' Perhaps a big one.'

The long pause suggested that Evans was giving some thought to *la corde paresseuse*. In fact he was digesting his pride. It was galling to be told what was *essential* by a twenty-five-year-old not long out of fishing boats. 'Now, Calvi, lad. Where would you be getting these ideas?'

The Corsican chuckled, knowing that Evans would hear him. 'From fishing boats, captain. Often we must tow in bad weather. If the mistral is blowing outside Ajaccio and the tow parts, there is not time to pass first one line then another before we drift on to Les Îles Sanguinaires.'

'Well then,' came the reply, 'have your lazy line. But mind you keep it out of my screw.'

'Thank you, captain. Is that all?'

'I think so. We'll be getting those men across. How's the food and fresh water over there?'

'We have enough, they say.'

'Enough for ten people for three or four weeks?'

Calvi looked at Dwala who was listening in. The African nodded.

'Yes, captain. Enough. Where do we go?' he added.

'Fremantle.'

'Australia?' The Corsican's surprise sounded through Evans' receiver.

'Yes. Five hundred miles closer than Durban. Wind, sea and current with us. We'd never make it to the South African coast in this weather. Even if we had the fuel.'

'Kerguelen, captain?'

'No repair facilities there. Who's paying salvage money for that?'

'You are right, captain. Fremantle is good.'

'Well, now. It's nice of you to agree.' The irony was not lost on the Corsican. 'Explain our intentions to Captain Stone right away,' said Evans.

'If he doesn't understand or agree?'

'Tell him you represent me. That he has accepted the offer of salvage. We already have a line aboard and I am in charge of the salvage operations.'

'*Bon*. I will do this.'

'Be tactful, Calvi.'

'But of course.' What does he think I am, thought the Corsican, an imbecile?

'And that reminds me. I have not yet mentioned it, Calvi.'

'What is that, captain?'

'That was a good swim.'

★   ★   ★

Frascatti's boat was sighted and picked up by a Sydney-bound container ship during the forenoon of 29th November, fifteen days after he and his men had abandoned the *Moonraker*. In that time they'd made good

300

over seven hundred and twenty miles but were still some five hundred miles south of Mauritius, which island they would certainly have missed since Frascatti's longitude by dead reckoning was three degrees in error.

When it was clear that the distant ship had sighted them, Frascatti gave his tattered crew, many of them weak from exposure, a final briefing. They would, he said, be questioned about the circumstances under which they had abandoned the *Moonraker*. Their interrogators would want to know, too, about Lopez's boat — and, of course, about Kantle's disappearance. Frascatti reminded them of the unanimity of their decision to abandon the ship. As to Lopez's boat they would remember, he said, that the towing painter had parted during a night of fierce squalls.

This the men believed. The flares fired by Lopez, and the Aldis lamp beam, had not been seen because of the curtain of rain which separated the two boats, then several miles apart. Before daybreak the next morning, when it was still dark, Frascatti had made the 'discovery' (which in no way surprised Achmed Khalif and one or two others) that the painter had parted.

'Must have chafed through on the transom,' Frascatti told his men, unhitching the inboard end from a bench thwart and throwing it over the side. Muttering with dismay that such a thing could have happened and gone unnoticed, he explained, 'We were too weak and tired. Otherwise we must have known from the speed of this boat.'

'How could we tell speed in the darkness? In any case we were sleeping or dozing,' complained a Senegalese fireman.

'I do not blame you,' said Frascatti humbly. 'I should have known from the feel of the steering.'

With the lugsail still set, drawing well before the southeasterly wind, and the petrol-engine at near full throttle, Frascatti had kept the boat on course for Mauritius while he and his companions discussed the pros and cons of turning back. All but two had agreed they should not, that it would be impossible to find the other boat in the darkness, especially heading into a fresh wind and sea against which a heavily-laden lifeboat would make little progress, even with an engine.

Lopez's boat, they pointed out, had a sail and adequate provisions; he was a good navigator and had with him men like Thoresen, Jenkins, Garrett the cook, the Dutch carpenter and the two Cape Verde islanders — among the best seamen in the ship. In short it was felt that he and his companions could fend for themselves.

'We have done everything possible for these peoples,' said one of Frascatti's men. 'Towed them many miles. Helped them when they lose sail. Stay with them every night in all weather. How must we go back now? Is not first duty to save this boat with many peoples in it?'

This proved to be a popular view and one with which Frascatti wholeheartedly agreed. He had, with some emphasis, told them that the chances of reaching Mauritius were *very good* on their own. He made no reference to the alternative, but his point was taken. The two who did not agree were Addu Batu the Nigerian third officer, and Kantle the radio operator. Addu Batu, much afraid, said little, but Kantle had spoken out: nervous, worried, stuttering, weak from exposure, he was certain it was their duty to go back. He had expressed himself in strong terms, saying it would be an act of cowardice to go on when they knew the other boat leaked so badly. There were angry growls of dissent and he was soon shouted down.

Next morning, at daybreak, he was missing. No one had seen him go. Two Senegalese firemen — they sat next to him

— said they had slept or dozed most of the night. Certainly they had seen and heard nothing until when, at first light, it was found he was no longer there.

'*Extraordinario*,' said a Paraguayan greaser, 'that he should have gone so quietly.'

'*Extraordinario*,' echoed Frascatti, looking beyond the men to the horizon ahead, his bearded face haggard in the grey light of morning.

★ ★ ★

Having picked up the survivors and hoisted their lifeboat inboard, the container ship resumed her journey to Sydney: course one-three-zero degrees, speed eighteen knots.

While the rescued men were being attended to by the crew, Frascatti was in the Norwegian captain's cabin making his report. The captain had his chief officer with him. Although suffering from exposure and visibly weak, Frascatti told the story well. He began with the cyclone, the damage suffered by *Moonraker*, the failure of the emergency generator after the flooding of the machinery spaces, the destruction of the standby batteries for the radio, the unfortunate circumstance of Captain Stone's attacks of alcoholism during and after the storm. Very tactful and understanding he was about this, speaking with compassion of the captain's hopeless struggle against his weakness. Frascatti, however, did not fail to refer to the *Donnington Wave* affair.

He emphasised how the officers and men of the *Moonraker*, convinced that survival lay in taking to the boats, had come to the unanimous decision that this should be done. He recounted how he, Thoresen and Jenkins had pleaded with the captain to come with them, only to meet with a blank refusal. Again, and with apparent reluctance, Frascatti spoke of the confused state of mind alcohol had induced in Stone. He explained with sorrow the decision of the girl and Dwala to remain behind. It was misplaced loyalty, he said, and fear of the long voyage in open boats. He told how the plan to take these three to the boats by force — for their own safety — had been thwarted by the captain's use of fire-arms. Despite every effort, said Frascatti, it had not been possible to get them to change their minds and so with heavy hearts he and his men had left them. Later they'd discovered that the Australian passage-worker was not in the boats, and concluded that he'd decided to remain on board.

Not only did Frascatti tell the story well

but it was, but for certain omissions, substantially true. He had not, however, mentioned Stone's orders that the ship should not be abandoned, nor the captain's charge of mutiny. Since none of the men in the boat, other than O'Halloran, had been present at the door of Stone's cabin, Frascatti felt these details could safely be omitted. He had, before they left the *Moonraker*, impressed upon O'Halloran, Thoresen and Jenkins the importance of concealing such details if charges of mutiny were to be avoided. Of course, he said, such charges were most unlikely, both because it was improbable that the captain would survive and — if he did — the circumstances were such that a charge of mutiny had little chance of succeeding. 'A man cannot,' Frascatti had said, 'be guilty of mutiny if he disobeys crazy orders from a drunken man.'

Briefly, with the omission of much detail, Frascatti told the Norwegian captain how they'd lost contact with Lopez's boat in a dark night of squalls a week back and how, on the following day, they'd discovered the loss of Kantle the radio operator. At this stage Frascatti tapped his forehead knowingly.

'Off his head was he?' asked the Norwegian captain.

Frascatti nodded. 'A good man,' he said

sadly. 'But I think the strains is too much. He was not young. Also not strong.' Then, pleading exhaustion and the onset of nausea, Frascatti had slumped in a chair, breathing heavily as if in distress.

The Norwegian watched him with keen blue eyes. 'It seems you require attention, Mr Frascatti. Thor Pedersen, my chief officer, will take you to the chief steward.'

When they'd gone, the captain wrote a radio message informing Durban, Port Louis and Sydney that he'd picked up a boatload of survivors from the missing ship *Moonraker*. He gave the latitude and longitude of the pick-up position, a brief outline of Frascatti's story, and recorded his intention to land the survivors in Sydney where he expected to arrive on 6th December. The message also gave the approximate position of the *Moonraker* on 14th November, the day upon which she'd been abandoned, and made known Frascatti's opinion that she could not have remained afloat for more than a few days at most.

When he'd handed the message to the radio operator the captain sat at his desk thinking. For reasons he could not pin down he did not like Carlo Frascatti. It wasn't, he thought, the shiftiness of the bloodshot eyes, the sore-ridden lips, the unpleasing aspect of

307

the haggard face, the rasping broken English ... after all the man was suffering from exposure, had just completed a long and difficult voyage in an open boat. No, it was something more than that. The Norwegian suspected it was his aversion to a chief officer who could leave his captain, a young woman and two men in a ship which, though damaged, had not apparently been in imminent danger of sinking.

The traditions of the sea lay deep in the Norwegian's bones.

19

Calvi reported to Captain Stone the results of his inspection of the *Moonraker*, and his radio discussions with Merfyr Evans. Stone niggled about the transfer of so many men to his ship. Patiently Calvi explained that the freighter could not be towed without them. The captain changed the subject to the weather. Later, he listened without comment to details of how the towing hawser would be rigged. Passive, silent, he sat hunched in a corner of the chart house, breathing heavily, his coat collar turned up against the wind which whistled in through a broken window, his eyes on the floor. He seemed not to understand Calvi's idea for pumping the flooded compartments. 'You can't pump them with the firemains pump.' The blood-shot eyes contemplated the chart house clock with gloomy displeasure. 'The intake pipe's outboard and well below sea level. Even in light trim.'

Calvi decided against repeating the explanation. There wasn't time.

'Anyway,' mumbled Stone. 'The emergency diesel's unserviceable.'

'I have already explained, captain. It was repaired by the Australian yesterday.'

'Ah, Casey. Good boy that. Not a seaman. But keen. Refused to join those mutinous devils. Had ideas about my niece. Got over that now. Cooks well, doesn't she?'

Calvi frowned in bewilderment. 'Excuse me, captain. We must have the ship in tow before dark.'

'Only twenty past eleven.' Stone looked at the clock. 'No hurry. I'll consider what you've told me. Let you have my decision later.'

Calvi decided there was no point in putting off the moment of confrontation. 'You've already made it, sir,' he said. 'Captain Evans wishes to begin at once.'

Stone stared blankly at his feet. The carpet slippers he wore were wet. 'Possibly,' he said. 'But I am in command here, Mr . . . ?'

'Calvi, sir. C-A-L-V-I. I must explain. You have accepted the salvage offer of Captain Evans. I am his representative. Your ship is disabled. We have a line aboard. Captain Evans commands the operation. *At both ends.*' It was a long statement for Calvi.

Stone was silent. He'd heard little of what the young man had said. In his mind's eye was the model in the cabin below. To-day he would get on with the sails. 'I wonder,' he said courteously, 'if you'd care to see the sail plan. Seven thousand square feet. Trysails and staysails. Can you imagine that in a steam ship?'

Calvi stared in confusion. 'Sail plan. I do not understand.'

'In my cabin. Been working on it for some time. We'll make four to five knots with this wind.'

'Thank you, sir. Later perhaps.' Calvi bowed politely. 'I must get the men across.'

★ ★ ★

Evans called for volunteers to transfer to *Moonraker*. More than needed came forward. First he chose Carelse, a middle-aged Cape coloured engineman, capable and popular. Then the seamen: two Zulus and a Cape coloured. Le Clerc, the French geologist — once he'd got over his shock on learning that Fremantle and not Amsterdam Island was his destination — had agreed cheerfully to go. He was a young man, keen and interested in all that went on now that he'd got his sea legs.

Evans had turned the coaster stern to wind in the lee of the freighter. He'd found she was easier to manœuvre that way. A life-raft was thrown over the side where it inflated automatically and the end of a coil of four-inch manilla was bent on to its stern. The end of the two-and-a-half-inch manila from *Moonraker* was made fast in the bows. Calvi's insistence on *la corde paresseuse* had won the day.

The five men to be transferred put on inflated life-jackets, took changes of warm clothing and climbed into the hooded raft. When all was ready Evans called Calvi on the walkie-talkie. 'All set. Haul away, now. But watch it.'

Those in the *Moonraker* bore on the rope and the loaded raft lurched and plunged towards the freighter. The bigger ship's rolling complicated taking the men from the raft. On Calvi's instructions it lay off clear of the ship's side, lines were thrown and a ladder put down. Watching *Moonraker*'s roll with a wary eye, Calvi barked his orders. First the engineman was hauled to the ladder and brought aboard. Then Le Clerc. After him the seamen. All arrived wet, some bruised, none badly hurt.

Finally the life-raft was hoisted on board. Evans had decided that *Moonraker* — having lost her boats and rafts in the cyclone — should keep it. The coaster had another, as well as two lifeboats. The new arrivals were shown to their quarters where they quickly changed into dry clothing before returning on deck.

* * *

Waiting for daylight the night before, Evans had discussed with Dai Williams the feasibility of towing. Ever cautious, Williams had said, 'Well, I don't rightly know, Merfyr. She's about eight thousand tons. Deep in the water. We're low-powered for that. And a bit light aft.'

When Evans suggested what the salvage money might be worth, Dai Williams had amended his judgment to: 'Well, Merfyr. It would be worth the trying, then.'

Fuel margins were finely balanced. Main fuel tanks were full, forty tons. Number one d.b. ballast tank, still had eleven to twelve tons. Fremantle was about one thousand eight hundred miles away. If with wind and current the tow could average five knots (Dai Williams thought the coaster's speed through the water might be three and a half) they'd have fifteen days' steaming *if all went well*. At three tons a day there would be a margin of six tons on arrival at Fremantle. It was risky, but the risk was worth taking. If they ran short of fuel it would be near the Australian coast where help should be forthcoming.

313

Evans worried most about the inability to flood the d.b. tank until the fuel there was used. That would take four days' steaming. Until then her trim aft would be getting lighter. The deeper in the water the coaster's stern, the better for towing. On the credit side stood Calvi's pumping plan. If one hundred and fifty tons could be pumped each day, the *Moonraker* would become progressively easier to tow, especially with a following wind. In five days she'd be seven hundred and fifty tons lighter. In ten, the flooded compartments could be dry.

* * *

The long rolling seas and force six wind continued throughout the day, adding to the problem of rigging and passing the towing hawser. First *Moonraker*'s starboard anchor had to be stoppered off in the hawse-pipe, the cable broken at the first shackle and passed through the Panama leads in the bow. The end was then brought inboard and made ready for the six-inch towing wire. That in turn had to be prepared for running; a difficult task in bad weather.

Downwind of the freighter, *Myfanwy*'s crew were busy making ready their end of the tow. Christopherson worked with Isak John

314

and two seamen, while Evans kept the coaster in position under the freighter's lee.

About four o'clock Calvi came on the air. 'We are ready, captain. The messenger is bent on to the six-inch wire. All set for running.'

'How's the end of the wire, Calvi? Got an eye?'

'Yes. We have spliced one in.'

'Good. Who did that then?'

'Msutu and myself, captain.'

'Ah. He's a good seaman.'

He taunts me, thought Calvi, who'd done most of the work. He swore softly in French.

'What's that?'

'*Rien du tout,*' said Calvi. 'Nussing.'

'Right, lad. We'll make a start.'

* * *

The coaster moved slowly ahead taking station on the freighter's bow but still enjoying the calmer water in her lee.

On the poop Christopherson and two seamen helped Isak John take turns off the after capstan as the manila messenger came inboard. Soon the six-inch wire came snaking across the water lifting and dipping as the seas rolled by. When it reached the coaster the eye was shackled on to the outboard end of her cable. Christopherson waved to the bridge. Evans spoke into the walkie-talkie. 'Hold on to that wire, Calvi. We'll pay out cable.'

Calvi acknowledged and the coaster went slowly ahead paying out cable. When Christopherson reported that twenty fathoms had gone, Evans called Calvi. 'Our cable is out. Ease away on the wire as we go ahead. Don't let it run.'

Myfanwy drew away from the freighter, rolling heavily as she came clear of the big ship's lee and began a slow turn to starboard. The walkie-talkie crackled. Calvi's voice came on the air: 'Only a few fathoms of wire left, captain.'

'Right. I'm stopping engines now.'

What seemed to Evans a long time later, Calvi reported, 'Our cable is beginning to run, captain. Slow ahead.'

I don't need you to tell me slow ahead, Evans grumbled to himself. 'Slow ahead, port a little,' he called to the seaman in the wheelhouse.

The arc of the towing wire diminished and the cable began to come clear of *Moonraker*'s bow leads.

Evans could hear over the walkie-talkie the metallic clatter of the big ship's cable running. Then Calvi's voice, 'Fifteen fathoms gone, captain.'

Evans ordered *stop engines* and the coaster lost way as the weight of the towline pulled on her stern. The rumble of the cable continued, Calvi's voice sounding above it: 'Twenty fathoms gone. Putting on stoppers.'

'Slow astern,' Evans called to the wheel-house. He spoke into the walkie-talkie. 'Let me know when the cable's fast, Calvi. Make it sharp, man.' He stood on the wing of the bridge watching anxiously through binoculars the activity on the freighter's foc'sle. Now and then he ordered a brief *slow ahead* to keep the towline sufficiently stretched to avoid fouling the *Myfanwy*'s screw.

At last came Calvi's voice: 'Cable made fast, captain. I go to the bridge.'

'Let me know when you're ready, then.'

A few minutes later an exultant Calvi reported: 'We are ready, captain. Hand-steering manned.'

'Put your wheel hard a-starboard, Calvi.' Evans turned the coaster downwind, moving her gently, until he was steaming almost at right angles to the line of the freighter's keel. He wanted to pivot the big ship first, to avoid the major strain of a direct pull as *Moonraker*'s inertia at rest was overcome.

The towing hawser lifted from the sea between waves and trembled, water streaming from it. Evans watched grimly. Everything depended on this. But the wire kept its arc and the *Moonraker's* bows moved slowly downwind. With infinite care and patience he increased the coaster's speed, and as the freighter's bows swung more quickly he reduced the angle of the tow. He pressed the mike's transmit button. 'We'll be coming round to north-sixty-east, Calvi. Course for Fremantle. See then how she lies on the hawser. Watch out for yawing, lad.'

The wheelhouse clock showed five-forty-seven as he steadied the coaster on her course and moved the engine-room telegraph from *slow* to *half-ahead*. She took it all right. During the next fifteen minutes he gradually increased the coaster's speed until her engine revolutions were those for full speed. This was, he knew, the moment of truth. Would the towing hawser hold? Could *Myfanwy* with her comparatively low power and light trim handle such a heavy tow in that weather, even with a following wind and sea? And could Calvi and those manning the hand-steering prevent dangerous yawing. If not there was one blinding certainty: the tow would part.

Evans soon knew some of the answers. And they were encouraging. The one hundred and fifty tons of ore stowed aft in number two hold, the full fuel tanks and the flooded ballast tanks were keeping *Myfanwy*'s stern sufficiently low in the water; the towing wire was holding; and though steering in both ships was difficult they were managing to cope.

★   ★   ★

Occasionally Evans caught a glimpse of the towing hawser between long crested seas, but most of the time nothing could be seen but the cables entering the water at *Moonraker*'s bow and the coaster's stern. All Evans' senses were keyed now to the freighter wallowing and rolling a couple of hundred yards astern, yawing at times as the wind and sea on her quarter threw her off course. Then he'd reduce speed, increasing it again when she came back.

On *Moonraker*'s bridge Calvi, in spite of the exertions of a long day, never relaxed his watch on the coaster's stern. Quickly he learnt how to anticipate a yaw, how much wheel to use and when to apply it. With him was Le Clerc, learning equally fast and enjoying himself.

Down in the steering flat the men on the handwheel, unable to see anything outside their steel compartment, were learning too. Not only about anticipation and timing in holding the ship to a given course, but how best to apply to the big handwheel the physical effort needed to move the ship's rudder.

★　★　★

Captain Stone stood morose and distant on the wing of *Moonraker*'s bridge. He was confused by the two young Frenchmen who seemed to have command of his ship. And he was sick and tired of the French language. For the last few hours he'd heard little else. It was humiliating that the *Moonraker* should be towed by this dirty rust-streaked coaster; that her men should be on *his* bridge, all over *his* ship. Given another week he'd have had the *Moonraker* under sail with no strangers to take from him the credit that was rightly his.

★　★　★

Towards evening the cloud ceiling lowered and rain began to fall. Evans and Calvi knew they would get no sleep that night for a new problem had to be faced. Towing in the dark. And they were not yet out of the area of icebergs and growlers. The *Moonraker* still displayed the red not-under-command lights

320

but now, in addition, she burnt port and starboard navigation lights and a stern light. As well as her side lights, the *Myfanwy* had two white lights on the foremast to show she had a ship in tow. On her poop an arc light had been rigged. It showed how the towing cable was leading, gave her crew light to work by if needed, and made Calvi's task of conning the freighter less difficult for *Myfanwy*'s illuminated stern showed up clearly in the darkness ahead in spite of the rain.

★ ★ ★

Joined by an unseen hawser the oddly assorted maritime cortège steamed slowly into the night, rolling, pitching and plunging, wind moaning through rigging, seas lifting and pushing, smothering the ships in spray and sometimes breaking aboard — course N 62 E, destination Fremantle, distance one thousand eight hundred and seventy-six miles.

Throughout that day and on into the night, despite moments of intense anxiety and frustration, Evans's respect for Calvi had grown. He still thought of him as 'The Fisherman', but the words now had a different connotation, a kinder meaning.

The night was warm and oppressive, the sea calm, its gentle undulations reflecting the moon and the stars. Lopez, half asleep, the water lapping at his calves, realised that something was wrong. The splash and metallic scrape of the bailers had ceased. He called to the men in the bows, 'Why are you not bailing?'

The Portuguese said, 'Tomas has passed out. I am holding him.'

Garrett the cook began to move forward. 'I'll see to 'im,' he said in a hoarse voice. He crawled over the thwarts pushing past hunched sleeping men who grunted and cursed. Garrett examined the wasted body of the Cape Verde Islander. He slapped the man's cheeks, felt his heart and pulse, lifted his eyelids, listened for breathing.

'Tomas is dead,' he said.

'If you are sure we shall have to — ' Lopez hesitated.

'Yes,' said Thoresen. 'Now. Before the sun comes.'

Garrett and the Portuguese bundled the corpse over the gunwale, grunting with their exertions. It stayed by the boat supported by the air trapped in its shirt and trousers.

The Portuguese began bailing again.

Scrape — splash — scrape — splash. Garrett tried to push the body beneath the water. It annoyed him that it should float there so close. It disappeared but soon re-surfaced. Garrett swore at it, then began bailing. A young man was whimpering. Lopez could not see who it was.

'Shut up,' said a Mexican fireman. 'How can one sleep with such a noise.' The whimperer, who was the brother of Tomas, fell silent.

'We must row a little,' said Lopez. 'To get away from it.' Oars were put out and the boat drew away from the floating body. Garrett and the Portuguese bailed hard. Much water had come into the boat during the interruption. Lopez sat hunched over the tiller thinking; first Jenkins, now Tomas. Who next?

One could understand about Tomas. He was not strong. With Jenkins it had been different. He was a big man, well covered. The trouble was in his mind, for he had not slept. He had spent the nights muttering to himself and each day his face had become more drawn, his eyes wilder. Quite suddenly, in the middle of a dark night, he'd dived over the side. Lopez and Thoresen had seen him go and shouted. He'd disappeared into the darkness, swimming strongly. They'd put out oars, turned the boat, searched with the Aldis lamp, but he was not seen again.

Two nights after Frascatti had cut the painter and deserted them, another storm had come suddenly in the darkness. Again the mast had broken. Where the splints were. The orange sail had torn clean across. Not that it mattered. The boat leaked so badly, it was not really possible to sail. The bows were always down and the energy of the men was consumed in bailing. It was after the mast had broken for the second time that Jenkins could no longer sleep.

For a few days now the sea had been calm and the currents had carried Lopez's boat far to the south and west under a blistering sun. There was food and water still, but men needed hope to survive and of that there was little. Perhaps, thought Lopez, it would be better to be with Jenkins and Tomas. At least their struggles were over.

20

Miss Kolbe's perfume fought Hassim Racher's cigar, the fragrance of one, the aroma of the other, masking the musty smell of old files, tired carpets and the car-like odour of artificial leather.

It wasn't that Mr Racher lacked fragrance for he was a much-scented man, sleek with well-creamed hair, carefully groomed moustache, expertly manicured hands quite unblemished by labour. Indeed, his appearance invariably suggested a recent visit to the barber. But his suits were too well cut, his ties too tightly knotted, his cuffs and handkerchiefs too formally on parade. In short his dress lacked the casual elegance he so much admired in others.

At the moment he was in a state of some excitement which arose neither from Miss Kolbe's perfume nor the pressure of her breasts as she leant over him to read the message he held; it was a cable from the agents in Port Louis announcing that Frascatti's boat had been picked up the day before by a Norwegian container ship.

Mr Racher put down the cable, looked at

Miss Kolbe, then at the *Daily Express* in which she had red pencilled a paragraph. Date-lined Sydney, it gave the same news. Both cable and press report referred to the *Moonraker* as *believed lost* after severe damage in a cyclone in the Indian Ocean early in November.

It was the *believed* which upset Mr Racher. 'Get me Lloyd's on the phone, Miss Kolbe. Mr Wilkinson. Casualty department.'

'Yes, Mr Racher.'

She dialled on the desk phone, got the casualty department and Mr Wilkinson to whom she spoke. He sighed, for there'd been many conversations with Mr Racher in recent weeks about the *Moonraker* which Lloyd's had first posted as *overdue* and latterly as *missing*.

''Morning, Mr Racher.'

'*Good* morning, Mr Wilkinson. You've heard the news?'

'About the *Moonraker*'s lifeboat. Yes. Splendid, isn't it?'

'Well,' Mr Racher was hesitant. 'What actually does *believed lost* mean?'

For a few moments Mr Wilkinson observed a shocked silence. 'I meant the rescue of those survivors was splendid,' he said.

'Ah, yes. Indeed. Of course. I was absolutely overcome when I heard the news.'

Mr Racher coughed discreetly. Behind his back Miss Kolbe made an unladylike gesture. He continued. 'I presume the *Moonraker* will now be posted on the casualty board as *lost*, Mr Wilkinson.'

'Not immediately, Mr Racher. Lloyd's Agents in Sydney will interview the survivors on arrival and report to us. Lloyd's Committee will consider the report and decide.'

'I see.' Mr Racher frowned. 'And once posted as lost — the underwriters will then pay out?'

'Not necessarily *immediately*, Mr Racher. Depends on the circumstances. The brokers and underwriters have to meet. Various procedures are involved.'

'What would you say in this case? There can be no doubt the ship is lost.'

'Not for me to say, Mr Racher. If the Committee decides she's lost I expect your claim will be met fairly quickly.'

Mr Racher beamed down the mouthpiece as if televising his pleasure. 'Of course, Mr Wilkinson. Thank you so much. But how astonishing. How truly remarkable that Frascatti and those fine fellows should be saved. I am so delighted.'

'Sad about the captain and his niece. And the others who didn't leave the ship.'

'Absolutely, Mr Wilkinson.' Mr Racher's

tone became sepulchral. 'The traditions of the sea, you know.'

'Yes,' said Mr Wilkinson. 'I know. Goodbye, Mr Racher.'

Mr Racher sat back in his chair, shot his cuffs, looked at his wristwatch, the desk calendar and Miss Kolbe in that order. The time was nine-fifty-seven a.m. The date, 30th November.

'I must fly to Sydney, Miss Kolbe. To arrive not later than the fifth of December.'

'You want to see Frascatti before . . .'

'I wish to meet him on arrival,' interrupted Mr Racher. 'And the other poor fellows. To make proper arrangements, you know. They have been through an absolutely frightful ordeal.'

Miss Kolbe wriggled her hips, pressing down the skirt with her hands. 'Of course. Will Lloyd's Underwriters pay out now?'

Mr Racher clicked his disapproval. 'It is the men I worry about. Only thirteen survivors. Think of the other poor fellows. What suffering.'

'Of course. I'll book you right away. To arrive on the fifth. The Norwegian ship gets there on the sixth, doesn't she?'

Mr Racher's eyes flickered. 'Better check with the Norwegian line before you make the reservation.'

'Certainly, *Mister* Racher.' She blew him a kiss as she minced out of the office, her bottom wiggling.

★ ★ ★

Bartot, the French geologist, brought interesting news to *Myfanwy*'s wheelhouse early in the afternoon of 30th November.

'Been listening to the Australian news service from Sydney,' he said. 'Yesterday a Norwegian ship picked up one of *Moonraker*'s lifeboats. Thirteen survivors including the first mate.'

Evans's eyes widened in surprise. 'Well then. That's good news.' He looked thoughtful. 'Did the report mention why they'd abandoned the ship? Leaving the master?'

Bartot said, 'Yes. It seems the captain, his niece, and two others would not go. How did you know this?'

'Calvi gave it me over the walkie-talkie yesterday. The *Moonraker*'s captain told him there was a mutiny led by the first mate. Afterwards they abandoned ship.'

Bartot whistled. 'Nothing was mentioned of mutiny. Sydney radio said the first mate had begged the captain to come with them. It seems the ship could not have survived for more than a day or so after they left.'

'Fine bloody seaman he must have been. They abandoned her on 14th November. She's still floating by the looks of her.' Evans jerked his thumb in *Moonraker*'s direction.

'Very strange, captain.' Bartot shook his head. 'They say there is still one lifeboat missing with fifteen men.'

Evans picked up his binoculars. 'That first mate's in for a surprise, isn't he? When we get this lot in.' He looked with affection at the freighter lumbering along astern. 'And now I'd better be passing the news to Calvi. No doubt Captain Stone . . . ' The radio telephone receiver in the wheelhouse crackled. It was Amsterdam Island calling *Myfanwy*. The call was repeated several times. 'You do not answer?' The Frenchman's eyebrows lifted in surprise. He did not know there'd been earlier calls which had gone unanswered.

'We can't,' said Evans. 'The transmitter's not working.' He removed the front of the set. 'See. Transmitting unit's gone. Dai Williams has it below.'

'What is the trouble?'

'Don't rightly know. First the fault was intermittent. Now it's packed up altogether. Expect he'll fix it. Clever fellow, Dai.'

Bartot said, 'That is unfortunate. I understand the *Moonraker* also cannot use radio.'

'That's right. Damaged in the cyclone.' Evans ran his hand over his beard. 'It would happen now, wouldn't it?' As he finished speaking they heard Amsterdam Island calling the weather station at Port-aux-Français. Contact was soon established.

'What is it they are saying, Bartot?'

The Frenchman held up his hand in a gesture of silence. 'A moment please.' The transmissions ceased. 'The man on Amsterdam Island is explaining that the *Myfanwy* was due there this morning but had not arrived. Also that he could get no radio response from you. Then they are agreeing that it is not necessary to worry. You had reported the transmitter trouble last night. Also that if the weather continued bad you might not call at Amsterdam Island because of the fuel problem.'

Evans was looking out of the wheelhouse windows at *Moonraker* rolling and pitching in the coaster's wake, sheets of white spray occasionally sweeping her. 'Yes,' he said. 'It's fortunate I spoke to them.'

★ ★ ★

By 3rd December those in *Myfanwy* and *Moonraker* had learnt a good deal about towing in bad weather. In particular the response of all concerned to yawing had speeded up after several hair-raising incidents on the first night when it had seemed certain the tow would part. Calvi and Le Clerc were now expert in detecting the first symptoms of a yaw, in knowing how much wheel to use and when to apply it. They had learned, too, the paramount importance of informing the coaster immediately of the onset of a yaw, and of not over-reacting with too much helm. The men in *Moonraker*'s steering compartment had mastered the muscular skills of turning the big wheel, and of keeping the freighter steady on a given course.

Evans had got star sights that morning and found the tow was making good close on four knots. One and a half of these he attributed to wind and current. If things went on as they were they'd be covering nearly one hundred miles a day. To his relief they were now north of latitude 39° south, clear of the northern limits of icebergs and growlers, and the air temperature was rising. Pumping was going well after initial difficulties which Calvi and Carelse the engineman had overcome. They estimated that one hundred and fifty tons of water was being got rid of each day. As a result the freighter's draught was decreasing and this lessened the towing burden. The diesel fuel in number one d.b. tank had been used up and the tank flooded thus increasing the coaster's draught aft. This, too, improved towing.

A close watch was being kept for chafing of the towing cables in the fairleads. Evans intended to halt the tow in a day or so to pay out a few cable links. That would ensure that chafing was not concentrated in the same places for too long.

*   *   *

In a befuddled way Captain Stone expressed pleasure on learning that Frascatti's boat had been picked up. And indeed he was pleased, but for different reasons. Kindly and humane by nature, he was pleased that so many lives had been saved. But he was also pleased because Frascatti, Thoresen and the rest would have to account for their conduct. Since *Moonraker* had not foundered and was now in tow, this was likely to prove difficult. Thinking about the mutiny, the anger and indignation he'd felt on that occasion returned. Through a veil of alcoholism he saw that he was a ruined man. Frascatti and others would testify to his drinking. The Italian had the deck logbook. The decisions which had caused *Moonraker* to blunder into the path of the cyclone would be only too clear from the logbook. Even if Frascatti had lost it, it would make no difference. The fair copy in the *Moonraker* had been written up regularly, latterly by the Australian. Stone, for all his weaknesses, was too decent a man to destroy or falsify a logbook. He had never intended to conceal his mistake. He had, in his alcoholic fuddle, hoped to absolve it by sailing the ship into Sydney.

'Frascatti will pay for his mutinous conduct,' he muttered. He did not really mind what happened to the others. Frascatti was the ringleader and it was he who had humiliated him. In his mind's eye he saw the dark scowling face. 'Insolent swine,' he muttered. 'Damned foreigner. Calling himself a first mate.'

The thought of foreigners brought to mind the two Frenchmen on the bridge. The events of the last few days had made him burn with injustice. He'd been pushed aside, disregarded in his own ship. Mostly by that fellow — what was his name? Calvin, Calvi? Another foreigner. And a youngster at that. What did he know about towage? Harold Stone had towed and been towed when the Frenchman was still sucking at his mother's teats.

Having worked himself into a high state of indignation he went to the sleeping cabin, locked the door and pulled out the mahogany drawer.

★ ★ ★

Dwala was a worried man. He could not find time in his two hour spells off watch to look after Captain Stone properly, to help Susie, and to sleep. Like others on board, notably Calvi and Casey, he was short of sleep. But despite Susie's insistence that she could manage the cooking (and that the captain, like the rest of them, must do his own cleaning and bed-making), Dwala persisted in his efforts.

One result of the shortage of sleep from which all suffered was their increasingly unkempt appearance. There was not enough time off watch to clean living spaces, wash clothes or attend to anything more than basic hygiene. The men, tired and hollow-eyed, had stubble-covered faces and unwashed bodies.

Susie, as cook, was a day worker and could have slept regularly. This seemed to her so unfair that during the night she would get up and prepare food and cocoa for those on watch. Never really dress conscious, her denim slacks, thick jersey and slip-on shoes showed increasing signs of neglect. Her only concession to femininity was the ribbon with which she tied her hair: 'to keep it out of the cooking,' she explained.

She was always cheerful, and alone in the galley she would sing or talk to herself or the parakeet. But, like Dwala, Susie had problems. One was her uncle. He seemed wholly lost now to alcohol. The cabin door was locked most of the time and she saw little of him. On those occasions when she did he would be asleep on his bunk, or sitting in an armchair staring vacantly at nothing, the smell of gin hanging over him like an invisible cloud. Sometimes she would find him working on the model. In slurred speech he would explain some detail of the rig or problem of getting the ship to Sydney under sail.

Her other worry was Napoleon Calvi. He lived on the bridge night and day and seemed rarely to sleep. When Le Clerc relieved him, the Corsican would rest on the chart house settee, but it was invariably broken rest. Every wheel order Le Clerc gave on the wheelhouse phone penetrated Calvi's subconscious, and if any sounded untoward he would run to the bridge to see what was happening.

If he were to crack up, if anything were to happen to him, Susie would ask herself, what would they do? There was no one to take his place. That subjective reasoning was valid enough. What she didn't acknowledge was that Calvi was important to her in another dimension. He was the hero in her saga. His dramatic entrance, the assuredness with which he'd taken command, his aura of authority: these things impressed themselves deeply on Susie's eighteen years. When she got up in the night to make cocoa and prepare snacks of ship's biscuits and tinned food for the men on watch, it was him she thought of. When a tray had to be taken to the bridge, day or night, then for her the important moment had arrived. If he was on watch and busy, as he mostly was, she would put the tray in the chart house, wedging it against the movement of the ship, and tell him it was there. If he was on the settee resting, he almost always seemed to hear her arrive. He would sit up then and take the tray from her, thanking her formally as if this were a service he expected. Despite her efforts to talk, to get to know him, he rarely responded.

Susie never felt rebuffed. On the bridge he is absorbed in his duties, she reasoned; and in the chart house he is in need of sleep. Of course he hasn't time to talk to me.

Casey, too, had his problems. One was Susie. Sometimes, off-watch, he would forgo sleeping to visit the galley or her cabin. But she was elusive and preoccupied. Her solicitude for Calvi was apparent — she wasn't good at hiding things — and Casey, tired and frustrated, grew jealous. This emotion wasn't helped by his knowledge that since Calvi's arrival on board *Moonraker*, he'd been pushed aside. Before that he'd virtually commanded the ship: taken noon sights, plotted the position, written up the logbook, and made such decisions as had to be made in the captain's absence. It was he who had dived for the missing part, got the diesel generator going, made the pumping possible and given them electric lights.

In taking command of the ship Napoleon Calvi had taken away *his* command, had assigned to him menial duties: like manning the hand-steering with Dwala — they worked in the same watch — and in his brief spells off duty attending if necessary to the diesel generator and pumping with Carelse the engineman.

Reflecting upon these imagined slights and real hardships the Australian managed to convince himself that Calvi had it in for him. Why else had the Corsican chosen the French geologist to work on the bridge with him? And why was Susie so offhand when he tried to chat her up, to discuss the problems of hand-steering and pumping? Only the night before, when putting things on a tray in the galley, she'd interrupted him. 'Sorry, Hank. I'm busy. Got to take these things along.'

'Along where?'

'To the bridge. For Napoleon.'

Casey scowled at her. 'Napoleon bloody Bonaparte. Tell him to shove them,' he'd added, walking away in disgust.

★　★　★

Casey came off the wheel at two o'clock on a dark wet morning and went to the galley for a brew of cocoa. The wooden tray with fiddles which Susie used for carrying meals was missing. He gave up the idea of cocoa and made for her cabin. It was empty.

In his own cabin, three doors away, he exchanged sea boots for rubber soled slip-ons. Then he made for the bridge, using the internal stairway. On the way he looked into the chart house. Le Clerc was asleep on the settee. Susie's tray was on the chart table, the things on it untouched. He went through the darkened wheelhouse, opened the lee-ward door and stepped out on to the bridge.

Serried ranks of cloud hurried overhead, driven by the westerly wind which whistled in the rigging in an unscored concerto with the sea. Ahead he could see the arc light on the coaster's stern. Before his eyes had become accustomed to the darkness he heard voices on the starboard side of the bridge.

One was Susie's. 'Oh, Napoleon. *Look out!*' She was laughing.

The Corsican laughed too, said something in his deep voice which Casey couldn't understand. The moon broke through the cloud ridges and he saw them on the bridge not far away.

Calvi was holding the girl in his arms.

21

The ship came up from the roll and Calvi put the girl down. '*Prenez-garde, mam'selle* — be careful,' he said. In the moonlight he saw, beyond her, a man. It was the Australian. The girl said, 'Hi Hank.'

Casey pushed her out of his way and faced Calvi. 'So Napoleon would a-wooing go,' he said hoarsely.

Susie sensed danger. 'Hank, what are you ... ' she broke off as he slapped the Corsican's face. 'You're here to salvage the ship,' he said. 'Not get fresh with my girl.'

'Stop it!' Susie shrilled. 'He was only ... '

What was happening was beyond Calvi's comprehension. He hadn't understood what the Australian was saying. The noise of the wind and sea had masked the girl's approach, and he'd not known she was there until the ship rolled to starboard and she'd fallen against him in the darkness. 'Oh, Napoleon. Look out!' she'd cried, laughing with embarrassment. The bridge was slippery from the rain and he'd caught her. '*Bon*,' he'd said. 'You shall not fall.' He, too, had laughed as he held her, waiting for the ship to come on to an even keel. Then he'd put her down and the Australian had appeared. While he rubbed his face, the truth dawned on him. 'You have made a mistake, *m'sieu*. You should not . . . '

Casey's reply was to hit him again. 'Come on lover boy. What's wrong? Chicken, huh?' The Australian was the bigger man but the Corsican, thickset and stocky, had grown up in a hard school. If the Australian was looking for a fight he'd got one. Calvi waded in, fists flailing.

Susie screamed. 'Stop it! Oh, please, stop it! You're both crazy.'

But they were past hearing. The roll and pitch of the ship, the waning and waxing of the moon as it filtered through the clouds, the girl hammering with clenched fists on the backs of the two men, screaming at them to stop, made the fight a bizarre affair of lunging figures, muttered oaths, the dull thud of punches, sudden snorting, the sharp intake of breath, the urgent scuffle of feet. In desperation the girl ran to the chart house and shook Le Clerc. 'Come,' she sobbed. 'Come at once. They're fighting.'

Le Clerc propped himself up on an elbow, rubbing his eyes. 'Who fights?'

'Napoleon and Hank Casey,' she said. 'Stop them! Please stop them!'

'*Sacré Dieu*,' he gasped. 'What of the ship?'

He ran into the wheelhouse and heard the coaster's siren sounding repeatedly. Evans's voice came crackling through the walkie-talkie. 'Starboard your wheel, Calvi. Starboard your wheel, man. You'll have the bloody tow parting.'

With one hand Le Clerc grabbed the phone to the steering-compartment. 'Hard-a-starboard,' he yelled. '*Vite!* Quick.' With the other he seized the walkie-talkie. 'Wheel's hard-a-starboard, Captain Evans.'

There was suppressed anger in Evans's voice. 'The wire's hove taut. I'm going astern. Maybe too late. Steady her on east-north-east. Smart as you can, Le Clerc.'

Outside on the bridge Calvi heard, dimly in the distance, the blast of the coaster's siren. It brought him to his senses, dissipated the sudden rage into which the Australian's assault had thrown him. Now he must finish quickly what the other had started.

The ship rolled towards him and he pretended to slip, going down on one knee. The Australian came rushing at him, using the roll of the ship. Calvi leapt forward and upwards to meet him in a crouching butt, his head hitting Casey's face with the combined weight of both men. Calvi heard more than felt the crunch of flesh and bone. The next moment he stood back, watching the

Australian swaying in front of him. As the ship rolled to port Calvi aimed a kick at Casey's groin.

That was the end of the fight.

The Australian lay on the bridge groaning, the girl bending over him. Calvi staggered to the wheelhouse. He saw Le Clerc talking into the phone. 'Le bon Dieu,' he gasped, going back to the bridge. With dismay he saw the bright glow of the coaster's arc light wide on the port bow. It should have been ahead.

★ ★ ★

It took all Evans's seamanship to prevent the tow parting, to get both ships back into station and steady on the course for Fremantle.

When this had been done his anger communicated itself all too clearly over the walkie-talkie. 'What the bloody hell's been happening over there? Where's Calvi?'

Wearily, Calvi replied, 'The Australian make a fight with me.'

'A fight? What for?'

'The girl.'

There was a pause and in the Moonraker's wheelhouse they could hear Evans's heavy breathing. Then his voice, cold and challenging. 'Have you gone bloody mad?'

'*Pas du tout*. It is he who is crazy. He makes the fight. For nothing.'

'Fine bloody nothing. Nearly parted the tow. What started it, for chrissake?'

'It is too much to explain, captain. Ask Le Clerc. He can tell you.' With an expression of disgust Calvi handed the mike to the Frenchman.

'Captain Evans? Le Clerc here. It was not at all the fault of Calvi. The girl herself says so. She brings the cocoa to the chart house, then slips on the bridge and Calvi catches her. The Australian comes at that moment to the bridge. He thinks it is love. He makes a fight.'

'Sounds a damn' fishy story to me. And who do they think watches the bloody tow while they fight?'

'It is not possible for Calvi to escape from the fight. The girl call me and I was taking charge.'

'Well, that was a good thing anyway. We came damn' near to parting.'

'I saw it, captain. The wire was lying straight. Shivering like . . . I don't know.' Le Clerc spread a hand in dismay. The receiver went silent but for the crackle of atmospherics. Then Evans came on the air again. 'Is everything settled there now?' It was still anger more than concern.

'Yes, captain. The Australian has left the bridge. He has some damage.'

'What damage?'

'When Calvi finish him. The face, you know. Also between the legs.'

'Nothing like a good kick in the balls,' said Evans unsympathetically. 'And how's Calvi?'

'He is all right. Just lose the wind. And have one black eye.

'The same one,' Le Clerc added significantly.

'You can tell him from me, any more of that and he'll get more than a bloody black eye.'

'It was not the fault of Calvi, captain.' Le Clerc was becoming impatient. 'I have already told you.' With quiet authority he added, 'The girl must go. If she stay there will be more trouble. Also the uncle drinks too much. It is bad for her here.'

'Go where?' said Evans.

'To your ship, captain. She cannot stay here. We have already discussed it. Calvi and myself. He insists.'

'Listen,' growled Evans. 'I'm the one around here who does the insisting.'

Le Clerc hesitated for a moment. 'Unless she goes Calvi will not accept responsibility. Myself also.'

'Right,' said Evans. 'She'll bloody go.

To-morrow. The glass is rising. Wind and sea moderating.'

'At what time, captain?'

'Don't worry about that. I'll let you know soon enough. Now let's get on with the tow.'

* * *

Towards dawn Le Clerc left Calvi on the bridge and went below to see how Casey was getting on. The Australian was stretched out on his bunk, the cabin light on, the girl sponging his face.

'You all right?' Le Clerc asked gently.

The Australian rolled his head towards him. 'That bastard doesn't fight clean. He butted. Then kicked.'

Le Clerc saw that a tooth was missing. He wondered what damage there was below. 'All right otherwise?'

Susie saw where the Frenchman was looking. She blushed. 'Yes. Just bruised. Very painful, I think.'

'I am sure.' There was the ghost of a smile at the corners of Le Clerc's mouth. 'Calvi also has damage. But let us forget. It is finished. The ship is the thing of importance. We have to save her.'

'That bastard butted and kicked.'

'Shush,' admonished Susie. 'Don't speak

347

like that, Hank. You started the fight.'

'Okay, so I did.' The Australian's speech was slurred by swollen lips. 'That's no reason to fight dirty.'

'Ah, the butt with the head, and the kick. It is the *coup de grâce*,' said Le Clerc philosophically. 'To make the end of the fight.'

'What's wrong with fists for that?'

Le Clerc smiled. 'You should 'ave seen my uncle Ferdinand. Then you would understand what is *coup de grâce*. He was magnificent. For him, after the head butt, the double kick. Left, then right. With both feet off the ground at the same time. Can you imagine? He was never losing the fight.' A reminiscent look came into Le Clerc's eyes. 'Yes. The double kick. Like the shuffle of Cassius Clay. But more dangerous.' He chuckled, leaning over to examine the Australian's face. '*Ma foi!* he exclaimed. '*Quel dommage!*'

★ ★ ★

On the afternoon of 3rd December, a Russian fishery survey vessel based on Port Louis sighted a water-logged lifeboat seven hundred and twenty miles south of Mauritius.

The Russian captain recorded in his logbook that the lifeboat was from the

Liberian registered steamship *Moonraker*, severely damaged in a cyclone 8/9th November, abandoned by her crew on 14th November. Her captain and three others had remained on board. There were nine survivors in the boat including one Martinho Lopez, the second mate; Nils Thoresen, the second engineer; and William Garrett, the cook. All were suffering from exposure in varying degree. Four were stretcher cases. Six men had perished according to the survivors' reports.

The Russian vessel landed the survivors in Port Louis on the night of 5th December. They were at once taken to hospital.

★   ★   ★

Five minutes after the take-off from London Airport, Hassim Racher leant back relaxed and unruffled for the first time that day. He disliked flying. The fuss and bother at airports, the irritations and indignities imposed by officialdom, the long waits while bored female voices made interminable announcements — tucked away among them one for you, so that you had to listen to all. But most of all he disliked the prolonged agony of the take-off. Taxiing out, sitting in that long metal tube, even in the comparative comfort of first class, speculating on the inflammability of the décor, the nearest emergency exit — and whom one might have to fight to reach it: these things played on Mr Racher's nerves. As for the take-off itself, it was an event which never failed to terrify him. To have to put one's life in the hands of so many people over whom one had absolutely no control: air crews, ground crews, flight controllers. Of course it was said the aircrew were as keen as the passengers on staying alive, but Mr Racher wasn't sure of this. If they were as keen as he was they wouldn't fly for a living. As for the ground crews and flight controllers? Well, they were taking absolutely no risks at all.

He undid the seat belt, loosened the waistband of his trousers and sat back looking through the papers Miss Kolbe had handed him at the airport, checking the flight schedules and the letter of introduction to Lloyd's agents in Sydney. He replaced everything neatly in the black pigskin briefcase and stuck it under his seat. Everything, that is, except the latest issues of *Playboy* and *The Director*. These he put on the empty aisle seat next to him, *The Director* on top. It was desirable that other passengers in the first class should be given some clue to his status. Later *Playboy* might be used for chatting up a hostess. He always concentrated on one. Made her feel special. Got her to sit next to him. Showed her the pictures. They were a useful catalyst.

With a critical eye he appraised these young ladies. The dark one with the severe fringe? No. Eyes too hard, legs too thin. The girl with the high cheek bones, green eyes and auburn hair? Yes. Nice legs, good thighs and firm breasts. She was coming down the aisle now with a bundle of newspapers. 'Paper, sir?' She smiled at him, leaning across the empty seat to offer him one. He took *The Financial Times* and *Daily Express*.

'I'd like a scotch-on-the-rocks,' Mr Racher told her. 'No hurry. Soon as you've time.' His teeth flashed like a white neon sign under the black moustache.

'Certainly, sir.' Soft red lips drew back over milk white teeth and he basked in the warmth of her smile. Elegant and refined, he decided. That was what she was. Back in the pantry she said to black fringe, 'There's a lecherous little bastard out there can't keep his eyes off my tits.'

'When he asks for your phone number give him the vice-squad's.'

'I'll do that, honey.'

Mr Racher, waiting for the scotch-on-the-rocks, devoted some thought to his mission.

The important thing was to see Frascatti before the press and Lloyd's agents got at him. Next priority was to make himself *persona grata* with those agents. It was largely upon their report to London that Lloyd's Committee would decide if and when to settle.

It was incredibly good luck, he reflected, that *Moonraker* had been lost at that moment in time when the affairs of Gimbal Ocean Carriers Limited were not exactly flourishing. The three dry cargo carriers he owned, built in the early fifties, were becoming an embarrassment. Costs had risen steeply for these elderly ships. They could not compete with containerisation. Full cargoes were increasingly difficult to come by, manning problems were formidable and now freight rates were falling. Of course a useful tax loss had been built up by the company but one couldn't operate indefinitely on that basis.

The *Moonraker* was well insured. It had always been in his mind — a hopeful possibility like the sudden demise of an aged benefactor — that the ship might be lost. That, indeed, had been why, knowing Captain Stone's weakness, he'd given him command. Mr Racher had tended to think in terms of a stranding. That had seemed the most likely mishap. Not an ideal one, of course, because there was always the chance of a refloating. But to founder in a cyclone. That was absolutely magnificent. A total loss. Final, decisive, irrevocable.

The funds he would receive in settlement of the claim were already earmarked for a property venture. He had recently taken over a small 'shell' company to that end. All that was required now was the injection of capital. With the eight hundred thousand pounds he hoped to get from Lloyd's he could raise a substantial sum in the City. The new project would be a big one. The biggest he'd yet tackled. Something beyond his wildest dreams ten years ago when, as a bank clerk in Beirut, he'd decided to put his expertise to the test in the City of London.

The scotch-on-the-rocks arrived and the auburn-haired girl leant over the empty seat proffering the tray. Mr Racher's eyes peered deeply into her blouse as he took the glass. Yes. They were a lovely pair. Firm, scarcely in need of support, the nipples small but prominent. There was plenty of time. Later he'd show her *Playboy*, ask for her opinion. Chat her up. Get her telephone number. No point in rushing one's jumps. Mr Racher was not to know that flight BA 718 would take on a new crew in Rome.

★ ★ ★

Hassim Racher was on the quay in Port Jackson Harbour, Sydney, when the container ship docked. It was a fine morning, hot after the chill of the London December from which he'd just escaped. He took this to be a good augury and was in high spirits. There were several groups of men on the quay. One he readily identified as press and broadcast. A flicker of annoyance crossed his face. Why did the mass media always poke their noses into other people's business? Two well-dressed men standing alone held his attention. Could they be the representatives of Lloyd's?

He had taken the precaution, through the Sydney agents of Gimbal Ocean Carriers Limited, of informing Frascatti by radio that he would meet the ship. With the assistance of the agents he'd obtained special permission to board the vessel immediately on arrival. Mr Racher was accompanied by a lugubrious young man, a clerk from the agents' office. It had been arranged that on boarding the ship Mr Racher would contact Frascatti and his men, whereas the clerk would go to the captain's cabin to inquire what formalities if any were required from the owners of *Moonraker* at that juncture.

With the aid of tugs the ship was warped

354

alongside, mooring ropes were made fast, cranes rumbled up their tracks, a gangway was lifted into position, and Mr Racher and the clerk went on board with the customs and immigration officials.

A scowling Frascatti, his face and lips still recovering from severe sunburn, met them at the head of the gangway. Mr Racher, who scarcely remembered him — they'd met once, briefly, in Captain Stone's cabin when the *Moonraker* was in London Docks — greeted him warmly. 'My dear Frascatti,' he said wringing the Italian's hand briskly and showing no signs of letting go. 'How absolutely splendid to see you, my dear boy. My heartfelt sympathy for your suffering. Tell me, where are the other brave fellows?'

Frascatti jerked a thumb in the direction of a small group of men leaning over the side gazing dully at the concrete-clad undulations of Sydney.

'Come, Mr Frascatti.' Mr Racher moved at once in their direction. 'I must speak to them.' With almost indecent haste, but quietly so that onlookers would not hear, he suggested that it would be much in their interests when questioned by reporters and others, to emphasise that *Moonraker* had been in imminent danger of sinking when they left her. 'Otherwise,' he said, looking round conspiratorially, 'there can be awkward questions. Why did you not stay with the captain and the others. Of course, *I* understand.' He nodded sympathetically. 'Men like you would never leave a ship unless it was absolutely certain she was about to sink. But you must not do yourselves an injustice by suggesting the *Moonraker* might have remained afloat.' He need not have worried. Frascatti had briefed them thoroughly. They had no intention of doing themselves an injustice.

Mr Racher switched from caution to geniality. 'You have had terrible sufferings,' he said. 'Now is the time to rest and relax. Enjoy yourselves. Forget your hardships. Reservations have been made for you in a hotel in Bourke Street (it was in fact a boarding house) where you will have every comfort — all at the expense of the Company. The agents will pay all wages due, and advance you other monies for clothing, etcetera.' Mr Racher paused to dab his lips with an unfolded white handkerchief of purest Irish linen. 'There is no hurry. Take your time. Enjoy the sun . . . ' He checked himself, they'd had rather too much of that lately. ' . . . I mean go down to Bondi Beach, see the girls, have fun.' He winked wickedly. It was not necessary, he felt, to inform them that since *Moonraker* was a Liberian registered ship, and they were not British, the prospects of a free passage home as Distressed British Seamen were remote. Sailors, however, were restless beings and once they'd spent their money they would, he fervently hoped, find berths in other ships and be off to sea again. That would be the cheapest solution for Gimbal Ocean Carriers Limited.

'And listen to this, boys.' Mr Racher beamed, holding an arm aloft to command silence. 'To-morrow night we celebrate your safe return. I give a dinner in your honour. At the Carlton-Rex. There will be champagne, caviar, cigars. The best of everything.'

The faint chorus of approval was interrupted by the arrival of immigration officials. Mr Racher left the survivors feeling he'd struck the right note. With Frascatti he set out for the captain's cabin. There he would express in suitable terms the heartfelt gratitude of Gimbal Ocean Carriers Limited.

★ ★ ★

Susie's transfer to the coaster on 7th December in much improved weather presented few technical problems though it was not without its human ones.

Evans slowed down the tow until the way

was almost off the *Moonraker*, keeping just sufficient weight on the tow-line to keep it clear of *Myfanwy*'s screw. The inflatable life-raft was hauled across from the freighter with the girl on board, accompanied by Msutu the Zulu seaman. Once she'd been delivered to the coaster, *Myfanwy*'s cook, Kleinbooi, a Cape coloured, joined Msutu on the life-raft and together they were hauled back to the *Moonraker*. During this time both ships eased their cables so that a new set of links took the chafing in the fairleads.

Susie had resolutely opposed the transfer. There had been angry scenes, tears and recriminations when Calvi told her of the decision. But he was adamant. And so, surprisingly, was Casey who liked the idea of getting her away from Calvi. Though he'd accepted her explanation of how she'd ended up in the Corsican's arms, he still had niggling doubts.

Since the *Moonraker* could not manage without a cook, Evans had agreed to exchange Kleinbooi for Susie on condition she cooked for the *Myfanwy*'s crew. Once on board she'd run up to the wheelhouse to tell him what she thought of the transfer. 'I was forced into this,' she protested, eyes flashing. 'Treated like a blooming bale of wool. I might have drowned in that rubber raft.'

'Not with Msutu around,' soothed Evans. 'He's a fine swimmer.'

'Well the whole thing's wrong.' She stamped her foot. 'Why should I be *forced* to leave the *Moonraker*. And my uncle wasn't even asked.'

Evans stared at her. 'You've been moved because you make trouble. Young men fighting over you.'

'That was a misunderstanding.' There was the faintest trace of a smile.

Evans was tired, worried and anxious to get the tow started. 'Well, then. With you here there'll be no more misunderstandings, will there? Now, I've work to do and no time to argue. There's work for you in the galley. Best get on with it.' He left the wheelhouse for the bridgewalk where he focused his binoculars on the freighter.

She followed him, at first defiant, then, on reflection, acquiescent. This was a rather frightening man. Uncompromising brown eyes and a bearded craggy face like a bit of rough-hewn rock. He was younger than she'd expected. 'Where am I to sleep?' she asked with new politeness.

With his back to her he said, 'In the mate's cabin.'

'And the mate? Where'll he sleep?'

'He's in the *Moonraker*, isn't he?'

She'd forgotten that Calvi was mate of the coaster. Somehow the knowledge that she would be sleeping in his cabin, among his things, pleased her. She was still angry with him about the transfer but he was, nonetheless, a heroic figure.

* * *

The tow was under way again by eleven-fifteen a.m., the operation of transferring Susie and easing the cables having taken just under two hours. The *Moonraker* towed better now with close on a thousand tons of water pumped out of the engine-room and stokehold and the coaster's stern deeper in the water thanks to the flooding of number one d.b. ballast tank, and the steadily improving weather.

* * *

That afternoon the thing Merfyr Evans had feared most, happened. They sighted a ship, hull down on the horizon. Watching it through binoculars he was a worried man for he saw that it was steering a southerly course, one which might bring it close to the coaster and her tow. And what sort of ship would it be, steering a southerly course in these

360

remote waters? An ocean salvage tug? The one class of ship which, above all others, he desired not to meet.

Fifteen minutes later he was able to identify the vessel: it was a whale-catcher. The season started in early December in southern waters. She would be bound for the Antarctic. This knowledge reassured him, particularly when he saw that her course would take her astern of the tow.

But his optimism was short-lived. When little more than two miles away the whale-catcher altered course and made directly for the *Myfanwy*. Soon after six o'clock she was steaming on an almost parallel course, a few hundred yards on the coaster's port beam. It was possible now to read her name and port of registration.

She was the whale-catcher *Shodo* 4 of Kobe, Japan.

22

The *Shodo 4* edged in closer, steaming on a parallel course until she was less than a hundred yards from the *Myfanwy*.

Merfyr Evans could see men in the whale-catcher's wheelhouse. A window there opened and a man called them by loud-hailer. His broken English was Jap-U.S. inflected. 'What place you from, captain? Where you go?'

'From Kerguelen, bound Fremantle,' Evans answered by loud-hailer.

'Is help necessary?'

'No, thank you, All is well.'

'What for trouble other ship?'

'Damaged in heavy weather. Flooded engine-room and stokehold.'

There was a pause while the Japanese captain considered the implications. 'What place you find other ship?'

'South of Amsterdam Island. Twenty-ninth November.'

'We see name *Moonraker*, Monrovia. Same time before we catch signal for this ship. They find already boats with crew.'

'That's right. But her captain and three

others are still aboard. And some of my crew.'
Evans didn't mention the mutiny. There was
only the word of a drunken master for that.
What's more the Welshman wasn't sure how a
mutiny — if there had been one — affected
the salvage award. The less said the better, he
decided.

'How we no catch signal if you report find
this ship?' asked *Shodo* 4.

Merfyr Evans didn't like that one, but there
was no way of ducking it. He couldn't say:
'Maybe you weren't keeping radio watch at
the time.' Bartot the geologist, standing next
to him, knew that no radio message had been
sent.

Evans raised the loud-hailer. 'Our radio
transmitter is out of order. We've been
working on it for days.' He added, 'Re-
assembling it right now.' He decided it was
time he asked some questions. 'What is your
ship doing here alone, captain?'

'Other catchers with factory ship one
hundred eighty miles south. We stop for
condenser trouble this morning. Now go
catch factory ship.'

'Good luck to you. And good hunting.'

'Same for you, captain. What time you
come Fremantle?'

'December sixteenth, I reckon.'

'Okay. I make radio report to factory ship.

She will inform all stations.'

Evans frowned. He feared this, yet there was nothing he could do about it. 'Thanks for the offer, captain, but please don't trouble. I'll be making a full radio report tonight. Soon as the transmitter's fixed.'

'No trouble, captain. Factory ship make report all same time. Maybe your transmitter not work good tonight.'

'Blast his oriental guts,' muttered Evans. 'Why doesn't he leave us alone.' Without enthusiasm he said, 'Thank you.'

'Good-bye, captain. Good tow.' The Japanese captain took off his cap and waved it as *Shodo* 4 sounded a long blast of farewell on her siren and turned away to the south. Within minutes they heard her calling the factory ship. An exchange in Japanese followed. Evans couldn't understand it but he didn't need to. The secret was out. In no time the information would be re-broadcast. Ship and shore stations throughout the Southern Ocean would be listening in. The world would know that the coaster *Myfanwy* of Cardiff had the missing *Moonraker* in tow, bound for Fremantle.

Evans cursed his luck. A salvage tug, maybe two, would have looked up *Myfanwy* in Lloyd's Register, seen that she was small and low-powered, and made their decision.

However, he'd got the freighter in tow and in terms of salvage, as in much else, possession was nine points of the law. But captains of ocean salvage tugs were not easily deterred from muscling in on a deal. Salvage was their business, they were fine seamen and their vessels were superbly equipped. They seldom missed a trick.

Evans went into the chart room and brought the coaster's position up to date: 37° 20′ S: 94° 42′ E by dead reckoning: distance to Fremantle one thousand and fifty-five miles. For some time he leant over the chart frowning at the new problem. Then he made up his mind. When the Japanese whale-catcher was out of sight he'd make a radical alteration of course. Steam to the south-east for twenty-four hours. That would add a day to the journey to Fremantle and eat a little more into his reserves of diesel oil, but it would confuse any searcher working on the position given by the factory ship. In twenty-four hours, on the new course, the tow would be a hundred miles south of its D.R. position had it maintained the north-easterly course. A salvage tug, failing to find the tow would, Evans hoped, suspect an evasive alteration of course to the north — away from the Roaring Forties, not towards them as he intended to go.

* * *

The dinner party in a private room in Sydney's fashionable Carlton-Rex had got off to a splendid start. In addition to Hassim Racher the host, the thirteen survivors and a junior partner from the agents' office, there were two ladies: the junior partner's wife, a pleasant smiling girl, and a tall strapping blonde, a receptionist at Mr Racher's hotel. Although he hoped later that night to acquaint himself more explicitly with the blonde's splendid proportions, he had in fact invited her so that the junior partner's wife would not be the only lady present. Mr Racher felt that the presence of ladies would exercise a restraining influence upon the survivors. Sailors, he knew, were a rough lot and when in wine no respecters of persons, even members of the Institute of Directors.

The long table in the mirrored dining-room gleamed with white napery, sparkling glass, shining silver, gay flowers and wine-oiled faces. At Mr Racher's request the chef had produced an impressive centre-piece: a model of the *Moonraker* in icing sugar and sweetmeats. Mr Racher, grateful that this was the last he would see of the old freighter — and yet not a little sentimental on that account — had instructed that no expense should be spared to make the dinner a success. Since the expense would be borne by Gimbal Ocean Carriers Limited directly, and by Lloyd's underwriters indirectly, Mr Racher's generosity was in no way inhibited.

Dressed in quaintly diverse fashion the guests had gathered in the ante-room before dinner and consumed considerable quantities of what Mr Racher had offered as 'a little apéritif, gentlemen, to freshen our taste buds.' The apéritif, served from cut-glass beakers, was a dry martini superbly mixed. One Mexican fireman, questioned by another as to the nature of the brew, thought it might be frozen kangaroo water from the outback, but nonetheless acceptable at that.

Numerous infusions of the apéritif had dissipated such diffidence as the guests might have felt on arrival and an atmosphere of warmth and geniality prevailed. Mr Racher sat at the head of the long table, Carlo Frascatti at the opposite end. The junior partner's wife sat on Mr Racher's right, the large blonde on Frascatti's.

Stories of a robustly permissive nature were producing howls of laughter, O'Halloran and the big blonde vying with each other with Eisteddfod-like zeal. Mr Racher was shocked. It seemed to him absolutely immoral that such stories should be told in front of ladies;

indeed, at times, by a lady. He wondered what the world was coming to.

For once Carlo Frascatti's scowl was absent. That morning he had bought another parakeet for Violetta. An even more beautiful bird. The thought of her joy when she saw it, the euphoria induced by the wine and occasional sorties under the table in the general direction of the blonde's thighs, all combined to put him in excellent humour.

The *Alaska Surprise* had come flaming, been consumed, washed away with champagne, and gone; the port had been passed (and a good deal else by the survivors who beat a general retreat after the *Surprise*, returning in animated groups shortly afterwards) cigars had been lit and a pleasantly relaxed atmosphere prevailed.

This, decided Mr Racher, was the moment. Rising to his feet he rapped the table firmly. 'Ladies and gentlemen,' he announced amid cries for silence. 'The time has come for me to say a few words. I can assure you I will be brief.'

There were shouts of approval, someone upset a wine glass, waiters came hurrying and the large blonde said, 'Bet your backside he won't.'

Mr Racher drew on his cigar as if to gather strength, inserted a hand Napoleon-like under the lapel of his coat, cleared his throat and launched forth. 'First, on behalf of Gimbal Ocean Carriers Limited, congratulations to you all on your magnificent achievement in surviving your great ordeal. I include in this your companions in Mauritius who, as you know, arrived there a day or so ago. They are still, alas, in hospital, but getting on fine.'

Carlo Frascatti's smile was wiped away by this reminder of news he would have preferred to forget.

'To make that voyage in open boats,' continued Mr Racher, pulling at the lobe of his ear. 'To survive as you did under such absolutely shocking conditions — that, gentlemen, required courage and leadership.' He put his hand to his mouth and coughed discreetly. 'Unhappily your ship was lost in the great depths of the ocean. Tragically, some of your brave companions — shipmates should I say — have died. Not least that fine gentleman Captain Stone, his beautiful niece and the — the other two.' Mr Racher had forgotten their names.

'But let me say that their efforts — and yours — have not been in vain. The finest traditions of the sea have been upheld . . . '

The door behind him flung open and a young man came into the room. The junior partner recognised him as a colleague from the office.

'Sorry to interrupt,' cried the newcomer, 'but there's fantastic news.' He handed Mr Racher a message. 'For you, sir.'

What Mr Racher read was commendably brief: *Japanese factory ship* SHODO *reports missing Liberian freighter* MOONRAKER *sighted to-day in tow British coaster* MYFANWY *approx. 1050 miles south-south-west of Fremantle. ETA that port 16th December. Captain and others on board freighter well.*

Mr Racher shook his head in disbelief. 'Impossible,' he muttered brokenly. 'Quite absolutely impossible.' But having read the message a second time, he realised that though impossible it must have happened. In sudden fury he turned on Frascatti. 'You have lied to me.' His face puckered with emotion. 'You and your *brave* companions. Now you have some explanations to make.'

The guests watched, some puzzled, some apprehensive, others amused, at their host's sudden discomfiture. All were wondering what could have caused it.

Frascatti said, 'I dunno of what you talk.'

'You soon will.' Mr Racher trembled with indignation. 'Listen to this.' He read the message aloud, slowly and with emphasis. A shocked silence followed. It was broken by the big blonde. 'But that's fabulous. Why aren't you dumb bums jumping for joy?'

Mr Racher collapsed into a chair, burying his face in his hands. But he soon recovered. 'I'm going now,' he called to the junior partner. 'Pack up this dinner. Get this lot out of here. No more drinks. No more smokes. Finished. *Kaput*.' To a chorus of boos and rather ruder noises he strode from the room, slamming the double doors behind him.

When he'd gone his astonished guests were left to consider the implications of what they'd heard.

★　★　★

The ocean salvage tug *Adventurer* returning to her base in Albany, Western Australia, after towing an oil rig to St Augustine Bay on the south-west coast of Madagascar, picked up an unusual signal at eight p.m. on 7th December.

It was from the whale-factory ship *Shodo* of Kobe, Japan, reporting that one of her catchers had that day spoken to the coaster *Myfanwy* of Cardiff with the freighter *Moonraker* in tow, position 37° 22′ S: 94° 40′ E, bound for Fremantle. The message recorded that both vessels' radio transmitters were at that time out of action.

The radio operator at once telephoned the signal to Captain John Brockman, master of the *Adventurer*, who was resting in his cabin. Brockman lost no time in plotting the position of the tow. It was just over six hundred miles SSW of the *Adventurer*. He then plotted the course from that position to Fremantle. Somewhere along that line, he decided, he would intercept the tow within the next thirty-six hours. His immediate problems were its speed and the possibility that other vessels, notably a Dutch salvage tug stationed at Fremantle, might make for the position. From the ETA for Fremantle given in the factory ship's signal, Brockman estimated the tow's speed at between four and five knots. As to the Dutch tug at Fremantle, the *Adventurer* was five hundred miles nearer the tow, so Brockman knew he had a good start.

His ship had read all the signals about the *Moonraker* from the time of the cyclone — when he'd been outward bound with the oil-rig — onwards. Disaster at sea was the *Adventurer*'s business. At the time of the cyclone, details of the *Moonraker* had been taken from Lloyd's Register and placed in the Current Casualty File in the chart room. Now Brockham consulted Lloyd's Register for details of the coaster *Myfanwy*. What he found was encouraging: displacement 956 tons: length overall 204 feet: beam 30 feet: mean draught, loaded 11′ 10″, light 8′ 0″: engines 650 HP single acting diesel, single screw: speed 10 ½ knots.

These were not good specifications for a small vessel faced with towing an eight thousand ton freighter with flooded compartments and no power. Indeed he wondered how the coaster had managed, particularly in the Roaring Forties.

Next he plotted the probable position of the tow at four-hourly intervals from the given position at six p.m. along the course line to Fremantle. He estimated that he would reach a position about thirty to forty miles ahead of the tow at between nine and eleven the following night. He would then carry out a line search using long range radar. He had no doubt of the *Adventurer*'s ability to find the two ships even if no radio signals emanated from them. If they did he would get D.F. bearings and the task would be that much easier.

Having made his decision, he turned the *Adventurer* on to course 175° and increased speed to eighteen knots. At the same time he gave orders that radio silence was not to be broken without his permission. He had no intention of making known the *Adventurer*'s movements to the coaster's captain or to the Dutch salvage tug.

★ ★ ★

It was in hospital in Port Louis on 6th December that Martinho Lopez learnt of the rescue of Frascatti and his men by the Norwegian container ship due in Sydney that day. The following day even more startling news reached him: the *Moonraker* had not sunk. She was on her way to Fremantle in tow of a British coaster. Captain Stone and his companions were on board and well. Weak though he was, Lopez's reaction was one of relief. He had never imagined that the freighter could survive and nothing had worried him more since they'd abandoned her than the fate of those on board. Nothing, that is, except Frascatti's treachery.

During those early days in hospital recovering his physical and mental strength he lived in a world of shifting nightmares. Of these some were curiously repetitive: in one he was on trial by what seemed to be a military court; at times the charge appeared to be treason, at others mutiny. Always he would see Felicia Perez, mistily, somewhere in the back of the courtroom, but he could never attract her attention. In another, and it predominated, he was pursued by Frascatti carrying a knife. The pursuit was always through a maze of dark alleys, with the Italian close on his heels. Lopez knew with fearful certainty that if Frascatti caught him the knife would be used. But he never did, for at the last moment Lopez, with a supreme effort, would wake himself from the dream. Its terror cut deeply into his mind.

★　★　★

Evans's decision to alter course to the south-east after meeting the Japanese whale-catcher, put wind and sea on the port beam. Although the weather had moderated there was still a swell and the ships rolled heavily. On the *Moonraker*'s bridge Calvi and Le Clerc, accustomed to dealing with yawing caused by wind and sea astern, were faced with new problems; so were the men on the hand-steering. The indication and duration of a yaw, the amount of wheel necessary to correct it, were no longer the same. Several times during that night the tow came near to parting, the walkie-talkie exchanges grew sharper and tempers frayed. But the difficulties were surmounted and night passed safely into day.

On the following morning *Moonraker's* diesel generator broke down and pumping had to be stopped. Carelse, the engineman, reported that repairs would take some time. The trouble was in the valve mechanism and dismantling was necessary. The interruption was no longer critical, however, for more than one thousand three hundred tons of water had been pumped from the flooded compartments: *Moonraker* rode noticeably higher and her rolling was no longer sluggish. The tow was making better progress through the water, though with less help from wind and current. Speed made good was still only four and a half knots.

Several times that day Evans heard shore stations calling the *Myfanwy*. In the late afternoon he and Dai Williams decided that since the secret of the tow was out, there was no point in not using the transmitter. On the contrary, if Evans could report that all was well and the tow making good progress, the likelihood of assistance being sent would be less.

At six p.m. the tow having then steamed to the south-east for twenty-four hours, Evans resumed course for Fremantle, N 68 E, distance one thousand and ten miles. Dai Williams came to the wheelhouse with the transmitting panel which, he reported, was now repaired. It was installed, and Evans called Fremantle but received no reply. He assumed it must be out of range. However, Amsterdam Island and several ships answered. Evans spoke to the island's operator, who undertook to relay a message to Fremantle.

'Tell them,' said Evans, 'that our transmitter is now serviceable. We are making good progress and should arrive sixteenth December. Most of the water in *Moonraker*'s stokehold and engine-room has been pumped out and all on board both ships are okay.' With Captain Stone in mind, he'd deliberately used the word *okay* in preference to *well*.

'*Magnifique*,' said the French operator. 'It is a fine achievement, captain. What is your ship's position?'

Evans was ready for that. 'Thirty-six fifty, south. Ninety-six thirty, east,' he replied. The position he'd given was that which the tow would have been in had they not steamed to the south-east. It was ninety-five miles north of their actual position. He was taking no chances.

'Thank you. I will inform Fremantle,' said the operator. 'How are the passengers — Le Clerc and Bartot?'

'Fine. Giving us a lot of help.'

'*Bon*. Anything further?'

'Yes. Tell Fremantle we do not, repeat *not*, require any assistance.'

'Certainly. I will tell them.' The French operator chuckled. '*Bon voyage et bon chance, mon capitaine.*'

'Thank you, Amsterdam Island.' Evans switched off the transmitter, yawned loudly and rubbed his eyes. He was a very tired man.

★ ★ ★

In the early hours of that morning the *Moonraker* yawed to port. Le Clerc was on watch in the wheelhouse, Dwala and Hank Casey were on the hand-steering in the poop. As soon as he detected the yaw, Le Clerc phoned the poop and ordered starboard wheel. At that moment he saw a pinpoint of light on the northern horizon and went out on to the bridge to examine it with binoculars. A few moments later exhaustion and distraction caused him to forget the starboard wheel he'd ordered.

Dwala and Hank Casey waiting for the next order, assumed that an alteration of course was taking place. When Le Clerc came to and discovered his mistake the *Moonraker* had already sheered well out to starboard. Alarmed, Le Clerc ordered *hard-a-starboard* when in fact he meant *hard-a-port*.

Christopherson's voice, urgent and insistent, crackled over the walkie-talkie, 'Bring her back to port, man. Shake it up!'

Calvi came hurrying in from the wheelhouse where he'd been resting. A glance at the coaster's lights was enough. '*Sacré Dieu!*' he blazed, reaching for the steering phone. Casey answered. 'Put the wheel hard-a-port. Quick. *Plus vite*,' shouted Calvi.

But it was too late. Calvi and Le Clerc stared helplessly at the arc light on the coaster's stern. The towing hawser lifted from the water and for long seconds shivered and trembled, throwing off water like a wet dog shaking itself. Then there was a sharp report and the wire fell back into the sea.

Calvi looked at Le Clerc as if he'd seen a ghost. '*Mon Dieu*. It has parted.' The brown eyes, smudged with exhaustion, widened in dismay. Pulling himself together he ordered, 'Wheel amidships. Steady on north sixty-eight east.' He pressed the transmit button and reported to the coaster, 'The tow has parted.' He expected to hear Christopherson's voice, but it was Evans. 'You're bloody right it has. What the hell are you playing at over there?'

★ ★ ★

379

Through dark and anxious hours the coaster stood by *Moonraker* waiting for daylight. Not until then would it be possible to repass the tow.

At six a.m. Amsterdam Island called *Myfanwy* to report that her message had been passed to Fremantle and acknowledged. Evans thanked the operator, said nothing about the parted towing wire and returned gloomily to the task of keeping the coaster close enough to the freighter to avoid parting the manila messenger between the two ships — Calvi's lazy line. It would be used for re-passing the tow.

When daylight came they found the towing hawser had parted where the wire was shackled on to *Moonraker*'s cable. The coaster, having power, had recovered her cable and the full length of the towing hawser without difficulty, but in *Moonraker* other means had to be used. When first rigging the tow, Calvi had attached a double-shackled wire strop to the inboard end of the freighter's cable. The problem now was to recover the heavy cable without steam. With Msutu he rigged a threefold purchase on the foc'sle head, one end secured to the after bitts, the other to the strop.

But for Captain Stone, every man in the ship — nine in all — manned the downhaul and pulling together like a tug-o'-war team they brought the cable home, heaving in twenty-foot lengths at a time, hand feeding them down the spurling pipe into the chain locker. They were still busy at nine-twenty-seven a.m. when a ship was observed to the north-east, steaming towards them at high speed. Shortly before ten o'clock it stopped within hailing distance of the *Moonraker*.

The newcomer was the ocean salvage tug *Adventurer*, based on Albany, Western Australia.

23

Evans frowned at the *Adventurer* where she lay stopped, the radar aerial on her bridge tower turning with slow insolence. In other circumstances he might have admired the eighteen hundred tons of gleaming stream-lined metal. He'd read about her: most powerful salvage tug in the southern hemisphere; twin diesels delivering sixteen thousand horse-power to a single controllable pitch propeller; bollard pull of eleven hundred tons; capable of towing a three-hundred-thousand-ton super-tanker at seven knots; air-conditioned, tropicalised, arcticised, computerised; bristling with every technological aid to navigation, communication and salvage. She made his weather-stained ageing little coaster look what she was: a small unimportant relation.

Dai Williams came to the wheelhouse. 'We've come a thousand miles through bad weather,' said Evans. 'Never parted the tow until this morning. Now this bloody vulture turns up.'

The chief engineer pointed his pipe at the *Moonraker*. 'Don't be worrying yourself then, Merfyr. We've men and a line aboard.'

'Aye. But it's only the messenger. It's under water. He'll not be seeing it now, will he?'

'It's there right enough.'

Evans shook his head. 'Salvage captains are bloody pirates, Dai. He'll be up to something soon. Be listening, too, when I talk to Calvi. I've a mind . . .'

At that moment the walkie-talkie crackled into life. '*Adventurer* calling *Moonraker*. Brockman, master here. I'm ready to put a line across. Do you accept Lloyd's Open Form?' It was more a statement than a question.

'The bastard,' exploded Evans, reaching for the R/T handset as Calvi's voice came on the air. 'I read you, *Adventurer*. *Myfanwy* has a line and crew aboard us. We've a signed contract with her. Your help not required.'

Evans's eyes gleamed. 'Good boy,' he said.

'Don't see any line,' Brockman challenged.

Merfyr Evans butted in. '*Myfanwy* to *Adventurer*. Keep clear. We have a line across. Adjusting tow for chafe. Your assistance not required.'

Brockman wasn't impressed. '*Adventurer* to *Moonraker*. I can tow you at twelve knots. *And* provide electric power for pumping.'

Calvi came back quickly. 'Possibly. But we respect contracts and have electric power.'

Evans thumped Dai Williams' back. 'Hear that? The lad's good.'

'Not bad for a fisherman.' Dai Williams had to suck his pipe vigorously to hide his smile.

Brockman's voice came on the air again. 'Is that *Moonraker*'s captain speaking?'

'I command the *Moonraker*.' Calvi's reply was quick and authoritative.

Dai Williams nudged Evans. 'Taking chances, isn't he?'

'Listen!' Evans held up a hand.

Adventurer's captain played his trump card. 'You speak with a French accent. Captain Stone is British.' He'd done his *Moonraker* homework at the time of the cyclone.

'Yes,' replied Calvi. 'But I command for the salvage. Wait please.' He phoned through to the foc'sle. 'Send Casey up here. Double quick.'

Over in *Myfanwy*, Evans was having a council of war with Dai Williams. 'What's he mean *wait please*. Not bringing that drunken Stone to the mike, is he?'

'You worry too much, Merfyr. What can Stone do? You've men and a line aboard his ship.'

Evans glared at the tug. He was tired, hollow-eyed. 'There's no policeman on the beat here, Dai. Anything can happen when there's big money at stake.' They were pondering these truths when an unknown voice came on the air. British all right, but surprising nevertheless. It hadn't occurred to them that Stone was an Australian.

''Morning *Adventurer*,' said the Australian voice. 'I've been listening to the conversation. We're on contract to Captain Evans. He's brought us a thousand miles through bad weather. I'm satisfied he'll get us to Fremantle. Thanks for your offer, but help is not required. We're making good progress.'

Irritation crept into Brockman's voice. 'Doesn't look like it from here, captain.'

'Closing down now, *Adventurer*,' replied Hank Casey. 'We're busy.'

Brockman wasn't got rid of as easily as that. 'I'll be standing by. Maybe your owners won't like your decision, captain. I'll ask them.'

That was too much for Evans. '*Myfanwy* to *Adventurer*. Owners or no bloody owners I've got a signed contract. Now get to hell out of it. We're busy.'

★ ★ ★

There had been more drama on *Moonraker*'s bridge than Evans or Brockman knew of.

Captain Stone, notwithstanding his alcoholic haze, was too much of a seaman not to have known that the tow had stopped when he looked out of his cabin windows that morning. Looking forward, he'd seen activity on the foc'sle and realised the tow must have parted. Later he saw the ocean salvage tug arrive. He'd gone up to the chart house then and through its open windows heard Calvi's end of the walkie-talkie exchanges. From them he knew of *Adventurer's* offer, its refusal, and Calvi's reference to men, a line aboard and the salvage contract. His indignation grew. Here was this Frenchman on *his* bridge presuming to act on his behalf and lying about a line aboard. The last straw was Calvi's *I command the* MOONRAKER. Captain Stone made unsteadily for the wing of the bridge where the Corsican stood facing the *Adventurer*. Another man was with him.

As Stone drew near he saw it was Casey. The Australian touched Calvi's shoulder and said something Stone couldn't hear. Calvi turned, saw Stone, and passed the walkie-talkie to the Australian. Then he came towards the captain, took his arm and firmly but gently led him back to the chart house. The captain's protests fell on deaf ears. Calvi opened the door and pushed him in.

Stone swung round. 'How dare you push

386

me, you foreign swine.' He trembled with fuzzy indignation. 'You'll have to account for this. Holding yourself out as commander of my ship. That's fraud.'

'I represent Captain Evans, sir.' Calvi's tone was patient, polite. 'He commands the salvage operation. In *both* ships. He cannot be in two ships at one time, so I act for him here. Therefore I command this ship for the salvage.'

'Lot of trumped up nonsense,' Stone's speech was slurred. 'Sea lawyer. That's what you are.' The ship rolled and he slumped on to the settee.

'I do my best to save your ship, captain.'

'Then let that salvage tug put a line aboard. Best way to save the ship. Her captain knows what he's about. *He* won't part towing hawsers. Have us in Sydney in a trice.'

Calvi didn't think it worth pointing out that Sydney was 1,000 miles farther away than Fremantle. 'You have signed a contract with Captain Evans. While he has crew or a line aboard he has not abandoned the tow.'

'That's another confounded lie,' fumed Stone. 'There's no line aboard this ship.'

Calvi's mouth tightened. 'There is a line, captain. A lazy-line.'

'Lazy-line? What the devil's that?'

'A manila messenger. Made fast in

Moonraker's bows and *Myfanwy*'s stern. We shall use it for passing the tow again.'

'I don't believe a word.'

'Look for yourself, captain,' said Calvi wearily.

★ ★ ★

The *Adventurer* withdrew to half a mile and settled down catlike to watch her mouse. On the *Moonraker*'s foc'sle Calvi was busy with all hands recovering the cable. It wasn't easy. Twice the wash of the sea snagged the cable under the flukes of an anchor and Msutu had to go down in a bosun's chair to clear it. Over in *Myfanwy* the cable was in and they were flaking large bits of the towing wire along the deck ready for running. Evans was worried. The barometer was falling, the cloud ceiling had lowered, the wind freshened. This was not his only problem: he was suffering from lack of sleep and it was affecting his judgment. Somehow he'd have to get five or six unbroken hours.

Knowing that the *Adventurer* would listen to walkie-talkie, Evans signalled Calvi by Aldis lamp: *Except in emergency use torch for signalling so that tug cannot read.* With the salvage tug out on the port beam the coaster and *Moonraker*, could, by screening their lights, signal each other unknown to the *Adventurer*.

It was not until five o'clock that afternoon that Calvi signalled: *ready to pass tow*. By then it was blowing hard with a biggish sea. Evans replied: *Weather deteriorating. Wait for daylight to-morrow*. Calvi acknowledged and Evans prepared for the night. With the salvage tug there they couldn't risk parting the messenger. He doubled up the watches: Christopherson and Bartot in one, he and Isak John in the other. Because he was short-handed he'd given Christopherson and Isak John more responsibility than usual. Both had responded well, handling the coaster with confidence, keeping her in station ahead of the *Moonraker*.

Before nightfall the end of the messenger and the arc light were moved from the coaster's stern to her foc'sle and Evans turned her bows-on to the *Moonraker* to keep the messenger clear of the coaster's screw. He hoped that with these changes he might get some sleep. Calvi, he knew, would get sleep. The *Moonraker* was drifting, steering not manned. There was little to do there save keep a look out.

★ ★ ★

At eight o'clock that night Evans went down for a wash and freshen up. Coming back he saw Susie in the saloon. He'd passed her when she called to him. 'Why don't you let that tug tow the *Moonraker*?'

The girl was staring at him: her face streaked with grease marks, hair untidy, eyes tired but challenging.

'I've towed the *Moonraker* close on a thousand miles,' he said. 'I'll finish the job.'

'We've spent all day stopped. Now we're stopping for the night. Never get there at this rate.'

A shadow crossed his face. 'We'll get there all right.'

'That tug's much better equipped to tow.'

'Maybe. But I'm not handing over.'

'No,' she said. 'You're after the money, aren't you. I've heard the crew talking. They're all after it.'

'What the hell's that got to do with you?' Evans was too tired, his nerves too frayed, to take cheek from this girl.

'Nothing,' she said. 'But with this miserable little ship we'll never get anywhere. That big tug must have *much* better seamen.'

Evans growled, moving towards her. The coaster pitched and the girl fell on to the saloon settee. She looked up fearfully, knowing she'd gone too far. He stood over her, red-rimmed eyes angry, lips compressed. 'More cheek like that,' he threatened, 'and I'll have the drawers off you and my belt to your backside. You look after the galley. Keep your thoughts to yourself.'

Susie burst into tears, burying her face in her hands. Evans looked with dismay at the crumpled figure on the settee, its shoulders heaving. He'd expected her to fight back, not give in like that. He didn't understand women. Not that she was really a woman. More a girl. Embarrassed, penitent, he patted her shoulder. She wriggled away. 'Leave me,' she sobbed.

He went back to the wheelhouse. Isak John was already there. 'Right then,' said Evans to Christopherson and Bartot. 'Carry on below. Get some rest.'

On and off until midnight, in between manœuvring the coaster, Evans was thinking of the girl. She'd been on board for four days and she was worrying him. The way she looked when she handed him something. The way he felt when their hands touched. In the chart room that day she'd brought him tea. He'd shown her where they were on the chart. She'd stood beside him and each time the ship rolled their bodies touched and he felt her breast against his arm and forgot what he was saying. Why did she affect him like that? Friendly grey eyes and a snub nose. Good complexion. Nice face, but nothing wonderful. Beneath the jersey and denim slacks there was a strong young body. But that wasn't special. Why was she on his mind then? Now, when he must concentrate all his energies on the tow. She was eighteen. He thirty-two. It was bloody absurd. A ship was no place for a woman. He'd not liked the idea when it was first mooted. He knew his instinct had been right.

What he didn't know was that Susie was aware that she disturbed him and rather liked it. Just as she'd liked being in Calvi's arms on *Moonraker*'s bridge. The Corsican had held her longer than he'd needed to. She knew that. And Hank? No doubt of the effect she had on him. She liked him best because she'd known him longest. But Napoleon Calvi was groovy. Those dark eyes and the French accent. Merfyr Evans, too. He was all right. Bit old. But strong and determined. Like iron, he seemed. A real man.

Whatever it was, she knew of her power over these men and it made her feel good.

★   ★   ★

Hank Casey came off watch at one o'clock in the morning having worked with Carelse for six hours on the diesel generator. This, after a day spent on the foc'sle head recovering the cable. Repairs to the diesel had been completed, the engine re-assembled and re-started. Pumping had been resumed and *Moonraker* again had electricity.

Before going below he sampled the fresh air on the upper deck. It was a cold night and the ship, drifting beam on to the weather, moved a good deal. Wind and sea were boisterous and spray drenched the decks. He saw the bright lights of the salvage tug to port, ahead the lights of the coaster. Deciding he'd seen enough he went below, straightened the blankets on the unmade bunk and took off his shoes and jersey. He hoped for four hours of unbroken sleep. In twelve days he'd never had more than two hours of that. Before turning in he went down the alleyway to the lavatory. Passing the saloon he saw a tall white-haired figure at the sideboard, back to the door.

It was Captain Stone. The captain's presence there at that time was not as remarkable as what he was doing: sharpening a carving knife on a metal sharpener. His curiosity aroused, Casey went back to his cabin, turned off the light and angled the door so that he could watch the saloon entrance without being seen. Presently Stone came out, carving knife in one hand, torch in the other. He wore a blue raincoat over pyjamas. Casey, bare-footed, took a torch and followed.

The captain went down the internal stairway and out through a door to the upper deck. It was a dark night and Casey kept close as Stone moved up forward. The captain reached the companion ladder and went on to the foc'sle. Fearful for the man on duty there watching the manila messenger, Casey shouted, 'Look out! He's got a knife.'

There was no reply, but he heard sounds of a scuffle followed by a thud. Then Msutu's voice. 'Okay. I catch him.' Casey switched on the torch. In the lee of the anchor windlass Captain Stone lay prostrate, the Zulu sitting astride him. Casey said, 'Where's the knife, Msutu?'

'I push it under warping drum, Hank.'

Casey shone the torch there and the knife blade gleamed. He picked it up. Captain Stone was struggling. 'Get off me, you black devil,' he gasped. 'You're breaking my back.'

'Let him up, Msutu,' said Casey.

The Zulu got up and helped Stone to his feet. Torchlight revealed a dishevelled Stone, eyes wild, white hair fluttering in the wind, temple bruised. Stone glared from Msutu to Casey. 'You and that black man dare attack me!' His voice choked. 'My God you'll pay for this. Don't imagine you can assault a British shipmaster in his own ship and get away with it.'

Casey was surprised at the steadiness of Stone's voice. It was not the slurred speech of recent weeks. He shone the torch on the knife. 'What was this for, captain? Murder?'

'Don't talk rubbish, man. I didn't know there was anyone here until this black fellow attacked me.'

Casey stuck to his point. 'What was the knife for, then?'

The captain's mouth set stubbornly as he glared at the young man in silence.

'I think captain want to cut rope,' said Msutu.

'What if I did?' demanded Stone. 'This is my ship. She hasn't been under tow for twenty-four hours. That messenger's a cheap trick to prevent me using the salvage tug.'

Casey said, 'Let the captain's arm free, Msutu.' He turned to Stone. 'We'd better get back amidships, captain.' Casey shone the torch towards the companion ladder. The old man appeared undecided. At last, muttering to himself, he moved off, followed by the Australian.

★ ★ ★

Le Clerc was on watch on *Moonraker's* bridge, Calvi asleep in the chart house. Casey knew how badly the Corsican needed sleep but had to waken him. Now that Susie had gone, they got on well. Casey, despite his bruised lips and missing tooth, liked Calvi, admitted that he knew his job, exercised iron authority, had guts and shouldered the lion's share of the work.

'What are the trouble?' yawned Calvi, rubbing his eyes.

Casey told him.

'And Captain Stone?'

'I've locked him in his cabin.'

'*Bon*. Excellent.' Calvi got up, yawned again and stretched. He saw the chart house clock. '*Merde!* Half past one.' Only one and a half of the four hours' sleep he'd hoped for. It is always like this, he reflected, putting on a duffle coat. They went down below and Casey unlocked the door of the cabin. Stone was slumped in an armchair, staring at the long legs poked out in front of him.

Calvi said, 'I have just heard what has happened, captain.'

Stone continued to stare at his feet.

'It is very serious for anyone to obstruct salvage work,' said Calvi. 'For this you can possibly lose your master's certificate.'

Captain Stone still gave no sign of having heard him.

'I regret very much, captain, that you must remain in your cabin until Fremantle. Please understand that I command this ship while the salvage operation lasts.'

That stung the old man. '*You* command my ship? You have the impertinence to order *me* to remain in my cabin.' He looked up from under bushy eyebrows. 'D'you know what that is, Frenchman?'

Calvi was silent.

Stone stood up, swaying to counter the ship's roll. Taller than the Corsican by inches, he looked down on him. 'I warn you. It is mutiny. D'you understand?'

'Jesus!' murmured Casey. 'Not again.'

'I shall enter the occurrence in the ship's logbook,' went on the captain. 'You will be brought to account.' He turned an icy stare on Hank Casey. 'You too, Casey. You have conspired to mutiny. The consequences are serious.' With a sudden, explosive cough, he pointed to the door. 'Get out,' he gasped. After they'd gone Stone dropped into the armchair and hid his face in his hands. For some time he sat there, shoulders shaking. Later he took out a handkerchief, blew his nose and dried his eyes. In the night cabin he ran water in the handbasin and bathed the bruise on his temple. Putting away the towel he pulled out the bunk drawer, opened the recess and brought out a bottle of gin. It was something of an occasion. The first drink for three days.

24

By daylight the weather had moderated and at ten o'clock Evans decided to re-pass the tow. The sky had cleared, the sun shone down on an indigo sea. 'Stand by,' he warned Calvi by walkie-talkie. In both ships men made ready to pass the tow. In the coaster the end of the manila messenger was taken from the bow to the stern and the coaster swung stern-on to the *Moonraker*.

Captain Brockman in the *Adventurer* had heard Evans's brief signal, correctly divined its purpose, and proceeded to make his own decisions. There was a froth of water under the salvage tug's counter and her bows began moving to starboard, towards the tow. Brockman had decided to do a Nelson. If there was a manila messenger between the coaster and the freighter — and he doubted it — it wasn't visible. What was more the coaster, turning now, had spent the entire night bows on to the freighter. That, too, encouraged his belief that there was no line between the ships. For a day and a night the coaster hadn't been towing so he could reasonably conclude, if asked to explain, that she appeared to have abandoned the tow.

This then was the moment. He headed the *Adventurer* for the three hundred yard gap between the two ships.

Standing on the starboard side of *Myfanwy*'s bridge engrossed in manœuvring his ship, the wheelhouse shutting out the salvage tug, Evans's first warning was Calvi's urgent:

'*Moonraker* to *Adventurer*: Keep clear. You will foul our line. We are passing tow.'

Evans ran into the wheelhouse, looked through the windows on the port side and saw the tug making for the gap. She was about a quarter of a mile away. He grabbed the handset. '*Myfanwy* to *Adventurer*: Keep clear of my tow or I ram.' His voice was cold, incisive. He phoned the poop. Christopherson answered. 'Bend on another line to that messenger. Double quick,' snapped Evans. 'Keep it clear of the screw. We need room to manœuvre.'

'Hard-a-starboard,' he ordered, ringing down *full-ahead*.

Brockman, misled by Evans's matter-of-fact voice, had taken the Welshman's threat as bluff. Merchant ships' captains didn't ram deliberately in the latter half of the twentieth century. *Adventurer* held her course. Brockman saw the *Myfanwy* turning towards him, white water under her stern. He realised with a shock that the coaster was on a collision course. It wasn't bluff. She was two hundred yards distant now — three points on the *Adventurer*'s port bow. A collision was less than a minute away . . . thirty, forty seconds, perhaps.

'Hard-a-port-full-ahead.' Brockman sounded two blasts on the tug's siren, his knuckles white where he gripped the bridge rail. If he went to starboard he'd collide with the *Moonraker* — it was too late to go astern. By increasing speed and turning hard to port a collision could be averted — but only if the coaster went hard-a-port. Drops of sweat formed on Brockman's forehead and his eyes widened.

'Thank God,' he breathed as he saw the coaster's bows moving to port. The seconds ticked by, each an eternity, as the two ships swung round to pass each other no more than twenty feet apart, their combined speeds close on twenty knots.

Brockman seized the loud-hailer. 'You bloody maniac,' he boomed at the bearded figure on the coaster's bridge. 'You could have sunk us.'

Amplified by loud-hailer, Evans's reply rolled back across the water: '*And* I will, if you try that again. Now get to hell out of here.' He was still shaking with anger when a cry of 'Man overboard!' came from the coaster's stern.

As he put the telegraph to *stop*, the phone buzzer sounded in the wheelhouse. Isak John's voice came through on the handset, hoarse, urgent. 'Christopherson overboard. Right aft.'

When, minutes before, Evans had turned the coaster on to a collision course with the *Adventurer*, Christopherson and Isak John were bending a rope on to the messenger. They were just in time, for the full length of the manila had run out. There were one hundred and twenty fathoms of it on the starboard reel. The bosun, seeing it was already running fast, shouted to a seaman, 'Get the line from the port reel.' Before the man could get back the last few turns were coming off the starboard reel. Christopherson grabbed a lifebuoy from its rack, threw it over the side as the bare end of the rope came clear, kicked off his seaboots and dived.

The coaster moved away.

A few powerful strokes took him to the buoy. A few more and he had found and grasped the rope's end. It was sinking slowly. Determined not to lose it, he took a turn round his body, making it fast with half hitches. Then he dived under the lifebuoy, came up through its centre and spread his arms. Away on his right the coaster was swinging to port. Beyond it, almost twice its size, loomed the shining bulk of the *Adventurer*. A collision seemed inevitable but, miraculously, the two vessels swung clear and drew rapidly apart. It was then that he first felt the pull of the line and realised that the two hundred and forty fathoms of manila messenger — Calvi's lazy-line, under water now for two weeks — was water-logged. It was dragging him down. With sudden fury he fought to free the line from his waist, but its pull forced the buoy against his armpits and he couldn't get his arms around it to work on the half-hitches.

The forces dragging him down were irresistible. The water grew darker. Jagged shafts of red and white light stabbed at his eyes as he twisted and clawed. His breath had gone, water choking the air out of his body as he inhaled, tearing at his lungs. Something, a dark shapeless object, came at him under the water, buffeting, but he was too far gone to struggle. With despair he realised it was a shark.

★ ★ ★

After the coaster's attempt to ram the *Adventurer*, Captain Brockman withdrew to a respectable distance to lick the wounds of his injured dignity and nurse his fright. He put his ship a mile astern of the *Moonraker*. He was not the man to give in easily. From long experience he knew that the place for business was where a ship was in trouble. Towing was fraught with imponderables. The coaster wasn't equipped for the job and a lot could go wrong. She might get the freighter to Fremantle but she might not. It was worth waiting.

From his position astern of the *Moonraker*, he'd caught glimpses of the coaster manœuvring and had heard the walkie-talkie exchanges. After trouble at the start — he was not clear what it was — the operation appeared to have gone smoothly and by noon the tow was under way. An hour later it was making three and a half knots, a speed which made Brockman thump his chart table in irritation. 'What a bloody waste of time,' he complained to the second mate. 'We could tow her at twelve knots.'

He'd no sooner said that than Evans's voice came over the loud speaker. He was calling Amsterdam Island. The French operator answered. Evans asked him to relay an urgent message to Fremantle. There was a tape-recorder under the tug's chart house speaker. Brockman switched it on.

The message began to come through: *Tug* ADVENTURER *based Albany arrived at tow yesterday. Tug's offer assistance refused and master informed* MYFANWY *had men and line aboard and written acceptance salvage Lloyd's Open Form signed by* MOON-RAKER'S *master. Tug has remained with tow ever since. To-day at 1005 tug attempted to steam between my ship and* MOONRAKER *to part line thereby endangering safety both ships and hazarding lives. Two of my men overboard as result tug master's disgraceful behaviour. Urgently request authorities call tug off and warn master consequences his gross irresponsibility. Message ends.*

Brockman's pulse rate quickened. He picked up a mike on the long range H.F. radio: '*Adventurer* calling *Myfanwy*. You bloody liar,' he said. 'You'll hear more of this.' He knew that Fremantle and Amsterdam Island would read the signal.

Evans made no reply but the rage in Brockman's voice gave him a good deal of pleasure. He knew that Brockman would signal a denial as soon as he'd worked it out. Sure enough it came on the air some minutes later. But the voice wasn't Brockman's.

'His radio operator,' said Evans to Dai Williams.

ADVENTURER *to* Port *Authorities,* Fremantle, began the anonymous voice. *Coaster's last message to you via Amsterdam Island grossly misstates the facts. Coaster was not towing at time nor did my vessel pass between the two ships. On arrival Albany intend laying charge against master* MYFANWY *for attempting ram my vessel following his threat to do so. Coaster underpowered and ill-equipped for towing freighter. Intend remaining with tow in case assistance needed. Message ends.*

Evans made a rude noise and winked at Dai Williams.

A soothing signal soon came from Fremantle. It urged all concerned to observe the rules of ocean salvage and international maritime law and warned of the dire consequences of contravention. There was to be no obstruction of any sort, said Fremantle, by one ship of another, nor was the towing operation to be interfered with or hazarded in any way. Finally Evans was asked to clarify his report that two men had gone overboard.

The composer of the signal had exercised masterly tact: no sides taken, no ships named, no blame allocated. Fremantle knew that the master of the *Adventurer* was perfectly within his rights in remaining with the tow. So did Merfyr Evans, but his signal had made his point: Brockman wouldn't be taking any more chances. In acknowledging the Fremantle signal via Amsterdam Island Evans reported that he'd recovered the two crewmen who'd gone overboard and that the tow's amended ETA was 17th December.

★　★　★

Christopherson lay on his bunk, Susie leaning over him, wiping his head with a soiled towel. 'Feeling better, Chris?' Her eyes were large. She'd thought he was dead but his eyelids had begun to flutter. The eyes opened and he smiled feebly. Then the pains in his head and chest became intolerable and he groaned. Exhaustion and pain overwhelmed him and he closed his eyes.

★　★　★

That evening Evans came to see him, told him what had happened. 'Isak John dived in as soon as he'd reported you overboard. He saw you tie that line round your body. Damn' fool thing you did, then. He had quite a way to swim. It was a race against time. He dived down, found you and cut the rope. Don't know how the hell he did. Said you were ten to fifteen feet under by the time he'd finished sawing through it.'

Christopherson shook his head in disbelief. 'Isak John,' he whispered. 'What did he want to save me for?'

Evans said, 'Force of habit, pulling sailors out of the drink. We all suffer from it.'

Christopherson grinned. 'I thought he was a shark.'

'Some shark,' said Evans.

'We lost the messenger?'

'Not for long. Tow re-passed and under way by noon.'

'That's great,' whispered Christopherson hoarsely. 'What's the time, captain?'

'Near to six. Susie'll be along with supper soon.'

The second mate tried to sit up but couldn't. 'Sorry, captain. I'll be okay for the middle watch.'

'You won't,' said Evans. 'We can manage without you tonight.'

'How's Isak John?'

'Fine,' said Evans. 'On watch now.'

'Give him a message, captain.'

'What's that, then?'

Christopherson closed his eyes. 'Tell him he's a crazy old bastard.'

★ ★ ★

408

The weather improved throughout the day, the tow making good progress. Evans and Isak John kept alternate watches, Bartot dividing his: two hours with Evans, two with Isak John.

By noon on 11th December they were seven hundred and eighty-five miles WSW of Fremantle and in direct radio contact. But Evans was a worried man. Not only was he close to the threshold of exhaustion, but the parting of the tow had cost them thirty-four hours. That loss made the *Myfanwy*'s fuel problem critical.

Two tons had been used during those thirty-four hours. Fuel remaining at noon on 11th December was twenty-one tons. If with wind and current the tow averaged five knots it would take six and a half days to Fremantle. At three tons a day that required nineteen to twenty tons, leaving enough for less than a day's steaming. If the tow averaged four and a half knots they'd run out of fuel a day away from Fremantle — if four knots, nearly two days away. The wind had dropped, the coaster's towing pull grew less as her fuel tanks emptied and she rode higher in the water. It looked more like being four knots than five.

Evans discussed the problem with Dai Williams. The chief engineer bit on the stem of his pipe. 'We've no margin left, Merfyr. And that's a fact. I doubt we've the fuel to make Fremantle.'

Evans's red-rimmed eyes held the chief's in a long frowning stare, but he said nothing.

★ ★ ★

With Christopherson back on duty, Evans got in five hours of unbroken sleep that afternoon. He woke at six-thirty, refreshed, his morale good and went to the wheelhouse. The weather was fine, the log-repeater showed speed through the water as three and a half knots. Star sights that evening gave speed made good since noon as five knots. The current was helping substantially.

Astern, beyond the *Moonraker*, Evans saw the *Adventurer*. She'd moved out on to the freighter's port quarter, a mile or more away.

Bartot said, 'Her captain. He is an optimist, *n'est ce pas?*'

'There's other names more appropriate,' growled Evans.

Susie came into the wheelhouse with a tray. 'Your supper, captain.'

He patted her shoulder and smiled. 'Thanks, Susie. I need it. Too much sleep this afternoon.'

She looked at him curiously. It was not like

410

him to smile and call her Susie. It was frowns and no names usually. 'Not enough sleep,' she said severely. 'You've been starved of it.'

'Don't worry. I feel fine now.' He looked at the tray with a critical eye. 'This for Bartot too?'

'No. He had his before he came on watch. I didn't want to wake you.'

★ ★ ★

Isak John and Christopherson relieved Evans and Bartot at ten o'clock that night. Bartot was fast asleep within minutes of reaching the cabin, but Evans sat at his small desk rechecking the fuel figures. He was engrossed in this when there was a subdued knock. He said, 'What is it?'

'Me,' said Susie, pushing the cabin curtains aside and coming in. 'Like some cocoa?' She smiled and he saw how white and even her teeth were under the moist red lips.

'Good for sleeping?' he asked.

'Great,' she said. 'Never seen the TV ads?'

He stood up, yawning and stretching. 'Right. I'll have some.'

She poured it and when she passed him the mug their hands touched. Like an electric shock, he thought, his one hand still covering hers. She was looking at him in a strange way.

411

It was a small cabin and she was beside him, her face close. The smell of her breath was young and warm. Before he knew it his arms were round her. For a moment she resisted, her body stiffening, her head turned away. Then she relaxed, sighed, her face came to his, mouth open, lips warm and inviting, body yielding. Evans's mind blurred and Susie was wondering mistily about her vow when there was a knock, the curtains were drawn aside and a man stood in the doorway.

It was Dai Williams, and he was glaring.

* * *

Dai brought bad news. Trouble with the engines. A main bearing running hot. They'd have to stop. For how long? six hours, maybe eight.

'Christ,' said Evans with sudden savagery. 'It would happen now. How long can you carry on, Dai?'

'Another ten fifteen minutes. I'll have to shut down then.'

'Make it fifteen.'

'I'll try.' Dai Williams threw an angry look at the girl and hurried away.

She said, 'He must have seen.'

'What of it?' Evans was sitting on the settee pulling on seaboots. 'It's no crime.'

412

'I shouldn't have let you.'

'I would have anyway.'

'It means nothing,' she said.

The brown eyes stared at her, hard and calculating. 'We'll see,' he said. 'I must get up top now.'

25

Two problems confronted Merfyr Evans: how to keep the news of the breakdown from Brockman in the *Adventurer*, and how to avoid casting off the tow. Any signal made by light would be read by the salvage tug astern of the *Moonraker*; the alternative was walkie-talkie, but then Brockman would get the story from both ends. With the coaster and the freighter unable to steam, the tow might well have to be cast: the last thing the Welshman wanted with Brockman waiting there like a hovering vulture. Evans broke the news to Isak John. There was a hurried discussion. It *had* to be with only ten minutes to go before the engines stopped. Isak John said, 'Pity Calvi doesn't speak Afrikaans.'

Evans knew it was the bosun's home language. 'What's that got to do with it?' he said with the irritation of despair.

'They wouldn't understand Afrikaans in the tug.'

Evans stared at the bosun as if he'd seen a ghost. 'That's it.' He slapped his thigh. 'My goodness, that's it, Isak! Should have thought of it long ago. Get Bartot here double quick.'

The Frenchman came to the wheelhouse, rubbing the sleep from his eyes.

'We must stop engines. Six or eight hours,' Evans shot at him. 'For repairs. Calvi must be told right away. After that we'll need to pass messages about the tow. May have to cast off. Depends on the drift.'

Bartot was puzzled. 'What is it you wish from me, captain?'

'Pass all those messages to Calvi in French. Not a word in English. The *Adventurer* mustn't know what's going on. Probably no one there speaks French.'

Bartot shrugged his shoulders. 'Possibly someone has learnt it at school. It is not an unknown language.'

'Speak it fast,' said Evans. 'I doubt schoolboy French will cope with that.' He handed over the walkie-talkie. 'Tell Calvi we're stopping any minute now. Explain why. Use personal names, not ship names. That'll fox Brockman.'

Bartot pressed the transmit button. '*Allo! Allo! Napoleon Calvi. Ici Jean Bartot. Le Capitaine Evans désire que tous signaux soient en Français seulement. Il faut parler vite. J'ai un signal pour vous. Terminé.*'

'*Allo! Jean. Ici François Le Clerc. Comment vas tu, mon vieil ami? Je comprends. Calvi se repose dans la chambre des cartes.*

Quel est ton message?'

Bartot passed it. Shortly afterwards Calvi arrived on *Moonraker*'s bridge and he and Bartot had a further conversation. It ended with Bartot's laughing, *'Tres bien. Je demandrai au capitaine. Au revoir, Napoleon. Vive La France.'* Bartot turned to Evans. 'First it was Le Clerc. Then Calvi. They understand very well. All messages shall be in French and no ships' names.'

Evans, about to say something, was interrupted by the buzzer from the engine-room. It was Dai Williams. 'We must shut down, Merfyr.'

Evans's mouth tightened. 'Right you are.' He put the engine-room telegraph to *stop*.

Nothing went more deeply against the grain.

★ ★ ★

It was the beginning of a long night. While Dai Williams and an engineman worked on the overheated bearing, Evans kept watch on the relative positions of the coaster and the *Moonraker*. There was little wind but it became evident that the coaster, lighter in draught, was drifting downwind faster than the freighter. This was what Evans hoped for. Nonetheless he feared that some quirk of wind and water, aided by the weight of the towing hawser, might draw the two ships together. This would mean casting the tow for with a swell running, moderate though it was, a collision between the two drifting ships could be serious.

By midnight, however, all was well, the *Myfanwy* down-wind of *Moonraker*, the freighter acting as a sea anchor, holding the small ship stern to wind — and the weight of the drifting coaster on the towing hawser hauling the freighter's bows to leeward so that she lay stern-to, four or five points off the wind.

★   ★   ★

Shortly after the coaster's engines stopped, Bartot had a message from the *Moonraker* for Evans.

'Le Clerc makes a suggestion.' Bartot grinned.

'It had better be a good one.'

'He suggests that between the messages for the tow we shall discuss problems of oceanic drift.'

'What the hell's that for?'

'We are scientists. We shall talk in scientific terms of winds and currents, their effects upon the movements of ocean waters. Also

417

the rate of drift of ships of different sizes in different conditions of loading.'

'Very interesting, I'm sure,' said Evans drily. 'But this is not a science convention, Bartot.'

The Frenchman smiled with quiet confidence. 'The *Adventurer* knows that the tow has stopped. Twice already Brockman has steamed round us with searchlights on. All that he hears is Frenchmen talking. Several times he calls *Moonraker* and this ship but he gets no answer. So he is puzzled, *n'est ce pas?* But it must be he suspects you have trouble.'

'And he's bloody right,' growled Evans.

'*Alors*. Let us before daylight make for him more puzzles.'

'What's it you're after?'

The Frenchman's eyes twinkled with pleasure. 'Le Clerc and myself we shall talk of these oceanic problems. Of the experiments we make with these ships. But we shall speak in English, with stronger accents than usual.'

'They couldn't be much stronger,' said Evans doubtfully.

'You see, captain,' Bartot went on. 'Brockman will think when we speak in French — when we make the real towing messages — he will think we are discussing oceanic problems.'

Merfyr Evans looked to where the *Adventurer*'s lights showed in the darkness. She'd come up from astern, to wide on the *Moonraker*'s bow. 'It's an idea.' His eyes gleamed. 'Brockman'll smell a rat. But he won't know what's happening.' He patted Bartot's shoulder. 'You and Le Clerc go ahead. Let Brockman feed that into his bloody computer.'

★ ★ ★

In the early hours of the morning Calvi left Le Clerc on *Moonraker*'s bridge and went to the chart house to snatch brief sleep. Hanging his duffle coat on the hook above the settee he lay down, drew up a blanket and switched off the light. It seemed only seconds later that an unfamiliar noise woke him. It was the sound of heavy breathing. He reached out and turned the switch.

The heavy breather was Captain Stone. The old man was going through the pockets of Calvi's coat. He turned, his watery eyes blinking.

Calvi sat up. 'If you're looking for the salvage acceptance you signed, it's not there, captain.'

Stone stared at him owlishly, sighed, leant over the bunk and replaced the duffle coat.

'You see,' explained Calvi. 'I sent it back to Captain Evans the same day. In the watertight canister.'

Stone shook his head. 'I was looking for my keys. Thought that was *my* duffle coat. Used to keep it there.' The speech was slurred, the smell of gin formidable.

Calvi said, 'I see, sir.'

Stone looked at him with disapproval. 'It is disgraceful,' he said. 'The tow stopped again. So much time lost.' He hiccoughed. 'That fine tug standing by . . . fobbed off with a pack of lies.' He hiccoughed again, lost his balance as the ship rolled, fell against the chart table and slithered to the floor.

Calvi helped him down to his cabin.

★ ★ ★

Daylight brought a mist which thickened as the climbing sun shone down on a cold sea. In the *Adventurer* and *Myfanwy*, the captains were at their radar screens, watching the same picture from different angles. Both screens told the same story: the coaster downwind of the freighter, their relative positions much as they had been through the night; the salvage tug on the *Moonraker*'s bow, half a mile to port, where she'd been since dawn.

Brockman knew that the towing hawser

was still made fast; that the coaster had drifted downwind faster than the freighter. He knew precisely the angles which the coaster and the freighter had assumed relative to wind, sea, current and each other. He knew the surface water temperature, sub-surface temperatures at various depths, relative humidity, wind speed and a good deal else he'd no desire to know. This was because throughout the night French scientists had been exchanging oceanic data. Much they'd said he couldn't understand because no one in *Adventurer* had more than a smattering of French and the scientists spoke too fast. Often, however, they broke into English and then, execrable though it was, they could be understood. Brockman, frustrated and suspicious, feared he was being taken for a ride but could not be sure.

What were French scientists doing in the coaster and the freighter? How had they got there in the first instance? He'd established from which ships the signals came as he steamed round them that night with radio D/F switched on. There were three different French voices — no doubt about that. But who'd ever heard of experiments in oceanic drift in the middle of a salvage operation? And the tow stopped so that this could be done.

It was crazy, yet the facts could not be controverted. There *were* two ships drifting, they *were* joined by a towing hawser and there *were* three Frenchmen exchanging messages in a scientific jargon. Twice one of them, the man with the deep voice, had urged the others to speed up their observations. 'The captain is impatient,' he'd said. 'We must finish quickly. He wishes to proceed with the tow.'

Baffled and impatient, Brockman didn't know what to make of it. It was quite outside his experience.

★ ★ ★

Some time after nine that morning the mist cleared, pulling aside like a stage curtain to reveal the three ships lying stopped, rolling easily to the swell from the south-west. Brockman manœuvred the *Adventurer* into a position where with glasses he could see the anchor cables of the coaster and freighter arcing into the sea. 'Tow's rigged all right,' he said to his chief officer. 'I'll nose up towards the gap. That'll bring the Welshman on the air.'

★ ★ ★

At nine-twenty-two a.m. Dai Williams reported repairs completed and main engines ready. Calvi was warned that the tow was about to be resumed. At nine-twenty-five a.m. the coaster's engines began to turn at slow speed as Evans coaxed the *Moonraker*'s bows downwind to line up the tow. He'd given the order *starboard wheel* when Christopherson reported that the *Adventurer* was getting under way, heading for the towing hawser.

Merfyr Evans turned to see the big tug making slowly for the gap. 'The bastard,' he muttered, switching on the long range R/T transmitter. Whatever he said now would be heard by Fremantle and Albany: '*Myfanwy* to *Adventurer*. Keep clear, repeat keep clear. You are heading for my towing hawser.'

With the transmit lever in the handset still depressed, he sounded a series of U's on the coaster's siren — the international signal for *you are standing into danger*. Fremantle and Albany would hear those too.

The *Adventurer* was several hundred yards away when Brockman made his reply. On long range R/T: he wasn't missing any points, either. '*Adventurer* to *Myfanwy*. Have no intention of passing between you and your tow. You appear unduly nervous and unable to judge distances. Is Fremantle aware tow has been stopped for last twelve hours? Have not heard you report.'

Merfyr Evans, white with anger, saw the *Adventurer* turning rapidly to port, away from the towing hawser. He switched on and called Fremantle. The operator answered. Evans said: 'Request you order tug *Adventurer* to keep at least one mile clear of towing hawser. Please record my formal charge of dangerous, irresponsible and unseamanlike behaviour on part of tugmaster.'

Fremantle acknowledged and Evans put down the handset. Now that he'd got that off his chest anger gave way to quiet satisfaction. There could be no greater insult than to call the captain of one of the world's largest and most powerful ocean salvage vessels a *tugmaster*. Many ships and shore stations would have read the signal. Their laughter would echo round the Southern Ocean for some time to come.

He was still grinning when Christopherson's voice broke in to report an aircraft approaching from the north-east. It was soon over them, circling the tow, big and impressive at a low altitude. It was a maritime reconaissance aircraft with the roundels and markings of the Royal Australian Air Force. The coaster's wheelhouse speaker reverberated suddenly to the sound of a new voice: 'Aircraft Charlie-Five-Zero calling *Myfanwy*.'

'*Myfanwy* answering Charlie-Five-Zero. Go ahead.'

'Hallo there *Myfanwy*. Have orders stand by you until mine-sweeper *Magpie* arrives. Her bearing one-seven-zero degrees, distance one-five-eight miles. Speed of advance thirteen knots. Over.'

'Roger Charlie-Five-Zero. Thank you. Glad to have you with us.'

The aircraft banked and went into a climbing turn, gaining height rapidly. The Australian voice came on the air again. 'Charlie-Five-Zero to *Myfanwy* and *Adventurer*. Be good boys down there. Uncle Charlie has big eyes and ears.' A chuckle followed. It wasn't only Fremantle, Albany and ships at sea who'd heard Brockman and Evans slanging each other.

Evans smiled with quiet satisfaction as he saw the salvage tug swing in a wide arc to take station astern of *Moonraker*.

★ ★ ★

By dawn on 14th December a number of changes had taken place. The Australian mine-sweeper *Magpie* had arrived during the preceding night, and Charlie-Five-Zero had departed.

This was not the only departure. An hour

after the mine-sweeper's arrival the salvage tug had left. Brockman made no announcement. The bright lights of the *Adventurer* came up from astern, swept past the tow at speed and disappeared in an easterly direction.

'A sailor's farewell to you,' muttered Evans as the tug's lights grew dim in the distance. He knew why Brockman had gone. With the mine-sweeper standing by there wasn't much chance of business.

'He'll be making for Albany,' said Dai Williams.

'Aye. And it's good to see the last of him.'

Dai Williams sucked at his pipe. 'Brockman was no more than doing his job, Merfyr.'

'Let him go and do it where he's welcome, then.' After that they got on with discussing the fuel problem . . . and it really was a problem. The stop for engine repairs had meant the loss of another half day.

It was Dai Williams who pointed out that the *Magpie* was diesel-powered. 'By God, Dai. That's it then.' Evans slapped him on the back in an unusual display of emotion.

Later that day Calvi reported that pumping of *Moonraker's* flooded compartments had been completed.

★ ★ ★

During the forenoon Evans called the mine-sweeper's captain on R/T. 'We're a bit low on diesel fuel. Can you let us have some, captain?'

'How many tons?' was the guarded reply.

'Thirty, if you can manage. It's for the ballast we need it. We tow better with full tanks. Increases the draught.'

'We're not the QE2,' said the *Magpie*'s captain.' Fifteen tons any good to you?'

'That would help,' said Evans.

'Ever refuelled under way?'

'No,' replied Evans. 'Can't say I have.'

'I'll send an officer across to explain the drill. He'll check your ship's fuel connections.'

'Thanks,' said Evans with studied calm. No point in explaining that *Myfanwy* would run out of fuel two days before Fremantle unless she got some oil. The *Magpie* lowered an inflatable skimmer, three men climbed into it and it swept across to the coaster, bumping and spraying, its outboard engine laying a carpet of foam astern. A young lieutenant clambered up the coaster's side. On reaching the bridge he congratulated Evans on towing the flooded *Moonraker* through the Roaring Forties. 'It's great,' he said. 'Got the press and public all steamed up. You know. Small coaster — big distances

— bad weather — missing ship.'

'H'm,' grunted Evans off-handedly. 'Is that so.' He was thinking about diesel fuel.

The lieutenant looked surprised. 'Don't you listen to the broadcast?'

Evans shook his head. 'Haven't had time to sleep let alone listen to broadcast.' He changed the subject. 'Now about this business of re-fuelling under way?'

The lieutenant took the hint. 'Sure. No trouble.'

Evans said, 'I'll get my chief and bosun up here.' He sent Christopherson off to fetch them. Dai Williams and Isak John arrived and after the lieutenant had explained the refuelling procedure, he and Williams went off to check the coaster's fuel lines. Passing the galley the Australian saw a girl tending the stove. He expressed surprise that there should be a woman on board. Dai Williams explained.

The lieutenant introduced himself and in a brief discussion questioned Susie about the *Moonraker*'s mutiny. Neither he nor the girl referred to her uncle's weakness. She spoke in glowing terms of the Australian passage-worker, Casey. But for him, she said, neither the *Moonraker* nor those in her could have survived. Before leaving the *Myfanwy* the lieutenant returned to the bridge to report to

428

Evans. 'My captain has ordered me to board the *Moonraker*. Have a look round. The authorities in Sydney want Captain Stone's story of how the crew came to abandon the ship after the cyclone.'

'You'll have a job.' Evans was unenthusiastic. 'Captain Stone's an alcoholic.'

The lieutenant nodded. 'That's what the survivors say. But we'd like to check up. You've no objection?'

'No,' said Evans. 'I've no objection. My first mate, Calvi, is in command over there. Five of my men with him. I'll tell him you're coming.'

'Thanks,' said the lieutenant. He looked at his watch. 'Just to recap before I go, captain. *Magpie* will take station ahead of you at 1400. We'll stream the buffs on the end of the pick-up line. Get a grapnel over the buffs and the line inboard as quick as you can. Then haul in the hose. Keep your course and speed dead steady. We'll look after the station keeping. When you've connected up the hoses give us the go ahead and we'll start pumping. Okay?'

'Fine,' said Evans. 'My compliments to your captain.'

The lieutenant went down the bridge companionway and along the main deck to the rope ladder over the bulwarks. He lowered himself into the skimmer, the engine spluttered into life, and it whirred and bumped towards the *Moonraker*.

★   ★   ★

The refuelling operation that afternoon was completed within the hour, despite the inexperience of the coaster's crew.

The captain of the *Magpie* informed Evans that the minesweeper would remain in company for the journey to Fremantle notwithstanding the Welshman's assurance that he required no assistance. In truth, he was pleased to have the naval vessel there. Its presence discouraged salvage tugs and other would-be helpers. But he'd emphasised that assistance was not required. He was determined to do nothing which might water down the salvage award.

★   ★   ★

That afternoon *Magpie* radioed a confidential report to Naval Headquarters in Sydney. It summarised the lieutenant's investigations on board the *Moonraker*. It referred, too, to Captain Stone's addiction to alcohol, to the fact that Napoleon Calvi, first mate of the coaster, was in *de facto* command of the

430

freighter which was manned largely by members of the coaster's crew. It recorded Captain Stone's allegation that the abandonment of the ship had constituted an act of mutiny under arms. The captain's steward, a Ghanaian, and an Australian passage-worker, Casey, had in most respects confirmed the accounts of Captain Stone and his niece. The passage-worker had been frank about the captain's weakness, but not the steward and niece. Both had made it clear that Frascatti, Nils Thoresen, O'Halloran and Jenkins had urged Captain Stone and the others to accompany them in the boats. Indeed, Frascatti was alleged to have threatened to use force to compel this.

★   ★   ★

In Sydney the Navy passed *Magpie*'s report to police headquarters where discreet inquiries were begun. Plain-clothes men interrogated Frascatti, O'Halloran, Houtman the Dutch carpenter and other survivors. They all told much the same story. Supported by *Moonraker*'s logbook — handed to the police by Frascatti — it was a plausible one: a drunken Captain Stone had led the *Moonraker* into the path of the cyclone, the ship had suffered severe damage and after a week of drifting with flooded compartments, the boats had seemed the only hope of survival. Repeated efforts to persuade Captain Stone and his companions to accompany the crew having failed — and the captain having resorted to the use of firearms — there had been no option but to leave them behind.

So plausible was this account that police H.Q. resolved to defer a decision on whether or not there had been mutiny to *Moonraker*'s arrival in Fremantle when Captain Stone and those with him could be questioned. Police H.Q. did, however, request the authorities in Mauritius to fly the *Moonraker*'s second officer and second engineer — Martinho Lopez and Nils Thoresen — to Sydney as soon as possible.

26

The Qantas flight from Mauritius touched down at Sydney Airport on the morning of 16th December.

Martinho Lopez and Nils Thoresen were met at the immigration desk by two plain-clothes policemen who took them by car to police headquarters. There they underwent separate and lengthy interrogation. In all material respects their accounts of the circumstances leading up to the abandonment of the *Moonraker* accorded with those of Frascatti and O'Halloran. Lopez acknowledged that he'd not been present at the discussions with the captain and could not vouch for what had transpired there.

The police found that in one important respect Frascatti's and O'Halloran's stories differed from those of Lopez and Thoresen: this had to do with how the two lifeboats had become separated. Frascatti and his men said that the towing painter had parted during a night of violent squalls. Lopez and Thoresen were adamant that it had been cut with a sharp knife. Their boat, they said, had been cast adrift deliberately because it was hindering the progress of Frascatti's boat.

Lopez made these allegations with passion and conviction. Thoresen, while supporting him on the facts, appeared to accept what had happened philosophically, acknowledging Frascatti's right to act in the interests of those in his own boat. The interrogations completed, the two men were given the address of a hotel in Palmer Street.

'I must ask you,' said the inspector, 'to stay there until our investigations are completed.'

Lopez frowned. 'When will that be?'

'Not long. The *Moonraker* is due in Fremantle the day after to-morrow. The captain and others on board will be questioned.'

Thoresen said, 'Why are the police handling this and not the Board of Trade?'

The inspector concentrated on the pad on which he was writing. 'Captain Stone has made an allegation of mutiny.'

'Mutiny!' echoed Lopez. 'That's absurd. Nobody mutinied.'

Thoresen said, 'I suppose you know that Captain Stone is an alcoholic.'

The inspector went on with his work. 'We have heard allegations to that effect. Leave it to us, gentlemen. We'll sort out the facts. Justice will be done.'

'I hope so,' said Thoresen doubtfully.

'One other thing.' The inspector looked up. 'Keep away from Frascatti and his lot. It'll be in your interests to do so.'

'Is that an order?' asked Thoresen.

'No,' said the inspector. 'It's advice.'

★ ★ ★

Outside police headquarters they flagged down a taxi and gave the driver the address of the hotel in Palmer Street. They got in and the taxi pulled out into the traffic stream.

'They can't charge us with mutiny,' said Thoresen quietly.

'I'm not so sure.' Lopez's face was drawn. 'As a moral issue, I don't believe it was mutiny. Technically it may have been.'

'What d'you mean technically?'

'I didn't hear the discussions with the captain. He has witnesses of what was said. Whether or not there was mutiny will depend upon that.'

'In what way?'

'If he gave a definite order that the ship was *not* to be abandoned, then it was mutiny. If he said, 'You may go, but I shall stay' it was not mutiny.'

In the time they'd been together in the lifeboat and afterwards in Mauritius, these two men had grown to like each other. They

435

were very different. Nils Thoresen: tough, practical, strong-willed, older than Lopez, a marine engineer who'd joined *Moonraker* in Manila on the outward voyage. Martinho Lopez: intellectual, radical, an aesthete for whom the old freighter provided sanctuary and anonymity at a critical time.

Thoresen looked out of the taxi window. 'It is difficult to remember the exact words. Much has happened since.'

'Did Stone say the ship was not to be abandoned?' Lopez stared at him. 'Did he use the word *mutiny*. Think, Nils.'

The knuckles on the Dane's hands whitened. 'It was not just a matter of words.' He spoke in a quiet concerned voice. 'You cannot isolate what happened like that. Perhaps he did say we must not abandon the ship. Perhaps he did talk of mutiny. But one must consider the circumstances. Stone was an alcoholic. It was his neglect — his stupidity — that landed the ship in that cyclone. He was responsible for what followed. We believed the ship would not remain afloat. That the boats were our only chance.' He turned on Lopez. 'You believed that, too.'

'I did,' said Lopez.

'Had that drunkard, then, the right to say 'No, you cannot go'. To accuse us of mutiny because we try to escape from a disaster he makes?'

'Morally, I think he had not,' said Lopez. 'But the courts take a juridical not a moral view. He was in command. If he said, 'You cannot go. If you do it is mutiny', then it will be found that we were guilty. That we conspired together to disobey his orders and so hazarded the ship and the lives of all on board.'

'That would be gross injustice.' Thoresen fiddled with his beard. 'Condemning the innocent. Letting the guilty go free.'

'The law of mutiny is not designed for special cases,' Lopez said. 'Without it the exercise of command at sea would be impossible. The courts do all they can to uphold it.'

Outside the taxi the roar of traffic muted as the lights went red and the rumbling columns halted.

Thoresen said, 'There were extenuating circumstances.'

Lopez smoothed away the dark locks of hair which had fallen across his forehead. 'In the lifeboats men lost their lives. The *Moonraker* did not sink. All who stayed in her were saved.' He looked away from Thoresen. 'It is these facts which will impress the court.'

'You think so?'

'Of course. What happened upheld the captain's judgment. That will count heavily against us.'

The lights went green and the traffic rolled forward, the clamour of its acceleration shutting out the other sounds of the big city.

★ ★ ★

When he made his telephone calls Lopez disguised his voice. First he called the office of the agents for Gimbal Ocean Carriers Limited to ask where the *Moonraker* survivors were staying. That was at half past four. At six o'clock he telephoned the boarding house in Bourke Street.

Yes. Mr Frascatti was staying there. No. He was not in. Where was he likely to be? At Bella's, said the girl. The café in Smith's Lane, off Wharf Road. Down near the loading berths in Woolloomooloo Bay. He went there for supper most nights.

When Lopez put the phone down he wondered why the name Bella was evocative. Soon he remembered. In moments of unsolicited confidence, in the night watches on *Moonraker*'s bridge, Frascatti would trot out erotic reminiscences. Bella, the Italian widow who ran a dockside café in Sydney, had figured prominently in them. According to Frascatti she was a woman of fine looks, her anatomy as notable in important places as his own virility.

★　★　★

Thoresen and Lopez sat drinking in the faded lounge of the Palmer Street hotel. They spoke little, their mood sober and restrained. There was much to think about. Thoresen announced his plan for an early night. 'What are you doing?' he asked Lopez.

'Pictures, I think.'

'What's on?'

'*War and Peace*. I've always just missed it.'

'Don't care for that sort of thing myself.' Thoresen looked at his watch. 'I go for comedy and Westerns.'

Lopez smiled thinly. 'See you in the morning.'

★　★　★

Smith's Lane was a narrow ill-lit thoroughfare snaking its way between warehouses, ships' chandlers and dusty shuttered shops. Towards its far end it became too narrow for traffic and here, where it was no more than an alley, dim light showed through the red-curtained windows of the Café Bella.

Lopez took up his vigil in a dark passageway between two warehouses, less than a hundred yards from the café. Anyone leaving would have to pass him, for Smith's Lane ended in a cul de sac. Often he'd visualised this moment and the imagery always recalled the old anger. He would think of Tomas and Jenkins and the others in his boat who had died. Some quietly, some noisily, some like Jenkins mysteriously. He would think, too, of those who'd nearly died, of their suffering, their deranged minds. The emotion these thoughts engendered seemed always to justify the vow he'd made that night in the boat.

He'd often wondered when if ever he'd see Frascatti again. Now events had delivered the Italian into his hands sooner and more easily than he'd expected. But waiting there in the shadows, gripping the rough boned handle of the sheath knife, the moment having come, he questioned what he was about to do. To have made such a vow under the stress of emotion when survival seemed remote, was understandable. But what were his motives now? To see justice done? Or simply to take revenge?

Frascatti had betrayed them and lives had been lost. Might those lives not have been lost anyway? Hadn't they all betrayed Captain Stone and his companions by leaving them in the derelict ship? Which was the greater betrayal? Yet he had made his vow publicly, meaning to implement it. If he failed now, would he not betray those who'd died? Frascatti had engineered the mutiny. It was he who was responsible for all the suffering there had been and for that which was still to come.

Lopez pulled up the collar of his coat against the wind which came in across the harbour, its swirling eddies sweeping leaves and paper up Smith's Lane, their rustling and scraping amplified by the high sides of the warehouses. From the Café Bella came the strident discords, the insistent drumming of pop music. Somewhere in the distance a ship's siren sounded and a dog barked. From time to time the door of the café opened and waves of sound rolled out into the street. Men and women came out, laughing and talking as they walked up the lane, passing the darkened passageway where Lopez waited. Before they reached him they had to pass beneath a street lamp and then he would examine their faces in its dim light.

At about eleven o'clock the door opened and he heard a man and woman bid each other good night. The woman stood for a moment in the open door, then went back into the café. Lopez pressed himself against the warehouse as the man walked under the lamplight. There was no mistaking the narrow shoulders, the slouching walk, the cadaverous face, the deep sunk eyes.

Lopez's fingers tightened round the knife handle. Frascatti began singing. Something from Verdi. In that moment of imminent confrontation, Lopez realised that he could not do it. It was not fear. It was simply that the reality, now that it had come, bore no relation to the fantasy. Everything in his nature revolted against violence and the ultimate violence was to kill a man in cold blood. With trembling hands he returned the knife to its sheath as Frascatti went by five or six feet from where he stood. Lopez's heart drummed against its ribcage, there was a dryness in his mouth, as he watched the Italian move away into the darkness.

Frascatti was passing out of the pool of light cast by the next street lamp when a dark shape came from the shadows at the far end of the warehouse and slipped into the lane behind him. An arm was raised, the yellow lamplight was reflected on a steel blade, and the singing stopped. The dark shape looked back for a moment before hurrying away into the shadows. On the edge of the pool of light

442

a crumpled figure lay on the ground twitching and gurgling.

The whole incident had the frozen quality of the isolated frames of a motion picture. It had occupied no more than a few seconds. In that time Lopez had caught a fleeting glance of a square bearded face turned towards the lamplight.

He could not be certain, but he was pretty sure it was Nils Thoresen.

27

At noon on 18th December the tow was fifty-eight miles west-south-west of Fremantle, distance covered in the preceding twenty-four hours ninety-four miles, an average of just under four knots. At that speed the ETA Fremantle would be two-thirty a.m. the next day. Since it was important to arrive in daylight, Evans reduced to three knots, informing Fremantle that the tow's amended ETA was seven-thirty a.m. 19th December.

In a radio conversation with the port authorities it was decided that the pilot would board the freighter before the Fairway Buoy in Gage Roads. If he was satisfied with the safety of the ship the tow would be slipped, harbour tugs would take over and she would be moved to a suitable berth in the inner harbour for survey and repairs.

★　★　★

During the afternoon of 18th December, the weather being then fine and the tow proceeding smoothly, Evans slept for five hours. It was his longest period of continuous sleep since taking the *Moonraker* in tow on 29th November. Soon after six-thirty that evening, having had supper, he went to the wheelhouse. A helicopter and a light aircraft were circling the tow. 'Been here long, have they?' he asked Christopherson.

'On and off most of the afternoon. Pictures for press and TV, I reckon,' said the second mate.

Evans frowned at the helicopter coming in on the starboard side. With its rotors whirring in the light of the dying sun, it looked like a giant dragonfly. 'Parasites,' he muttered. 'Why don't they leave us alone and get on with their business?'

The second mate didn't like to point out that they were getting on with their business.

Evans looked at the younger man's drawn face and hollow eyes. 'Go down now and get some sleep,' he said. 'You need it.'

★ ★ ★

A few minutes after nine Evans sighted a pinpoint of light winking in the darkness ahead. He noted the time interval between the tiny blinks, seven to eight seconds, and knew it was the lighthouse on Rottnest Island outside Fremantle. The tow was still

445

twenty-two miles from the island and since they were making good three knots it would be another seven hours before the light was abeam.

But that distant flicker of light was the first visual evidence of the imminence of their arrival and Evans experienced a sudden exultation, a surge of inner excitement. He wanted to shout, to dance, to somehow express what he felt. But he was a taciturn man who mistrusted emotion, so he went out to the bridgewalk to be alone with his thoughts.

It was three weeks since that stormy night south of Amsterdam Island when he'd sighted the ghost ship drifting before the high wind and seas of the Roaring Forties. In that time the coaster had towed the *Moonraker* close on two thousand miles. As he saw it, this was *Myfanwy*'s achievement not his, and he felt a warmth of affection for the small ship. But it had been a long and tiring journey. More like three months and twenty thousand miles it seemed now.

With a heavy sigh he focused the night glasses on Rottnest Island, then turned them to the port beam where, a mile away, the mine-sweeper was drawing ahead as she increased speed. The lights of other ships were in sight, some inward bound, others outward. The *Magpie*, acting as policeman, was ensuring that traffic kept clear of the tow. Evans, normally sceptical of naval vessels, thought well of this mine-sweeper. Not only had she discouraged the *Adventurer*, but she'd provided the diesel fuel he'd so urgently needed. Not that he or Dai Williams would ever let on what would have happened without it.

It was a fine night, no moon, the stars shining, the remains of a westerly swell coming from astern, the sea ruffled by a light breeze. Looking aft he could see *Moonraker's* side-lights shining beneath the not-under-command lights. He knew Calvi was on the bridge for he'd spoken to him earlier. He was thinking of him now. What a fine seaman the man had turned out to be. Resourceful, determined, tireless. He seemed rarely to sleep, ready always to respond to a call.

Evans knew that without Calvi the tow would not have been possible. The Welshman felt a nagging sense of guilt. His judgment of the young man had been harsh: he'd been too quick to criticise, too slow to encourage, too insensitive to his feelings. He resolved to make amends. Calvi must get a good share of the salvage money. More than his legal due. And if he wanted to buy an interest in the coaster and stay with her, why he'd be more than welcome. It was something they could discuss in Fremantle.

There'd be much to do there and it'd have to be done quickly. Time cost money. The *Myfanwy* needed a quick turn round: he'd have to take on fuel, stores and water, attend to the salvage formalities — then make for Amsterdam Island to land Le Clerc, Bartot and their equipment. After that to Durban to discharge the Kerguelen ore samples; then Cape Town. There he'd pay off the crew, terminate the charter contract and sign on a small steaming party for the journey home to Cardiff.

For the immediate future the important thing was the salvage claim. He'd have to discuss that with Lloyd's agents in Fremantle. Get them to put him in touch with a good firm of solicitors. Not the sort of thing he could handle himself. It would all have to be referred to London. The underwriters there would ask the Salvage Association to conduct a survey of the ship and cargo. Lloyd's in London would have to be asked to see that adequate security was put up before he released the *Moonraker* to her owners. The Arbitration Panel in London would have to consider the evidence and decide the award. Specialist solicitors would represent him on the panel.

Evans breathed deeply, rubbing his eyes with his hands in an attempt to banish exhaustion. There were so many details which nagged at him. How was the Kerguelen-Amsterdam Island-Durban voyage contract affected? Would the cost of running the coaster for the extra time incurred by the salvage operation be met from the award, or was that a separate item? By the time *Myfanwy* got back to Amsterdam Island the extra time could be thirty days. At two hundred and fifty pounds a day, a lot of money was involved. It was a complicated business and it bore heavily on his weariness, so that he turned his thoughts to Susie. He'd seen little of her since that night in the cabin when Dai Williams had burst in on them. He'd been too busy since, too exhausted for anything but work and sleep. On those occasions when he had seen her, when she'd brought his meals, she'd looked at him in a strangely disconcerting way. What was it, he wondered? Shyness, regret, reproach? What he did know was that he was getting used to having her around — that, somehow, she'd become important to him. He imagined that he must mean something to her, too. How else could the incident in the cabin be explained?

After his long sleep that afternoon Susie

had brought his supper to the cabin before he'd come on watch. She'd put the tray down and whereas she normally went straight back to the galley, this time she'd stood in the doorway watching him, her head cocked on one side, the grey eyes expressing something he couldn't fathom.

'Well. And what is it then?' he asked.

'Bartot has been telling me about the salvage money.'

He looked up sharply. 'What about it?'

'He heard it being discussed on the Australian broadcast.'

'And so?'

'Well, it's . . . ' She looked embarrassed. 'It'll be a fortune they say.'

'What's a fortune?' He was guarded.

'Hundreds of thousands of pounds, perhaps. It's based on the value of the ship *and* the cargo, they say. Something like that.'

Evans had known all along that if he got the *Moonraker* to Fremantle the award would be a big one but he'd never thought of anything of that magnitude. It was characteristic of him that he said nothing, showed no surprise.

'You'll be rich, won't you?' she went on. 'I mean you're captain *and* owner.' Again that searching look. What was she after? The money?

'Maybe.' He spoke slowly, pulling on a seaboot. 'But there'll be shares for all of the crew. Something for you, too. Being in this ship makes you part of the salvage crew.'

'I wasn't thinking of myself.' She frowned.

'What's it then?'

'Le Clerc and Bartot. Will they get anything?'

So Bartot had put her up to it. 'Yes,' he said. 'They're passengers but they volunteered for crew work. They're entitled to shares.'

'And the Australian passage-worker?'

Evans dug into the mince and mashed potatoes she'd brought him. 'You mean that chap in the *Moonraker*?'

'Yes.'

'Well, now. I'm not sure of that.'

'Why?' she challenged. 'He's done terrific things. Dived for the missing part of that diesel. Got it going. They couldn't have pumped but for him. Before you found us he ran the ship. We'd never have survived without him.'

Evans munched away at his meal. 'There's no denying,' he said with a full mouth. 'He's done a good job. But he's a member of *Moonraker*'s crew. Not of the salvage crew.'

She looked at him doubtfully. 'So he could get nothing?'

'Why, then, it could be that way,' said Evans.

Pink patches formed on Susie's cheeks and her voice hardened. 'That's the most unfair thing I've ever heard.'

'Look,' said Evans brusquely. 'You asked me about entitlement. I've done my best to answer. I'm not responsible for the salvage laws.'

She'd said nothing, just stood there staring at him, a blank look on her face. Then she'd gone.

Funny girl, he thought. Worrying like that about the others. That was the young nowadays. Always looking for what they called social justice. Worrying about other people's problems instead of minding their own. Anyway, if it meant all that to her, he'd see that the young fellow got something. He'd certainly helped.

She was a fine girl. A hard worker. And plenty of guts. It couldn't have been easy for her. First in the *Moonraker* and then in the coaster. Yet he'd never heard her complain. Never, that is, but for that first day when she'd objected to coming to the *Myfanwy*. He considered the difference in their ages. Thirty-two and eighteen. Must be a lot of couples the same. And there'd be plenty of money now. He'd pay off *Myfanwy's* bondholders and there'd still be more than enough to spare. Buy a small farm in the Vale of Teivi, close to Llandyssul, and lease off the fields. She could live there and bring up the family. Later, when he tired of the sea, he'd sell the coaster and take on the farming himself. In the morning he would tell her she could have a free passage home in the *Myfanwy*. There'd be time enough during that long voyage for them to get better acquainted. Before they reached Cardiff he'd ask her to marry him.

His mother would approve. Susie was a strong healthy girl with a happy disposition — and a good cook at that.

★ ★ ★

Deeply immersed in his fantasy world, Captain Stone sat at the desk, a bottle of gin at his elbow, a part filled tumbler in front of him. He was writing the speech he would make in reply to the Lord Mayor of Sydney's welcome after *Moonraker*'s triumphant entry under sail through the Sydney Heads.

He paid much attention to detail, crossing out and rewriting, reading aloud, standing at times to declaim in front of the mirror. He was not happy about the bit in which he thanked the Governor-General's representative for conveying to him Her Most Gracious Majesty's decision to confer a knighthood. He was not quite sure whether he should say, 'Pray convey to Her Majesty my humble duty' or whether that phrase was not archaic and the sentiment better expressed by 'Please convey to Her Majesty my humble gratitude.' But why should gratitude be humble? Uncertain about this, he groped for other words.

Satisfied at last that he could no longer improve upon a speech which seemed both eloquent and sincere, he decided that the occasion called for celebration. Tired of his quarters in which he'd so long been confined he decided that the place for celebration was out in God's fresh air. With these thoughts in mind he took the speech in one hand, the gin bottle in the other, opened the door quietly, tiptoed along the alleyway, down a staircase and out on to the boat-deck.

It was somewhere between one and two o'clock in the morning, the cloudless sky bright with stars. A little chilly, he decided, but fresh and invigorating. Moving gingerly, he felt his way towards the chocks that had been occupied by number one boat. His searching hands found the foremost set and he sat down with his back to them, looking out across the sea. *Moonraker* rolled gently to the swell and far down below him the water sucked and gurgled along her side, sparkling with phosphorescence as it tumbled past.

Captain Stone felt at peace with the world, and the more gin he drank the more grandiose his thoughts became. Snatches of immortal verse passed through his mind accompanied by orchestrations of great music. He drained the last of the gin, threw the bottle over the side and felt in the darkness for the speech. Somehow it eluded him. He went forward on hands and knees until his fingers touched the sheets. Grasping them, he raised himself to his feet, lost his balance as *Moonraker* rolled, and toppled over the side.

In the instant that it took to fall those twenty-five to thirty feet it was not clear to him what had happened, but as he hit the water he registered the last thought that was to be his — concern that such a fine speech would not, after all, be delivered.

★   ★   ★

Calvi picked up the phone and called the steering compartment.

'Yeh?' came back Casey's tired voice. 'What's it?'

'I have the news for you,' said Calvi. 'We see already the light on Rottnest Island.'

'Whacko sport! That's great. How far?'

'About twenty miles.'

'ETA still seven-thirty to-morrow?' There was a tremor of excitement in the Australian's voice.

'Yes,' said Calvi. 'If the imbeciles who steer this ship do not break the towing hawser.'

'Don't give me that,' said Casey. 'It was the bridge's fault last time.'

'Yes,' Calvi agreed. 'I remember very well. Also another time when you make the fight.'

'Yeh. And you put the boot in.'

'Ah, the double kick.' Calvi chuckled. 'Maybe they fight for her now in the coaster.'

'Cool it,' warned Casey. 'She's my girl.'

'Too good for a low type Australian.'

'Get stuffed,' said Casey.

Calvi smiled to himself, put down the phone and went back to the bridge. He stood in the forepart watching the arc light on the coaster's stern. Like Merfyr Evans he had slept well that day. Nearly five hours before coming on watch. Now Le Clerc, asleep in the chart house, was having his turn.

Already Calvi was visualising the arrival. The casting off of the tow, the harbour tugs taking over the *Moonraker*, shepherding her into a berth in the inner harbour. He went once again through the technicalities of seamanship involved. He'd already discussed them with Msutu, the Zulu seaman, who'd rigged the three-fold purchase on the foc'sle head ready for recovering the anchor cable.

★　★　★

At midnight Le Clerc came on watch. For some time he and Calvi discussed the impending arrival in Fremantle. Afterwards Calvi wrote up the log-book in the chart house. He wrote carefully, not hurrying, knowing with a certain melancholy that after to-morrow he would not do it again. When he'd finished he went to the starboard wing of the bridge and stood there in the darkness.

Le Clerc was nominally in charge of the watch but Calvi had no intention of leaving the bridge that night. There would be time for sleep in Fremantle. He knew that Evans was on watch in the coaster. They'd spoken to each other a few minutes before. Indeed, over these last weeks they'd spoken to each other many times each day and night. Always what was said had to do with the ships, with the tow: laconic, cryptic, technical exchanges. Sometimes, when there was trouble, there had been anger in Evans's voice. Only once had the Welshman commended him. That was south of Amsterdam Island, after the swim across to the *Moonraker*.

Calvi knew that Evans didn't think much of him, that he held his fishing origins against him. '*Sacré bleu!*' the Corsican muttered. 'Why should I care.' He snapped his fingers in the darkness. 'To the devil with the man.'

In the time that Calvi had been in the *Myfanwy*, Evans had all but destroyed his self confidence. It was the *Moonraker* which had restored it. Calvi thought of the battered old freighter with affection. She had made a difference to his life. To-morrow he would part with her and it would hurt. She'd been his first command and by morning, the Holy Mother willing, she would be safely in harbour. Maybe Evans was right. Maybe he, Calvi, was not a good seaman. But they had got the *Moonraker* to within sight of Rottnest Island, and Calvi knew that without him it might not have been so.

He thought with compassion of the English captain down in the cabin below. For him the arrival in Fremantle meant more humiliation, more personal disaster, whereas for Calvi and Evans it spelt success and reward. Such different ends to a shared journey, reflected the Corsican, wondering at the part chance played in the affairs of men.

458

His thoughts turned to more practical things. He knew enough about salvage to realise that there would be a substantial award. But for the fortuitous encounter south of Amsterdam Island, the *Moonraker* would have foundered with her cargo. Much money was involved. The coaster's captain, who was also owner, would get the lion's share but Calvi knew that he, too, would get something. Not much maybe, but enough with what he'd saved already to marry Marie Louise when he got back to Ajaccio, to buy a share in a fishing boat, or a small farm on the terraces in the mountains. He would have to discuss that with her. Either way he would live at home. There would be no more trudging the high seas.

★   ★   ★

Dwala the Ghanaian was having a disturbing dream. He was back in the West African village where he'd been born, where he'd spent the first years of his life and where his father had died. But the village was not as he had known it. It was deserted and the huts, those of his mother and grandmother, his uncles and aunts and the other people of the tribe, stood empty and decaying, the thatch rotting and falling away. There was a bad smell about the place and all the tribe had gone.

While he stood alone and frightened in the village he became aware of ghosts in the trees and bushes around him. The eyes of these ghosts were turned upon him and the worst of them were the green snakes. Snakes as large as pythons but of another kind with fire in their eyes and knives on their tails. There were also dogs of an unusual sort, gaunt animals, huge, with shaggy coats and bullock-like horns on which rattled empty bottles. They barked ferociously, baring their teeth, and the snakes hissed.

Dwala fled, knowing that the village had been taken over by the bad ghosts and was now a place of evil. But the green snakes and the horned dogs pursued him and as they came close upon him his terror was great for he could feel their hot breath and to his nose came the bad smell of it, and above the barking and the hissing he could hear the rattle of the bottles against the horns of the dogs.

When it seemed that he could not in any way escape he heard someone calling and knew it was Captain Stone whom he could now see in the distance standing beneath a high tree.

With his last strength Dwala ran towards

the captain who was smiling in a most pleasant fashion and waving encouragement, so that Dwala gained on the green snakes and horned dogs and came near to his master. Then from that distance he could see that his mother and grandmother, his uncle and aunts were with the captain and they were laughing and talking together, while around them stood the men of the tribe, their spears shining in the sunlight as they brandished them, calling to him.

Dwala knew at once that these were good ghosts so he ran faster and had all but reached them when he woke up. Now that he was awake he was greatly disturbed for he was not sure whether the sound of Captain Stone's voice had come from the dream or whether the captain had really summoned him. In great haste he put on a singlet and trousers and made for the captain's cabin.

★ ★ ★

At three o'clock in the morning Calvi heard someone hurrying up the bridge ladder. A voice in the darkness called 'Mister Calvi, sah.' It was the steward Dwala to report that Captain Stone had disappeared. The Ghanaian explained how, in a dream, he had heard the captain calling and had gone to his cabin

461

but he was not there. He had looked everywhere after that but could not find him. Having ordered Le Clerc to accompany the steward on a thorough search of the ship, Calvi called Evans on the walkie-talkie to report what had happened. The *Magpie* broke in to announce that she would steam back along the tow's track in case Captain Stone had gone overboard. These measures were without result. By daylight it was assumed that Captain Stone had been lost overboard and Fremantle was informed accordingly.

Calvi was not distressed for he believed the English captain had made the right decision. It was better for the old man to have finished his life in the sea where he belonged than face the future ashore.

While Dwala grieved deeply at this separation from a man for whom he had worked for so long and to whom he had been devoted for reasons he could not explain, he was consoled by the recollection of the dream. The good ghosts, the members of his family and the men of the tribe whom he'd seen round the captain waving their spears, had come to rescue him. They would by now have taken him to a place where he could no longer be troubled by the bad ghosts, a place where he would be with all his ancestors, very safe and secure.

28

To the uninformed bystander in Fremantle that morning there could be no conceivable connection between the weather-stained coaster at the Victoria Quay and the brine encrusted freighter on the opposite side of the harbour at the North Quay. But to Merfyr Evans looking out through a porthole to where the *Moonraker* lay, the visual evidence that the two ships were no longer joined was as significant as the severance of an umbilical cord.

He was so much a part of his ship, they were so closely integrated, that over the long weeks of the tow the impression had grown in his mind that it was to *him* that the *Moonraker*'s towing hawser was attached. Every helm and engine order he'd given, every decision made, had been conditioned by the effect it would have on the ship astern. She had always been there, lumbering along, wallowing helplessly, utterly dependent, dominating his thoughts, disturbing his sleep. Now that was all over and he knew that just as he'd had to accustom himself to a deck that no longer pitched and rolled, to engines that no longer thumped and pulsated, so he must accommodate the reality that the *Moonraker* was no longer tied to him.

There had been no drama about the arrival that morning. Some of the ships alongside had sounded their sirens when the rusty coaster entered harbour soon after seven-thirty, but that was all the outward notice taken. Once she'd berthed, there'd been activity of another kind. An exigent, determined press, radio and TV had descended upon Evans and when he'd escaped from them — and that had not been easy — another never-ending human stream had to be dealt with: shipping agents, Lloyd's agents, chandlers, fuel suppliers, literary agents, publishers' agents, and others determined to batten on to what for him was now ended.

He didn't understand the fuss nor a lot of the questions and he didn't much like the pushing presumptuous characters who put them. But he knew that he had to go through with the ritual: that others now wanted to share *Myfanwy*'s experience, however vicariously. His questioners had not seemed to know or care that he'd been on the bridge throughout the night, that he was — after weeks without proper sleep — near to

464

exhaustion. Neither did they appear to know or care that he'd not had breakfast, nor time for the wash, shave and clean-up so long overdue. Only now could he do these things and then only by locking the cabin door and refusing to see anyone until later in the day. As he washed himself down, shaved, trimmed his beard and made ready his shore-going clothes, a sense of anti-climax overcame him. To his tired mind there seemed only three things left of real importance: to have breakfast, to see Susie, and to visit the *Moonraker*.

It wouldn't be the first time that morning that he'd seen the girl. At daybreak she'd come to the wheelhouse with coffee. He'd sensed she wanted to say something, but he'd been immensely busy at that time with Rottnest Island abeam, the pilot vessel ahead, the mine-sweeper making a signal, and the tow coming round on to the new course for the Fairway Buoy.

He knew, however, that he had to break the news to her so, perfunctorily, between giving a wheel-order and watching the *Moonraker* follow round, he'd said, 'I'm sorry to have to tell you that your uncle was lost overboard last night. The mine-sweeper searched back along the course but couldn't find him.'

She made a choking noise and he'd put

465

down the binoculars to look at her, but she wasn't crying. Just staring at him in a blank frozen way, a hand in front of her mouth. She'd hurried off the bridge without saying a word and he'd got on with the job of bringing the tow on to the new course. Afterwards, feeling that he could perhaps have broken the news more tactfully, he'd sent the second mate down to see if she was all right. Christopherson came back to report that she'd locked herself in her cabin and wished to be left alone.

As he dressed, Merfyr Evans thought over the incident. He could understand her shock, the desire to be alone. But that was hours ago. She ought to be all right now. It was only an uncle and by all accounts a drunk at that. As soon as he'd had breakfast, he'd go and comfort her. Let her know she could travel home with him in the *Myfanwy*. He'd not mention marriage yet — just make it clear that she'd nothing to worry about. Maybe she'd guess what he had in mind. Women had an instinct about those things. Like a sailor's nose for the weather. He stood before the mirror brushing his hair, the sun through the portholes playing on his face, magnifying the blemishes, the enlarged pores, the moles and scars.

Outside, above the subdued roar of city

traffic, he heard the familiar reassuring sounds of the port, of cranes working, stevedores shouting, trains shunting. Somewhere a ship sounded three short blasts on her siren — *going astern*, a part of his brain registered without intruding on his thoughts. In the distance the sonorous boom of a city clock struck the hour. He looked at his watch. It was eleven.

At that moment a closer more urgent sound intruded: the racket of a two-stroke slowing down, then pop-popping as it idled. He looked out of the porthole and saw a young man astride a motor scooter, stopped near the gangway. He was wearing a blue denim shirt and jeans, a red handkerchief round his neck. Very bronzed and sunburnt he was, with tousled sandy hair. A tall strong-looking young man with a guitar slung across his back. He sat on the stationary scooter, his feet on the ground, his arms folded, the two-stroke pop-popping away. He was looking at the *Myfanwy* with evident interest. Heard the news of the tow and come down to the docks out of curiosity, decided Evans. The Welshman was about to turn away when he saw Susie running down the gangway, a faded blue beach bag over her shoulder.

She and the young man shouted joyous

'Hi's', he got off the scooter and she ran into his arms. They were less than fifty feet away and Evans could see the girl's shoulders shaking and he knew she was crying. The young man pushed a grubby handkerchief into her hand and said, 'Hey. What's wrong with you?' and she said, 'Oh, Hank. It's so good to see you,' and looked up, laughing through her tears.

Hank pulled the guitar strap over his head and put it around hers so that she had the beach bag over one shoulder and the guitar over the other. He straddled the scooter, she climbed on behind, the engine popped and crackled into rasping life and they wobbled off down the quay, the girl's arms round his waist.

Above the whirr of the engine, Evans thought he heard the cheerful sound of her laughter. They disappeared round the corner of the cargo shed as a taxi drew up opposite the *Myfanwy*'s stern. A door opened and its human cargo bundled out, noisy and boisterous. One of the passengers thrust money into the driver's hand, the door was slammed hard, the driver swore, and the taxi moved off. The men waved after it, shouting and laughing, before coming up the quay towards the gangway. A dark-bearded, broad-shouldered young man led the way. The beard was unfamiliar and it was moments before Evans recognised Napoleon Calvi.

The Corsican was carrying a skin-diver's suit over his shoulder, flippers and goggles in one hand, a bottle of wine in the other. Behind him came Le Clerc the geologist, Msutu the Zulu seaman, and Carelse the engineman. Msutu was carrying a cage in which the bright colours of a parakeet reflected the sunlight.

Calvi's walk suggested that the bottle of wine was not the first of the morning but there was nothing wrong with the voice booming the *Marseillaise* in a deep-throated bass, Le Clerc, Msutu and Carelse singing seconds and thirds.

Evans's instinct was to call out but he did not at that moment trust his voice. Disillusionment, the feeling that he had been let down by Susie, in some way diminished, gave way to a more powerful emotion. As the four men came up the gangway, their anthem swelling to its finale, he perceived that this was what was important, what really mattered. These were men. Tough, uncomplicated, resourceful men. His sort of men. It was a homecoming. A family reunion.

He unlocked the door of the cabin and went down to meet them. For the first time that day he was smiling.

We do hope that you have enjoyed reading this large print book.

Did you know that all of our titles are available for purchase?

We publish a wide range of high quality large print books including:
Romances, Mysteries, Classics
General Fiction
Non Fiction and Westerns

Special interest titles available in large print are:
The Little Oxford Dictionary
Music Book
Song Book
Hymn Book
Service Book

Also available from us courtesy of Oxford University Press:
Young Readers' Dictionary
(large print edition)
Young Readers' Thesaurus
(large print edition)

For further information or a free brochure, please contact us at:
Ulverscroft Large Print Books Ltd.,
The Green, Bradgate Road, Anstey,
Leicester, LE7 7FU, England.
Tel: (00 44) **0116 236 4325**
Fax: (00 44) **0116 234 0205**

Other titles published by
The House of Ulverscroft:

TWO HOURS TO DARKNESS

Antony Trew

For most of her crew the *Retaliate*'s Baltic cruise is a routine one, and her sixteen nuclear missiles no more than a silent threat to the Russians. But the submarine's captain, Commander Shadde, is obsessed with the communist menace and haunted by the memory of his one act of cowardice. As the submarine approaches the end of her voyage, a letter from his wife threatening divorce pushes Shadde to the brink of madness — in a vessel where nuclear war is just a touch of the button away . . .

THE SEA BREAK

Antony Trew

Lieutenant Commander Widmark had truly earned his nickname, 'The Butcher', in Mediterranean waters. He derided the Geneva Convention: in his view, war was a bloody business in which those who stopped at nothing would be victorious. And in November 1942 his greatest adventure begins: the organization and execution of a private cutting-out operation, designed — regardless of any consequences — to strike a telling blow for his own side. Widmark plans to seize and sail an 8,000-tonne German vessel, *Hagenfels*, from the neutral East African port of Lourenço Marques . . .